The Jaguar Hunter

LUCIUS SHEPARD

THE JAGUAR HUNTER

With a foreword by Michael Bishop

BANTAM BOOKS
NEW YORK · TORONTO · LONDON · SYDNEY · AUCKLAND

*This edition contains the complete text
of the original hardcover edition.*
NOT ONE WORD HAS BEEN OMITTED.

THE JAGUAR HUNTER
*A Bantam Book / published by arrangement with
Arkham House Publishers, Inc.*

*PRINTING HISTORY
Arkham House edition published May 1987*

ACKNOWLEDGMENTS

"Black Coral," copyright © 1984 by Terry Carr for *Universe 14*.
"The End of Life As We Know It," copyright © 1984 by Davis Publications, Inc., for *Isaac Asimov's Science Fiction Magazine*, January 1985.
"How the Wind Spoke at Madaket," copyright © 1985 by Davis Publications, Inc., for *Isaac Asimov's Science Fiction Magazine*, April 1985.
"The Jaguar Hunter," copyright © 1985 by Mercury Press, Inc., for *The Magazine of Fantasy and Science Fiction*, May 1985.
"The Man Who Painted the Dragon Griaule," copyright © 1984 by Mercury Press, Inc., for *The Magazine of Fantasy and Science Fiction*, December 1984.
"Mengele," copyright © 1985 by Terry Carr for *Universe 15*.
"The Night of White Bhairab," copyright © 1984 by Mercury Press, Inc., for *The Magazine of Fantasy and Science Fiction*, October 1984.
"Salvador," copyright © 1984 by Mercury Press, Inc., for *The Magazine of Fantasy and Science Fiction*, April 1984.
"A Spanish Lesson," copyright © 1985 by Mercury Press, Inc., for *The Magazine of Fantasy and Science Fiction*, December 1985.
"A Traveler's Tale," copyright © 1984 by Davis Publications, Inc., for *Isaac Asimov's Science Fiction Magazine*, July 1984.
"Foreword," copyright © 1987 by Michael Bishop.

Bantam edition / May 1989

Library of Congress Cataloging-in-Publication Data

Shepard, Lucius.
   The jaguar hunter / Lucius Shepard ; with a foreword by Michael
Bishop —Bantam ed.
     p. cm.
   ISBN 0-553-34695-4 (pbk.)
   1. Fantastic fiction, American. I. Title.
[PS3569.H3939J3 1989]
813'.54—dc19   88-27502
                                    CIP

Published simultaneously in the United States and Canada

---

*Bantam Books are published by Bantam Books, a division of Bantam
Doubleday Dell Publishing Group, Inc. Its trademark, consisting of the
words "Bantam Books" and the portrayal of a rooster, is Registered in
U.S. Patent and Trademark Office and in other countries. Marca Regis-
trada, Bantam Books, 666 Fifth Avenue, New York, New York 10103.*

PRINTED IN THE UNITED STATES OF AMERICA

FG   0 9 8 7 6 5 4 3 2 1

For Gullivar

Contents

Foreword

〜〜〜〜〜〜〜〜〜〜〜〜〜 **S**eldom do new writers arrive
〜〜〜〜〜〜〜〜〜〜〜〜〜 on the scene—whether amid
the Scotch and evening-wear ads in *The New Yorker* or in the
grainy double columns of *Fantasy and Science Fiction*—with a
convincing command of language, a deft display of storytelling techniques, and an authoritative auctorial presence.
Attention-grabbing newcomers may write like seraphs in disguise. Or they may expertly set you up for stinger endings that
you never once expect. Or (the least likely of these three sce-
narios) they may show you a hard-won compassion or a with-
it worldliness narrowly compensating for their deficiencies as
either stylists or spellbinders.

Rarely, though, will you find yourself reading a newcomer
whose work manages to combine all three of these virtues.
The reason is simple. Except for a few literary prodigies who
take to it like termites to timber, writing requires blood, sweat,
and tears. It wants not only a developable talent but also a
fingers-to-the-nub apprenticeship that may occasionally prove
more humbling than uplifting. Because most writers begin to
sell their work in their late teens or early twenties, they do part
of their apprenticeship in public, keyboarding marginally sal-
able work while struggling to improve their craft and to grow
as persons. Little wonder, then, that neophyte writers produce
a catch-as-catch-can commodity, now singing exquisite arias,
now crudely caterwauling—but even in moments of full-

throated triumph betraying more tonsil than tone, more raw power than rigor.

All of which I note by way of introducing, roundabout, Lucius Shepard—who, like Athena stepping magnificently entire from the forehead of Zeus, arrived on the fantasy and science-fiction scene a fully formed talent. (On the other hand, how long did Athena gestate before inflicting her daddy's migraine?) His first stories—"The Taylorsville Reconstruction" from Terry Carr's *Universe 13* and "Solitario's Eyes" from *Fantasy and Science Fiction*—appeared in 1983; they showed him to be both an accomplished and a versatile storyteller. In 1984, at least seven more tales (short stories, novelettes, novellas) bearing the Shepard byline cropped up in the field's best magazines and anthologies. These tales displayed a range of experience, and a mature insight into the complexities of human behavior, astonishing in a "beginner." In May 1984, his novel *Green Eyes* appeared as the second title in the revived Ace Science Fiction Special series; and in 1985, at the World Science Fiction Convention in Melbourne, Australia, the John W. Campbell Award for Best New Writer went to Lucius Shepard—with total and therefore gratifying justice.

Okay. Who is this guy? I've never met him, but I *have* read nearly everything he has published to date. Moreover, letters have been exchanged. (I wrote him one, and he wrote me back.) Beyond these glancing run-ins, I've talked to Lucius Shepard twice, long distance, on the telephone; and all my not-quite-close encounters with the man have probably given me the mistaken impression that I know something vital about the person behind the name, when what I chiefly know is really only what you are going to discover when you begin reading this collection of stories—namely, that Lucius Shepard field-marshals the language with the best of them, that he knows not just the tricks but also some of the deeper mysteries of the trade, and that he has lived long enough and intensely enough to have acquired a gut feel for the best ways to use his knowledge of both people and craft to transfigure honest entertainment into unpretentious art. *All* the stories in *The Jaguar Hunter* are fun to read, but several of them—maybe as many as half—rise toward the Keatsian beauty and truth of the long-enduring.

How so? Well, Shepard came somewhat tardily to writing (i.e., in his mid- to late-thirties), after a worldly apprenticeship that included an enforced introduction to the English classics at the hands of his father; a teenage rebellion against institutionalized learning; expatriate sojourns in Europe, the Middle East, India, and Afghanistan, among other exotic places; an intermittent but serious commitment to rock 'n' roll with bands such as The Monsters, Mister Right, Cult Heroes, The Average Joes, Alpha Ratz, and Villain ("We Have Ways of Making You Rock"); occasional trips to Latin America, where he has granted Most Favored Hideaway status to an island off the coast of Honduras; marriage, fatherhood, and divorce; and some stints both employed and unemployed that he may one day decide to narrate in his autobiography but that I know too little about even to mention in passing. Total immersion in the Clarion workshop for budding fantasy and science-fiction writers in the Summer of '80 led him to begin testing his talents, and not too long thereafter his first stories achieved print. In short, Lucius Shepard is so far from a novice—although he may yet qualify as a Young Turk—that even middle-aged professionals with more than a book or two behind them have to acknowledge him as a peer. Indeed, he has already shown signs of outright mastery that both humble and enormously cheer all of us who believe in the power of imaginative fiction to speak to the human heart.

Haunting echoes of the Vietnam conflict reverberate through the distinctive stories "Salvador" and "Mengele." Meanwhile, "Black Coral," "The End of Life as We Know It," "A Traveler's Tale," and "The Jaguar Hunter" illuminate this same lush Latin American landscape in a fashion vaguely suggestive of Graham Greene, Paul Theroux, and Gabriel García Márquez. Nevertheless, Shepard's voice remains determinedly his own. In both "The Night of White Bhairab" and "How the Wind Spoke at Makadet," he plays unusual variations on the contemporary horror story. In the latter tale, for instance, he says of the wind, "It was of nature, not of some netherworld.

It was ego without thought, power without morality." And in the novelette "A Spanish Lesson," Shepard dares to conclude his baroque narrative with a practical moral that "makes the story resonate beyond the measure of the page." My own favorite in this collection, by the way, is "The Man Who Painted the Dragon Griaule"—a tale that, in the indirect way of a parable, implies a great deal about both love and creativity. Seldom, though, do you find a parable so vivid or so involvingly sustained.

So pick a story at random, read it, and go helplessly on to all the others at hand. Lucius Shepard has arrived. *The Jaguar Hunter* beautifully announces this fact.

MICHAEL BISHOP

The Jaguar Hunter

It was his wife's debt to Onofrio Esteves, the appliance dealer, that brought Esteban Caax to town for the first time in almost a year. By nature he was a man who enjoyed the sweetness of the countryside above all else; the placid measures of a farmer's day invigorated him, and he took great pleasure in nights spent joking and telling stories around a fire, or lying beside his wife, Encarnación. Puerto Morada, with its fruit company imperatives and sullen dogs and cantinas that blared American music, was a place he avoided like the plague: indeed, from his home atop the mountain whose slopes formed the northernmost enclosure of Bahía Onda, the rusted tin roofs ringing the bay resembled a dried crust of blood such as might appear upon the lips of a dying man.

On this particular morning, however, he had no choice but to visit the town. Encarnación had—without his knowledge—purchased a battery-operated television set on credit from Onofrio, and he was threatening to seize Esteban's three milk cows in lieu of the eight hundred *lempira* that was owed; he refused to accept the return of the television, but had sent word that he was willing to discuss an alternate method of payment. Should Esteban lose the cows, his income would drop below a subsistence level and he would be forced to take up his old occupation, an occupation far more onerous than farming.

As he walked down the mountain, past huts of thatch and brushwood poles identical to his own, following a trail that wound through sun-browned thickets lorded over by banana trees, he was not thinking of Onofrio but of Encarnación. It was in her nature to be frivolous, and he had known this when he had married her; yet the television was emblematic of the differences that had developed between them since their children had reached maturity. She had begun to put on sophisticated airs, to laugh at Esteban's country ways, and she had become the doyenne of a group of older women, mostly widows, all of whom aspired to sophistication. Each night they would huddle around the television and strive to outdo one another in making sagacious comments about the American detective shows they watched; and each night Esteban would sit outside the hut and gloomily ponder the state of his marriage. He believed Encarnación's association with the widows was her manner of telling him that she looked forward to adopting the black skirt and shawl, that—having served his purpose as a father—he was now an impediment to her. Though she was only forty-one, younger by three years than Esteban, she was withdrawing from the life of the senses; they rarely made love anymore, and he was certain that this partially embodied her resentment to the fact that the years had been kind to him. He had the look of one of the Old Patuca— tall, with chiseled features and wide-set eyes; his coppery skin was relatively unlined and his hair jet black. Encarnación's hair was streaked with gray, and the clean beauty of her limbs had dissolved beneath layers of fat. He had not expected her to remain beautiful, and he had tried to assure her that he loved the woman she was and not merely the girl she had been. But that woman was dying, infected by the same disease that had infected Puerto Morada, and perhaps his love for her was dying, too.

The dusty street on which the appliance store was situated ran in back of the movie theater and the Hotel Circo del Mar, and from the inland side of the street Esteban could see the bell towers of Santa María del Onda rising above the hotel roof like the horns of a great stone snail. As a young man, obeying his mother's wish that he become a priest, he had spent three years cloistered beneath those towers, preparing for the seminary under the tutelage of old Father Gonsalvo. It was the part of his life he most regretted, because the academic disciplines he had mastered seemed to have stranded him between the world of the Indian and that of contemporary society; in his heart he held to his father's teachings—the principles of magic, the history of the tribe, the lore of nature—and yet he could never escape the feeling that such wisdom was either superstitious or simply unimportant. The shadows of the towers lay upon his soul as surely as they did upon the cobbled square in front of the church, and the sight of them caused him to pick up his pace and lower his eyes.

Farther along the street was the Cantina Atómica, a gathering place for the well-to-do youth of the town, and across from it was the appliance store, a one-story building of yellow stucco with corrugated metal doors that were lowered at night. Its facade was decorated by a mural that supposedly represented the merchandise within: sparkling refrigerators and televisions and washing machines, all given the impression of enormity by the tiny men and women painted below them, their hands upflung in awe. The actual merchandise was much less imposing, consisting mainly of radios and used kitchen equipment. Few people in Puerto Morada could afford more, and those who could generally bought elsewhere. The majority of Onofrio's clientele were poor, hard-pressed to meet his schedule of payments, and to a large degree his wealth derived from selling repossessed appliances over and over.

Raimundo Esteves, a pale young man with puffy cheeks and heavily lidded eyes and a petulant mouth, was leaning against the counter when Esteban entered; Raimundo smirked and let out a piercing whistle, and a few seconds later his father emerged from the back room: a huge slug of a man, even paler than Raimundo. Filaments of gray hair were slicked down across his mottled scalp, and his belly stretched the front of a starched *guayabera*. He beamed and extended a hand.

"How good to see you," he said. "Raimundo! Bring us coffee and two chairs."

Much as he disliked Onofrio, Esteban was in no position to be uncivil: he accepted the handshake. Raimundo spilled coffee in the saucers and clattered the chairs and glowered, angry at being forced to serve an Indian.

"Why will you not let me return the television?" asked Esteban after taking a seat; and then, unable to bite back the words, he added, "Is it no longer your policy to swindle my people?"

Onofrio sighed, as if it were exhausting to explain things to a fool such as Esteban. "I do not swindle your people. I go beyond the letter of the contracts in allowing them to make returns rather than pursuing matters through the courts. In your case, however, I have devised a way whereby you can keep the television without any further payments and yet settle the account. Is this a swindle?"

It was pointless to argue with a man whose logic was as facile and self-serving as Onofrio's. "Tell me what you want," said Esteban.

Onofrio wetted his lips, which were the color of raw sausage. "I want you to kill the jaguar of Barrio Carolina."

"I no longer hunt," said Esteban.

"The Indian is afraid," said Raimundo, moving up behind Onofrio's shoulder. "I told you."

Onofrio waved him away and said to Esteban, "That is unreasonable. If I take the cows, you will once again be hunting jaguars. But if you do this, you will have to hunt only one jaguar."

"One that has killed eight hunters." Esteban set down his coffee cup and stood. "It is no ordinary jaguar."

Raimundo laughed disparagingly, and Esteban skewered him with a stare.

"Ah!" said Onofrio, smiling a flatterer's smile. "But none of the eight used your method."

"Your pardon, Don Onofrio," said Esteban with mock formality. "I have other business to attend."

"I will pay you five hundred *lempira* in addition to erasing the debt," said Onofrio.

"Why?" asked Esteban. "Forgive me, but I cannot believe it is due to a concern for the public welfare."

Onofrio's fat throat pulsed, his face darkened.

"Never mind," said Esteban. "It is not enough."

"Very well. A thousand." Onofrio's casual manner could not conceal the anxiety in his voice.

Intrigued, curious to learn the extent of Onofrio's anxiety, Esteban plucked a figure from the air. "Ten thousand," he said. "And in advance."

"Ridiculous! I could hire ten hunters for this much! Twenty!"

Esteban shrugged. "But none with my method."

For a moment Onofrio sat with hands enlaced, twisting them, as if struggling with some pious conception. "All right," he said, the words squeezed out of him. "Ten thousand!"

The reason for Onofrio's interest in Barrio Carolina suddenly dawned on Esteban, and he understood that the profits involved would make his fee seem pitifully small. But he was possessed by the thought of what ten thousand *lempira* could mean: a herd of cows, a small truck to haul produce, or—and as he thought it, he realized this was the happiest possibility— the little stucco house in Barrio Clarín that Encarnación had set her heart on. Perhaps owning it would soften her toward him. He noticed Raimundo staring at him, his expression a knowing smirk; and even Onofrio, though still outraged by the fee, was beginning to show signs of satisfaction, adjusting the fit of his *guayabera,* slicking down his already-slicked-down hair. Esteban felt debased by their capacity to buy him, and to preserve a last shred of dignity, he turned and walked to the door.

"I will consider it," he tossed back over his shoulder. "And I will give you my answer in the morning."

"Murder Squad of New York," starring a bald American actor, was the featured attraction on Encarnación's television that night, and the widows sat cross-legged on the floor, filling the hut so completely that the charcoal stove and the sleeping hammock had been moved outside in order to provide good viewing angles for the latecomers. To Esteban, standing in the doorway, it seemed his home had been invaded by a covey of large black birds with cowled heads, who were receiving evil instruction from the core of a flickering gray jewel. Reluctantly, he pushed between them and made his way to the shelves mounted on the wall behind the set; he reached up to the top shelf and pulled down a long bundle wrapped in oil-stained newspapers. Out of the corner of his eye, he saw Encarnación watching him, her lips thinned, curved in a smile, and that cicatrix of a smile branded its mark on Esteban's heart. She knew what he was about, and she was delighted! Not in the least worried! Perhaps she had known of Onofrio's plan to kill the jaguar, perhaps she had schemed with Onofrio to entrap him. Infuriated, he barged through the widows, setting them to gabbling, and walked out into his banana grove and sat on a stone amidst it. The night was cloudy, and only a handful of stars showed between the tattered dark shapes of the leaves; the wind sent the leaves slithering together, and he heard one of his cows snorting and smelled the ripe odor of the corral. It was as if the solidity of his life had been reduced to this isolated perspective, and he bitterly felt the isolation. Though he would admit to fault in the marriage, he could think of nothing he had done that could have bred Encarnación's hateful smile.

After a while, he unwrapped the bundle of newspapers and drew out a thin-bladed machete of the sort used to chop banana stalks, but which he used to kill jaguars. Just holding it renewed his confidence and gave him a feeling of strength. It had been four years since he had hunted, yet he knew he had not lost the skill. Once he had been proclaimed the greatest hunter in the province of Nueva Esperanza, as had his father before him, and he had not retired from hunting because of age or infirmity, but because the jaguars were beautiful, and their beauty had begun to outweigh the reasons he had for killing them. He had no better reason to kill the jaguar of Barrio Carolina. It menaced no one other than those who hunted it, who sought to invade its territory, and its death would profit only a dishonorable man and a shrewish wife, and would spread the contamination of Puerto Morada. And besides, it was a black jaguar.

"Black jaguars," his father had told him, "are creatures of

the moon. They have other forms and magical purposes with which we must not interfere. Never hunt them!"

His father had not said that the black jaguars lived on the moon, simply that they utilized its power; but as a child, Esteban had dreamed about a moon of ivory forests and silver meadows through which the jaguars flowed as swiftly as black water; and when he had told his father of the dreams, his father had said that such dreams were representations of a truth, and that sooner or later he would discover the truth underlying them. Esteban had never stopped believing in the dreams, not even in face of the rocky, airless place depicted by the science programs on Encarnación's television: that moon, its mystery explained, was merely a less enlightening kind of dream, a statement of fact that reduced reality to the knowable.

But as he thought this, Esteban suddenly realized that killing the jaguar might be the solution to his problems, that by going against his father's teaching, that by killing his dreams, his Indian conception of the world, he might be able to find accord with his wife's; he had been standing halfway between the two conceptions for too long, and it was time for him to choose. And there was no real choice. It was this world he inhabited, not that of the jaguars; if it took the death of a magical creature to permit him to embrace as joys the television and trips to the movies and a stucco house in Barrio Clarín, well, he had faith in this method. He swung the machete, slicing the dark air, and laughed. Encarnación's frivolousness, his skill at hunting, Onofrio's greed, the jaguar, the television . . . all these things were neatly woven together like the elements of a spell, one whose products would be a denial of magic and a furthering of the unmagical doctrines that had corrupted Puerto Morada. He laughed again, but a second later he chided himself: it was exactly this sort of thinking he was preparing to root out.

Esteban waked Encarnación early the next morning and forced her to accompany him to the appliance store. His machete swung by his side in a leather sheath, and he carried a burlap sack containing food and the herbs he would need for the hunt. Encarnación trotted along beside him, silent, her face hidden by a shawl. When they reached the store, Esteban had Onofrio stamp the bill PAID IN FULL, then he handed the bill and the money to Encarnación.

"If I kill the jaguar or if it kills me," he said harshly, "this will be yours. Should I fail to return within a week, you may assume that I will never return."

She retreated a step, her face registering alarm, as if she had seen him in a new light and understood the consequences of her actions; but she made no move to stop him as he walked out the door.

Across the street, Raimundo Esteves was leaning against the wall of the Cantina Atómica, talking to two girls wearing jeans and frilly blouses; the girls were fluttering their hands and dancing to the music that issued from the cantina, and to Esteban they seemed more alien than the creature he was to hunt. Raimundo spotted him and whispered to the girls; they peeked over their shoulders and laughed. Already angry at Encarnación, Esteban was washed over by a cold fury. He crossed the street to them, rested his hand on the hilt of the machete, and stared at Raimundo; he had never before noticed how soft he was, how empty of presence. A crop of pimples straggled along his jaw, the flesh beneath his eyes was pocked by tiny indentations like those made by a silversmith's hammer, and, unequal to the stare, his eyes darted back and forth between the two girls.

Esteban's anger dissolved into revulsion. "I am Esteban Caax," he said. "I have built my own house, tilled my soil, and brought four children into the world. This day I am going to hunt the jaguar of Barrio Carolina in order to make you and your father even fatter than you are." He ran his gaze up and down Raimundo's body, and, letting his voice fill with disgust, he asked, "Who are you?"

Raimundo's puffy face cinched in a knot of hatred, but he offered no response. The girls tittered and skipped through the door of the cantina; Esteban could hear them describing the incident, laughter, and he continued to stare at Raimundo.

Several other girls poked their heads out the door, giggling and whispering. After a moment Esteban spun on his heel and walked away. Behind him there was a chorus of unrestrained laughter, and a girl's voice called mockingly, "Raimundo! Who are you?" Other voices joined in, and it soon became a chant.

Barrio Carolina was not truly a barrio of Puerto Morada; it lay beyond Punta Manabique, the southernmost enclosure of the bay, and was fronted by a palm hammock and the loveliest stretch of beach in all the province, a curving slice of white sand giving way to jade-green shallows. Forty years before, it had been the headquarters of the fruit company's experimental farm, a project of such vast scope that a small town had been built on the site: rows of white frame houses with shingle roofs and screen porches, the kind you might see in a magazine illustration of rural America. The company had touted the project as being the keystone of the country's future and had promised to develop high-yield crops that would banish starvation; but in 1947 a cholera epidemic had ravaged the coast and the town had been abandoned. By the time the cholera scare had died down, the company had become well entrenched in national politics and no longer needed to maintain a benevolent image; the project had been dropped and the property abandoned until—in the same year that Esteban had retired from hunting—developers had bought it, planning to build a major resort. It was then the jaguar had appeared. Though it had not killed any of the workmen, it had terrorized them to the point that they had refused to begin the job. Hunters had been sent, and these the jaguar *had* killed. The last party of hunters had been equipped with automatic rifles, all manner of technological aids; but the jaguar had picked them off one by one, and this project, too, had been abandoned. Rumor had it that the land had recently been resold (now Esteban knew to whom), and that the idea of a resort was once more under consideration.

The walk from Puerto Morada was hot and tiring, and upon arrival Esteban sat beneath a palm and ate a lunch of cold banana fritters. Combers as white as toothpaste broke on the

shore, and there was no human litter, just dead fronds and
driftwood and coconuts. All but four of the houses had been
swallowed by the jungle, and only sections of those four remained visible, embedded like moldering gates in a blackish
green wall of vegetation. Even under the bright sunlight, they
were haunted-looking: their screens ripped, boards weathered
gray, vines cascading over their facades. A mango tree had
sprouted from one of the porches, and wild parrots were eating its fruit. He had not visited the barrio since childhood: the
ruins had frightened him then, but now he found them appealing, testifying to the dominion of natural law. It distressed him
that he would help transform it all into a place where the parrots would be chained to perches and the jaguars would be
designs on tableclothes, a place of swimming pools and tourists sipping from coconut shells. Nonetheless, after he had finished lunch, he set out to explore the jungle and soon
discovered a trail used by the jaguar: a narrow path that
wound between the vine-matted shells of the houses for about
a half mile and ended at the Río Dulce. The river was a murk-
ier green than the sea, curving away through the jungle walls;
the jaguar's tracks were everywhere along the bank, especially
thick upon a tussocky rise some five or six feet above the water.
This baffled Esteban. The jaguar could not drink from the
rise, and it certainly would not sleep there. He puzzled over it
awhile, but eventually shrugged it off, returned to the beach,
and, because he planned to keep watch that night, took a nap
beneath the palms.

Some hours later, around midafternoon, he was started
from his nap by a voice hailing him. A tall, slim, copper-
skinned woman was walking toward him, wearing a dress of
dark green—almost the exact color of the jungle walls—that
exposed the swell of her breasts. As she drew near, he saw that
though her features had a Patucan cast, they were of a lapidary
fineness uncommon to the tribe; it was as if they had been
refined into a lovely mask: cheeks planed into subtle hollows,
lips sculpted full, stylized feathers of ebony inlaid for eyebrows, eyes of jet and white onyx, and all this given a human
gloss. A sheen of sweat covered her breasts, and a single curl of

black hair lay over her collarbone, so artful-seeming it appeared to have been placed there by design. She knelt beside him, gazing at him impassively, and Esteban was flustered by her heated air of sensuality. The sea breeze bore her scent to him, a sweet musk that reminded him of mangoes left ripening in the sun.

"My name is Esteban Caax," he said, painfully aware of his own sweaty odor.

"I have heard of you," she said. "The jaguar hunter. Have you come to kill the jaguar of the barrio?"

"Yes," he said, and felt shame at admitting it.

She picked up a handful of sand and watched it sift through her fingers.

"What is your name?" he asked.

"If we become friends, I will tell you my name," she said. "Why must you kill the jaguar?"

He told her about the television set, and then, to his surprise, he found himself describing his problems with Encarnación, explaining how he intended to adapt to her ways. These were not proper subjects to discuss with a stranger, yet he was lured to intimacy; he thought he sensed an affinity between them, and that prompted him to portray his marriage as more dismal than it was, for though he had never once been unfaithful to Encarnación, he would have welcomed the chance to do so now.

"This is a black jaguar," she said. "Surely you know they are not ordinary animals, that they have purposes with which we must not interfere?"

Esteban was startled to hear his father's words from her mouth, but he dismissed it as coincidence and replied, "Perhaps. But they are not mine."

"Truly, they are," she said. "You have simply chosen to ignore them." She scooped up another handful of sand. "How will you do it? You have no gun. Only a machete."

"I have this as well," he said, and from his sack he pulled out a small parcel of herbs and handed it to her.

She opened it and sniffed the contents. "Herbs? Ah! You plan to drug the jaguar."

"Not the jaguar. Myself." He took back the parcel. "The herbs slow the heart and give the body a semblance of death. They induce a trance, but one that can be thrown off at a moment's notice. After I chew them, I will lie down in a place that the jaguar must pass on its nightly hunt. It will think I am dead, but it will not feed unless it is sure that the spirit has left the flesh, and to determine this, it will sit on the body so it can feel the spirit rise up. As soon as it starts to settle, I will throw off the trance and stab it between the ribs. If my hand is steady, it will die instantly."

"And if your hand is unsteady?"

"I have killed nearly fifty jaguars," he said. "I no longer fear unsteadiness. The method comes down through my family from the Old Patuca, and it has never failed, to my knowledge."

"But a black jaguar . . ."

"Black or spotted, it makes no difference. Jaguars are creatures of instinct, and one is like another when it comes to feeding."

"Well," she said, "I cannot wish you luck, but neither do I wish you ill." She came to her feet, brushing the sand from her dress.

He wanted to ask her to stay, but pride prevented him, and she laughed as if she knew his mind.

"Perhaps we will talk again, Esteban," she said. "It would be a pity if we did not, for more lies between us than we have spoken of this day."

She walked swiftly down the beach, becoming a diminutive black figure that was rippled away by the heat haze.

That evening, needing a place from which to keep watch, Esteban pried open the screen door of one of the houses facing the beach and went onto the porch. Chameleons skittered into the corners, and an iguana slithered off a rusted lawn chair sheathed in spiderweb and vanished through a gap in the floor. The interior of the house was dark and forbidding, except for the bathroom, the roof of which was missing, webbed over by vines that admitted a gray-green infusion of twilight. The cracked toilet was full of rainwater and dead insects. Uneasy, Esteban returned to the porch, cleaned the lawn chair, and sat.

Out on the horizon the sea and sky were blending in a haze of silver and gray; the wind had died, and the palms were as still as sculpture; a string of pelicans flying low above the waves seemed to be spelling a sentence of cryptic black syllables. But the eerie beauty of the scene was lost on him. He could not stop thinking of the woman. The memory of her hips rolling beneath the fabric of her dress as she walked away was repeated over and over in his thoughts, and whenever he tried to turn his attention to the matter at hand, the memory became more compelling. He imagined her naked, the play of muscles rippling her haunches, and this so enflamed him that he started to pace, unmindful of the fact that the creaking boards were signaling his presence. He could not understand her effect upon him. Perhaps, he thought, it was her defense of the jaguar, her calling to mind of all he was putting behind him . . . and then a realization settled over him like an icy shroud.

It was commonly held among the Patuca that a man about to suffer a solitary and unexpected death would be visited by an envoy of death, who—standing in for family and friends—would prepare him to face the event; and Esteban was now very sure that the woman had been such an envoy, that her allure had been specifically designed to attract his soul to its imminent fate. He sat back down in the lawn chair, numb with the realization. Her knowledge of his father's words, the odd flavor of her conversation, her intimation that more lay between them: it all accorded perfectly with the traditional wisdom. The moon rose three-quarters full, silvering the sands of the barrio, and still he sat there, rooted to the spot by his fear of death.

He had been watching the jaguar for several seconds before he registered its presence. It seemed at first that a scrap of night sky had fallen onto the sand and was being blown by a fitful breeze; but soon he saw that it was the jaguar, that it was inching along as if stalking some prey. Then it leaped high into the air, twisting and turning, and began to race up and down the beach: a ribbon of black water flowing across the silver sands. He had never before seen a jaguar at play, and this alone was cause for wonder; but most of all, he wondered at the fact that here were his childhood dreams come to life. He might have been peering out onto a silvery meadow of the moon, spying on one of its magical creatures. His fear was eroded by the sight, and like a child he pressed his nose to the screen, trying not to blink, anxious that he might miss a single moment.

At length the jaguar left off its play and came prowling up the beach toward the jungle. By the set of its ears and the purposeful sway of its walk, Esteban recognized that it was hunting. It stopped beneath a palm about twenty feet from the house, lifted its head, and tested the air. Moonlight frayed down through the fronds, applying liquid gleams to its haunches; its eyes, glinting yellow-green, were like peepholes into a lurid dimension of fire. The jaguar's beauty was heart-stopping—the embodiment of a flawless principle—and Esteban, contrasting this beauty with the pallid ugliness of his employer, with the ugly principle that had led to his hiring, doubted that he could ever bring himself to kill it.

All the following day he debated the question. He had hoped the woman would return, because he had rejected the idea that she was death's envoy—that perception, he thought, must have been induced by the mysterious atmosphere of the barrio—and he felt that if she was to argue the jaguar's cause again, he would let himself be persuaded. But she did not put in an appearance, and as he sat upon the beach, watching the evening sun decline through strata of dusky orange and lavender clouds, casting wild glitters over the sea, he understood once more that he had no choice. Whether or not the jaguar was beautiful, whether or not the woman had been on a supernatural errand, he must treat these things as if they had no substance. The point of the hunt had been to deny mysteries of this sort, and he had lost sight of it under the influence of old dreams.

He waited until moonrise to take the herbs, and then lay down beneath the palm tree where the jaguar had paused the previous night. Lizards whispered past in the grasses, sand fleas hopped onto his face: he hardly felt them, sinking deeper into the languor of the herbs. The fronds overhead showed an ashen green in the moonlight, lifting, rustling; and the stars between their feathered edges flickered crazily as if the breeze were fanning their flames. He became immersed in the land-scape, savoring the smells of brine and rotting foliage that were blowing across the beach, drifting with them; but when he heard the pad of the jaguar's step, he came alert. Through narrowed eyes he saw it sitting a dozen feet away, a bulky shadow craning its neck toward him, investigating his scent. After a moment it began to circle him, each circle a bit tighter than the one before, and whenever it passed out of view he had to repress a trickle of fear. Then, as it passed close on the sea-ward side, he caught a whiff of its odor.

A sweet, musky odor that reminded him of mangoes left ripening in the sun.

Fear welled up in him, and he tried to banish it, to tell him-self that the odor could not possibly be what he thought. The jaguar snarled, a razor stroke of sound that slit the peaceful mesh of wind and surf, and realizing it had scented his fear, he sprang to his feet, waving his machete. In a whirl of vision he saw the jaguar leap back, then he shouted at it, waved the ma-chete again, and sprinted for the house where he had kept watch. He slipped through the door and went staggering into the front room. There was a crash behind him, and turning, he had a glimpse of a huge black shape struggling to extricate itself from a moonlit tangle of vines and ripped screen. He darted into the bathroom, sat with his back against the toilet bowl, and braced the door shut with his feet.

The sound of the jaguar's struggles subsided, and for a mo-ment he thought it had given up. Sweat left cold trails down his sides, his heart pounded. He held his breath, listening, and it seemed the whole world was holding its breath as well. The noises of wind and surf and insects were a faint seething; moonlight shed a sickly white radiance through the enlaced vines overhead, and a chameleon was frozen among peels of wallpaper beside the door. He let out a sigh and wiped the sweat from his eyes. He swallowed.

Then the top panel of the door exploded, shattered by a black paw. Splinters of rotten wood flew into his face, and he screamed. The sleek wedge of the jaguar's head thrust through the hole, roaring. A gateway of gleaming fangs guarding a plush red throat. Half-paralyzed, Esteban jabbed weakly with the machete. The jaguar withdrew, reached in with its paw, and clawed at his leg. More by accident than design, he managed to slice the jaguar, and the paw, too, was withdrawn. He heard it rumbling in the front room, and then, seconds later, a heavy thump against the wall behind him. The jaguar's head appeared above the edge of the wall; it was hanging by its forepaws, trying to gain a perch from which to leap down into the room. Esteban scrambled to his feet and slashed wildly, severing vines. The jaguar fell back, yowling. For a while it prowled along the wall, fuming to itself. Finally there was silence.

When sunlight began to filter through the vines, Esteban walked out of the house and headed down the beach to Puerto Morada. He went with his head lowered, desolate, thinking of the grim future that awaited him after he returned the money to Onofrio: a life of trying to please an increasingly shrewish Encarnación, of killing lesser jaguars for much less money. He was so mired in depression that he did not notice the woman until she called to him. She was leaning against a palm about thirty feet away, wearing a filmy white dress through which he could see the dark jut of her nipples. He drew his machete and backed off a pace.

"Why do you fear me, Esteban?" she called, walking toward him.

"You tricked me into revealing my method and tried to kill me," he said. "Is that not reason for fear?"

"I did not know you or your method in that form. I knew only that you were hunting me. But now the hunt has ended, and we can be as man and woman."

He kept his machete at point. "What are you?" he asked.

She smiled. "My name is Miranda. I am Patuca."

"Patucas do not have black fur and fangs."

"I am of the Old Patuca," she said. "We have this power."

"Keep away!" He lifted the machete as if to strike, and she stopped just beyond his reach.

"You can kill me if that is your wish, Esteban." She spread her arms, and her breasts thrust forward against the fabric of her dress. "You are stronger than I, now. But listen to me first."

He did not lower the machete, but his fear and anger were being overridden by a sweeter emotion.

"Long ago," she said, "there was a great healer who foresaw that one day the Patuca would lose their place in the world, and so, with the help of the gods, he opened a door into another world where the tribe could flourish. But many of the tribe were afraid and would not follow him. Since then, the door has been left open for those who would come after." She waved at the ruined houses. "Barrio Carolina is the site of the door, and the jaguar is its guardian. But soon the fevers of this world will sweep over the barrio, and the door will close forever. For though our hunt has ended, there is no end to hunters or to greed." She came a step nearer. "If you listen to the sounding of your heart, you will know this is the truth."

He half believed her, yet he also believed her words masked a more poignant truth, one that fitted inside the other the way his machete fitted into its sheath.

"What is it?" she asked. "What troubles you?"

"I think you have come to prepare me for death," he said, "and that your door leads only to death."

"Then why do you not run from me?" She pointed toward Puerto Morada. "That is death, Esteban. The cries of the gulls are death, and when the hearts of lovers stop at the moment of greatest pleasure, that, too, is death. This world is no more than a thin covering of life drawn over a foundation of death, like a scum of algae upon a rock. Perhaps you are right, perhaps my world lies beyond death. The two ideas are not opposed. But if I am death to you, Esteban, then it is death you love."

He turned his eyes to the sea, not wanting her to see his face. "I do not love you," he said.

"Love awaits us," she said. "And someday you will join me in my world."

He looked back to her, ready with a denial, but was shocked to silence. Her dress had fallen to the sand, and she was smiling. The litheness and purity of the jaguar were reflected in every line of her body; her secret hair was so absolute a black that it seemed an absence in her flesh. She moved close, pushing aside the machete. The tips of her breasts brushed against him, warm through the coarse cloth of his shirt; her hands cupped his face, and he was drowning in her heated scent, weakened by both fear and desire.

"We are of one soul, you and I," she said. "One blood and one truth. You cannot reject me."

Days passed, though Esteban was unclear as to how many. Night and day were unimportant incidences of his relationship with Miranda, serving only to color their lovemaking with a spectral or a sunny mood; and each time they made love, it was as if a thousand new colors were being added to his senses. He had never been so content. Sometimes, gazing at the haunted facades of the barrio, he believed that they might well conceal shadowy avenues leading to another world; however, whenever Miranda tried to convince him to leave with her, he refused: he could not overcome his fear and would never admit—even to himself—that he loved her. He attempted to fix his thoughts on Encarnación, hoping this would undermine his fixation with Miranda and free him to return to Puerto Morada; but he found that he could not picture his wife except as a black bird hunched before a flickering gray jewel. Miranda, however, seemed equally unreal at times. Once as they sat on the bank of the Río Dulce, watching the reflection of the moon—almost full—floating upon the water, she pointed to it and said, "My world is that near, Esteban. That touchable. You may think the moon above is real and this is only a reflection, but the thing most real, that most illustrates the real, is the surface that permits the illusion of reflection. Passing through this surface is what you fear, and yet it is so insubstantial, you would scarcely notice the passage."

"You sound like the old priest who taught me philosophy," said Esteban. "His world—his heaven—was also philosophy.

Is that what your world is? The idea of a place? Or are there birds and jungles and rivers?"

Her expression was in partial eclipse, half-moonlit, half-shadowed, and her voice revealed nothing of her mood. "No more than there are here," she said.

"What does that mean?" he said angrily. "Why will you not give me a clear answer?"

"If I were to describe my world, you would simply think me a clever liar." She rested her head on his shoulder. "Sooner or later you will understand. We did not find each other merely to have the pain of being parted."

In that moment her beauty—like her words—seemed a kind of evasion, obscuring a dark and frightening beauty beneath; and yet he knew that she was right, that no proof of hers could persuade him contrary to his fear.

One afternoon, an afternoon of such brightness that it was impossible to look at the sea without squinting, they swam out to a sandbar that showed as a thin curving island of white against the green water. Esteban floundered and splashed, but Miranda swam as if born to the element; she darted beneath him, tickling him, pulling at his feet, eeling away before he could catch her. They walked along the sand, turning over starfish with their toes, collecting whelks to boil for their dinner, and then Esteban spotted a dark stain hundreds of yards wide that was moving below the water beyond the bar: a great school of king mackerel.

"It is too bad we have no boat," he said. "Mackerel would taste better than whelks."

"We need no boat," she said. "I will show you an old way of catching fish."

She traced a complicated design in the sand, and when she had done, she led him into the shallows and had him stand facing her a few feet away.

"Look down at the water between us," she said. "Do not look up, and keep perfectly still until I tell you."

She began to sing with a faltering rhythm, a rhythm that put him in mind of the ragged breezes of the season. Most of the words were unfamiliar, but others he recognized as Patuca.

After a minute he experienced a wave of dizziness, as if his legs had grown long and spindly, and he was now looking down from a great height, breathing rarefied air. Then a tiny dark stain materialized below the expanse of water between him and Miranda. He remembered his grandfather's stories of the Old Patuca, how—with the help of the gods—they had been able to shrink the world, to bring enemies close and cross vast distances in a matter of moments. But the gods were dead, their powers gone from the world. He wanted to glance back to shore and see if he and Miranda had become coppery giants taller than the palms.

"Now," she said, breaking off her song, "you must put your hand into the water on the seaward side of the school and gently wiggle your fingers. Very gently! Be sure not to disturb the surface."

But when Esteban made to do as he was told, he slipped and caused a splash. Miranda cried out. Looking up, he saw a wall of jade-green water bearing down on them, its face thickly studded with the fleeting dark shapes of the mackerel. Before he could move, the wave swept over the sandbar and carried him under, dragging him along the bottom and finally casting him onto shore. The beach was littered with flopping mackerel; Miranda lay in the shallows, laughing at him. Esteban laughed, too, but only to cover up his rekindled fear of this woman who drew upon the powers of dead gods. He had no wish to hear her explanation; he was certain she would tell him that the gods lived on in her world, and this would only confuse him further.

Later that day as Esteban was cleaning the fish, while Miranda was off picking bananas to cook with them—the sweet little ones that grew along the riverbank—a Land-Rover came jouncing up the beach from Puerto Morada, an orange fire of the setting sun dancing on its windshield. It pulled up beside him, and Onofrio climbed out the passenger side. A hectic flush dappled his cheeks, and he was dabbing his sweaty brow with a handkerchief. Raimundo climbed out the driver's side and leaned against the door, staring hatefully at Esteban.

"Nine days and not a word," said Onofrio gruffly. "We thought you were dead. How goes the hunt?"

Esteban set down the fish he had been scaling and stood. "I have failed," he said. "I will give you back the money."

Raimundo chuckled—a dull, cluttered sound—and Onofrio grunted with amusement. "Impossible," he said. "Encarnación has spent the money on a house in Barrio Clarín. You must kill the jaguar."

"I cannot," said Esteban. "I will repay you somehow."

"The Indian has lost his nerve, Father." Raimundo spat in the sand. "Let me and my friends hunt the jaguar."

The idea of Raimundo and his loutish friends thrashing through the jungle was so ludicrous that Esteban could not restrain a laugh.

"Be careful, Indian!" Raimundo banged the flat of his hand on the roof of the car.

"It is you who should be careful," said Esteban. "Most likely the jaguar will be hunting you." Esteban picked up his machete. "And whoever hunts this jaguar will answer to me as well."

Raimundo reached for something in the driver's seat and walked around in front of the hood. In his hand was a silvered automatic. "I await your answer," he said.

"Put that away!" Onofrio's tone was that of a man addressing a child whose menace was inconsequential, but the intent surfacing in Raimundo's face was not childish. A tic marred the plump curve of his cheek, the ligature of his neck was cabled, and his lips were drawn back in a joyless grin. It was, thought Esteban—strangely fascinated by the transformation—like watching a demon dissolve its false shape: the true lean features melting up from the illusion of the soft.

"This son of a whore insulted me in front of Julia!" Raimundo's gun hand was shaking.

"Your personal differences can wait," said Onofrio. "This is a business matter." He held out his hand. "Give me the gun."

"If he is not going to kill the jaguar, what use is he?" said Raimundo.

"Perhaps we can convince him to change his mind." Onofrio beamed at Esteban. "What do you say? Shall I let my son collect his debt of honor, or will you fulfill our contract?"

"Father!" complained Raimundo; his eyes flicked sideways. "He . . ."

Esteban broke for the jungle. The gun roared, a white-hot claw swiped at his side, and he went flying. For an instant he did not know where he was; but then, one by one, his impressions began to sort themselves. He was lying on his injured side, and it was throbbing fiercely. Sand crusted his mouth and eyelids. He was curled up around his machete, which was still clutched in his hand. Voices above him, sand fleas hopping on his face. He resisted the urge to brush them off and lay without moving. The throb of his wound and his hatred had the same red force behind them.

". . . carry him to the river," Raimundo was saying, his voice atremble with excitement. "Everyone will think the jaguar killed him!"

"Fool!" said Onofrio. "He might have killed the jaguar, and you could have had a sweeter revenge. His wife . . ."

"This was sweet enough," said Raimundo.

A shadow fell over Esteban, and he held his breath. He needed no herbs to deceive this pale, flabby jaguar who was bending to him, turning him onto his back.

"Watch out!" cried Onofrio.

Esteban let himself be turned and lashed out with the machete. His contempt for Onofrio and Encarnación, as well as his hatred of Raimundo, was involved in the blow, and the blade lodged deep in Raimundo's side, grating on bone. Raimundo shrieked and would have fallen, but the blade helped to keep him upright; his hands fluttered around the machete as if he wanted to adjust it to a more comfortable position, and his eyes were wide with disbelief. A shudder vibrated the hilt of the machete—it seemed sensual, the spasm of a spent passion—and Raimundo sank to his knees. Blood spilled from his mouth, adding tragic lines to the corners of his lips. He pitched forward, not falling flat but remaining kneeling, his face pressed into the sand: the attitude of an Arab at prayer.

Esteban wrenched the machete free, fearful of an attack by Onofrio, but the appliance dealer was squirming into the Land-Rover. The engine caught, the wheels spun, and the car lurched off, turning through the edge of the surf and heading for Puerto Morada. An orange dazzle flared on the rear window, as if the spirit who had lured it to the barrio was now harrying it away.

Unsteadily, Esteban got to his feet. He peeled his shirt back from the bullet wound. There was a lot of blood, but it was only a crease. He avoided looking at Raimundo and walked down to the water and stood gazing out at the waves; his thoughts rolled in with them, less thoughts than tidal sweeps of emotion.

It was twilight by the time Miranda returned, her arms full of bananas and wild figs. She had not heard the shot. He told her what had happened as she dressed his wounds with a poultice of herbs and banana leaves. "It will mend," she said of the wound. "But this"—she gestured at Raimundo—"this will not. You must come with me, Esteban. The soldiers will kill you."

"No," he said. "They will come, but they are Patuca . . . except for the captain, who is a drunkard, a shell of a man. I doubt he will even be notified. They will listen to my story, and we will reach an accommodation. No matter what lies Onofrio tells, his word will not stand against theirs."

"And then?"

"I may have to go to jail for a while, or I may have to leave the province. But I will not be killed."

She sat for a minute without speaking, the whites of her eyes glowing in the half-light. Finally she stood and walked off along the beach.

"Where are you going?" he called.

She turned back. "You speak so casually of losing me. . . ." she began.

"It is not casual!"

"No!" She laughed bitterly. "I suppose not. You are so afraid of life, you call it death and would prefer jail or exile to living it. That is hardly casual." She stared at him, her expression a cypher at that distance. "I will not lose you, Esteban," she said. She walked away again, and this time when he called she did not turn.

· · ·

Twilight deepened to dusk, a slow fill of shadow graying the world into negative, and Esteban felt himself graying along with it, his thougths reduced to echoing the dull wash of the receding tide. The dusk lingered, and he had the idea that night would never fall, that the act of violence had driven a nail through the substance of his irresolute life, pinned him forever to this ashen moment and deserted shore. As a child he had been terrified by the possibility of such magical isolations, but now the prospect seemed a consolation for Miranda's absence, a remembrance of her magic. Despite her parting words, he did not think she would be back—there had been sadness and finality in her voice—and this roused in him feelings of both relief and desolation, feelings that set him to pacing up and down the tidal margin of the shore.

The full moon rose, the sands of the barrio burned silver, and shortly thereafter four soldiers came in a jeep from Puerto Morada. They were gnomish copper-skinned men, and their uniforms were the dark blue of the night sky, bearing no device or decoration. Though they were not close friends, he knew them each by name: Sebastian, Amador, Carlito, and Ramón. In their headlights Raimundo's corpse—startlingly pale, the blood on his face dried into intricate whorls—looked like an exotic creature cast up by the sea, and their inspection of it smacked more of curiosity than of a search for evidence. Amador unearthed Raimundo's gun, sighted along it toward the jungle, and asked Ramón how much he thought it was worth.

"Perhaps Onofrio will give you a good price," said Ramón, and the others laughed.

They built a fire of driftwood and coconut shells, and sat around it while Esteban told his story; he did not mention either Miranda or her relation to the jaguar, because these men—estranged from the tribe by their government service—had grown conservative in their judgments, and he did not want them to consider him irrational. They listened without comment; the firelight burnished their skins to reddish gold and glinted on their rifle barrels.

"Onofrio will take his charge to the capital if we do nothing," said Amador after Esteban had finished.

"He may in any case," said Carlito. "And then it will go hard with Esteban."

"And," said Sebastian, "if an agent is sent to Puerto Morada and sees how things are with Captain Portales, they will surely replace him and it will go hard with us."

They stared into the flames, mulling over the problem, and Esteban chose the moment to ask Amador, who lived near him on the mountain, if he had seen Encarnación.

"She will be amazed to learn you are alive," said Amador. "I saw her yesterday in the dressmaker's shop. She was admiring the fit of a new black skirt in the mirror."

It was as if a black swath of Encarnación's skirt had folded around Esteban's thoughts. He lowered his head and carved lines in the sand with the point of his machete.

"I have it," said Ramón. "A boycott!"

The others expressed confusion.

"If we do not buy from Onofrio, who will?" said Ramón. "He will lose his business. Threatened with this, he will not dare involve the government. He will allow Esteban to plead self-defense."

"But Raimundo was his only son," said Amador. "It may be that grief will count more than greed in this instance."

Again they fell silent. It mattered little to Esteban what was decided. He was coming to understand that without Miranda, his future held nothing but uninteresting choices; he turned his gaze to the sky and noticed that the stars and the fire were flickering with the same rhythm, and he imagined each of them ringed by a group of gnomish copper-skinned men, debating the question of his fate.

"Aha!" said Carlito. "I know what to do. We will occupy Barrio Carolina—the entire company—and *we* will kill the jaguar. Onofrio's greed cannot withstand this temptation."

"That you must not do," said Esteban.

"But why?" asked Amador. "We may not kill the jaguar, but with so many men we will certainly drive it away."

Before Esteban could answer, the jaguar roared. It was prowling down the beach toward the fire, like a black flame itself shifting over the glowing sand. Its ears were laid back, and silver drops of moonlight gleamed in its eyes. Amador grabbed his rifle, came to one knee, and fired: the bullet sprayed sand a dozen feet to the left of the jaguar.

"Wait!" cried Esteban, pushing him down.

But the rest had begun to fire, and the jaguar was hit. It leaped high as it had that first night while playing, but this time it landed in a heap, snarling, snapping at its shoulder; it regained its feet and limped toward the jungle, favoring its right foreleg. Excited by their success, the soldiers ran a few paces after it and stopped to fire again. Carlito dropped to one knee, taking careful aim.

"No!" shouted Esteban, and as he hurled his machete at Carlito, desperate to prevent further harm to Miranda, he recognized the trap that had been sprung and the consequences he would face.

The blade sliced across Carlito's thigh, knocking him onto his side. He screamed, and Amador, seeing what had happened, fired wildly at Esteban and called to the others. Esteban ran toward the jungle, making for the jaguar's path. A fusillade of shots rang out behind him, bullets whipped past his ears. Each time his feet slipped in the soft sand, the moonstruck facades of the barrio appeared to lurch sideways as if trying to block his way. And then, as he reached the verge of the jungle, he was hit.

The bullet seemed to throw him forward, to increase his speed, but somehow he managed to keep his feet. He careened along the path, arms waving, breath shrieking in his throat. Palmetto fronds swatted his face, vines tangled his legs. He felt no pain, only a peculiar numbness that pulsed low in his back; he pictured the wound opening and closing like the mouth of an anemone. The soldiers were shouting his name. They would follow, but cautiously, afraid of the jaguar, and he thought he might be able to cross the river before they could catch up. But when he came to the river, he found the jaguar waiting.

It was crouched on the tussocky rise, its neck craned over the water, and below, half a dozen feet from the bank, floated the reflection of the full moon, huge and silvery, an unblemished circle of light. Blood glistened scarlet on the jaguar's shoulder, like a fresh rose pinned in place, and this made it look even more an embodiment of principle: the shape a god might choose, that some universal constant might assume. It gazed calmly at Esteban, growled low in its throat, and dove into the river, cleaving and shattering the moon's reflection, vanishing beneath the surface. The ripples subsided, the image of the moon re-formed. And there, silhouetted against it, Esteban saw the figure of a woman swimming, each stroke causing her to grow smaller and smaller until she seemed no more than a character incised upon a silver plate. It was not only Miranda he saw, but all mystery and beauty receding from him, and he realized how blind he had been not to perceive the truth sheathed inside the truth of death that had been sheathed inside her truth of another world. It was clear to him now. It sang to him from his wound, every syllable a heartbeat. It was written by the dying ripples, it swayed in the banana leaves, it sighed on the wind. It was everywhere, and he had always known it: if you deny mystery—even in the guise of death—then you deny life and you will walk like a ghost through your days, never knowing the secrets of the extremes. The deep sorrows, the absolute joys.

He drew a breath of the rank jungle air, and with it drew a breath of a world no longer his, of the girl Encarnación, of friends and children and country nights . . . all his lost sweetness. His chest tightened as with the onset of tears, but the sensation quickly abated, and he understood that the sweetness of the past had been subsumed by a scent of mangoes, that nine magical days—a magical number of days, the number it takes to sing the soul to rest—lay between him and tears. Freed of those associations, he felt as if he were undergoing a subtle refinement of form, a winnowing, and he remembered having felt much the same on the day when he had run out the door of Santa María del Onda, putting behind him its dark geometries and cobwebbed catechisms and generations of swallows that had never flown beyond the walls, casting off his acolyte's robe and racing across the square toward the mountain and Encarnación: it had been she who had lured him then, just as his mother had lured him to the church and as Miranda was luring him now, and he laughed at seeing how easily these three women had diverted the flow of his life, how like other men he was in this.

The strange bloom of painlessness in his back was sending out tendrils into his arms and legs, and the cries of the soldiers had grown louder. Miranda was a tiny speck shrinking against a silver immensity. For a moment he hesitated, experiencing a resurgence of fear; then Miranda's face materialized in his mind's eye, and all the emotion he had suppressed for nine days poured through him, washing away the fear. It was a silvery, flawless emotion, and he was giddy with it, light with it; it was like thunder and fire fused into one element and boiling up inside him, and he was overwhelmed by a need to express it, to mold it into a form that would reflect its power and purity. But he was no singer, no poet. There was but a single mode of expression open to him. Hoping he was not too late, that Miranda's door had not shut forever, Esteban dove into the river, cleaving the image of the full moon; and—his eyes still closed from the shock of the splash—with the last of his mortal strength, he swam hard down after her.

The Night of White Bhairab

Whenever Mr. Chatterji went to Delhi on business, twice yearly, he would leave Eliot Blackford in charge of his Katmandu home, and prior to each trip the transfer of keys and instructions would be made at the Hotel Anapurna. Eliot—an angular sharp-featured man in his mid-thirties, with thinning blond hair and a perpetually ardent expression—knew Mr. Chatterji for a subtle soul, and he suspected that this subtlety had dictated the choice of meeting place. The Anapurna was the Nepalese equivalent of a Hilton, its bar equipped in vinyl and plastic, with a choirlike arrangement of bottles fronting the mirror. Lights were muted, napkins monogrammed. Mr. Chatterji, plump and prosperous in a business suit, would consider it an elegant refutation of Kipling's famous couplet ("East is East," etc.) that he was at home here, whereas Eliot, wearing a scruffy robe and sandals, was not; he would argue that not only had the twain met, they had actually exchanged places. It was Eliot's own measure of subtlety that restrained him from pointing out what Mr. Chatterji could not perceive: that the Anapurna was a skewed version of the American Dream. The carpeting was indoor-outdoor runner; the menu was rife with ludicrous misprints (*Skotch Miss, Screwdiver*); and the lounge act—two turbaned, tuxedoed Indians on electric guitar and traps—was managing to turn "Evergreen" into a doleful raga.

"There will be one important delivery." Mr. Chatterji hailed the waiter and nudged Eliot's shot glass forward. "It should have been here days ago, but you know these customs people." He gave an effeminate shudder to express his distaste for the bureaucracy, and cast an expectant eye on Eliot, who did not disappoint.

"What is it?" he asked, certain that it would be an addition to Mr. Chatterji's collection: he enjoyed discussing the collection with Americans; it proved that he had an overview of their culture.

"Something delicious!" said Mr. Chatterji. He took the tequila bottle from the waiter and—with a fond look—passed it to Eliot. "Are you familiar with the Carversville Terror?"

"Yeah, sure." Eliot knocked back another shot. "There was a book about it."

"Indeed," said Mr. Chatterji. "A best-seller. The Cousineau mansion was once the most notorious haunted house of your New England. It was torn down several months ago, and I've succeeded in acquiring the fireplace, which"—he sipped his drink—"which was the locus of power. I'm very fortunate to have obtained it." He fitted his glass into the circle of moisture on the bar and waxed scholarly. "Aimée Cousineau was a most unusual spirit, capable of a variety of. . . ."

Eliot concentrated on his tequila. These recitals never failed to annoy him, as did—for different reasons—the sleek Western disguise. When Eliot had arrived in Katmandu as a member of the Peace Corps, Mr. Chatterji had presented a far less pompous image: a scrawny kid dressed in Levi's that he had wheedled from a tourist. He'd been one of the hangers-on—mostly young Tibetans—who frequented the grubby tearooms on Freak Street, watching the American hippies giggle over their hash yogurt, lusting after their clothes, their women, their entire culture. The hippies had respected the Tibetans: they were a people of legend, symbols of the occultism then in vogue, and the fact that they liked James Bond movies, fast cars, and Jimi Hendrix had increased the hippies' self-esteem. But they had found laughable the fact that Ranjeesh Chatterji—another Westernized Indian—had liked these same things, and they had treated him with mean condescension. Now, thirteen years later, the roles had been reversed; it was Eliot who had become the hanger-on.

He had settled in Katmandu after his tour was up, his idea being to practice meditation, to achieve enlightenment. But it had not gone well. There was an impediment in his mind—he pictured it as a dark stone, a stone compounded of worldly attachments—that no amount of practice could wear down, and his life had fallen into a futile pattern. He would spend ten months of the year living in a small room near the temple of Swayambhunath, meditating, rubbing away at the stone; and then, during March and September, he would occupy Mr. Chatterji's house and debauch himself with liquor and sex and drugs. He was aware that Mr. Chatterji considered him a burnout, that the position of caretaker was in effect a form of revenge, a means by which his employer could exercise his own brand of condescension; but Eliot minded neither the label nor the attitude. There were worse things to be than a burnout in Nepal. It was beautiful country, it was inexpensive, it was far from Minnesota (Eliot's home). And the concept of personal failure was meaningless here. You lived, died, and were reborn over and over until at last you attained the ultimate success of nonbeing: a terrific consolation for failure.

". . . yet in your country," Mr. Chatterji was saying, "evil has a sultry character. Sexy! It's as if the spirits were adopting vibrant personalities in order to contend with pop groups and movie stars."

Eliot thought of a comment, but the tequila backed up on him and he belched instead. Everything about Mr. Chatterji— teeth, eyes, hair, gold rings—seemed to be gleaming with extraordinary brilliance. He looked as unstable as a soap bubble, a fat little Hindu illusion.

Mr. Chatterji clapped a hand to his forehead. "I nearly forgot. There will be another American staying at the house. A girl. Very shapely!" He shaped an hourglass in the air. "I'm quite mad for her, but I don't know if she's trustworthy. Please see she doesn't bring in any strays."

"Right," said Eliot. "No problem."

"I believe I will gamble now," said Mr. Chatterji, standing and gazing toward the lobby. "Will you join me?"

"No, I think I'll get drunk. I guess I'll see you in October."

"You're drunk already, Eliot." Mr. Chatterji patted him on the shoulder. "Hadn't you noticed?"

Early the next morning, hung over, tongue cleaving to the roof of his mouth, Eliot sat himself down for a final bout of trying to visualize the Avalokitesvara Buddha. All the sounds outside—the buzzing of a motor scooter, birdsong, a girl's laughter—seemed to be repeating the mantra, and the gray stone walls of his room looked at once intensely real and yet incredibly fragile, papery, a painted backdrop he could rip with his hands. He began to feel the same fragility, as if he were being immersed in a liquid that was turning him opaque, filling him with clarity. A breath of wind could float him out the window, drift him across the fields, and he would pass through the trees and mountains, all the phantoms of the material world . . . but then a trickle of panic welled up from the bottom of his soul, from that dark stone. It was beginning to smolder, to give off poison fumes: a little briquette of anger and lust and fear. Cracks were spreading across the clear substance he had become, and if he didn't move soon, if he didn't break off the meditation, he would shatter.

He toppled out of the lotus position and lay propped on his elbows. His heart raced, his chest heaved, and he felt very much like screaming his frustration. Yeah, that was a temptation. To just say the hell with it and scream, to achieve through chaos what he could not through clarity: to empty himself into the scream. He was trembling, his emotions flowing between self-hate and self-pity. Finally, he struggled up and put on jeans and a cotton shirt. He knew he was close to a breakdown, and he realized that he usually reached this point just before taking up residence at Mr. Chatterji's. His life was a frayed thread stretched tight between those two poles of debauchery. One day it would snap.

"The hell with it," he said. He stuffed the remainder of his clothes into a duffel bag and headed into town.

. . .

Walking through Durbar Square—which wasn't really a square but a huge temple complex interspersed with open areas and wound through by cobbled paths—always put Eliot in mind of his brief stint as a tour guide, a career cut short when the agency received complaints about his eccentricity. (". . . As you pick your way among the piles of human waste and fruit rinds, I caution you not to breathe too deeply of the divine afflatus; otherwise, it may forever numb you to the scent of Prairie Cove or Petitpoint Gulch or whatever citadel of gracious living it is that you call home. . . .") It had irked him to have to lecture on the carvings and history of the square, especially to the just-plain-folks who only wanted a Polaroid of Edna or Uncle Jimmy standing next to that weird monkey god on the pedestal. The square was a unique place, and in Eliot's opinion such unenlightened tourism demeaned it.

Pagoda-style temples of red brick and dark wood towered on all sides, their finials rising into brass lightning bolts. They were alien-looking—you half expected the sky above them to be of an otherworldly color and figured by several moons. Their eaves and window screens were ornately carved into the images of gods and demons, and behind a large window screen on the temple of White Bhairab lay the mask of that god. It was almost ten feet high, brass, with a fanciful headdress and long-lobed ears and a mouth full of white fangs; its eyebrows were enameled red, fiercely arched, but the eyes had the goofy quality common to Newari gods—no matter how wrathful they were, there was something essentially friendly about them, and they reminded Eliot of cartoon germs. Once a year—in fact, a little more than a week from now—the screens would be opened, a pipe would be inserted into the god's mouth, and rice beer would jet out into the mouths of the milling crowds; at some point a fish would be slipped into the pipe, and whoever caught it would be deemed the luckiest soul in the Katmandu Valley for the next year. It was one of Eliot's traditions to make a try for the fish, though he knew that it wasn't luck he needed.

Beyond the square, the streets were narrow, running between long brick buildings three and four stories tall, each divided into dozens of separate dwellings. The strip of sky between the roofs was bright, burning blue—a void color— and in the shade the bricks looked purplish. People hung out the windows of the upper stories, talking back and forth: an exotic tenement life. Small shrines—wooden enclosures containing statuary of stucco or brass—were tucked into wall niches and the mouths of alleys. The gods were everywhere in Katmandu, and there was hardly a corner to which their gaze did not penetrate.

On reaching Mr. Chatterji's, which occupied half a block-long building, Eliot made for the first of the interior courtyards; a stair led up from it to Mr. Chatterji's apartment, and he thought he would check on what had been left to drink. But as he entered the courtyard—a phalanx of jungly plants arranged around a lozenge of cement—he saw the girl and stopped short. She was sitting in a lawn chair, reading, and she was indeed very shapely. She wore loose cotton trousers, a T-shirt, and a long white scarf shot through with golden threads. The scarf and the trousers were the uniform of the young travelers who generally stayed in the expatriate enclave of Temal: it seemed that they all bought them immediately upon arrival in order to identify themselves to each other. Edging closer, peering between the leaves of a rubber plant, Eliot saw that the girl was doe-eyed, with honey-colored skin and shoulder-length brown hair interwoven by lighter strands. Her wide mouth had relaxed into a glum expression. Sensing him, she glanced up, startled; then she waved and set down her book.

"I'm Eliot," he said, walking over.

"I know. Ranjeesh told me." She stared at him incuriously.

"And you?" He squatted beside her.

"Michaela." She fingered the book, as if she were eager to get back to it.

"I can see you're new in town."

"How's that?"

He told her about the clothes, and she shrugged. "That's what I am," she said. "I'll probably always wear them." She folded her hands on her stomach: it was a nicely rounded

stomach, and Eliot—a connoisseur of women's stomachs—
felt the beginnings of arousal.

"Always?" he said. "You plan on being here that long?"

"I don't know." She ran a finger along the spine of the book.
"Ranjeesh asked me to marry him, and I said maybe."

Eliot's infant plan of seduction collapsed beneath this
wrecking ball of a statement, and he failed to hide his incredulity. "You're in love with Ranjeesh?"

"What's that got to do with it?" A wrinkle creased her brow:
it was the perfect symptom of her mood, the line a cartoonist
might have chosen to express petulant anger.

"Nothing. Not if it doesn't have anything to do with it." He
tried a grin, but to no effect. "Well," he said after a pause.
"How do you like Katmandu?"

"I don't get out much," she said flatly.

She obviously did not want conversation, but Eliot wasn't
ready to give up. "You ought to," he said. "The festival of Indra
Jatra's about to start. It's pretty wild. Especially on the night
of White Bhairab. Buffalo sacrifices, torchlight . . ."

"I don't like crowds," she said.

Strike two.

Eliot strained to think of an enticing topic, but he had the
idea it was a lost cause. There was something inert about her, a
veneer of listlessness redolent of Thorazine, of hospital routine. "Have you ever seen the Khaa?" he asked.

"The what?"

"The Khaa. It's a spirit . . . though some people will tell you
it's partly animal, because over here the animal and spirit
worlds overlap. But whatever it is, all the old houses have one,
and those that don't are considered unlucky. There's one here."

"What's it look like?"

"Vaguely anthropomorphic. Black, featureless. Kind of a
living shadow. They can stand upright, but they roll instead of
walk."

She laughed. "No, I haven't seen it. Have you?"

"Maybe," said Eliot. "I thought I saw it a couple of times,
but I was pretty stoned."

She sat up straighter and crossed her legs; her breasts jiggled, and Eliot fought to keep his eyes centered on her face. "Ranjeesh tells me you're a little cracked," she said.

Good ol' Ranjeesh! He might have known that the son of a bitch would have sandbagged him with his new lady. "I guess I am," he said, preparing for the brush-off. "I do a lot of meditation, and sometimes I teeter on the edge."

But she appeared more intrigued by this admission than by anything else he had told her; a smile melted up from her carefully composed features. "Tell me some more about the Khaa," she said.

Eliot congratulated himself. "They're quirky sorts," he said. "Neither good nor evil. They hide in dark corners, though now and then they're seen in the streets or in the fields out near Jyapu. And the oldest ones, the most powerful ones, live in the temples in Durbar Square. There's a story about the one here that's descriptive of how they operate . . . if you're interested."

"Sure." Another smile.

"Before Ranjeesh bought this place, it was a guesthouse, and one night a woman with three goiters on her neck came to spend the night. She had two loaves of bread that she was taking home to her family, and she stuck them under her pillow before going to sleep. Around midnight the Khaa rolled into her room and was struck by the sight of her goiters rising and falling as she breathed. He thought they'd make a beautiful necklace, so he took them and put them on his own neck. Then he spotted the loaves sticking out from her pillow. They looked good, so he took them as well and replaced them with two loaves of gold. When the woman woke, she was delighted. She hurried back to her village to tell her family, and on the way she met a friend, a woman, who was going to market. This woman had four goiters. The first woman told her what had happened, and that night the second woman went to the guesthouse and did exactly the same things. Around midnight the Khaa rolled into her room. He'd grown bored with his necklace, and he gave it to the woman. He'd also decided that bread didn't taste very good, but he still had a loaf and he figured he'd give it another chance. So in exchange for the necklace, he took the woman's appetite for bread. When she woke, she had seven goiters, no gold, and she could never eat bread again the rest of her life."

Eliot had expected a response of mild amusement and had hoped that the story would be the opening gambit in a game with a foregone and pleasurable conclusion; but he had not expected her to stand, to become walled off from him again.

"I've got to go," she said, and with a distracted wave she made for the front door. She walked with her head down, hands thrust into her pockets as if counting the steps.

"Where are you going?" called Eliot, taken back.

"I don't know. Freak Street, maybe."

"Want some company?"

She turned back at the door. "It's not your fault," she said, "but I don't really enjoy your company."

Shot down!

Trailing smoke, spinning, smacking into the hillside, and blowing up into a fireball.

Eliot didn't understand why it had hit him so hard. It had happened before, and it would again. Ordinarily he would have headed for Temal and found himself another long white scarf and pair of cotton trousers, one less morbidly self-involved (that, in retrospect, was how he characterized Michaela), one who would help him refuel for another bout of trying to visualize Avalokitesvara Buddha. He did, in fact, go to Temal; but he merely sat and drank tea and smoked hashish in a restaurant, and watched the young travelers pairing up for the night. Once he caught the bus to Patan and visited a friend, an old hippie pal named Sam Chipley who ran a medical clinic; once he walked out to Swayambhunath, close enough to see the white dome of the stupa, and atop it, the gilt structure on which the all-seeing eyes of Buddha were painted: they seemed squinty and mean-looking, as if taking unfavorable notice of his approach. But mostly over the next week he wandered through Mr. Chatterji's house, carrying a bottle, maintaining a buzz, and keeping an eye on Michaela.

The majority of the rooms were unfurnished, but many bore signs of recent habitation: broken hash pipes, ripped sleeping

bags, empty packets of incense. Mr. Chatterji let travelers—
those he fancied sexually, male and female—use the rooms for
up to months at a time, and to walk through them was to take
a historical tour of the American counterculture. The graffiti
spoke of concerns as various as Vietnam, the Sex Pistols,
women's lib, and the housing shortage in Great Britain, and
also conveyed personal messages: "Ken Finkel please get in
touch with me at Am. Ex. in Bangkok . . . love Ruth." In one
of the rooms was a complicated mural depicting Farrah Faw-
cett sitting on the lap of a Tibetan demon, throttling his
barbed phallus with her fingers. It all conjured up the image of
a moldering, deranged milieu. Eliot's milieu. At first the tour
amused him, but eventually it began to sour him on himself,
and he took to spending more and more time on a balcony
overlooking the courtyard that was shared with the connecting
house, listening to the Newari women sing at their chores and
reading books from Mr. Chatterji's library. One of the books
was titled *The Carversville Terror*.

"Bloodcurdling, chilling . . ." said *the New York Times* on
the front flap; ". . . the Terror is unrelenting . . ." commented
Stephen King; ". . . riveting, gut-wrenching, mind-bending
horror . . ." gushed *People* magazine. In neat letters, Eliot
appended his own blurb: ". . . piece of crap . . ." The text—
written to be read by the marginally literate—was a fic-
tionalized treatment of purportedly real events, dealing with
the experiences of the Whitcomb family, who had attempted
to renovate the Cousineau mansion during the sixties. Following the usual buildup of apparitions, cold spots, and noisome
odors, the family—Papa David, Mama Elaine, young sons
Tim and Randy, and teenage Ginny—had met to discuss the
situation.

> . . . *even the kids, thought David, had been aged by the
> house. Gathered around the dining room table, they
> looked like a company of the damned—haggard, shadows
> under their eyes, grim-faced. Even with the windows open
> and the light streaming in, it seemed there was a pall in the
> air that no light could dispel. Thank God the damned
> thing was dormant during the day!*

"Well," he said, "I guess the floor's open for arguments."

"I wanna go home!" Tears sprang from Randy's eyes, and on cue, Tim started crying, too.

"It's not that simple," said David. "This is home, and I don't know how we'll make it if we do leave. The savings account is just about flat."

"I suppose I could get a job," said Elaine unenthusiastically.

"I'm not leaving!" Ginny jumped to her feet, knocking over her chair. "Every time I start to make friends, we have to move!"

"But Ginny!" Elaine reached out a hand to calm her. "You were the one. . . ."

"I've changed my mind!" She backed away, as if she had just recognized them all to be mortal enemies. "You can do what you want, but I'm staying!" And she ran from the room.

"Oh, God," said Elaine wearily. "What's gotten into her?"

What had gotten into Ginny, what was in the process of getting into her and was the only interesting part of the book, was the spirit of Aimée Cousineau. Concerned with his daughter's behavior, David Whitcomb had researched the house and learned a great deal about the spirit. Aimée Cousineau, née Vuillemont, had been a native of St. Berenice, a Swiss village at the foot of the mountain known as the Eiger (its photograph, as well as one of Aimée—a coldly beautiful woman with black hair and cameo features—was included in the central section of the book). Until the age of fifteen she had been a sweet, unexceptional child; in the summer of 1889, however, while hiking on the slopes of the Eiger, she had become lost in a cave.

The family had all but given up hope when, to their delight—three weeks later—she had turned up on the steps of her father's store. Their delight was short-lived. This Aimée was far different from the one who had entered the cave. Violent, calculating, slatternly.

Over the next two years she succeeded in seducing half the

men of the village, including the local priest. According to his testimony, he had been admonishing her that sin was not the path to happiness when she began to undress. "I'm wed to Happiness," she told him. "I've entwined my limbs with the God of Bliss and kissed the scaly thighs of Joy." Throughout the ensuing affair, she made cryptic comments concerning "the God below the mountain," whose soul was now forever joined to hers.

At this point the book reverted to the gruesome adventures of the Whitcomb family, and Eliot, bored, realizing it was noon and that Michaela would be sunbathing, climbed to Mr. Chatterji's apartment on the fourth floor. He tossed the book onto a shelf and went out onto the balcony. His continued interest in Michaela puzzled him. It occurred to him that he might be falling in love, and he thought that would be nice. Though it would probably lead nowhere, love would be a good kind of energy to have. But he doubted this was the case. Most likely his interest was founded on some fuming product of the dark stone inside him. Simple lust. He looked over the edge of the balcony. She was lying on a blanket—her bikini top beside her—at the bottom of a well of sunlight: thin, pure sunlight like a refinement of honey spreading down and congealing into the mold of a little gold woman. It seemed that her heat was in the air.

That night Eliot broke one of Mr. Chatterji's rules and slept in the master bedroom. It was roofed by a large skylight mounted in a ceiling painted midnight blue. The normal display of stars had not been sufficient for Mr. Chatterji, and so he'd had the skylight constructed of faceted glass that multiplied the stars, making it appear that you were at the heart of a galaxy, gazing out between the interstices of its blazing core. The walls consisted of a photomural of the Khumbu Glacier and Chomolungma; and, bathed in the starlight, the mural had acquired the illusion of depth and chill mountain silence. Lying there, Eliot could hear the faint sounds of Indra Jatra: shouts and cymbals, oboes and drums. He was drawn to the sounds; he wanted to run out into the streets, become an element of the drunken crowds, be whirled through torchlight

and delirium to the feet of an idol stained with sacrificial
blood. But he felt bound to the house, to Michaela. Marooned
in the glow of Mr. Chatterji's starlight, floating above Chomolungma and listening to the din of the world below, he could
almost believe he was a bodhisattva awaiting a call to action,
that his watchfulness had some purpose.

The shipment arrived late in the afternoon of the eighth day.
Five enormous crates, each requiring the combined energies of
Eliot and three Newari workmen to wrangle up to the third-
floor room that housed Mr. Chatterji's collection. After tip-
ping the men, Eliot—sweaty, panting—sat down against the
wall to catch his breath. The room was about twenty-five feet
by fifteen, but looked smaller because of the dozens of curious
objects standing around the floor and mounted one above the
other on the walls. A brass doorknob; a shattered door; a
straight-backed chair whose arms were bound with a velvet
rope to prevent anyone from sitting; a discolored sink; a mirror
streaked by a brown stain; a slashed lampshade. They were all
relics of some haunting or possession, some grotesque violence, and there were cards affixed to them testifying to the
details and referring those who were interested to materials in
Mr. Chatterji's library. Sitting amidst these relics, the crates
looked innocuous. Bolted shut, chest-high, branded with customs stamps.

When he had recovered, Eliot strolled around the room,
amused by the care that Mr. Chatterji had squandered on his
hobby; the most amusing thing was that no one except Mr.
Chatterji was impressed by it: it provided travelers with a foot-
note for their journals. Nothing more.

A wave of dizziness swept over him—he had stood too
soon—and he leaned against one of the crates for support.
Jesus, he was in lousy shape! And then, as he blinked away the
tangles of opaque cells drifting across his field of vision, the
crate shifted. Just a little shift, as if something inside had
twitched in its sleep. But palpable, real. He flung himself
toward the door, backing away. A chill mapped every knob
and articulation of his spine, and his sweat had evaporated,

leaving clammy patches on his skin. The crate was motionless. But he was afraid to take his eyes off it, certain that if he did, it would release its pent-up fury. "Hi," said Michaela from the doorway.

Her voice electrified Eliot. He let out a squawk and wheeled around, his hands outheld to ward off attack.

"I didn't mean to startle you," she said. "I'm sorry."

"Goddamn!" he said. "Don't sneak up like that!" He remembered the crate and glanced back at it. "Listen, I was just locking. . . ."

"I'm sorry," she repeated, and walked past him into the room. "Ranjeesh is such an idiot about all this," she said, running her hand over the top of the crate. "Don't you think?"

Her familiarity with the crate eased Eliot's apprehension. Maybe he had been the one who had twitched: a spasm of overstrained muscles. "Yeah, I guess."

She walked over to the straight-backed chair, slipped off the velvet rope, and sat down. She was wearing a pale brown skirt and a plaid blouse that made her look schoolgirlish. "I want to apologize about the other day," she said; she bowed her head, and the fall of her hair swung forward to obscure her face. "I've been having a bad time lately. I have trouble relating to people. To anything. But since we're living here together, I'd like to be friends." She stood and spread the folds of her skirt. "See? I even put on different clothes. I could tell the others offended you."

The innocent sexuality of the pose caused Eliot to have a rush of desire. "Looks nice," he said with forced casualness. "Why've you been having a bad time?"

She wandered to the door and gazed out. "Do you really want to hear about it?"

"Not if it's painful for you."

"It doesn't matter," she said, leaning against the doorframe. "I was in a band back in the States, and we were doing okay. Cutting an album, talking to record labels. I was living with the guitarist, in love with him. But then I had an affair. Not even an affair. It was stupid. Meaningless. I still don't know why I did it. The heat of the moment, I guess. That's what rock 'n' roll's all about, and maybe I was just acting out the myth. One of the other musicians told my boyfriend. That's the way bands are—you're friends with everyone, but never at the same time. See, I told this guy about the affair. We'd always confided. But one day he got mad at me over something. Something else stupid and meaningless." Her chin was struggling to stay firm; the breeze from the courtyard drifted fine strands of hair across her face. "My boyfriend went crazy and beat up my. . . ." She gave a dismal laugh. "I don't know what to call him. My lover. Whatever. My boyfriend killed him. It was an accident, but he tried to run, and the police shot him."

Eliot wanted to stop her; she was obviously seeing it all again, seeing blood and police flashers and cold white morgue lights. But she was riding a wave of memory, borne along by its energy, and he knew that she had to crest with it, crash with it.

"I was out of it for a while. Dreamy. Nothing touched me. Not the funerals, the angry parents. I went away for months, to the mountains, and I started to feel better. But when I came home, I found that the musician who'd told my boyfriend had written a song about it. The affair, the killings. He'd cut a record. People were buying it, singing the hook when they walked down the street or took a shower. Dancing to it! They were dancing on blood and bones, humming grief, shelling out $5.98 for a jingle about suffering. Looking back, I realize I was crazy, but at the time everything I did seemed normal. More than normal. Directed, inspired. I bought a gun. A ladies' model, the salesman said. I remember thinking how strange it was that there were male and female guns, just like with electric razors. I felt enormous carrying it. I had to be meek and polite or else I was sure people would notice how large and purposeful I was. It wasn't hard to track down Ronnie—that's the guy who wrote the song. He was in Germany, cutting a second album. I couldn't believe it, I wasn't going to be able to kill him! I was so frustrated that one night I went down to a park and started shooting. I missed everything. Out of all the bums and joggers and squirrels, I hit leaves and air. They locked me up after that. A hospital. I think it helped, but. . . ." She blinked, waking from a trance. "But I still feel so disconnected, you know?"

Eliot carefully lifted away the strands of hair that had blown across her face and laid them back in place. Her smile flickered. "I know," he said. "I feel that way sometimes."

She nodded thoughtfully, as if to verify that she had recognized this quality in him.

They ate dinner in a Tibetan place in Temal; it had no name and was a dump with flyspecked tables and rickety chairs, specializing in water buffalo and barley soup. But it was away from the city center, which meant they could avoid the worst of the festival crowds. The waiter was a young Tibetan wearing jeans and a T-shirt that bore the legend MAGIC IS THE ANSWER; the earphones of personal stereo dangled about his neck. The walls—visible through a haze of smoke—were covered with snapshots, most featuring the waiter in the company of various tourists, but a few showing an older Tibetan in blue robes and turquoise jewelry, carrying an automatic rifle; this was the owner, one of the Khampa tribesmen who had fought a guerrilla war against the Chinese. He rarely put in an appearance at the restaurant, and when he did, his glowering presence tended to dampen conversation.

Over dinner, Eliot tried to steer clear of topics that might unsettle Michaela. He told her about Sam Chipley's clinic, the time the Dalai Lama had come to Katmandu, the musicians at Swayambhunath. Cheerful, exotic topics. Her listlessness was such an inessential part of her that Eliot was led to chip away at it, curious to learn what lay beneath; and the more he chipped away, the more animated her gestures, the more luminous her smile became. This was a different sort of smile than she had displayed on their first meeting. It came so suddenly over her face, it seemed an autonomic reaction, like the opening of a sunflower, as if she were facing not you but the principle of light upon which you were grounded. It was aware of you, of course, but it chose to see past the imperfections of the flesh and know the perfected thing you truly were. It boosted your sense of worth to realize that you were its target, and Eliot—whose sense of worth was at low ebb—would have done pratfalls to sustain it. Even when he told his own story, he told it as a joke, a metaphor for American misconceptions of oriental pursuits.

"Why don't you quit it?" she asked. "The meditation, I mean. If it's not working out, why keep on with it?"

"My life's in perfect suspension," he said. "I'm afraid that if I quit practicing, if I change anything, I'll either sink to the bottom or fly off." He tapped his spoon against his cup, signaling for more tea. "You're not really going to marry Ranjeesh, are you?" he asked, and was surprised at the concern he felt that she actually might.

"Probably not." The waiter poured their tea, whispery drumbeats issuing from his earphones. "I was just feeling lost. You see, my parents sued Ronnie over the song, and I ended up with a lot of money—which made me feel even worse. . . ."

"Let's not talk about it," he said.

"It's all right." She touched his wrist, reassuring, and the skin remained warm after her fingers had withdrawn. "Anyway," she went on, "I decided to travel, and all the strangeness . . . I don't know. I was starting to slip away. Ranjeesh was a kind of sanctuary."

Eliot was vastly relieved.

Outside, the streets were thronged with festivalgoers, and Michaela took Eliot's arm and let him guide her through the crowds. Newars wearing Nehru hats and white trousers that bagged at the hips and wrapped tightly around the calves; groups of tourists, shouting and waving bottles of rice beer; Indians in white robes and saris. The air was spiced with incense, and the strip of empurpled sky above was so regularly patterned with stars that it looked like a banner draped between the roofs. Near the house, a wild-eyed man in a blue satin robe rushed past, bumping into them, and he was followed by two boys dragging a goat, its forehead smeared with crimson powder: a sacrifice.

"This is crazy!" Michaela laughed.

"It's nothing. Wait'll tomorrow night."

"What happens then?"

"The night of White Bhairab." Eliot put on a grimace. "You'll have to watch yourself. Bhairab's a lusty, wrathful sort."

She laughed again and gave his arm an affectionate squeeze.

Inside the house, the moon—past full, blank and golden—floated dead center on the square of night sky admitted by the roof. They stood close together in the courtyard, silent, suddenly awkward.

"I enjoyed tonight," said Michaela; she leaned forward and brushed his cheek with her lips. "Thank you," she whispered.

Eliot caught her as she drew back, tipped her chin, and kissed her mouth. Her lips parted, her tongue darted out. Then she pushed him away. "I'm tired," she said, her face tightened with anxiety. She walked off a few steps, but stopped and turned back. "If you want to . . . to be with me, maybe it'll be all right. We could try."

Eliot went to her and took her hands. "I want to make love with you," he said, no longer trying to hide his urgency. And that *was* what he wanted: to make love. Not to ball or bang or screw or any other inelegant version of the act.

But it was not love they made.

Under the starlit blaze of Mr. Chatterji's ceiling, she was very beautiful, and at first she was very loving, moving with a genuine involvement; then abruptly, she quit moving altogether and turned her face to the pillow. Her eyes were glistening. Left alone atop her, listening to the animal sound of his breathing, the impact of his flesh against hers, Eliot knew he should stop and comfort her. But the months of abstinence, the eight days of wanting her, all this fused into a bright flare in the small of his back, a reactor core of lust that irradiated his conscience, and he continued to plunge into her, hurrying to completion. She let out a gasp when he withdrew, and curled up, facing away from him.

"God, I'm so sorry," she said, her voice cracking.

Eliot shut his eyes. He felt sickened, reduced to the bestial. It had been like two mental patients doing nasty on the sly, two fragments of people who together didn't form a whole. He understood now why Mr. Chatterji wanted to marry her: he planned to add her to his collection, to enshrine her with the other splinters of violence. And each night he would complete his revenge, substantiate his cultural overview, by making something less than love with this sad, inert girl, this American ghost. Her shoulders shook with muffled sobs. She needed someone to console her, to help her find her own strength and capacity for love. Eliot reached out to her, willing to do his best. But he knew it shouldn't be him.

Several hours later, after she had fallen asleep, unconsolable, Eliot sat in the courtyard, thoughtless, dejected, staring at a rubber plant. It was mired in shadow, its leaves hanging limp. He had been staring for a couple of minutes when he noticed that a shadow in back of the plant was swaying ever so slightly; he tried to make it out, and the swaying subsided. He stood. The chair scraped on the concrete, sounding unnaturally loud. His neck prickled, and he glanced behind him. Nothing. Ye Olde Mental Fatigue, he thought. Ye Olde Emotional Strain. He laughed, and the clarity of the laugh—echoing up through the empty well—alarmed him; it seemed to stir little flickers of motion everywhere in the darkness. What he needed was a drink! The problem was how to get into the bedroom without waking Michaela. Hell, maybe he should wake her. Maybe they should talk more before what had happened hardened into a set of unbreakable attitudes.

He turned toward the stairs . . . and then, yelling out in panic, entangling his feet with the lawn chairs as he leaped backward midstep, he fell onto his side. A shadow—roughly man-shaped and man-sized—was standing a yard away; it was undulating the way a strand of kelp undulates in a gentle tide. The patch of air around it was rippling, as if the entire image had been badly edited into reality. Eliot scrambled away, coming to his knees. The shadow melted downward, puddling on the concrete; it bunched in the middle like a caterpillar, folded over itself, and flowed after him: a rolling sort of motion. Then it reared up, again assuming its manlike shape, looming over him.

Eliot got to his feet, still frightened, but less so. If he had previously been asked to testify as to the existence of the Khaa, he would have rejected the evidence of his bleared senses and come down on the side of hallucination, folktale. But now, though he was tempted to draw that same conclusion, there was too much evidence to the contrary. Staring at the featureless black cowl of the Khaa's head, he had a sense of something staring back. More than a sense. A distinct impression of personality. It was as if the Khaa's undulations were producing a breeze that bore its psychic odor through the air. Eliot began to picture it as a loony, shy old uncle who liked to sit under the basement steps and eat flies and cackle to himself, but who could tell when the first frost was due and knew how to fix the tail on your kite. Weird, yet harmless. The Khaa stretched out an arm: the arm just peeled away from its torso, its hand a thumbless black mitten. Eliot edged back. He wasn't quite prepared to believe it was harmless. But the arm stretched farther than he had thought possible and enveloped his wrist. It was soft, ticklish, a river of furry moths crawling over his skin.

In the instant before he jumped away, Eliot heard a whining note inside his skull, and that whining—seeming to flow through his brain with the same suppleness that the Khaa's arm had displayed—was translated into a wordless plea. From it he understood that the Khaa was afraid. Terribly afraid. Suddenly it melted downward and went rolling, bunching, flowing up the stairs; it stopped on the first landing, rolled halfway down, then up again, repeating the process over and over. It came clear to Eliot *(Oh, Jesus! This is nuts!)* that it was trying to convince him to follow. Just like Lassie or some other ridiculous TV animal, it was trying to tell him something, to lead him to where the wounded forest ranger had fallen, where the nest of baby ducks was being threatened by the brush fire. He should walk over, rumple its head, and say, "What's the matter, girl? Those squirrels been teasing you?" This time his laughter had a sobering effect, acting to settle his thoughts. One likelihood was that his experience with Michaela had been sufficient to snap his frayed connection with consensus reality; but there was no point in buying that. Even if that were the case, he might as well go with it. He crossed to the stairs, and climbed toward the rippling shadow on the landing.

"Okay, Bongo," he said. "Let's see what's got you so excited."

On the third floor the Khaa turned down a hallway, moving fast, and Eliot didn't see it again until he was approaching the room that housed Mr. Chatterji's collection. It was standing beside the door, flapping its arms, apparently indicating that he should enter. Eliot remembered the crate.

"No, thanks," he said. A drop of sweat slid down his rib cage, and he realized that it was unusually warm next to the door.

The Khaa's hand flowed over the doorknob, enveloping it, and when the hand pulled back, it was bulging, oddly deformed, and there was a hole through the wood where the lock mechanism had been. The door swung open a couple of inches. Darkness leaked out of the room, adding an oily essence to the air. Eliot took a backward step. The Khaa dropped the lock mechanism—it materialized from beneath the black formless hand and clattered to the floor—and latched onto Eliot's arm. Once again he heard the whining, the plea for help, and since he did not jump away, he had a clearer understanding of the process of translation. He could feel the wining as a cold fluid coursing through his brain, and as the whining died, the message simply appeared—the way an image might appear in a crystal ball. There was an undertone of reassurance to the Khaa's fear, and though Eliot knew this was the mistake people in horror movies were always making, he reached inside the room and fumbled for the wall switch, half-expecting to be snatched up and savaged. He flicked on the light and pushed the door open with his foot.

And wished that he hadn't.

The crates had exploded. Splinters and shards of wood were scattered everywhere, and the bricks had been heaped at the center of the room. They were dark red, friable bricks like crumbling cakes of dried blood, and each was marked with black letters and numbers that signified its original position in the fireplace. But none were in their proper position now, though they were quite artfully arranged. They had been piled into the shape of a mountain, one that—despite the crudity of its building blocks—duplicated the sheer faces and chimneys and gentle slopes of a real mountain. Eliot recognized it from its photograph. The Eiger. It towered to the ceiling, and under the glare of the lights, it gave off a radiation of ugliness and barbarity. It seemed alive, a fang of dark red meat, and the charred smell of the bricks was like a hum in Eliot's nostrils.

Ignoring the Khaa, who was again flapping its arms, Eliot broke for the landing; there he paused, and after a brief struggle between fear and conscience, he sprinted up the stairs to the bedroom, taking them three at a time. Michaela was gone! He stared at the starlit billows of the sheets. Where the hell . . . her room! He hurtled down the stairs and fell sprawling on the second-floor landing. Pain lanced through his kneecap, but he came to his feet running, certain that something was behind him.

A seam of reddish orange light—not lamplight—edged the bottom of Michaela's door, and he heard a crispy chuckling noise like a fire crackling in a hearth. The wood was warm to the touch. Eliot's hand hovered over the doorknob. His heart seemed to have swelled to the size of a basketball and was doing a fancy dribble against his chest wall. The sensible thing to do would be to get out quick, because whatever lay beyond the door was bound to be too much for him to handle. But instead he did the stupid thing and burst into the room.

His first impression was that the room was burning, but then he saw that though the fire looked real, it did not spread; the flames clung to the outlines of things that were themselves unreal, that had no substance of their own and were made of the ghostly fire: belted drapes, an overstuffed chair and sofa, a carved mantelpiece, all of antique design. The actual furniture—production-line junk—was undamaged. Intense reddish orange light glowed around the bed, and at its heart lay Michaela. Naked, her back arched. Lengths of her hair lifted into the air and tangled, floating in an invisible current; the muscles of her legs and abdomen were coiling, bunching, as if she were shedding her skin. The crackling grew louder, and the light began to rise from the bed, to form into a column of even brighter light; it narrowed at the midpoint, bulged in an approximation of hips and breasts, gradually assuming the shape of a burning woman. She was faceless, a fiery silhouette. Her flickering gown shifted as with the movements of walking, and flames leaped out behind her head like windblown hair.

Eliot was pumped full of terror, too afraid to scream or run. Her aura of heat and power wrapped around him. Though she was within arm's length, she seemed a long way off, inset into a great distance and walking toward him down a tunnel that conformed exactly to her shape. She stretched out a hand, brushing his cheek with a finger. The touch brought more pain than he had ever known. It was luminous, lighting every circuit of his body. He could feel his skin crisping, cracking, fluids leaking forth and sizzling. He heard himself moan: a gush of rotten sound like something trapped in a drain.

Then she jerked back her hand, as if *he* had burned *her*.

Dazed, his nerves screaming, Eliot slumped to the floor and—through blurred eyes—caught sight of a blackness rippling by the door. The Khaa. The burning woman stood facing it a few feet away. It was such an uncanny scene, this confrontation of fire and darkness, of two supernatural systems, that Eliot was shocked to alertness. He had the idea that neither of them knew what to do. Surrounded by its patch of disturbed air, the Khaa undulated; the burning woman crackled and flickered, embedded in her eerie distance. Tentatively, she lifted her hand; but before she could complete the gesture, the Khaa reached with blinding swiftness and its hand enveloped hers.

A shriek like tortured metal issued from them, as if some iron-clad principle had been breached. Dark tendrils wound through the burning woman's arm, seams of fire striped the Khaa, and there was a high-pitched humming, a vibration that jarred Eliot's teeth. For a moment he was afraid that spiritual versions of antimatter and matter had been brought into conjunction, that the room would explode. But the hum was sheared off as the Khaa snatched back its hand: a scrap of reddish orange flame glimmered within it. The Khaa melted downward and went rolling out the door. The burning woman—and every bit of flame in the room—shrank to an incandescent point and vanished.

Still dazed, Eliot touched his face. It felt burned, but there was no apparent damage. He hauled himself to his feet, staggered to the bed, and collapsed next to Michaela. She was breathing deeply, unconscious. "Michaela!" He shook her. She moaned, her head rolled from side to side. He heaved her over his shoulder in a fireman's lift and crept out into the hall. Moving stealthily, he eased along the hall to the balcony overlooking the courtyard and peered over the edge . . . and bit his lip to stifle a cry. Clearly visible in the electric blue air of the predawn darkness, standing in the middle of the courtyard, was a tall, pale woman wearing a white nightgown. Her black hair fanned across her back. She snapped her head around to stare at him, her cameo features twisted by a gloating smile, and that smile told Eliot everything he had wanted to know about the possibility of escape. Just try to leave, Aimée Cousineau was saying. Go ahead and try. I'd like that. A shadow sprang erect about a dozen feet away from her, and she turned to it. Suddenly there was a wind in the courtyard: a violent whirling wind of which she was the calm center. Plants went flapping up into the well like leathery birds; pots shattered, and the shards flew toward the Khaa. Slowed by Michaela's weight, wanting to get as far as he could from the battle, Eliot headed up the stairs toward Mr. Chatterji's bedroom.

It was an hour later, an hour of peeking down into the courtyard, watching the game of hide-and-seek that the Khaa was playing with Aimée Cousineau, realizing that the Khaa was protecting them by keeping her busy . . . it was then that Eliot remembered the book. He retrieved it from the shelf and began to skim through it, hoping to learn something helpful. There was nothing else to do. He picked up at the point of Aimée's rap about her marriage to Happiness, passed over the transformation of Ginny Whitcomb into a teenage monster, and found a second section dealing with Aimée.

In 1895 a wealthy Swiss-American named Armand Cousineau had returned to St. Berenice—his birthplace—for a visit. He was smitten with Aimée Vuillemont, and her family, seizing the opportunity to be rid of her, allowed Cousineau to marry Aimée and sail her off to his home in Carversville, New

Hampshire. Aimée's taste for seduction had not been curbed by the move. Lawyers, deacons, merchants, farmers: they were all grist for her mill. But in the winter of 1905, she fell in love—obsessively, passionately in love—with a young schoolmaster. She believed that the schoolmaster had saved her from her unholy marriage, and her gratitude knew no bounds. Unfortunately, when the schoolmaster fell in love with another woman, neither did her fury. One night while passing the Cousineau mansion, the town doctor spotted a woman walking the grounds: ". . . a woman of flame, not burning but composed of flame, her every particular a fiery construct. . . ." Smoke was curling from a window; the doctor rushed inside and discovered the schoolmaster wrapped in chains, burning like a log in the vast fireplace. He put out the small blaze spreading from the hearth, and on going back onto the grounds, he stumbled over Aimée's charred corpse.

It was not clear whether Aimée's death had been accidental, a stray spark catching on her nightgown, or the result of suicide; but it *was* clear that thereafter the mansion had been haunted by a spirit who delighted in possessing women and driving them to kill their men. The spirit's supernatural powers were limited by the flesh but were augmented by immense physical strength. Ginny Whitcomb, for example, had killed her brother Tim by twisting off his arm, and then had gone after her other brother and her father, a harrowing chase that had lasted a day and a night: while in possession of a body, the spirit was not limited to nocturnal activity. . . .

Christ!

The light coming through the skylight was gray.

They were safe!

Eliot went to the bed and began shaking Michaela. She moaned, her eyes blinked open. "Wake up!" he said. "We've got to get out!"

"What?" She batted at his hands. "What are you talking about?"

"Don't you remember?"

"Remember what?" She swung her legs onto the floor, sitting with her head down, stunned by wakefulness; she stood, swayed, and said, "God, what did you do to me? I feel. . . ." A dull, suspicious expression washed over her face.

"We have to leave." He walked around the bed to her. "Ranjeesh hit the jackpot. Those crates of his had an honest-to-God spirit packed in with the bricks. Last night it tried to possess you." He saw her disbelief. "You must have blanked out. Here." He offered the book. "This'll explain. . . ."

"Oh, God!" she shouted. "What did you do? I'm all raw inside!" She backed away, eyes wide with fright.

"I didn't do anything." He held out his palms as if to prove he had no weapons.

"You raped me! While I was asleep!" She looked left, right, in a panic.

"That's ridiculous!"

"You must have drugged me or something! Oh, God! Go away!"

"I won't argue," he said. "We have to get out. After that you can turn me in for rape or whatever. But we're leaving, even if I have to drag you."

Some of her desperation evaporated, her shoulders sagged.

"Look," he said, moving closer. "I didn't rape you. What you're feeling is something that goddamn spirit did to you. It was. . . ."

She brought her knee up into his groin.

As he writhed on the floor, curled up around the pain, Eliot heard the door open and her footsteps receding. He caught at the edge of the bed, hauled himself to his knees, and vomited all over the sheets. He fell back and lay there for several minutes until the pain had dwindled to a powerful throbbing, a throbbing that jolted his heart into the same rhythm; then, gingerly, he stood and shuffled out into the hall. Leaning on the railing, he eased down the stairs to Michaela's room and lowered himself into a sitting position. He let out a shuddering sigh. Actinic flashes burst in front of his eyes.

"Michaela," he said. "Listen to me." His voice sounded feeble: the voice of an old, old man.

"I've got a knife," she said from just behind the door. "I'll use it if you try to break in."

"I wouldn't worry about that," he said. "And I sure as hell wouldn't worry about being raped. Now will you listen?"

No response.

He told her everything, and when he was done, she said, "You're insane. You raped me."

"I wouldn't hurt you. I . . ." He had been on the verge of telling her he loved her, but decided it probably wasn't true. He probably just wished that he had a good, clean truth like love. The pain was making him nauseated again, as if the blackish purple stain of his bruises were seeping up into his stomach and filling him with bad gases. He struggled to his feet and leaned against the wall. There was no point in arguing, and there was not much hope that she would leave the house on her own, not if she reacted to Aimée like Ginny Whitcomb. The only solution was to go to the police, accuse her of some crime. Assault. She would accuse him of rape, but with luck they would both be held overnight. And he would have time to wire Mr. Chatterji . . . who would believe him. Mr. Chatterji was by nature a believer: it simply hadn't fit his notion of sophistication to give credence to his native spirits. He'd be on the first flight from Delhi, eager to document the Terror.

Himself eager to get it over, Eliot negotiated the stairs and hobbled across the courtyard; but the Khaa was waiting, flapping its arms in the shadowed alcove that led to the street. Whether it was an effect of the light or of its battle with Aimée, or, specifically, of the pale scrap of fire visible within its hand, the Khaa looked less substantial. Its blackness was somewhat opaque, and the air around it was blurred, smeary, like waves washing over a lens: it was as if the Khaa were being submerged more deeply in its own medium. Eliot felt no compunction about allowing it to touch him; he was grateful to it, and his relaxed attitude seemed to intensify the communication. He began to see images in his mind's eye: Michaela's face, Aimée's, and then the two faces were superimposed. He was shown this over and over, and he understood from it that the Khaa wanted the possession to take place. But he didn't understand why. More images. Himself running, Michaela running, Durbar Square, the mask of White Bhairab, the Khaa. Lots of

Khaa. Like black hieroglyphs. These images were repeated, too, and after each sequence the Khaa would hold its hand up to his face and display the glimmering scrap of Aimée's fire. Eliot thought he understood, but whenever he tried to convey that he wasn't sure, the Khaa merely repeated the images.

At last, realizing that the Khaa had reached the limits of its ability to communicate, Eliot headed for the street. The Khaa melted down, reared up in the doorway to block his path, and flapped its arms desperately. Once again Eliot had a sense of its weird-old-man-ness. It went against logic to put his trust in such an erratic creature, especially in such a dangerous plan; but logic had little hold on him, and this was a permanent solution. If it worked. If he hadn't misread it. He laughed. The hell with it!

"Take it easy, Bongo," he said. "I'll be back as soon as I get my shootin' iron fixed."

The waiting room of Sam Chipley's clinic was crowded with Newari mothers and children, who giggled as Eliot did a bow-legged shuffle through their midst. Sam's wife led him into the examination room, where Sam—a burly, bearded man, his long hair tied in a ponytail—helped him onto a surgical table.

"Holy shit!" he said after inspecting the injury. "What you been into, man?" He began rubbing ointment into the bruises.

"Accident," gritted Eliot, trying not to cry out.

"Yeah, I bet," said Sam. "Maybe a sexy little accident who had a change of heart when it come down to strokes. You know, not gettin' it steady might tend to make you a tad intense for some ladies, man. Ever think about that?"

"That's not how it was. Am I all right?"

"Yeah, but you ain't gonna be superstud for a while." Sam went to the sink and washed his hands. "Don't gimme that innocent bullshit. You were tryin' to slip it to Chatterji's new squeeze, right?"

"You know her?"

"He brought her over one day, showin' her off. She's a head case, man. You should know better."

"Will I be able to run?"

Sam laughed. "Not hardly."

"Listen, Sam." Eliot sat up, winced. "Chatterji's lady. She's in bad trouble, and I'm the only one who can help her. I have to be able to run, and I need something to keep me awake. I haven't slept for a couple of days."

"I ain't givin' you pills, Eliot. You can stagger through your doper phase without my help." Sam finished drying his hands and went to sit on a stool beside the window; beyond the window was a brick wall, and atop it a string of prayer flags snapped in the breeze.

"I'm not after a supply, damn it! Just enough to keep me going tonight. This is important, Sam!"

Sam scratched his neck. "What kind of trouble she in?"

"I can't tell you now," said Eliot, knowing that Sam would laugh at the idea of something as metaphysically suspect as the Khaa. "But I will tomorrow. It's not illegal. Come on, man! There's got to be something you can give me."

"Oh, I can fix you up. I can make you feel like King Shit on Coronation Day." Sam mulled it over. "Okay, Eliot. But you get your ass back here tomorrow and tell me what's happenin'." He gave a snort of amusement. "All I can say is, it must be some strange damn trouble for you to be the only one who can save her."

After wiring Mr. Chatterji, urging him to come home at once, Eliot returned to the house and unscrewed the hinges of the front door. He was not certain that Aimée would be able to control the house, to slam doors and make windows stick as she had with her house in New Hampshire, but he didn't want to take any chances. As he lifted the door and set it against the wall of the alcove, he was amazed by its lightness; he felt possessed of a giddy strength, capable of heaving the door up through the well of the courtyard and over the roofs. The cocktail of pain-killers and speed was working wonders. His groin ached, but the ache was distant, far removed form the center of his consciousness, which was a fount of well-being. When he had finished with the door, he grabbed some fruit juice from the kitchen and went back to the alcove to wait.

In midafternoon Michaela came downstairs. Eliot tried to talk to her, to convince her to leave, but she warned him to keep away and scuttled back to her room. Then, around five o'clock, the burning woman appeared, floating a few feet above the courtyard floor. The sun had withdrawn to the upper third of the well, and her fiery silhouette was inset into slate-blue shadow, the flames of her hair dancing about her head. Eliot, who had been hitting the pain-killers heavily, was dazzled by her: had she been a hallucination, she would have made his All-Time Top Ten. But even realizing that she was not, he was too drugged to relate to her as a threat. He snickered and shied a piece of broken pot at her. She shrank to an incandescent point, vanished, and that brought home to him his foolhardiness. He took more speed to counteract his euphoria, and did stretching exercises to loosen the kinks and to rid himself of the cramped sensation in his chest.

Twilight blended the shadows in the courtyard, celebrants passed in the street, and he could hear distant drums and cymbals. He felt cut off from the city, the festival. Afraid. Not even the presence of the Khaa, half-merged with the shadows along the wall, served to comfort him. Near dusk, Aimée Cousineau walked into the courtyard and stopped about twenty feet away, staring at him. He had no desire to laugh or throw things. At this distance he could see that her eyes had no whites or pupils or irises. They were dead black. One moment they seemed to be the bulging heads of black screws threaded into her skull; the next they seemed to recede into blackness, into a cave beneath a mountain where something waited to teach the joys of hell to whoever wandered in. Eliot sidled closer to the door. But she turned, climbed the stairs to the second landing, and walked down Michaela's hallway.

Eliot's waiting began in earnest.

An hour passed. He paced between the door and the courtyard. His mouth was cottony; his joints felt brittle, held together by frail wires of speed and adrenaline. This was insane! All he had done was to put them in worse danger. Finally he heard a door close upstairs. He backed into the street, bumping into two Newari girls, who giggled and skipped away. Crowds of people were moving toward Durbar Square.

"Eliot!"

Michaela's voice. He'd expected a hoarse demon voice, and when she walked into the alcove, her white scarf glowing palely against the dark air, he was surprised to see that she was unchanged. Her features held no trace of anything other than her usual listlessness.

"I'm sorry I hurt you," she said, walking toward him. "I know you didn't do anything. I was just upset about last night."

Eliot continued to back away.

"What's wrong?" She stopped in the doorway.

It might have been his imagination, the drugs, but Eliot could have sworn that her eyes were much darker than normal. He trotted off a dozen yards or so and stood looking at her.

"Eliot!"

It was a scream of rage and frustration, and he could scarcely believe the speed with which she darted toward him. He ran full tilt at first, leaping sideways to avoid collisions, veering past alarmed dark-skinned faces; but after a couple of blocks he found a more efficient rhythm and began to antici-pate obstacles, to glide in and out of the crowd. Angry shouts were raised behind him. He glanced back. Michaela was clos-ing the distance, beelining for him, knocking people sprawling with what seemed effortless blows. He ran harder. The crowd grew thicker, and he kept near the walls of the houses, where it was thinnest; but even there it was hard to maintain a good pace. Torches were waved in his face; young men—singing, their arms linked—posed barriers that slowed him further. He could no longer see Michaela, but he could see the wake of her passage. Fists shaking, heads jerking. The entire scene was starting to lose cohesiveness to Eliot. There were screams of torchlight, bright shards of deranged shouts, jostling waves of incense and ordure. He felt like the only solid chunk in a glit-tering soup that was being poured through a stone trough.

At the edge of Durbar Square he had a brief glimpse of a shadow standing by the massive gilt doors of Degutale Temple.

It was larger and a more anthracitic black than Mr. Chatterji's Khaa: one of the old ones, the powerful ones. The sight buoyed his confidence and restored his equilibrium. He had not misread the plan. But he knew that this was the most dangerous part. He had lost track of Michaela, and the crowd was sweeping him along; if she caught up to him now, he would not be able to run. Fighting for elbow room, struggling to keep his feet, he was borne into the temple complex. The pagoda roofs sloped up into darkness like strangely carved mountains, their peaks hidden by a moonless night; the cobbled paths were narrow, barely ten feet across, and the crowd was being squeezed along them, a lava flow of humanity. Torches bobbed everywhere, sending wild licks of shadow and orange light up the walls, revealing scowling faces on the eaves. Atop its pedestal, the gilt statue of Hanuman—the monkey god—looked to be swaying. Clashing cymbals and arrhythmic drumming scattered Eliot's heartbeat; the sinewy wail of oboes seemed to be graphing the fluctuations of his nerves.

As he swept past Hanuman Dhoka Temple, he caught sight of the brass mask of White Bhairab shining over the heads of the crowd like the face of an evil clown. It was less than a hundred feet away, set in a huge niche in a temple wall and illuminated by light bulbs that hung down among strings of prayer flags. The crowd surged faster, knocking him this way and that; but he managed to spot two more Khaa in the doorway of Hanuman Dhoka. Both melted downward, vanishing, and Eliot's hopes soared. They must have located Michaela, they must be attacking! By the time he had been carried to within a few yards of the mask, he was sure that he was safe. They must have finished her exorcism by now. The only problem left was to find her. That, he realized, had been the weak link in the plan. He'd been an idiot not to have foreseen it. Who knows what might happen if she were to fall in the midst of the crowd. Suddenly he was beneath the pipe that stuck out of the god's mouth; the stream of rice beer arching from it looked translucent under the lights, and as it splashed his face (no fish), its coldness acted to wash away his veneer of chemical strength. He was dizzy, his groin throbbed. The great face, with its fierce fangs and goofy, startled eyes, appeared to be swelling and rocking back and forth. He took a deep breath. The thing to do would be to find a place next to a wall where he could wedge himself against the flow of the crowd, wait until it had thinned, and then search for her. He was about to do that very thing when two powerful hands gripped his elbows from behind.

Unable to turn, he craned his neck and peered over his shoulder. Michaela smiled at him: a gloating "gotcha!" smile. Her eyes were dead-black ovals. She shaped his name with her mouth, her voice inaudible above the music and shouting, and she began to push him ahead of her, using him as a battering ram to forge a path through the crowd. To anyone watching, it might have appeared that he was running interference for her, but his feet were dangling just off the ground. Angry Newars yelled at him as he knocked them aside. He yelled, too. No one noticed. Within seconds they had got clear into a side street, threading between groups of drunkards. People laughed at Eliot's cries for help, and one guy imitated the awkward loose-limbed way he was running.

Michaela turned into a doorway, carrying him down a dirt-floored corridor whose walls were carved into ornate screens; the dusky orange lamplight shining through the screens cast a lacework of shadow on the dirt. The corridor widened to a small courtyard, the age-darkened wood of its walls and doors inlaid with intricate mosaics of ivory. Michaela stopped and slammed him against a wall. He was stunned, but he recognized the place to be one of the old Buddhist temples that surrounded the square. Except for a life-sized statue of a golden cow, the courtyard was empty.

"Eliot." The way she said it, it was more of a curse than a name.

He opened his mouth to scream, but she drew him into an embrace; her grip on his right elbow tightened, and her other hand squeezed the back of his neck, pinching off the scream.

"Don't be afraid," she said. "I only want to kiss you."

Her breasts crushed into his chest, her pelvis ground against him in a mockery of passion, and inch by inch she forced his face down to hers. Her lips parted, and—*oh, Christ Jesus!*—Eliot writhed in her grasp, enlivened by a new horror. The inside of her mouth was as black as her eyes. She wanted him to kiss that blackness, to taste the evil she had kissed beneath the Eiger. He kicked and clawed with his free hand, but she was irresistible, her hands like iron. His elbow cracked, and brilliant pain shot through his arm. Something else was cracking in his neck. Yet none of that compared to what he felt as her tongue—a burning black poker—pushed between his lips. His chest was bursting with the need to scream, and everything was going dark. Thinking this was death, he experienced a peevish resentment that death was not—as he'd been led to believe—an end to pain, that it merely added a tickling sensation to all his other pain. Then the searing heat in his mouth diminished, and he thought that death must just have been a bit slower than usual.

Several seconds passed before he realized that he was lying on the ground, several more before he noticed Michaela lying beside him, and—because darkness was tattering the edges of his vision—it was considerably longer before he distinguished the six undulating darknesses that had ringed Aimée Cousineau. They towered over her; their blackness gleamed like thick fur, and the air around them was awash with vibration. In her fluted white nightgown, her cameo face composed in an expression of calm, Aimée looked the antithesis of the vaguely male giants that were menacing her, delicate and finely worked in contrast to their crudity. Her eyes appeared to mirror their negative color. After a moment, a little wind kicked up, swirling about her. The undulations of the Khaa increased, becoming rhythmic, the movements of boneless dancers, and the wind subsided. Puzzled, she darted between two of them and took a defensive stance next to the golden cow; she lowered her head and stared up through her brows at the Khaa. They melted downward, rolled forward, sprang erect, and hemmed her in against the statue. But the stare was doing its damage. Pieces of ivory and wood were splintering, flying off the walls toward the Khaa, and one of them was fading, a mist of black particles accumulating around its body; then, with a shrill noise that reminded Eliot of a jet passing overhead, it misted away.

Five Khaa remained in the courtyard. Aimée smiled and turned her stare on another. Before the stare could take effect, however, the Khaa moved close, blocking Eliot's view of her; and when they pulled back, it was Aimée who showed signs of damage. Rills of blackness were leading from her eyes, webbing her cheeks, making it look as if her face were cracking. Her nightgown caught fire, her hair began to leap. Flames danced on her fingertips, spread to her arms, her breast, and she assumed the form of the burning woman.

As soon as the transformation was complete, she tried to shrink, to dwindle to her vanishing point; but, acting in unison, the Khaa extended their hands and touched her. There was that shriek of tortured metal, lapsing to a high-pitched hum, and to Eliot's amazement, the Khaa were sucked inside her. It was a rapid process. The Khaa faded to a haze, to nothing, and veins of black marbled the burning woman's fire; the blackness coalesced, forming into five tiny stick figures, a hieroglyphic design patterning her gown. With a fuming sound she expanded again, regaining her normal dimensions, and the Khaa flowed back out, surrounding her. For an instant she stood motionless, dwarfed: a schoolgirl helpless amidst a circle of bullies. Then she clawed at the nearest of them. Though she had no features with which to express emotion, it seemed to Eliot there was desperation in her gesture, in the agitated leaping of her fiery hair. Unperturbed, the Khaa stretched out their enormous mitten hands, hands that spread like oil and enveloped her.

The destruction of the burning woman, of Aimée Cousineau, lasted only a matter of seconds; but to Eliot it occurred within a bubble of slow time, a time during which he achieved a speculative distance. He wondered if—as the Khaa stole portions of her fire and secreted it within their bodies—they were removing disparate elements of her soul, if she consisted of psychologically distinct fragments: the girl who had wandered into the cave, the girl who had returned from it, the betrayed lover. Did she embody gradations of innocence and sinfulness, or was she a contaminated essence, an unfractionated evil? While still involved in this speculation, half a reaction to pain, half to the metallic shriek of her losing battle, he lost consciousness, and when he reopened his eyes, the courtyard was deserted. He could hear music and shouting from Durbar Square. The golden cow stared contentedly into nowhere.

He had the idea that if he moved, he would further break all the broken things inside him; but he inched his left hand across the dirt and rested it on Michaela's breast. It was rising and falling with a steady rhythm. That made him happy, and he kept his hand there, exulting in the hits of her life against his palm. Something shadowy above him. He strained to see it. One of the Khaa . . . No! It was Mr. Chatterji's Khaa. Opaquely black, scrap of fire glimmering in its hand. Compared to its big brothers, it had the look of a skinny, sorry mutt. Eliot felt camaraderie toward it.

"Hey, Bongo," he said weakly. "We won."

A tickling at the top of his head, a whining note, and he had an impression not of gratitude—as he might have expected—but of intense curiosity. The tickling stopped, and Eliot suddenly felt clear in his mind. Strange. He was passing out once again, his consciousness whirling, darkening, and yet he was calm and unafraid. A roar came from the direction of the square. Somebody—the luckiest somebody in the Katmandu Valley—had caught the fish. But as Eliot's eyelids fluttered shut, as he had a last glimpse of the Khaa looming above them and felt the warm measure of Michaela's heartbeat, he thought maybe that the crowd was cheering the wrong man.

Three weeks after the night of White Bhairab, Ranjeesh Chatterji divested himself of all worldly possessions (including the gift of a year's free rent at his house to Eliot) and took up residence at Swayambhunath where—according to Sam Chipley, who visited Eliot in the hospital—he was attempting to visualize the Avalokitesvara Buddha. It was then that Eliot understood the nature of his newfound clarity. Just as it had done long ago with the woman's goiters, the Khaa had tried his habituation to meditation on for size, had not cared for it, and sloughed it off in a handy repository: Ranjeesh Chatterji.

It was such a delicious irony that Eliot had to restrain himself from telling Michaela when she visited that same afternoon; she had no memory of the Khaa, and news of it tended to unsettle her. But otherwise she had been healing right along with Eliot. All her listlessness had eroded over the weeks, her capacity for love was returning and was focused solely on Eliot. "I guess I needed someone to show me that I was worth an effort," she told him. "I'll never stop trying to repay you." She kissed him. "I can hardly wait till you come home." She brought him books and candy and flowers; she sat with him each day until the nurses shooed her away. Yet being the center of her devotion disturbed him. He was still uncertain whether or not he loved her. Clarity, it seemed, made a man dangerously versatile, his conscience flexible, and instituted a cautious approach to commitment. At least this was the substance of Eliot's clarity. He didn't want to rush into anything.

When at last he did come home, he and Michaela made love beneath the starlight glory of Mr. Chatterji's skylight. Because of Eliot's neck brace and cast, they had to manage the act with extreme care, but despite that, despite the ambivalence of his feelings, this time it *was* love they made. Afterward, lying with his good arm around her, he edged nearer to commitment. Whether or not he loved her, there was no way this part of things could be improved by any increment of emotion. Maybe he'd give it a try with her. If it didn't work out, well, he was not going to be responsible for her mental health. She would have to learn to live without him.

"Happy?" he asked, caressing her shoulder.

She nodded and cuddled closer and whispered something that was partially drowned out by the crinkling of the pillow. He was sure he had misheard her, but the mere thought that he hadn't was enough to lodge a nugget of chill between his shoulder blades.

"What did you say?" he asked.

She turned to him and propped herself on an elbow, silhouetted by the starlight, her features obscured. But when she spoke, he realized that Mr. Chatterji's Khaa had been true to its erratic traditions of barter on the night of White Bhairab; and he knew that if she were to tip back her head ever so slightly and let the light shine into her eyes, he would be able to resolve all his speculations about the composition of Aimée Cousineau's soul.

"I'm wed to Happiness," she said.

Salvador

━━〜〜〜〜〜〜〜〜〜〜〜〜〜 Three weeks before they
━━〜〜〜〜〜〜〜〜〜〜〜〜〜 wasted Tecolutla, Dantzler
had his baptism of fire. The platoon was crossing a meadow at
the foot of an emerald-green volcano, and being a dreamy
sort, he was idling along, swatting tall grasses with his rifle
barrel and thinking how it might have been a first-grader with
crayons who had devised this elementary landscape of a perfect cone rising into a cloudless sky, when cap-pistol noises
sounded on the slope. Someone screamed for the medic, and
Dantzler dove into the grass, fumbling for his ampules. He
slipped one from the dispenser and popped it under his nose,
inhaling frantically; then, to be on the safe side, he popped
another—"A double helpin' of martial arts," as DT would
say—and lay with his head down until the drugs had worked
their magic. There was dirt in his mouth, and he was very
afraid.

Gradually his arms and legs lost their heaviness, and his
heart rate slowed. His vision sharpened to the point that he
could see not only the pinpricks of fire blooming on the slope,
but also the figures behind them, half-obscured by brush. A
bubble of grim anger welled up in his brain, hardened to a
fierce resolve, and he started moving toward the volcano. By
the time he reached the base of the cone, he was all rage and
reflexes. He spent the next forty minutes spinning acrobati-
cally through the thickets, spraying shadows with bursts of his

M-18; yet part of his mind remained distant from the action, marveling at his efficiency, at the comic-strip enthusiasm he felt for the task of killing. He shouted at the men he shot, and he shot them many more times than was necessary, like a child playing soldier.

"Playin' my ass!" DT would say. "You just actin' natural."

DT was a firm believer in the ampules; though the official line was that they contained tailored RNA compounds and pseudoendorphins modified to an inhalant form, he held the opinion that they opened a man up to his inner nature. He was big, black, with heavily muscled arms and crudely stamped features, and he had come to the Special Forces direct from prison, where he had done a stretch for attempted murder; the palms of his hands were covered by jail tattoos—a pentagram and a horned monster. The words DIE HIGH were painted on his helmet. This was his second tour in Salvador, and Moody—who was Dantzler's buddy—said the drugs had addled DT's brains, that he was crazy and gone to hell.

"He collects trophies," Moody had said. "And not just ears like they done in 'Nam."

When Dantzler had finally gotten a glimpse of the trophies, he had been appalled. They were kept in a tin box in DT's pack and were nearly unrecognizable; they looked like withered brown orchids. But despite his revulsion, despite the fact that he was afraid of DT, he admired the man's capacity for survival and had taken to heart his advice to rely on the drugs.

On the way back down the slope they discovered a live casualty, an Indian kid about Dantzler's age, nineteen or twenty. Black hair, adobe skin, and heavy-lidded brown eyes. Dantzler, whose father was an anthropologist and had done fieldwork in Salvador, figured him for a Santa Ana tribesman; before leaving the States, Dantzler had pored over his father's notes, hoping this would give him an edge, and had learned to identify the various regional types. The kid had a minor leg wound and was wearing fatigue pants and a faded COKE ADDS LIFE T-shirt. This T-shirt irritated DT no end.

"What the hell you know 'bout Coke?" he asked the kid as they headed for the chopper that was to carry them deeper into

Morazán Province. "You think it's funny or somethin'?" He whacked the kid in the back with his rifle butt, and when they reached the chopper, he slung him inside and had him sit by the door. He sat beside him, tapped out a joint from a pack of Kools, and asked, "Where's Infante?"

"Dead," said the medic.

"Shit!" DT licked the joint so it would burn evenly. "Goddamn beaner ain't no use 'cept somebody else know Spanish."

"I know a little," Dantzler volunteered.

Staring at Dantzler, DT's eyes went empty and unfocused. "Naw," he said. "You don't know no Spanish."

Dantzler ducked his head to avoid DT's stare and said nothing; he thought he understood what DT meant, but he ducked away from the understanding as well. The chopper bore them aloft, and DT lit the joint. He let the smoke out his nostrils and passed the joint to the kid, who accepted gratefully.

"*Qué sabor!*" he said, exhaling a billow; he smiled and nodded, wanting to be friends.

Dantzler turned his gaze to the open door. They were flying low between the hills, and looking at the deep bays of shadow in their folds acted to drain away the residue of the drugs, leaving him weary and frazzled. Sunlight poured in, dazzling the oil-smeared floor.

"Hey, Dantzler!" DT had to shout over the noise of the rotors. "Ask him whass his name!"

The kid's eyelids were drooping from the joint, but on hearing Spanish he perked up; he shook his head, though, refusing to answer. Dantzler smiled and told him not to be afraid.

"Ricardo Quu," said the kid.

"Kool!" said DT with false heartiness. "Thass my brand!" He offered his pack to the kid.

"*Gracias, no.*" The kid waved the joint and grinned.

"Dude's named for a goddamn cigarette," said DT disparagingly, as if this were the height of insanity.

Dantzler asked the kid if there were more soldiers nearby, and once again received no reply; but, apparently sensing in Dantzler a kindred soul, the kid leaned forward and spoke rapidly, saying that his village was Santander Jiménez, that his father was—he hesitated—a man of power. He asked where they were taking him. Dantzler returned a stony glare. He found it easy to reject the kid, and he realized later this was because he had already given up on him.

Latching his hands behind his head, DT began to sing—a wordless melody. His voice was discordant, barely audible above the rotors; but the tune had a familiar ring and Dantzler soon placed it. The theme from "Star Trek." It brought back memories of watching TV with his sister, laughing at the low-budget aliens and Scotty's Actors' Equity accent. He gazed out the door again. The sun was behind the hills, and the hillsides were unfeatured blurs of dark green smoke. Oh, God, he wanted to be home, to be anywhere but Salvador! A couple of the guys joined in the singing at DT's urging, and as the volume swelled, Dantzler's emotion peaked. He was on the verge of tears, remembering tastes and sights, the way his girl Jeanine had smelled, so clean and fresh, not reeking of sweat and perfume like the whores around Ilopango—finding all this substance in the banal touchstone of his culture and the illusions of the hillsides rushing past. Then Moody tensed beside him, and he glanced up to learn the reason why.

In the gloom of the chopper's belly, DT was as unfeatured as the hills—a black presence ruling them, more the leader of a coven than a platoon. The other two guys were singing their lungs out, and even the kid was getting into the spirit of things. *"Música!"* he said at one point, smiling at everybody, trying to fan the flame of good feeling. He swayed to the rhythm and essayed a "la-la" now and again. But no one else was responding.

The singing stopped, and Dantzler saw that the whole platoon was staring at the kid, their expressions slack and dispirited.

"Space!" shouted DT, giving the kid a little shove. "The final frontier!"

The smile had not yet left the kid's face when he toppled out the door. DT peered after him; a few seconds later he smacked his hand against the floor and sat back, grinning. Dantzler felt like screaming, the stupid horror of the joke was so at odds with the languor of his homesickness. He looked to the others for reaction. They were sitting with their heads down, fiddling with trigger guards and pack straps, studying their bootlaces, and seeing this, he quickly imitated them.

Morazán Province was spook country. Santa Ana spooks. Flights of birds had been reported to attack patrols; animals appeared at the perimeters of campsites and vanished when you shot at them; dreams afflicted everyone who ventured there. Dantzler could not testify to the birds and animals, but he did have a recurring dream. In it the kid DT had killed was pinwheeling down through a golden fog, his T-shirt visible against the roiling backdrop, and sometimes a voice would boom out of the fog, saying, "You are killing my son." No, no, Dantzler would reply, it wasn't me, and besides, he's already dead. Then he would wake covered with sweat, groping for his rifle, his heart racing.

But the dream was not an important terror, and he assigned it no significance. The land was far more terrifying. Pine-forested ridges that stood out against the sky like fringes of electrified hair; little trails winding off into thickets and peter-ing out, as if what they led to had been magicked away; gray rock faces along which they were forced to walk, hopelessly exposed to ambush. There were innumerable booby traps set by the guerrillas, and they lost several men to rockfalls. It was the emptiest place of Dantzler's experience. No people, no an-imals, just a few hawks circling the solitudes between the ridges. Once in a while they found tunnels, and these they blew with the new gas grenades; the gas ignited the rich con-centrations of hydrocarbons and sent flame sweeping through the entire system. DT would praise whoever had discovered the tunnel and would estimate in a loud voice how many beaners they had "refried." But Dantzler knew they were tra-versing pure emptiness and burning empty holes. Days, under debilitating heat, they humped the mountains, traveling seven, eight, even ten klicks up trails so steep that frequently the feet of the guy ahead of you would be on a level with your face; nights, it was cold, the darkness absolute, the silence so profound that Dantzler imagined he could hear the great humming vibration of the earth. They might have been anywhere or nowhere. Their fear was nourished by the isolation, and the only remedy was "martial arts."

Dantzler took to popping the pills without the excuse of combat. Moody cautioned him against abusing the drugs, citing rumors of bad side effects and DT's madness; but even he was using them more and more often. During basic training, Dantzler's D.I. had told the boots that the drugs were available only to the Special Forces, that their use was optional; but there had been too many instances of lackluster battlefield performance in the last war, and this was to prevent a reoccurrence.

"The chickenshit infantry should take 'em," the D.I. had said. "You bastards are brave already. You're born killers, right?"

"Right, sir!" they had shouted.

"What are you?"

"Born killers, sir!"

But Dantzler was not a born killer; he was not even clear as to how he had been drafted, less clear as to how he had been manipulated into the Special Forces, and he had learned that nothing was optional in Salvador, with the possible exception of life itself.

The platoon's mission was reconnaissance and mop-up. Along with other Special Forces platoons, they were to secure Morazán prior to the invasion of Nicaragua; specifically, they were to proceed to the village of Tecolutla, where a Sandinista patrol had recently been spotted, and following that they were to join up with the First Infantry and take part in the offensive against León, a provincial capital just across the Nicaraguan border. As Dantzler and Moody walked together, they frequently talked about the offensive, how it would be good to get down into flat country; occasionally they talked about the possibility of reporting DT, and once, after he had led them on a forced night march, they toyed with the idea of killing him. But most often they discussed the ways of the Indians and the land, since this was what had caused them to become buddies.

Moody was slightly built, freckled, and red-haired; his eyes had the "thousand-yard stare" that came from too much war. Dantzler had seen winos with such vacant, lusterless stares. Moody's father had been in 'Nam, and Moody said it had been worse than Salvador because there had been no real commitment to win; but he thought Nicaragua and Guatemala might be the worst of all, especially if the Cubans sent in troops as they had threatened. He was adept at locating tunnels and detecting booby traps, and it was for this reason Dantzler had cultivated his friendship. Essentially a loner, Moody had resisted all advances until learning of Dantzler's father; thereafter he had buddied up, eager to hear about the field notes, believing they might give him an edge.

"They think the land has animal traits," said Dantzler one day as they climbed along a ridgetop. "Just like some kinds of fish look like plants or sea bottom, parts of the land look like plain ground, jungle . . . whatever. But when you enter them, you find you've entered the spirit world, the world of *Sukias*."

"What's *Sukias*?" asked Moody.

"Magicians." A twig snapped behind Dantzler, and he spun around, twitching off the safety of his rifle. It was only Hodge—a lanky kid with the beginnings of a beer gut. He stared hollow-eyed at Dantzler and popped an ampule.

Moody made a noise of disbelief. "If they got magicians, why ain't they winnin'? Why ain't they zappin' us off the cliffs?"

"It's not their business," said Dantzler. "They don't believe in messing with worldly affairs unless it concerns them directly. Anyway, these places—the ones that look like normal land but aren't—they're called. . . ." He drew a blank on the name. "*Aya*-something. I can't remember. But they have different laws. They're where your spirit goes to die after your body dies."

"Don't they got no Heaven?"

"Nope. It just takes longer for your spirit to die, and so it goes to one of these places that's between everything and nothing."

"Nothin'," said Moody disconsolately, as if all his hopes for an afterlife had been dashed. "Don't make no sense to have spirits and not have no Heaven."

"Hey," said Dantzler, tensing as wind rustled the pine boughs. "They're just a bunch of damn primitives. You know what their sacred drink is? Hot chocolate! My old man was a guest at one of their funerals, and he said they carried cups of hot chocolate balanced on these little red towers and acted like drinking it was going to wake them to the secrets of the universe." He laughed, and the laughter sounded tinny and psychotic to his own ears. "So you're going to worry about fools who think hot chocolate's holy water?"

"Maybe they just like it," said Moody. "Maybe somebody dyin' just give 'em an excuse to drink it."

But Dantzler was no longer listening. A moment before, as they emerged from pine cover onto the highest point of the ridge, a stony scarp open to the winds and providing a view of rumpled mountains and valleys extending to the horizon, he had popped an ampule. He felt so strong, so full of righteous purpose and controlled fury, it seemed only the sky was around him, that he was still ascending, preparing to do battle with the gods themselves.

Tecolutla was a village of whitewashed stone tucked into a notch between two hills. From above, the houses—with their shadow-blackened windows and doorways—looked like an unlucky throw of dice. The streets ran uphill and down, diverging around boulders. Bougainvilleas and hibiscuses speckled the hillsides, and there were tilled fields on the gentler slopes. It was a sweet, peaceful place when they arrived, and after they had gone it was once again peaceful; but its sweetness had been permanently banished. The reports of Sandinistas had proved accurate, and though they were casualties left behind to recuperate, DT had decided their presence called for extreme measures. Fu gas, frag grenades, and such. He had fired an M-60 until the barrel melted down, and then had manned the flamethrower. Afterward, as they rested atop the next ridge, exhausted and begrimed, having radioed in a chopper for resupply, he could not get over how one of the houses he had torched had come to resemble a toasted marshmallow.

"Ain't that how it was, man?" he asked, striding up and
down the line. He did not care if they agreed about the house;
it was a deeper question he was asking, one concerning the
ethics of their actions.

"Yeah," said Dantzler, forcing a smile. "Sure did."

DT grunted with laughter. "You *know* I'm right, don'tcha
man?"

The sun hung directly behind his head, a golden corona rimming a black oval, and Dantzler could not turn his eyes away.
He felt weak and weakening, as if threads of himself were being spun loose and sucked into the blackness. He had popped
three ampules prior to the firefight, and his experience of Tecolutla had been a kind of mad whirling dance through the
streets, spraying erratic bursts that appeared to be writing
weird names on the walls. The leader of the Sandinistas had
worn a mask—a gray face with a surprised hole of a mouth
and pink circles around the eyes. A ghost face. Dantzler had
been afraid of the mask and had poured round after round into
it. Then, leaving the village, he had seen a small girl standing
beside the shell of the last house, watching them, her colorless
rag of a dress tattering in the breeze. She had been a victim of
that malnutrition disease, the one that paled your skin and
whitened your hair and left you retarded. He could not recall
the name of the disease—things like names were slipping away
from him—nor could he believe anyone had survived, and for
a moment he had thought the spirit of the village had come out
to mark their trail.

That was all he could remember of Tecolutla, all he wanted
to remember. But he knew he had been brave.

Four days later, they headed up into a cloud forest. It was the
dry season, but dry season or not, blackish gray clouds always
shrouded these peaks. They were shot through by ugly glimmers of lightning, making it seem that malfunctioning neon
signs were hidden beneath them, advertisements for evil.
Everyone was jittery, and Jerry LeDoux—a slim dark-haired
Cajun kid—flat-out refused to go.

"It ain't reasonable," he said. "Be easier to go through the
passes."

"We're on recon, man! You think the beaners be waitin' in the passes, wavin' their white flags?" DT whipped his rifle into firing position and pointed it at LeDoux. "C'mon, Louisiana man. Pop a few, and you feel different."

As LeDoux popped the ampules, DT talked to him.

"Look at it this way, man. This is your big adventure. Up there it be like all them animal shows on the tube. The savage kingdom, the unknown. Could be like Mars or somethin'. Monsters and shit, with big red eyes and tentacles. You wanna miss that, man? You wanna miss bein' the first grunt on Mars?"

Soon LeDoux was raring to go, giggling at DT's rap.

Moody kept his mouth shut, but he fingered the safety of his rifle and glared at DT's back. When DT turned to him, however, he relaxed. Since Tecolutla he had grown taciturn, and there seemed to be a shifting of lights and darks in his eyes, as if something were scurrying back and forth behind them. He had taken to wearing banana leaves on his head, arranging them under his helmet so the frayed ends stuck out the sides like strange green hair. He said this was camouflage, but Dantzler was certain it bespoke some secretive irrational purpose. Of course DT had noticed Moody's spiritual erosion, and as they prepared to move out, he called Dantzler aside.

"He done found someplace inside his head that feel good to him," said DT. "He's tryin' to curl up into it, and once he do that he ain't gon' be responsible. Keep an eye on him."

Dantzler mumbled his assent, but was not enthused.

"I know he your fren', man, but that don't mean shit. Not the way things are. Now me, I don't give a damn 'bout you personally. But I'm your brother-in-arms, and thass somethin' you can count on . . . y'understand."

To Dantzler's shame, he did understand.

They had planned on negotiating the cloud forest by nightfall, but they had underestimated the difficulty. The vegetation beneath the clouds was lush—thick, juicy leaves that mashed underfoot, tangles of vines, trees with slick, pale bark and waxy leaves—and the visibility was only about fifteen feet. They were gray wraiths passing through grayness. The vague shapes of the foliage reminded Dantzler of fancifully engraved letters, and for a while he entertained himself with the notion that they were walking among the half-formed phrases of a constitution not yet manifest in the land. They barged off the trail, losing it completely, becoming veiled in spiderwebs and drenched by spills of water; their voices were oddly muffled, the tag ends of words swallowed up. After seven hours of this, DT reluctantly gave the order to pitch camp. They set electric lamps around the perimeter so they could see to string the jungle hammocks; the beam of light illuminated the moisture in the air, piercing the murk with jeweled blades. They talked in hushed tones, alarmed by the eerie atmosphere. When they had done with the hammocks, DT posted four sentries— Moody, LeDoux, Dantzler, and himself. Then they switched off the lamps.

It grew pitch-dark, and the darkness was picked out by plips and plops, the entire spectrum of dripping sounds. To Dantzler's ears they blended into a gabbling speech. He imagined tiny Santa Ana demons talking about him, and to stave off paranoia he popped two ampules. He continued to pop them, trying to limit himself to one every half hour; but he was uneasy, unsure where to train his rifle in the dark, and he exceeded his limit. Soon it began to grow light again, and he assumed that more time had passed than he had thought. That often happened with the ampules—it was easy to lose yourself in being alert, in the wealth of perceptual detail available to your sharpened senses. Yet on checking his watch, he saw it was only a few minutes after two o'clock. His system was too inundated with the drugs to allow panic, but he twitched his head from side to side in tight little arcs to determine the source of the brightness. There did not appear to be a single source; it was simply that filaments of the cloud were gleaming, casting a diffuse golden glow, as if they were elements of a nervous system coming to life. He started to call out, then held back. The others must have seen the light, and they had given no cry; they probably had a good reason for their silence. He scrunched down flat, pointing his rifle out from the campsite.

Bathed in the golden mist, the forest had acquired an alchemic beauty. Beads of water glittered with gemmy brilliance; the leaves and vines and bark were gilded. Every surface shimmered with light . . . everything except a fleck of blackness hovering between two of the trunks, its size gradually increasing. As it swelled in his vision, he saw it had the shape of a bird, its wings beating, flying toward him from an inconceivable distance—inconceivable, because the dense vegetation did not permit you to see very far in a straight line, and yet the bird was growing larger with such slowness that it must have been coming from a long way off. It was not really flying, he realized; rather, it was as if the forest were painted on a piece of paper, as if someone were holding a lit match behind it and burning a hole, a hole that maintained the shape of a bird as it spread. He was transfixed, unable to react. Even when it had blotted out half the light, when he lay before it no bigger than a mote in relation to its huge span, he could not move or squeeze the trigger. And then the blackness swept over him. He had the sensation of being borne along at incredible speed, and he could no longer hear the dripping of the forest.

"Moody!" he shouted. "DT!"

But the voice that answered belonged to neither of them. It was hoarse, issuing from every part of the surrounding blackness, and he recognized it as the voice of his recurring dream.

"You are killing my son," it said. "I have led you here, to this *ayahuamaco,* so he may judge you."

Dantzler knew to his bones the voice was that of the *Sukia* of the village of Santander Jiménez. He wanted to offer a denial, to explain his innocence, but all he could manage was, "No." He said it tearfully, hopelessly, his forehead resting on his rifle barrel. Then his mind gave a savage twist, and his soldiery self regained control. He ejected an ampule from his dispenser and popped it.

The voice laughed—malefic, damning laughter whose vibrations shuddered Dantzler. He opened up with the rifle, spraying fire in all directions. Filigrees of golden holes appeared in the blackness, tendrils of mist coiled through them. He kept on firing until the blackness shattered and fell in jagged sections toward him. Slowly. Like shards of black glass dropping through water. He emptied the rifle and flung himself flat, shielding his head with his arms, expecting to be sliced into bits; but nothing touched him. At last he peeked between his arms; then—amazed, because the forest was now a uniform lustrous yellow—he rose to his knees. He scraped his hand on one of the crushed leaves beneath him, and blood welled from the cut. The broken fibers of the leaf were as stiff as wires. He stood, a giddy trickle of hysteria leaking up from the bottom of his soul. It was no forest, but a building of solid gold worked to resemble a forest—the sort of conceit that might have been fabricated for the child of an emperor. Canopied by golden leaves, columned by slender golden trunks, carpeted by golden grasses. The water beads were diamonds. All the gleam and glitter soothed his apprehension; here was something out of a myth, a habitat for princesses and wizards and dragons. Almost gleeful, he turned to the campsite to see how the others were reacting.

Once, when he was nine years old, he had sneaked into the attic to rummage through the boxes and trunks, and he had run across an old morocco-bound copy of *Gulliver's Travels*. He had been taught to treasure old books, and so he had opened it eagerly to look at the illustrations, only to find that the centers of the pages had been eaten away, and there, right in the heart of the fiction, was a nest of larvae. Pulpy, horrid things. It had been an awful sight, but one unique in his experience, and he might have studied those crawling scraps of life for a very long time if his father had not interrupted. Such a sight was now before him, and he was numb with it.

They were all dead. He should have guessed they would be; he had given no thought to them while firing his rifle. They had been struggling out of their hammocks when the bullets hit, and as a result they were hanging half-in, half-out, their limbs dangling, blood pooled beneath them. The veils of golden mist made them look dark and mysterious and malformed, like monsters killed as they emerged from their cocoons. Dantzler could not stop staring, but he was shrinking inside himself. It was not his fault. That thought keep swooping in and out of a flock of less acceptable thoughts; he wanted it to stay put, to be true, to alleviate the sick horror he was beginning to feel.

"What's your name?" asked a girl's voice behind him.

She was sitting on a stone about twenty feet away. Her hair was a tawny shade of gold, her skin a half-tone lighter, and her dress was cunningly formed out of the mist. Only her eyes were real. Brown heavy-lidded eyes—they were at variance with the rest of her face, which had the fresh, unaffected beauty of an American teenager.

"Don't be afraid," she said, and patted the ground, inviting him to sit beside her.

He recognized the eyes, but it was no matter. He badly needed the consolation she could offer; he walked over and sat down. She let him lean his head against her thigh.

"What's your name?" she repeated.

"Dantzler," he said. "John Dantzler." And then he added, "I'm from Boston. My father's . . ." It would be too difficult to explain about anthropology. "He's a teacher."

"Are there many soldiers in Boston?" She stroked his cheek with a golden finger.

The caress made Dantzler happy. "Oh, no," he said. "They hardly know there's a war going on."

"This is true?" she said, incredulous.

"Well, they *do* know about it, but it's just news on the TV to them. They've got more pressing problems. Their jobs, families."

"Will you let them know about the war when you return home?" she asked. "Will you do that for me?"

Dantzler had given up hope of returning home, of surviving, and her assumption that he would do both acted to awaken his gratitude. "Yes," he said fervently. "I will."

"You must hurry," she said. "If you stay in the *ayahuamaco* too long, you will never leave. You must find the way out. It is a way not of directions or trails, but of events."

"Where is this place?" he asked, suddenly aware of how much he had taken it for granted.

She shifted her leg away, and if he had not caught himself on the stone, he would have fallen. When he looked up, she had vanished. He was surprised that her disappearance did not alarm him; in reflex he slipped out a couple of ampules, but after a moment's reflection he decided not to use them. It was impossible to slip them back into the dispenser, so he tucked them into the interior webbing of his helmet for later. He doubted he would need them, though. He felt strong, competent, and unafraid.

Dantzler stepped carefully between the hammocks, not wanting to brush against them; it might have been his imagination, but they seemed to be bulged down lower than before, as if death had weighed out heavier than life. That heaviness was in the air, pressuring him. Mist rose like golden steam from the corpses, but the sight no longer affected him—perhaps because the mist gave the illusion of being their souls. He picked up a rifle with a full magazine and headed off into the forest.

The tips of the golden leaves were sharp, and he had to ease past them to avoid being cut; but he was at the top of his form, moving gracefully, and the obstacles barely slowed his pace. He was not even anxious about the girl's warning to hurry; he was certain the way out would soon present itself. After a minute or so he heard voices, and after another few seconds he came to a clearing divided by a stream, one so perfectly reflecting that its banks appeared to enclose a wedge of golden mist. Moody was squatting to the left of the stream, staring at the blade of his survival knife and singing under his breath—a wordless melody that had the erratic rhythm of a trapped fly. Beside him lay Jerry LeDoux, his throat slashed from ear to ear. DT was sitting on the other side of the stream; he had been shot just above the knee, and though he had ripped up his shirt for bandages and tied off the leg with a tourniquet, he was not in good shape. He was sweating, and a gray chalky pallor infused his skin. The entire scene had the weird vitality of something that had materialized in a magic mirror, a bubble of reality enclosed within a gilt frame.

DT heard Dantzler's footfalls and glanced up. "Waste him!" he shouted, pointing to Moody.

Moody did not turn from contemplation of the knife. "No,"

he said, as if speaking to someone whose image was held in the blade.

"Waste him, man!" screamed DT. "He killed LeDoux!"

"Please," said Moody to the knife. "I don't want to."

There was blood clotted on his face, more blood on the banana leaves sticking out of his helmet.

"Did you kill Jerry?" asked Dantzler; while he addressed the question to Moody, he did not relate to him as an individual, only as part of a design whose message he had to unravel.

"Jesus Christ! Waste him!" DT smashed his fist against the ground in frustration.

"Okay," said Moody. With an apologetic look, he sprang to his feet and charged Dantzler, swinging the knife.

Emotionless, Dantzler stitched a line of fire across Moody's chest; he went sideways into the bushes and down.

"What the hell was you waitin' for!" DT tried to rise, but winced and fell back. "Damn! Don't know if I can walk."

"Pop a few," Dantzler suggested mildly.

"Yeah. Good thinkin', man." DT fumbled for his dispenser.

Dantzler peered into the bushes to see where Moody had fallen. He felt nothing, and this pleased him. He was weary of feeling.

DT popped an ampule with a flourish, as if making a toast, and inhaled. "Ain't you gon' to do some, man?"

"I don't need them," said Dantzler. "I'm fine."

The stream interested him; it did not reflect the mist, as he had supposed, but was itself a seam of the mist.

"How many you think they was?" asked DT.

"How many what?"

"Beaners, man! I wasted three or four after they hit us, but I couldn't tell how many they was."

Dantzler considered this in light of his own interpretation of events and Moody's conversation with the knife. It made sense. A Santa Ana kind of sense.

"Beats me," he said. "But I guess there's less than there used to be."

DT snorted. "You got *that* right!" He heaved to his feet and limped to the edge of the stream. "Gimme a hand across."

Dantzler reached out to him, but instead of taking his hand, he grabbed his wrist and pulled him off-balance. DT teetered on his good leg, then toppled and vanished beneath the mist. Dantzler had expected him to fall, but he surfaced instantly, mist clinging to his skin. Of course, thought Dantzler; his body would have to die before his spirit would fall.

"What you doin', man?" DT was more disbelieving than enraged.

Dantzler planted a foot in the middle of his back and pushed him down until his head was submerged. DT bucked and clawed at the foot and managed to come to his hands and knees. Mist slithered from his eyes, his nose, and he choked out the words ". . . kill you . . ." Dantzler pushed him down again; he got into pushing him down and letting him up, over and over. Not so as to torture him. Not really. It was because he had suddenly understood the nature of the *ayahuamaco*'s laws, that they were approximations of normal laws, and he further understood that his actions had to approximate those of someone jiggling a key in a lock. DT was the key to the way out, and Dantzler was jiggling him, making sure all the tumblers were engaged.

Some of the vessels in DT's eyes had burst, and the whites were occluded by films of blood. When he tried to speak, mist curled from his mouth. Gradually his struggles subsided; he clawed runnels in the gleaming yellow dirt of the bank and shuddered. His shoulders were knobs of black land foundering in a mystic sea.

For a long time after DT sank from view, Dantzler stood beside the stream, uncertain of what was left to do and unable to remember a lesson he had been taught. Finally he shouldered his rifle and walked away from the clearing. Morning had broken, the mist had thinned, and the forest had regained its usual coloration. But he scarcely noticed these changes, still troubled by his faulty memory. Eventually, he let it slide—it would all come clear sooner or later. He was just happy to be alive. After a while he began to kick the stones as he went, and to swing his rifle in a carefree fashion against the weeds.

· · ·

When the First Infantry poured across the Nicaraguan border and wasted León, Dantzler was having a quiet time at the VA hospital in Ann Arbor, Michigan; and at the precise moment the bulletin was flashed nationwide, he was sitting in the lounge, watching the American League playoffs between Detroit and Texas. Some of the patients ranted at the interruption, while others shouted them down, wanting to hear the details. Dantzler expressed no reaction whatsoever. He was solely concerned with being a model patient; however, noticing that one of the staff was giving him a clinical stare, he added his weight on the side of the baseball fans. He did not want to appear too controlled. The doctors were as suspicious of that sort of behavior as they were of its contrary. But the funny thing was—at least it was funny to Dantzler—that his feigned annoyance at the bulletin was an exemplary proof of his control, his expertise at moving through life the way he had moved through the golden leaves of the cloud forest. Cautiously, gracefully, efficiently. Touching nothing, and being touched by nothing. That was the lesson he had learned—to be as perfect a counterfeit of a man as the *ayahuamaco* had been of the land; to adopt the various stances of a man, and yet, by virtue of his distance from things human, to be all the more prepared for the onset of crisis or a call to action. He saw nothing aberrant in this; even the doctors would admit that men were little more than organized pretense. If he was different from other men, it was only that he had a deeper awareness of the principles on which his personality was founded.

When the battle of Managua was joined, Dantzler was living at home. His parents had urged him to go easy in readjusting to civilian life, but he had immediately gotten a job as a management trainee in a bank. Each morning he would drive to work and spend a controlled, quiet eight hours; each night he would watch TV with his mother, and before going to bed, he would climb to the attic and inspect the trunk containing his souvenirs of war—helmet, fatigues, knife, boots. The doctors had insisted he face his experiences, and this ritual was his way of following their instructions. All in all, he was quite pleased with his progress, but he still had problems. He had not been able to force himself to venture out at night, remembering too well the darkness in the cloud forest, and he had rejected his friends, refusing to see them or answer their calls—he was not secure with the idea of friendship. Further, despite his methodical approach to life, he was prone to a nagging restlessness, the feeling of a chore left undone.

One night his mother came into his room and told him that an old friend, Phil Curry, was on the phone. "Please talk to him, Johnny," she said. "He's been drafted, and I think he's a little scared."

The word *drafted* struck a responsive chord in Dantzler's soul, and after brief deliberation he went downstairs and picked up the receiver.

"Hey," said Phil. "What's the story, man? Three months, and you don't even give me a call."

"I'm sorry," said Dantzler. "I haven't been feeling so hot."

"Yeah, I understand." Phil was silent a moment. "Listen, man. I'm leaving', y'know, and we're having a big send-off at Sparky's. It's goin' on right now. Why don't you come down?"

"I don't know."

"Jeanine's here, man. Y'know, she's still crazy 'bout you, talks 'bout you alla time. She don't go out with nobody."

Dantzler was unable to think of anything to say.

"Look," said Phil, "I'm pretty weirded out by this soldier shit. I hear it's pretty bad down there. If you got anything you can tell me 'bout what it's like, man, I'd 'preciate it."

Dantzler could relate to Phil's concern, his desire for an edge, and besides, it felt right to go. Very right. He would take some precautions against the darkness.

"I'll be there," he said.

It was a foul night, spitting snow, but Sparky's parking lot was jammed. Dantzler's mind was flurried like the snow, crowded like the lot—thoughts whirling in, jockeying for position, melting away. He hoped his mother would not wait up, he wondered if Jeanine still wore her hair long, he was worried because the palms of his hands were unnaturally warm. Even with the car windows rolled up, he could hear loud music coming from inside the club. Above the door the words

SPARKY'S ROCK CITY were being spelled out a letter at a time in red neon, and when the spelling was complete, the letters flashed off and on and a golden neon explosion bloomed around them. After the explosion, the entire sign went dark for a split second, and the big ramshackle building seemed to grow large and merge with the black sky. He had an idea it was watching him, and he shuddered—one of those sudden lurches downward of the kind that take you just before you fall asleep. He knew the people inside did not intend him any harm, but he also knew that places have a way of changing people's intent, and he did not want to be caught off guard. Sparky's might be such a place, might be a huge black presence camouflaged by neon, its true substance one with the abyss of the sky, the phosphorescent snowflakes jittering in his headlights, the wind keening through the side vent. He would have liked very much to drive home and forget about his promise to Phil; however, he felt a responsibility to explain about the war. More than a responsibility, an evangelistic urge. He would tell them about the kid falling out of the chopper, the white-haired girl in Tecolutla, the emptiness. God, yes! How you went down chock-full of ordinary American thoughts and dreams, memories of smoking weed and chasing tail and hanging out and freeway flying with a case of something cold, and how you smuggled back a human-shaped container of pure Salvadorian emptiness. Primo grade. Smuggled it back to the land of silk and money, of mindfuck video games and topless tennis matches and fast-food solutions to the nutritional problem. Just a taste of Salvador would banish all those trivial obsessions. Just a taste. It would be easy to explain.

Of course, some things beggared explanation.

He bent down and adjusted the survival knife in his boot so the hilt would not rub against his calf. From his coat pocket he withdrew the two ampules he had secreted in his helmet that long-ago night in the cloud forest. As the neon explosion flashed once more, glimmers of gold coursed along their shiny surfaces. He did not think he would need them; his hand was steady, and his purpose was clear. But to be on the safe side, he popped them both.

How the Wind Spoke at Madaket

I

~~~~~~~~~~~~~~~~~~~~~~~~~~~~~~ *Softly at dawn, rustling dead*
~~~~~~~~~~~~~~~~~~~~~~~~~~~~~~ *leaves in the roof gutters,*
ticking the wires of the television antenna against the shingled
wall, seething through the beach grasses, shifting the bare twigs
of a hawthorn to claw at the toolshed door, playfully flipping a
peg off the clothesline, snuffling the garbage and tattering the
plastic bags, creating a thousand nervous flutters, a thousand
more shivery whispers, then building, keening in the window
cracks and rattling the panes, smacking down a sheet of ply-
board that has been leaning against the woodpile, swelling to a
pour off the open sea, its howl articulated by throats of narrow
streets and teeth of vacant houses, until you begin to imagine a
huge invisible animal throwing back its head and roaring, and
the cottage is creaking like the timbers of an old ship. . . .

II

Waking at first light, Peter Ramey lay abed awhile and listened
to the wind; then, steeling himself against the cold, he threw
off the covers, hurriedly pulled on jeans, tennis shoes, and a
flannel shirt, and went into the front room to kindle a fire in
the wood stove. Outside, the trees were silhouetted by a backdrop of slate clouds, but the sky wasn't yet bright enough to

cast the shadow of the window frame across the picnic-style table beneath it; the other furniture—three chewed-up wicker chairs and a sofa bunk—hunched in their dark corners. The tinder caught, and soon the fire was snapping inside the stove. Still cold, Peter beat his arms against his shoulders and hopped from one foot to another, setting dishes and drawers to rattling. He was a pale, heavyset man of thirty-three, with ragged black hair and beard, so tall that he had to duck through the doors of the cottage; and because of his size he had never really settled into the place: he felt like a tramp who had appropriated a child's abandoned treehouse in which to spend the winter.

The kitchen was an alcove off the front room, and after easing the chill, his face stinging with heat, he lit the gas stove and started breakfast. He cut a hole in a slice of bread, laid it in the frying pan, then cracked an egg and poured it into the hole (usually he just opened cans and cereal boxes or heated frozen food, but Sara Tappinger, his current lover, had taught him to fix eggs this way, and it made him feel like a competent bachelor to keep up the practice). He shoveled down the egg and bread standing at the kitchen window, watching the gray-shingled houses across the street melt from the darkness, shadowy clumps resolving into thickets of bayberry and sheep laurel, a picket line of Japanese pines beyond them. The wind had dropped and it looked as if the clouds were going to hang around, which was fine by Peter. Since renting the cottage in Madaket eight months before, he had learned that he thrived on bleakness, that the blustery, overcast days nourished his imagination. He had finished one novel here, and he planned to stay until the second was done. And maybe a third. What the hell? There wasn't much point in returning to California. He turned on the water to do the dishes, but the thought of LA had soured him on being competent. Screw it! Let the roaches breed. He pulled on a sweater, stuffed a notebook in his pocket, and stepped out into the cold.

As if it had been waiting for him, a blast of wind came swerving around the corner of the cottage and numbed his face. He tucked his chin onto his chest and set out walking, turning left on Tennessee Avenue and heading toward Smith Point, past more gray-shingled houses with quarterboards bearing cutesy names above their doors: names like Sea Shanty and Tooth Acres (the vacation home of a New Jersey dentist). When he had arrived on Nantucket he'd been amused by the fact that almost every structure on the island, even the Sears, Roebuck store, had gray shingles, and he had written his ex-wife a long humorous let's-be-friends letter telling about the shingles, about all the odd characters and quirkiness of the place. His ex-wife had not answered, and Peter couldn't blame her, not after what he had done. Solitude was the reason he gave for having moved to Madaket, but while this was superficially true, it would have been more accurate to say that he had been fleeing the ruins of his life. He had been idling along, content with his marriage, churning out scripts for a PBS children's show, when he had fallen obsessively in love with another woman, herself married. Plans and promises had been made, as a result of which he had left his wife; but then, in a sudden reversal of form, the woman—who had never expressed any sentiment other than boredom and resentment concerning her husband—had decided to honor her vows, leaving Peter alone and feeling both a damned fool and a villain. Desperate, he had fought for her, failed, tried to hate her, failed, and finally, hoping a change of geography would provoke a change of heart—hers or his—he had come to Madaket. That had been in September, directly after the exodus of the summer tourists; it was now May, and though the cold weather still lingered, the tourists were beginning to filter back. But no hearts had changed.

Twenty minutes of brisk walking brought him to the top of a dune overlooking Smith Point, a jut of sand extending a hundred yards or so into the water, with three small islands strung out beyond it; the nearest of these had been separated from the Point during a hurricane, and had the island still been attached, it—in conjunction with Eel Point, some three-quarters of a mile distant—would have given the western end of the land mass the shape of a crab's claw. Far out at sea a ray of sunlight pierced the overcast and dazzled the water beneath to such brilliance that it looked like a laving of fresh white paint. Sea gulls made curving flights overhead, hovered and dropped scallops onto the gravelly shingle to break the shells, then swooped down to pluck the meat. Sad-voweled gusts of wind sprayed a fine grit through the air.

Peter sat in the lee of a dune, choosing a spot from which he could see the ocean between stalks of the pale green beach grass, and opened his notebook. The words HOW THE WIND SPOKE AT MADAKET were printed on the inside cover. He had no illusions that the publishers would keep the title; they would change it to *The Keening* or *The Huffing and Puffing,* package it with a garish cover, and stick it next to *Love's Tormenting Itch* by Wanda LaFontaine on the grocery store racks. But none of that mattered as long as the words were good, and they were, though it hadn't gone well at first, not until he had started walking each morning to Smith Point and writing longhand. Then everything had snapped into focus. He had realized that it was *his* story he wanted to tell—the woman, his loneliness, his psychic flashes, the resolution of his character—all wrapped in the eerie metaphor of the wind; the writing had flowed so easily that it seemed the wind was collaborating on the book, whispering in his ear and guiding his hand across the page. He flipped the pages and noticed a paragraph that was a bit too formal, that he should break up and seed throughout the story:

> *Sadler had spent much of his life in Los Angeles, where the sounds of nature were obscured, and to his mind the constancy of the wind was Nantucket's most remarkable feature. Morning, noon, and night it flowed across the island, giving him a sense of being a bottom-dweller in an ocean of air, buffeted by currents that sprang from exotic quarters of the globe. He was a lonely soul, and the wind served to articulate his loneliness, to point up the immensity of the world in which he had become isolated; over the months he had come to feel an affinity with it, to consider it a fellow-traveler through emptiness and time. He half believed its vague speechlike utterances to be exactly that—*

an oracular voice whose powers of speech were not yet fully developed—and from listening to them he derived an impression of impending strangeness. He did not discount the impression, because as far back as he could recall he had received similar ones, and most had been borne out by reality. It was no great prophetic gift, no foreshadowings of earthquakes or assassinations; rather, it was a low-grade psychic ability: flashes of vision often accompanied by queasiness and headaches. Sometimes he could touch an object and know something about its owner, sometimes he would glimpse the shape of an upcoming event. But these premonitions were never clear enough to do him any good, to prevent broken arms or—as he had lately discovered— emotional disaster. Still, he hearkened to them. And now he thought the wind might actually be trying to tell him something of his future, of a new factor about to compli-cate his existence, for whenever he staked himself out on the dune at Smith Point he would feel. . . .

Gooseflesh pebbling his skin, nausea, an eddying sensation behind his forehead as if his thoughts were spinning out of control. Peter rested his head on his knees and took deep breaths until the spell had abated. It was happening more and more often, and while it was most likely a product of sug- gestibility, a side effect of writing such a personal story, he couldn't shake the notion that he had become involved in some Twilight Zone irony, that the story was coming true as he wrote it. He hoped not: it wasn't going to be a very pleasant story. When the last of his nausea had passed, he took out a blue felt-tip, turned to a clean page, and began to detail the unpleasantness.

Two hours and fifteen pages later, hands stiff with cold, he heard a voice hailing him. Sara Tappinger was struggling up the side of the dune from the blacktop, slipping in the soft sand. She was, he thought with a degree of self-satisfaction, a damned pretty woman. Thirtyish; long auburn hair and nice cheekbones; endowed with what one of Peter's islander ac- quaintances called "big chest problems." That same acquaintance had congratulated him for having scored with Sara, saying that she'd blue-balled half the men on the island after her divorce, and wasn't he the lucky son of a bitch. Peter supposed he *was:* Sara was witty, bright, independent (she ran the local Montessori school), and they were compatible in every way. Yet it was not a towering passion. It was friendly, comfortable, and this Peter found alarming. Although being with her only glossed over his loneliness, he had come to depend on the relationship, and he was concerned that this signaled an overall reduction of his expectations, and that this in turn signaled the onset of middle age, a state for which he was unprepared.

"Hi," she said, flinging herself down beside him and planting a kiss on his cheek. "Wanna play?"

"Why aren't you in school?"

"It's Friday. I told you, remember? Parent-teacher conferences." She took his hand. "You're cold as ice! How long have you been here?"

"Couple of hours."

"You're insane." She laughed, delighted by his insanity. "I was watching you for a bit before I called. With your hair flying about, you looked like a mad Bolshevik hatching a plot."

"Actually," he said, adopting a Russian accent, "I come here to make contact with our submarines."

"Oh? What's up? An invasion?"

"Not exactly. You see, in Russia we have many shortages. Grain, high technology, blue jeans. But the Russian soul can fly above such hardships. There is, however, a shortage of one commodity that we must solve immediately, and this is why I have lured you here."

She pretended bewilderment. "You need school administrators?"

"No, no. It is more serious. I believe the American word for it is. . . ." He caught her by the shoulders and pushed her down on the sand, pinning her beneath him. "Poontang. We cannot do without."

Her smile faltered, then faded to a look of rapt anticipation. He kissed her. Through her coat he felt the softness of her breasts. The wind ruffled his hair, and he had the idea that it was leaning over his shoulder, spying on them; he broke off the kiss. He was queasy again. Dizzy.

"You're sweating," she said, dabbing at his brow with a gloved hand. "Is this one of those spells?"

He nodded and lay back against the dune.

"What do you see?" She continued to pat his brow dry, a concerned frown etching delicate lines at the corners of her mouth.

"Nothing," he said.

But he did see something. Something glinting behind a cloudy surface. Something that attracted him yet frightened him at the same time. Something he knew would soon fall to his hand.

Though nobody realized it at the time, the first sign of trouble was the disappearance of Ellen Borchard, age thirteen, on the evening of Tuesday, May 19—an event Peter had written into his book just prior to Sara's visit on Friday morning; but it didn't really begin for him until Friday night while drinking at the Atlantic Cafe in the village of Nantucket. He had gone there with Sara for dinner, and since the restaurant section was filled to capacity, they had opted for drinks and sandwiches at the bar. They had hardly settled on their stools when Jerry Highsmith—a blond young man who conducted bicycle tours of the island (" . . . the self-proclaimed Hunk of Hunks," was Sara's description of him)—latched onto Peter; he was a regular at the cafe and an aspiring writer, and he took every opportunity to get Peter's advice. As always, Peter offered encouragement, but he secretly felt that anyone who liked to do their drinking at the Atlantic could have little to say to the reading public: it was a typical New England tourist trap, decorated with brass barometers and old life preservers, and it catered to the young summer crowd, many of whom—evident by their Bahama tans—were packed around the bar. Soon Jerry moved off in pursuit of a redhead with a honeysuckle drawl, a member of his latest tour group, and his stool was taken by Mills Lindstrom, a retired fisherman and a neighbor of Peter's.

"Damn wind out there's sharp enough to carve bone," said

Mills by way of a greeting, and ordered a whiskey. He was a big red-faced man stuffed into overalls and a Levi's jacket; white curls spilled from under his cap, and a lacing of broken blood vessels webbed his cheeks. The lacing was more prominent than usual, because Mills had a load on.

"What are you doing here?" Peter was surprised that Mills would set foot in the cafe; it was his conviction that tourism was a deadly pollution, and places like the Atlantic were its mutant growths.

"Took the boat out today. First time in two months." Mills knocked back half his whiskey. "Thought I might set a few lines, but then I run into that thing off Smith Point. Didn't feel like fishin' anymore." He emptied his glass and signaled for a refill. "Carl Keating told me it was formin' out there a while back. Guess it slipped my mind."

"What thing?" asked Peter.

Mills sipped at his second whiskey. "Offshore pollution aggregate," he said grimly. "That's the fancy name, but basically it's a garbage dump. Must be pretty near a kilometer square of water covered in garbage. Oil slick, plastic bottles, driftwood. They collect at slack points in the tides, but not usually so close to land. This one ain't more'n fifteen miles off the Point."

Peter was intrigued. "You're talking about something like the Sargasso Sea, right?"

"'Spose so. 'Cept these ain't so big and there ain't no seaweed."

"Are they permanent?"

"This one's new, the one off Smith Point. But there's one about thirty miles off the Vineyard that's been there for some years. Big storm'll break it up, but it'll always come back." Mills patted his pockets, trying unsuccessfully to find his pipe. "Ocean's gettin' like a stagnant pond. Gettin' to where a man throws in a line and more'n likely he'll come up with an ol' boot 'stead of a fish. I 'member twenty years ago when the mackerel was runnin', there'd be so many fish the water would look black for miles. Now you spot a patch of dark water and you know some damn tanker's taken a shit!"

Sara, who had been talking to a friend, put her arm around

Peter's shoulder and asked what was up; after Peter had explained, she gave a dramatic shudder and said, "It sounds spooky to me." She affected a sepulchral tone. "Strange magnetic zones that lure sailors to their dooms."

"Spooky!" Mills scoffed. "You got better sense than that, Sara. Spooky!" The more he considered the comment, the madder he became. He stood and made a flailing gesture that spilled the drink of a tanned college-age kid behind him; he ignored the kid's complaint and glared at Sara. "Maybe you think this place is spooky. It's the same damn thing! A garbage dump! 'Cept here the garbage walks and talks"—he turned his glare on the kid—"and thinks it owns the goddamn world!"

"Shit," said Peter, watching Mills shoulder his way through the crowd. "I was going to ask him to take me to see it."

"Ask him tomorrow," said Sara. "Though I don't know why you'd want to see it." She grinned and held up her hands to ward off his explanation. "Sorry. I should realize that anyone who'll spend all day staring at sea gulls would find a square kilometer of garbage downright erotic."

He made a grab for her breasts. "I'll show you erotic!"

She laughed and caught his hand and—her mood suddenly altered—brushed the knuckles against her lips. "Show me later," she said.

They had a few more drinks, talked about Peter's work, about Sara's, and discussed the idea of taking a weekend together in New York. Peter began to acquire a glow. It was partly the drinks, yet he realized that Sara, too, was responsible. Though there had been other women since he had left his wife, he had scarcely noticed them; he had tried to be honest with them, had explained that he was in love with someone else, but he had learned that this was simply a sly form of dishonesty, that when you went to bed with someone—no matter how frank you had been as to your emotional state—they would refuse to believe there was any impediment to commitment that their love could not overcome; and so, in effect, he had used those women. But he did notice Sara, he did appreciate her, and he had not told her about the woman back in LA: once he had thought this a lie, but now he was beginning to suspect it was a sign that the passion was over. He had been in love for such a long time with a woman absent from him that perhaps he had grown to believe absence was a precondition for intensity, and perhaps it was causing him to overlook the birth of a far more realistic yet equally intense passion closer at hand. He studied Sara's face as she rambled on about New York. Beautiful. The kind of beauty that sneaks up on you, that you assumed was mere prettiness. But then, noticing her mouth was a bit too full, you decided that she was interestingly pretty; and then, noticing the energy of the face, how her eyes widened when she talked, how expressive her mouth was, you were led feature by feature to a perception of her beauty. Oh, he noticed her all right. The trouble was that during those months of loneliness *(Months? Christ, it had been over a year!)* he had become distanced from his emotions; he had set up surveillance systems inside his soul, and every time he started to twitch one way or the other, instead of completing the action he analyzed it and thus aborted it. He doubted he would ever be able to lose himself again.

Sara glanced questioningly at someone behind him. Hugh Weldon, the chief of police. He nodded at them and settled onto the stool. "Sara," he said. "Mr. Ramey. Glad I caught you."

Weldon always struck Peter as the archetypal New Englander. Gaunt; weatherbeaten; dour. His basic expression was so bleak you assumed his gray crewcut to have been an act of penance. He was in his fifties but had a habit of sucking at his teeth that made him seem ten years older. Usually Peter found him amusing; however, on this occasion he experienced nausea and a sense of unease, feelings he recognized as the onset of a premonitory spell.

After exchanging pleasantries with Sara, Weldon turned to Peter. "Don't want you to go takin' this wrong, Mr. Ramey. But I got to ask where you were last Tuesday evenin' 'round six o'clock."

The feelings were growing stronger, evolving into a sluggish panic that roiled inside Peter like the effects of a bad drug. "Tuesday," he said. "That's when the Borchard girl disappeared."

"My God, Hugh," said Sara testily. "What is this? Roust out the bearded stranger every time somebody's kid runs away? You know damn well that's what Ellen did. I'd run away myself if Ethan Borchard was my father."

"Mebbe." Weldon favored Peter with a neutral stare. "Did you happen to see Ellen last Tuesday, Mr. Ramey?"

"I was home," said Peter, barely able to speak. Sweat was popping out on his forehead, all over his body, and he knew he must look as guilty as hell; but that didn't matter, because he could almost see what was going to happen. He was sitting somewhere, and just out of reach below him something glinted.

"Then you musta seen her," said Weldon. "'Cordin' to witnesses she was mopin' 'round your woodpile for pretty near an hour. Wearin' bright yellow. Be hard to miss that."

"No," said Peter. He was reaching for that glint, and he knew it was going to be bad in any case, very bad, but it would be even worse if he touched it and he couldn't stop himself.

"Now that don't make sense," said Weldon from a long way off. "That cottage of yours is so small, it 'pears to me a man would just naturally catch sight of somethin' like a girl standin' by his woodpile while he was movin' 'round. Six o'clock's dinnertime for most folks, and you got a nice view of the woodpile out your kitchen window."

"I didn't see her." The spell was starting to fade, and Peter was terribly dizzy.

"Don't see how that's possible." Weldon sucked at his teeth, and the glutinous sound caused Peter's stomach to do a slow flip-flop.

"You ever stop to think, Hugh," said Sara angrily, "that maybe he was otherwise occupied?"

"You know somethin', Sara, why don't you say it plain?"

"I was with him last Tuesday. He was moving around, all right, but he wasn't looking out any window. Is that plain enough?"

Weldon sucked at his teeth again. "I 'spect it is. You sure 'bout this?"

Sara gave a sarcastic laugh. "Wanna see my hickey?"

"No reason to be snitty, Sara. I ain't doin' this for pleasure."

Weldon heaved to his feet and gazed down at Peter. "You lookin' a bit peaked, Mr. Ramey. Hope it ain't somethin' you ate." He held the stare a moment longer, then pushed off through the crowd.

"God, Peter!" Sara cupped his face in her hands. "You look awful!"

"Dizzy," he said, fumbling for his wallet; he tossed some bills on the counter. "C'mon, I need some air."

With Sara guiding him, he made it through the front door and leaned on the hood of a parked car, head down, gulping in the cold air. Her arm around his shoulders was a good weight that helped steady him, and after a few seconds he began to feel stronger, able to lift his head. The street—with its cobblestones and newly budded trees and old-fashioned lampposts and tiny shops—looked like a prop for a model railroad. Wind prowled the sidewalks, spinning paper cups and fluttering awnings. A strong gust shivered him and brought a flashback of dizziness and vision. Once more he was reaching down toward that glint, only this time it was very close, so close that its energies were tingling his fingertips, pulling at him, and if he could just stretch out his hand another inch or two. . . . Dizziness overwhelmed him. He caught himself on the hood of the car; his arm gave way, and he slumped forward, feeling the cold metal against his cheek. Sara was calling to someone, asking for help, and he wanted to reassure her, to say he'd be all right in a minute, but the words clogged in his throat and he continued lying there, watching the world tip and spin, until someone with arms stronger than Sara's lifted him and said, "Hey, man! You better stop hittin' the sauce, or I might be tempted to snake your ol' lady."

Streetlight angled a rectangle of yellow glare across the foot of Sara's bed, illuminating her stockinged legs and half of Peter's bulk beneath the covers. She lit a cigarette, then—exasperated at having given into the habit again—she stubbed it out, turned on her side, and lay watching the rise and fall of Peter's chest. Dead to the world. Why, she wondered, was she such a sucker for the damaged ones? She laughed at herself; she knew the answer. She wanted to be the one to make them forget whatever had hurt them, usually another woman. A combination Florence Nightingale and sex therapist, that was her, and she could never resist a new challenge. Though Peter had not talked about it, she could tell some LA ghost owned half his heart. He had all the symptoms. Sudden silences, distracted stares, the way he jumped for the mailbox as soon as the postman came and yet was always disappointed by what he had received. She believed that she owned the other half of his heart, but whenever he started to go with it, to forget the past and immerse himself in the here and now, the ghost would rear up and he'd create a little distance. His approach to lovemaking, for instance. He'd come on soft and gentle, and then, just as they were on the verge of a new level of intimacy, he'd draw back, crack a joke, or do something rough—like tackling her on the beach that morning—and she would feel cheap and sluttish. Sometimes she thought that the thing to do would be to tell him to get the hell out of her life, to come back and see her when his head was clear. But she knew she wouldn't. He owned more than half her heart.

She eased off the bed, careful not to wake him, and slipped out of her clothes. A branch scraped the window, startling her, and she held her blouse up to cover her breasts. Oh, right! A Peeping Tom at a third-floor window. In New York, maybe, but not in Nantucket. She tossed the blouse into the laundry hamper and caught sight of herself in the full-length mirror affixed to the closet door. In the dim light the reflection looked elongated and unfamiliar, and she had a feeling that Peter's ghost woman was watching her from across the continent, from another mirror. She could almost make her out. Tall, long-legged, a mournful expression. Sara didn't need to see her to know the woman had been sad: it was the sad ones who were the real heartbreakers, and the men whose hearts they had broken were like fossil records of what the women were. They offered their sadness to be cured, yet it wasn't a cure they wanted, only another reason for sadness, a spicy bit to mix in with the stew they had been stirring all their lives. Sara moved closer to the mirror, and the illusion of the other woman was replaced by the conformation of her own body. "That's what I'm going to do to you, lady," she whispered. "Blot you out." The words sounded empty.

She turned back the bedspread and slid in beside Peter. He made a muffled noise, and she saw gleams of the streetlights in his eyes. "Sorry about earlier," he said.

"No problem," she said brightly. "I got Bob Frazier and Jerry Highsmith to help bring you home. Do you remember?"

"Vaguely. I'm surprised Jerry could tear himself away from his redhead. Him and his sweet Ginger!" He lifted his arm so Sara could burrow in against his shoulder. "I guess your reputation's ruined."

"I don't know about that, but it's certainly getting more exotic all the time."

He laughed.

"Peter?" she said.

"Yeah?"

"I'm worried about these spells of yours. That's what this was, wasn't it?"

"Yeah." He was silent a moment. "I'm worried, too. I've been having them two and three times a day, and that's never happened before. But there's nothing I can do except try not to think about them."

"Can you see what's going to happen?"

"Not really, and there's no point in trying to figure it out. I can't ever use what I see. It just happens, whatever's going to, and then I understand that *that* was what the premonition was about. It's a pretty worthless gift."

Sara snuggled closer, throwing her leg across his hip. "Why don't we go over to the Cape tomorrow?"

"I was going to check out Mills's garbage dump."

"Okay. We can do that in the morning and still catch the three o'clock boat. It might be good for you to get off the island for a day or so."

"All right. Maybe that's not such a bad idea."

Sara shifted her leg and realized that he was erect. She eased her hand beneath the covers to touch him, and he turned so as to allow her better access. His breath quickened and he kissed her—gentle, treasuring kisses on her lips, her throat, her eyes—and his hips moved in counterpoint to the rhythm of her hand, slowly at first, becoming insistent, convulsive, until he was prodding against her thigh and she had to take her hand away and let him slip between her legs, opening her. Her thoughts were dissolving into a medium of urgency, her consciousness being reduced to an awareness of heat and shadows. But when he lifted himself above her, that brief separation broke the spell, and she could suddenly hear the fretful sounds of the wind, could see the particulars of his face and the light fixture on the ceiling behind him. His features seemed to sharpen, to grow alert, and he opened his mouth to speak. She put a finger to his lips. *Please, Peter! No jokes. This is serious.* She beamed the thoughts at him, and maybe they sank in. His face slackened, and as she guided him into place he moaned, a despairing sound such as a ghost might make at the end of its earthly term; and then she was clawing at him, driving him deeper inside, and talking to him, not words, just breathy noises, sighs and whispers, but having meanings that he would understand.

III

That same night while Peter and Sara were asleep, Sally McColl was driving her jeep along the blacktop that led to Smith Point. She was drunk and not giving a good goddamn where she wandered, steering in a never-ending S, sending the headlights veering across low gorsey hills and gnarled hawthorns. With one hand she kept a choke hold on a pint of cherry brandy, her third of the evening. 'Sconset Sally, they called her. Crazy Sally. Seventy-four years old and still able to shell scallops and row better than most men on the island. Wrapped in a couple of Salvation Army dresses, two moth-eaten sweaters, a tweed jacket gone at the elbows, and generally looking like a bag lady from hell. Brambles of white hair sticking out from under a battered fisherman's hat. Static fizzled on the radio, and Sally accompanied it with mutters, curses, and fitful bursts of song, all things that echoed the jumble of her thoughts. She parked near the spot where the blacktop gave out, staggered from the jeep and stumped through the soft sand to the top of a dune. There she swayed for a moment, dizzied by the pour of wind and the sweep of darkness broken only by a few stars on the horizon. "Whoo-ooh!" she screeched; the wind sucked up her yell and added it to its sound. She lurched forward, slipped, and went rolling down the face of the dune. Sand adhering to her tongue, spitting, she sat up and found that somehow she'd managed to hold on to the bottle, that the cap was still on even though she hadn't screwed it tight. A flicker of paranoia set her to jerking her head from side to side. She didn't want anybody spying on her, spreading more stories about old drunk Sally. The ones they told were bad enough. Half were lies, and the rest were slanted to make her seem loopy . . . like the one about how she'd bought herself a mail-order husband and he'd run off after two weeks, stowed away on a boat, scared to death of her, and she had come riding on horseback through Nantucket, hoping to bring him home. A swarthy little bump of a man, Eyetalian, no English, and he hadn't known shit from shortcake in bed. Better to do yourself than fool with a pimple like him. All she'd wanted had been the goddamn trousers she'd dressed him in, and the tale-tellers had cast her as a desperate woman. Bastards! Buncha goddamn . . .

Sally's train of thought pulled into a tunnel, and she sat staring blankly at the dark. Damn cold, it was, and windy a bit as well. She took a swig of brandy; when it hit bottom she felt ten degrees warmer. Another swig put her legs under her, and she started walking along the beach away from the Point, searching for a nice lonesome spot where nobody was likely to happen by. That was what she wanted. Just to sit and spit and feel the night on her skin. You couldn't hardly find such a place nowadays, what with all the summer trash floating in from the mainland, the Gucci-Pucci sissies and the little swish-tailed chick-women eager to bend over and butter their behinds for the first five-hundred-dollar suit that showed interest, probably some fat-boy junior executive who couldn't get it up and would marry 'em just for the privilege of being humiliated every night. . . . That train of thought went spiraling off, and Sally spiraled after it. She sat down with a thump. She gave out with a cackle, liked the sound of it, and cackled louder. She sipped at the brandy, wishing that she had brought another bottle, letting her thoughts subside into a crackle of half-formed images and memories that seemed to have been urged upon her by the thrashings and skitterings of the wind. As her eyes adjusted, she made out a couple of houses lumped against the lesser blackness of the sky. Vacant summer places. No, wait! Those were them whatchamacallems. Condominiums. What had that Ramey boy said about 'em? Iniums with a condom slipped over each. Prophylactic lives. He was a good boy, that Peter. The first person she'd met with the gift for dog's years, and it was strong in him, stronger than her gift, which wasn't good for much except for guessing the weather, and she was so old now that her bones could do that just as well. He'd told her how some people in California had blown up condominiums to protect the beauty of their coastline, and it had struck her as a fine idea. The thought of condominiums ringing the island caused her to tear up, and with a burst of drunken nostalgia she remembered what a wonder the sea had been when she was a girl. Clean, pure, rife with spirits. She'd been able to sense those spirits. . . .

Battering and crunching from somewhere off in the dunes. She staggered to her feet, cocking an ear. More sounds of breakage. She headed toward them, toward the condominiums. Might be some kids vandalizing the place. If so, she'd cheer 'em on. But as she climbed to the top of the nearest dune, the sounds died away. Then the wind picked up, not howling or roaring, but with a weird ululation, almost a melody, as if it were pouring through the holes of an enormous flute.

The back of Sally's neck prickled, and a cold slimy worm of fear wriggled the length of her spine. She was close enough to the condominiums to see their rooflines against the sky, but she could see nothing else. There was only the eerie music of the wind, repeating the same passage of five notes over and over. Then it, too, died. Sally took a slug of brandy, screwed up her courage, and started walking again; the beach grass swayed and tickled her hands, and the tickling spread goose-flesh up her arms. About twenty feet from the first condominium she stopped, her heartbeat ragged. Fear was turning the brandy to a sour mess in her stomach. What was there to be afraid of, she asked herself. The wind? Shit! She had another slug of brandy and went forward. It was so dark she had to grope her way along the wall, and she was startled to find a hole smack in the middle of it. Bigger than a damn door, it was. Edged by broken boards and ripped shingles. Like a giant fist had smashed it through. Her mouth was cottony, but she stepped inside. She rummaged in her pockets, dug out a box of kitchen matches, lit one and cupped it with her hands until it burned steadily. The room was unfurnished, just carpeting and telephone fixtures and paint-spattered newspapers and rags. Sliding glass doors were inset into the opposite wall, but most of the glass had been blown out, crunching under her feet; as she drew near, an icicle-shaped piece hanging from the frame caught the glow of the match and for a second was etched on the dark like a fiery tooth. The match scorched her fingers. She dropped it and lit another and moved into the next room. More holes and a heaviness in the air, as if the house were holding its breath. Nerves, she thought. Goddamn old-woman nerves. Maybe it *had* been kids, drunk and ramming a car into the walls. A breeze eeled from somewhere and puffed out the match. She lit a third one. The breeze extinguished it, too, and she realized that kids hadn't been responsible for the damage, because the breeze didn't blow away this time: it fluttered around her, lifting her dress, her hair, twining about her legs, patting and frisking her all over, and in the breeze was a feeling, a knowledge, that turned her bones to splinters of black ice. Something had come from the sea, some evil thing with the wind for a body had smashed holes in the walls to play its foul, spine-chilling music, and it was surrounding her, toying with her, getting ready to whirl her off to hell and gone. It had a clammy, bitter smell, and that smell clung to her skin everywhere it touched.

Sally backed into the first room, wanting to scream but only able to manage a feeble squawk. The wind flowed after her, lifting the newspapers and flapping them at her like crinkly white bats, matting them against her face and chest. Then she screamed. She dove for the hole in the wall and flung herself into a frenzied heart-busting run, stumbling, falling, scrambling to her feet, and waving her arms and yelling. Behind her, the wind gushed from the house, roaring, and she imagined it shaping itself into a towering figure, a black demon who was laughing at her, letting her think she might make it before swooping down and tearing her apart. She rolled down the face of the last dune, and, her breath sobbing, clawed at the door handle of the jeep; she jiggled the key in the ignition, prayed until the engine turned over, and then, gears grinding, swerved off along the Nantucket road.

She was halfway to 'Sconset before she grew calm enough to think what to do, and the first thing she decided was to drive straight to Nantucket and tell Hugh Weldon. Though God only knew what *he'd* do. Or what he'd say. That scrawny flint of a man! Like as not he'd laugh in her face and be off to share the latest 'Sconset Sally story with his cronies. No, she told herself. There weren't going to be any more stories about ol' Sally drunk as the moon and seeing ghosts and raving about the wind. They wouldn't believe her, so let 'em think kids had done it. A little sun of gleeful viciousness rose in her thoughts, burning away the shadows of her fear and heating her blood even quicker than would a jolt of cherry brandy. Let it happen, whatever was going to happen, and *then* she'd tell her story, *then* she'd say I would have told you sooner, but you would have called me crazy. Oh, no! She wouldn't be the butt of their jokes this time. Let 'em find out for themselves that some new devil had come from the sea.

IV

Mills Lindstrom's boat was a Boston whaler, about twenty feet of blue squarish hull with a couple of bucket seats, a control pylon, and a fifty-five-horsepower outboard racketing behind. Sara had to sit on Peter's lap, and while he wouldn't have minded that in any case, in this case he appreciated the extra warmth. Though it was calm, the sea rolling in long swells, heavy clouds and a cold front had settled over the island; farther out the sun was breaking through, but all around them crumbling banks of whitish mist hung close to the water. The gloom couldn't dampen Peter's mood, however; he was anticipating a pleasant weekend with Sara and gave hardly a thought to their destination, carrying on a steady stream of chatter. Mills, on the other hand, was brooding and taciturn, and when they came in sight of the offshore pollution aggregate, a dirty brown stain spreading for hundreds of yards across the water, he pulled his pipe from beneath his rain gear and set to chomping the stem, as if to restrain impassioned speech.

Peter borrowed Mills's binoculars and peered ahead. The surface of the aggregate was pocked by thousands of white objects; at this distance they looked like bones sticking up from thin soil. Streamers of mist were woven across it, and the edge was shifting sluggishly, an obscene cap sliding over the dome of a swell. It was a no-man's-land, an ugly blot, and as they drew near, its ugliness increased. The most common of the white objects were Clorox bottles such as fishermen used to mark the spread of their nets; there were also a great many fluorescent tubes, other plastic debris, torn pieces of netting, and driftwood, all mired in a pale brown jelly of decayed oil products. It was a Golgotha of the inorganic world, a plain of ultimate spiritual malaise, of entropy triumphant, and perhaps, thought Peter, the entire earth would one day come to resemble it. The briny, bitter stench made his skin crawl.

"God," said Sara as they began cruising along the edge; she opened her mouth to say more but couldn't find the words.

"I see why you felt like drinking last night," said Peter to Mills, who just shook his head and grunted.

"Can we go into it?" asked Sara.

"All them torn nets'll foul the propeller." Mills stared at her askance. "Ain't it bad enough from out here?"

"We can tip up the motor and row in," Peter suggested. "Come on, Mills. It'll be like landing on the moon."

And, indeed, as they rowed into the aggregate, cutting through the pale brown stuff, Peter felt that they had crossed some intangible border into uncharted territory. The air seemed heavier, full of suppressed energy, and the silence seemed deeper; the only sound was the slosh of the oars. Mills had told Peter that the thing would have roughly a spiral shape, due to the actions of opposing currents, and that intensified his feeling of having entered the unknown; he pictured them as characters in a fantasy novel, creeping across a great device inlaid on the floor of an abandoned temple. Debris bobbed against the hull. The brown glop had the consistency of Jell-O that hadn't set properly, and when Peter dipped his hands into it, beads accumulated on his fingers. Some of the textures on the surface had a horrid, almost organic, beauty: bleached, wormlike tendrils of netting mired in the slick, reminding Peter of some animal's diseased spoor; larval chips of wood matted on a bed of glistening cellophane; a blue plastic lid bearing a girl's sunbonneted face embedded in a spaghetti of Styrofoam strips. They would point out such oddities to each other, but nobody was eager to talk. The desolation of the aggregate was oppressive, and not even a ray of sunlight fingering the boat, as if a searchlight were keeping track of them from the real world, not even that could dispel the gloom. Then, about two hundred yards in, Peter saw something shiny inside an opaque plastic container, reached down and picked it up.

The instant he brought it on board he realized that this was the object about which he had experienced the premonition, and he had the urge to throw it back; but he felt such a powerful attraction to it that instead he removed the lid and lifted out a pair of silver combs, the sort Spanish women wear in their hair. Touching them, he had a vivid mental image of a young woman's face: a pale, drawn face that might have been beautiful but was starved-thin and worn by sorrows. Gabriela. The name seeped into his consciousness the way a paw track frozen in the ground melts up from beneath the snow during a thaw. Gabriela Pa . . . Pasco . . . Pascual. His finger traced the design etched on the combs, and every curlicue conveyed a sense of her personality. Sadness, loneliness, and—most of all—terror. She'd been afraid for a very long time. Sara asked to see the combs, took them, and his ghostly impression of Gabriela Pascual's life flew apart like a creature of foam, leaving him disoriented.

"They're beautiful," said Sara. "And they must be really old."

"Looks like Mexican work," said Mills. "Hmph. What we got here?" He stretched out his oar, trying to snag something; he hauled the oar back in and Sara lifted the thing from the blade: a rag showing yellow streaks through its coating of slick.

"It's a blouse." Sara turned it in her hands, her nose wrinkling at having to touch the slick; she stopped turning it and stared at Peter. "Oh, God! It's Ellen Borchard's."

Peter took it from her. Beneath the manufacturer's label was Ellen Borchard's name tag. He closed his eyes, hoping to read some impression as he had with the silver combs. Nothing. His gift had deserted him. But he had a bad feeling that he knew exactly what had happened to the girl.

"Better take that to Hugh Weldon," said Mills. "Might . . ." He broke off and stared out over the aggregate.

At first Peter didn't see what had caught Mills's eyes; then he noticed that a wind had sprung up. A most peculiar wind. It was moving slowly around the boat about fifty feet away, its path evident by the agitation of the debris over which it passed; it whispered and sighed, and with a sucking noise a couple of Clorox bottles popped out of the slick and spun into the air. Each time the wind made a complete circuit of the boat, it seemed to have grown a little stronger.

"What the hell!" Mills's face was drained of color, the web of broken blood vessels on his cheeks showing like a bright red tattoo.

Sara's nails bit into Peter's arm, and he was overwhelmed by the knowledge that this wind was what he had been warned against. Panicked, he shook Sara off, scrambled to the back of the boat, and tipped down the outboard motor.

"The nets . . ." Mills began.

"Fuck the nets! Let's get out of here!"

The wind was keening, and the entire surface of the aggregate was starting to heave. Crouched in the stern, Peter was again struck by its resemblance to a graveyard with bones sticking out of the earth, only now all the bones were wiggling, working themselves loose. Some of the Clorox bottles were rolling sluggishly along, bouncing high when they hit an obstruction. The sight froze him for a moment, but as Mills fired the engine, he crawled back to his seat and pulled Sara down with him. Mills turned the boat toward Madaket. The slick glubbed and smacked against the hull, and brown flecks splashed onto the windshield and oozed sideways. With each passing second the wind grew stronger and louder, building to a howl that drowned out the motor. A fluorescent tube went twirling up beside them like a cheerleader's baton; bottles and cellophane and splatters of oil slick flew at them from every direction. Sara ducked her face into Peter's shoulder, and he held her tight, praying that the propeller wouldn't foul. Mills swerved the boat to avoid a piece of driftwood that sailed past the bow, and then they were into clear water, out of the wind—though they could still hear it raging—and running down the long slope of a swell.

Relieved, Peter stroked Sara's hair and let out a shuddering breath; but when he glanced behind them all his relief went glimmering. Thousands upon thousands of Clorox bottles and fluorescent tubes and other debris were spinning in midair above the aggregate—an insane mobile posed against the gray sky—and just beyond the edge narrow tracks of water were being lashed up, as if a windy knife were slicing back and forth across it, undecided whether or not to follow them home.

Hugh Weldon had been out in Madaket investigating the vandalism of the condominiums, and after receiving the radio call it had only taken him a few minutes to get to Peter's cottage. He sat beside Mills at the picnic table, listening to their story, and from the perspective of the sofa bunk, where Peter was sitting, his arms around Sara, the chief presented an angular mantislike silhouette against the gray light from the window; the squabbling of the police radio outside seemed part of his persona, a radiation emanating from him. When they had finished he stood, walked to the wood stove, lifted the lid, and spat inside it; the stove crackled and spat back a spark.

"If it was just you two," he said to Peter and Sara, "I'd run you in and find out what you been smokin'. But Mills here don't have the imagination for this kind of foolishness, so I guess I got to believe you." He set down the lid with a clank and squinted at Peter. "You said you wrote somethin' 'bout Ellen Borchard in your book. What?"

Peter leaned forward, resting his elbows on his knees. "She was down at Smith Point just after dark. She was angry at her parents, and she wanted to scare them. So she took off her blouse—she had extra clothes with her, because she was planning to run away—and was about to rip it up, to make them think she'd been murdered, when the wind killed her."

"Now how'd it do that?" asked Weldon.

"In the book the wind was a sort of elemental. Cruel, capricious. It played with her. Knocked her down, rolled her along the shingle. Then it would let her up and knock her down again. She was bleeding all over from the shell-cuts, and screaming. Finally it whirled her up and out to sea." Peter stared down at his hands; the inside of his head felt heavy, solid, as if his brains were made of mercury.

"Jesus Christ!" said Weldon. "What you got to say 'bout that, Mills?"

"It wasn't no normal wind," said Mills. "That's all I know."

"Jesus Christ!" repeated Weldon; he rubbed the back of his neck and peered at Peter. "I been twenty years at this job, and I've heard some tall tales. But this . . . what did you say it was? An elemental?"

"Yeah, but I don't really know for sure. Maybe if I could handle those combs again. I could learn more about it."

"Peter." Sara put her hand on his arm; her brow was furrowed. "Why don't we let Hugh deal with it?"

Weldon was amused. "Naw, Sara. You let Mr. Ramey see what he can do." He chuckled. "Maybe he can tell me how the Red Sox are gonna do this year. Me and Mills can have another look at that mess off the Point."

Mills's neck seemed to retract into his shoulders. "I ain't goin' back out there, Hugh. And if you want my opinion, you better keep clear of it yourself."

"Damn it, Mills." Weldon smacked his hand against his hip. "I ain't gonna beg, but you sure as hell could save me some trouble. It'll take me an hour to get the Coast Guard boys off their duffs. Wait a minute!" He turned to Peter. "Maybe you people were seein' things. There musta been all kinds of bad chemicals fumin' up from that mess. Could be you breathed somethin' in." Brakes squealed, a car door slammed, and seconds later the bedraggled figure of Sally McColl strode past the window and knocked on the door.

"What in God's name does she want?" said Weldon.

Peter opened the door, and Sally gave him a gap-toothed grin. "Mornin', Peter," she said. She was wearing a stained raincoat over her usual assortment of dresses and sweaters, and a gaily colored man's necktie for a scarf. "Is that skinny ol' fart Hugh Weldon inside?"

"I ain't got time for your crap today, Sally," called Weldon.

Sally pushed past Peter. "Mornin', Sara. Mills."

"Hear one of your dogs just had a litter," said Mills.

"Yep. Six snarly little bastards." Sally wiped her nose with the back of her hand and checked it to see what had rubbed off. "You in the market?"

"I might drop 'round and take a look," said Mills. "Dobermans or Shepherds?"

"Dobermans. Gonna be fierce."

"What's on your mind, Sally?" said Weldon, stepping between them.

"Got a confession to make."

Weldon chuckled. "What'd you do now? You sure as hell didn't burglarize no dress shop."

A frown etched the wrinkles deeper on Sally's face. "You stupid son of a bitch," she said flatly. "I swear, God musta been runnin' short of everything but horseshit when He made you."

"Listen, you ol' . . ."

"Musta ground up your balls and used 'em for brains," Sally went on. "Musta . . ."

"Sally!" Peter pushed them apart and took the old woman by the shoulders. A glaze faded from her eyes as she looked at him. At last she shrugged free of his grasp and patted down her hair: a peculiarly feminine gesture for someone so shapeless and careworn.

"I shoulda told you sooner," she said to Weldon. "But I was sick of you laughin' at me. Then I decided it might be important and I'd have to risk listenin' to your jackass bray. So I'm tellin' you." She looked out the window. "I know what done them condominiums. It was the wind." She snapped a hateful glance at Weldon. "And I ain't crazy, neither!"

Peter felt weak in the knees. They were surrounded by trouble; it was in the air as it had been off Smith Point, yet stronger, as if he were becoming sensitized to the feeling.

"The wind," said Weldon, acting dazed.

"That's right," said Sally defiantly. "It punched holes in them damn buildin's and was whistlin' through 'em like it was playin' music." She glared at him. "Don't you believe me?"

"He believes you," said Peter. "We think the wind killed Ellen Borchard."

"Now don't be spreadin' that around! We ain't sure!" Weldon said it desperately, clinging to disbelief.

Sally crossed the room to Peter. "It's true 'bout the Borchard girl, ain't it?"

"I think so," he said.

"And that thing what killed her, it's here in Madaket. You feel it, don'tcha?"

He nodded. "Yeah."

Sally headed for the door.

"Where you goin'?" asked Weldon. She mumbled and went outside; Peter saw her pacing back and forth in the yard. "Crazy ol' bat," said Weldon.

"Mebbe she is," said Mills. "But you ought not to be treatin' her so harsh after all she's done."

"What's she done?" asked Peter.

"Sally used to live up in Madaket," said Mills. "And whenever a ship would run up on Dry Shoals or one of the others, she'd make for the wreck in that ol' lobster boat of hers. Most times she'd beat the Coast Guard to 'em. Musta saved fifty or sixty souls over the years, sailin' out in the worst kind of weather."

"Mills!" said Weldon emphatically. "Run me out to that garbage dump of yours."

Mills stood and hitched up his pants. "Ain't you been listenin', Hugh? Peter and Sally say that thing's 'round here somewhere."

Weldon was a frustrated man. He sucked at his teeth, and his face worked. He picked up the container holding the combs, glanced at Peter, then set the container down.

"You want me to see what I can learn from those?" asked Peter.

Weldon shrugged. "Can't hurt nothin', I guess." He stared out the window as if unconcerned with the issue.

Peter took the container and sat down next to Sara. "Wait," she said. "I don't understand. If this thing is nearby, shouldn't we get away from here?" Nobody answered.

The plastic container was cold, and when Peter pried off the lid, the cold welled out at him. Intense, aching cold, as if he had opened the door to a meat locker.

Sally burst into the room and pointed at the container. "What's that?"

"Some old combs," said Peter. "They didn't feel like this when I found them. Not as strong."

"Feel like what?" asked Weldon; every new mystery seemed to be unnerving him further, and Peter suspected that if the mysteries weren't cleared up soon, the chief would start disbelieving them on purely practical grounds.

Sally came over to Peter and looked into the container. "Gimme one," she said, extending a grimy hand. Weldon and Mills moved up behind her, like two old soldiers flanking their mad queen.

Reluctantly, Peter picked up one of the combs. Its coldness flowed into his arm, his head, and for a moment he was in the midst of a storm-tossed sea, terrified, waves crashing over the bows of a fishing boat and the wind singing around him. He dropped the comb. His hands were trembling, and his heart was doing a jig against his chest wall.

"Oh, shit," he said to no one in particular. "I don't know if I want to do this."

Sara gave Sally her seat beside Peter, and as they handled the combs, setting them down every minute or so to report what they had learned, she chewed her nails and fretted. She could relate to Hugh Weldon's frustration; it was awful just to sit and watch. Each time Peter and Sally handled the combs their respiration grew shallow and their eyes rolled back, and when they laid them aside they appeared drained and frightened.

"Gabriela Pascual was from Miami," said Peter. "I can't tell exactly when all this happened, but it was years ago . . . because in my image of her, her clothes look a little old-fashioned. Maybe ten or fifteen years back. Something like that. Anyway, there was trouble for her onshore, some emotional entanglement, and her brother didn't want to leave her alone, so he took her along on a fishing voyage. He was a commercial fisherman."

"She had the gift," Sally chimed in. "That's why there's so much of her in the combs. That, and because she killed herself and died holdin' 'em."

"Why'd she kill herself?" asked Weldon.

"Fear," said Peter. "Loneliness. Crazy as it sounds, the wind was holding her prisoner. I think she cracked up from being alone on a drifting boat with only this thing—the elemental—for company."

"Alone?" said Weldon. "What happened to her brother?"

"He died." Sally's voice was shaky. "The wind came down and killed 'em all 'cept this Gabriela. It wanted her."

As the story unfolded, gusts of wind began to shudder the cottage and Sara tried to remain unconcerned as to whether or not they were natural phenomena. She turned her eyes from the window, away from the heaving trees and bushes, and concentrated on what was being said; but that in itself was so eerie that she couldn't keep from jumping whenever the panes rattled. Gabriela Pascual, said Peter, had been frequently seasick during the cruise; she had been frightened of the crew, most of whom considered her bad luck, and possessed by a feeling of imminent disaster. And, Sally added, that premonition had been borne out. One cloudless calm day the elemental had swept down and killed everyone. Everyone except Gabriela. It had whirled the crew and her brother into the air, smashed them against bulkheads, dropped them onto the decks. She had expected to die as well, but it had seemed interested in her. It had caressed her and played with her, knocking her down and rolling her about; and at night it had poured through the passageways and broken windows, making a chilling music that—as the days passed and the ship drifted north—she came to half-understand.

"She didn't think of it as a spirit," said Peter. "There wasn't anything mystical about it to her mind. It struck her as being kind of a . . ."

"An animal," interrupted Sally. "A big, stupid animal. Vicious, it was. But not evil. 'Least it didn't feel evil to her."

Gabriela, Peter went on, had never been sure what it wanted of her—perhaps her presence had been all. Most of the time it had left her alone. Then, suddenly, it would spring up out of a calm to juggle splinters of glass or chase her about. Once the ship had drifted near to shore, and when she had attempted to jump over the side, the elemental had battered her and driven her below-decks. Though at first it had controlled the drift of the ship, gradually it lost interest in her and on several occasions the ship almost foundered. Finally, no longer caring to prolong the inevitable, she had cut her wrists and died clutching the container holding her most valued possessions, her grandmother's silver combs, with the wind howling in her ears.

Peter leaned back against the wall, his eyes shut, and Sally sighed and patted her breast. For a long moment no one spoke.

"Wonder why it's hangin' 'round that garbage out there," said Mills.

"Maybe no reason," said Peter dully. "Or maybe it's attracted to slack points in the tides, to some condition of the air."

"I don't get it," said Weldon. "What the hell is it? It can't be no animal."

"Why not?" Peter stood, swayed, then righted himself. "What's wind, anyway? Charged ions, vacating air masses. Who's to say that some stable form of ions couldn't approximate a life? Could be there's one of these at the heart of every storm, and they've always been mistaken for spirits, given an anthropomorphic character. Like Ariel." He laughed disconsolately. "It's no sprite, that's for sure."

Sally's eyes looked unnaturally bright, like watery jewels lodged in her weathered face. "The sea breeds 'em," she said firmly, as if that were explanation enough of anything strange.

"Peter's book was right," said Sara. "It's an elemental. That's what you're describing, anyway. A violent, inhuman creature, part spirit and part animal." She laughed, and the laugh edged a bit high, bordering on the hysteric. "It's hard to believe."

"Right!" said Weldon. "Damned hard! I got an ol' crazy woman and a man I don't know from Adam tellin' me. . . ."

"Listen!" said Mills; he walked to the door and swung it open.

It took Sara a second to fix on the sound, but then she realized that the wind had died, had gone from heavy gusts to trifling breezes in an instant, and farther away, coming from the sea, or nearer, maybe as close as Tennessee Avenue, she heard a roaring.

V

A few moments earlier Jerry Highsmith had been both earning his living and looking forward to a night of exotic pleasures in the arms of Ginger McCurdy. He was standing in front of one of the houses on Tennessee Avenue, its quarterboard reading AHAB-ITAT, and a collection of old harpoons and whalebones mounted on either side of the door; his bicycle leaned against a rail fence behind him, and ranged around him, straddling their bikes, dolled up in pastel-hued jogging suits and sweat clothes, were twenty-six members of the Peach State Ramblers Bicycle Club. Ten men, sixteen women. The women were all in good shape, but most were in their thirties, a bit long in the tooth for Jerry's taste. Ginger, on the other hand, was prime. Twenty-three or twenty-four, with red hair down to her ass and a body that wouldn't quit. She had peeled off her sweats and was blooming out a halter and shorts cut so high that each time she dismounted you could see right up to the Pearly Gates. And she knew what she was doing: every jiggle of those twin jaloobies was aimed at his crotch. She had pressed to the front of the group and was attending to his spiel about the bullshit whaling days. Oh, yeah! Ginger was ready. A couple of lobsters, a little wine, a stroll along the waterfront, and then by God he'd pump her so full of the Nantucket Experience that she'd breach like a snow-white hill.

Thar she fuckin' blows!

"Now, y'all . . ." he began.

They tittered; they liked him mocking their accent.

He grinned abashedly as if he hadn't known what he was doing. "Must be catchin'," he said. "Now you people probably haven't had a chance to visit the Whaling Museum, have you?"

A chorus of Nos.

"Well then, I'll give you a course in harpoonin'." He pointed at the wall of the AHAB-ITAT. "That top one with the single barb stickin' off the side, that's the kind most commonly used during the whalin' era. The shaft's of ash. That was the preferred wood. It stands up to the weather"—he stared pointedly at Ginger—"and it won't bend under pressure." Ginger tried to constrain a smile. "Now that one," he continued, keeping an eye on her, "the one with the arrow point and no barbs, that was favored by some whalers. They said it allowed for deeper penetration."

"What about the one with two barbs?" asked someone.

Jerry peered over heads and saw that the questioner was his second choice. Ms. Selena Persons. A nice thirtyish brunette, flat-chested, but with killer legs. Despite the fact that he was obviously after Ginger, she hadn't lost interest. Who knows? A double-header might be a possibility.

"That was used toward the end of the whalin' era," he said. "But generally two-barbed harpoons weren't considered as effective as single-barbed ones. I don't know why, exactly. Might have just been stubbornness on the whalers' part. Resistance to change. They knew the ol' single-barb could give satisfaction."

Ms. Persons met his gaze with the glimmer of a smile.

"'Course," Jerry continued, addressing all the Ramblers, "now the shaft's tipped with a charge that explodes inside the whale." He winked at Ginger and added *sotto voce,* "Must be a rush."

She covered her mouth with her hand.

"Okay, folks!" Jerry swung his bike away from the fence. "Mount up, and we'll be off to the next thrillin' attraction."

Laughing and chattering, the Ramblers started to mount, but just then a powerful gust of wind swept down Tennessee Avenue, causing squeals and blowing away hats. Several of the riders overbalanced and fell, and several more nearly did. Ginger stumbled forward and clung to Jerry, giving him chest-to-chest massage. "Nice catch," she said, doing a little writhe as she stepped away.

"Nice toss," he replied.

She smiled, but the smile faded and was replaced by a bewildered look. "What's that?"

Jerry turned. About twenty yards away a column of whirling leaves had formed above the blacktop; it was slender, only a few feet high, and though he had never seen anything similar, it alarmed him no more than had the freakish gust of wind. Within seconds, however, the column had grown to a height of fifteen feet; twigs and gravel and branches were being sucked into it, and it sounded like a miniature tornado. Someone screamed. Ginger clung to him in genuine fright. There was a rank smell in the air, and a pressure was building in Jerry's ears. He couldn't be sure, because the column was spinning so rapidly, but it seemed to be assuming a roughly human shape, a dark green figure made of plant litter and stones. His mouth had gone dry, and he restrained an urge to throw Ginger aside and run.

"Come on!" he shouted.

A couple of the Ramblers managed to mount their bicycles, but the wind had grown stronger, roaring, and it sent them wobbling and crashing into the weeds. The rest huddled together, their hair whipping about, and stared at the great Druid thing that was taking shape and swaying above them, as tall as the treetops. Shingles were popping off the sides of the houses, sailing up and being absorbed by the figure; and as Jerry tried to outvoice the wind, yelling at the Ramblers to lie flat, he saw the whalebones and harpoons ripped from the wall of the AHAB-ITAT. The windows of the house exploded outward. One man clutched the bloody flap of his cheek, which had been sliced open by a shard of glass; a woman grabbed the back of her knee and crumpled. Jerry shouted a final warning and pulled Ginger down with him into the road-side ditch. She squirmed and struggled, in a panic, but he forced her head down and held tight. The figure had risen much higher than the trees, and though it was still swaying, its form had stabilized somewhat. It had a face now: a graveyard smile of gray shingles and two circular patches of stones for eyes: a terrible blank gaze that seemed responsible for the in-creasing air pressure. Jerry's heart boomed in his inner ear, and his blood felt like sludge. The figure kept swelling, up and up; the roar was resolving into an oscillating hum that shivered the ground. Stones and leaves were beginning to spray out of it. Jerry knew, *knew,* what was going to happen, and he couldn't keep from watching. Amid a flurry of leaves he saw one of the harpoons flit through the air, impaling a woman who had been trying to stand. The force of the blow drove her out of Jerry's field of vision. Then the great figure exploded. Jerry squeezed his eyes shut. Twigs and balls of dirt and gravel stung him. Ginger leaped sideways and collapsed atop him, clawing at his hip. He waited for something worse to happen, but nothing did. "You okay?" he asked, pushing Ginger away by the shoulders.

She wasn't okay.

A splintered inch of whalebone stuck out from the center of her forehead. Shrieking with revulsion, Jerry wriggled from beneath her and came to his hands and knees. A moan. One of the men was crawling toward him, his face a mask of blood, a ragged hole where his right eye had been; his good eye looked glazed like a doll's. Horrified, not knowing what to do, Jerry scrambled to his feet and backed away. All the harpoons, he saw, had found targets. Most of the Ramblers lay unmoving, their blood smeared over the blacktop; the rest were sitting up, dazed and bleeding. Jerry's heel struck something, and he spun about. The quarterboard of the AHAB-ITAT had nailed Ms. Selena Persons vampire-style to the roadside dirt; the board had been driven so deep into the ground that only the letter *A* was showing above the mired ruin of her jogging suit, as if she were an exhibit. Jerry began to tremble, and tears started from his eyes.

A breeze ruffled his hair.

Somebody wailed, shocking him from his daze. He should call the hospital, the police. But where was a phone? Most of the houses were empty, waiting for summer tenants, and the phones wouldn't be working. Somebody must have seen what had happened, though. He should just do what he could until help arrived. Gathering himself, he walked toward the man whose eye was missing; but before he had gone more than a few paces a fierce gust of wind struck him in the back and knocked him flat.

This time the roaring was all around him, the pressure so intense that it seemed a white-hot needle had pierced him from ear to ear. He shut his eyes and clamped both hands to his ears, trying to smother the pain. Then he felt himself lifted. He couldn't believe it at first. Even when he opened his eyes and saw that he was being borne aloft, revolving in a slow circle, it made no sense. He couldn't hear, and the quiet added to his sense of unreality; further adding to it, a riderless bicycle ped-aled past. The air was full of sticks and leaves and pebbles, a threadbare curtain between him and the world, and he imag-ined himself rising in the gorge of that hideous dark figure. Ginger McCurdy was flying about twenty feet overhead, her red hair streaming, arms floating languidly as if in a dance. She was revolving faster than he, and he realized that his rate of spin was increasing as he rose. He saw what was going to happen: you went higher and higher, faster and faster, until you were spewed out, shot out over the village. His mind re-belled at the prospect of death, and he tried to swim back down the wind, flailing, kicking, bursting with fear. But as he whirled higher, twisting and turning, it became hard to breathe, to think, and he was too dizzy to be afraid any longer.

Another woman sailed by a few feet away. Her mouth was open, her face contorted; blood dripped from her scalp. She clawed at him, and he reached out to her, not knowing why he bothered. Their hands just missed touching. Thoughts were coming one at a time. Maybe he'd land in the water. MIRACULOUS SURVIVOR OF FREAK TORNADO. Maybe he'd fly across the island and settle gently in a Nantucket treetop. A broken leg, a bruise or two. They'd set up drinks for him in the Atlantic Cafe. Maybe Connie Keating would finally come across, would finally recognize the miraculous potential of Jerry Highsmith. Maybe. He was tumbling now, limbs jerking about, and he gave up thinking. Flash glimpses of the gapped houses below, of the other dancers on the wind, moving with spasmodic abandon. Suddenly, as he was bent backward by a violent updraft, there was a wrenching pain inside him, a grating, then a vital dislocation that delivered him from pain. Oh, Christ Jesus! Oh, God! Dazzles exploded behind his eyes. Something bright blue flipped past him, and he died.

VI

After the column of leaves and branches looming up from Tennessee Avenue had vanished, after the roaring had died, Hugh Weldon sprinted for his squad car with Peter and Sara at his heels. He frowned as they piled in but made no objection, and this, Peter thought, was probably a sign that he had stopped trying to rationalize events, that he accepted the wind as a force to which normal procedures did not apply. He switched on the siren, and they sped off. But less than fifty yards from the cottage he slammed on the brakes. A woman was hanging in a hawthorn tree beside the road, an old-fashioned harpoon plunged through her chest. There was no point in checking to see if she was alive. All her major bones were quite obviously broken, and she was painted with blood head to foot, making her look like a horrid African doll set out as a warning to trespassers.

Weldon got on the radio. "Body out in Madaket," he said. "Send a wagon."

"You might need more than one," said Sara; she pointed to three dabs of color farther up the road. She was very pale, and she squeezed Peter's hand so hard that she left white imprints on his skin.

Over the next twenty-five minutes they found eighteen bodies: broken, mutilated, several pierced by harpoons or fragments of bone. Peter would not have believed that the human form could be reduced to such grotesque statements, and though he was horrified, nauseated, he became increasingly numbed by what he saw. Odd thoughts flocked to his brain, most persistent among them being that the violence had been done partly for his benefit. It was a sick, nasty idea, and he tried to dismiss it; but after a while he began to consider it in light of other thoughts that had lately been striking him out of the blue. The manuscript of *How the Wind Spoke at Madaket*, for instance. As improbable as it sounded, it was hard to escape the conclusion that the wind had been seeding all this in his brain. He didn't want to believe it, yet there it was, as believable as anything else that had happened. And given that, was his latest thought any less believable? He was beginning to understand the progression of events, to understand it with the same sudden clarity that had helped him solve the problems of his book, and he wished very much that he could have obeyed his premonition and not touched the combs. Until then the elemental had not been sure of him; it had been nosing around him like—as Sally had described it—a big, stupid animal, sensing something familiar about him but unable to remember what. And when he had found the combs, when he had opened the container, there must have been some kind of circuit closed, a flash point sparked between his power and Gabriela Pascual's, and the elemental had made the connection. He recalled how excited it had seemed, darting back and forth beyond the borders of the aggregate.

As they turned back onto Tennessee Avenue, where a small group of townsfolk were covering bodies with blankets, Weldon got on the radio again, interrupting Peter's chain of logic. "Where the hell are them ambulances?" he snapped.

"Sent 'em a half hour ago," came the reply. "Shoulda been there by now."

Weldon cast a grim look at Peter and Sara. "Try 'em on the radio," he told the operator.

A few minutes later the report came that none of the ambulances were answering their radios. Weldon told his people to stay put, that he'd check it out himself. As they turned off Tennessee Avenue onto the Nantucket road, the sun broke through the overcast, flooding the landscape in a thin yellow light and warming the interior of the car. The light seemed to be illuminating Peter's weaknesses, making him realize how tense he was, how his muscles ached with the poisons of adrenaline and fatigue. Sara leaned against him, her eyes closed, and the pressure of her body acted to shore him up, to give him a burst of vitality.

Weldon kept the speed at thirty, glancing left and right, but nothing was out of the ordinary. Deserted streets, houses with blank-looking windows. Many of the homes in Madaket were vacant, and the occupants of many of the rest were away at work or off on errands. About two miles out of town, as they crested a low rise just beyond the dump, they spotted the ambulances. Weldon pulled onto the shoulder, letting the engine idle, and stared at the sight. Four ambulances were strewn across the blacktop, forming an effective roadblock a hundred feet away. One had been flipped over on its roof like a dead white bug; another had crashed into a light pole and was swathed in electrical lines whose broken ends were sticking in through the driver's window, humping and writhing and sparking. The other two had been smashed together and were burning; transparent licks of flame warped the air above their blackened husks. But the wrecked ambulances were not the reason that Weldon had stopped so far away, why they sat silent and hopeless. To the right of the road was a field of bleached weeds and grasses, an Andrew Wyeth field glowing yellow in the pale sun, figured by a few stunted oaks and extending to a hill overlooking the sea, where three gray houses were posed against a faded blue sky. Though only fitful breezes played about the squad car, the field was registering the passage of heavy winds; the grasses were rippling, eddying, bending, and swaying in contrary directions, as if thousands of low-slung animals were scampering through them to and fro, and this rippling was so constant, so furious, it seemed that the shadows of the clouds passing overhead were standing still and the land was flowing away. The sound of the wind was a mournful whistling rush. Peter was entranced. The scene had a fey power that weighed upon him, and he had trouble catching his breath.

"Let's go," said Sara tremulously. "Let's . . ." She stared past Peter, a look of fearful comprehension forming on her face.

The wind had begun to roar. Less than thirty feet away a patch of grass had been flattened, and a man wearing an orderly's uniform was being lifted into the air, revolving slowly. His head flopped at a ridiculous straw-man angle, and the front of his tunic was drenched with blood. The car shuddered in the turbulence.

Sara shrieked and clutched at Peter. Weldon tried to jam the gearshift into reverse, missed, and the car stalled. He twisted the key in the ignition. The engine sputtered, dieseled, and went dead. The orderly continued to rise, assuming a vertical position. He spun faster and faster, blurring like an ice skater doing a fancy finish, and at the same time drifted closer to the car. Sara was screaming, and Peter wished he could scream, could do something to release the tightness in his chest. The engine caught. But before Weldon could put the car in gear, the wind subsided and the orderly fell onto the hood. Drops of blood sprinkled the windshield. He lay spread-eagled for a moment, his dead eyes staring at them. Then, with the obscene sluggishness of a snail retracting its foot, he slumped down onto the road, leaving a red smear across the white metal.

Weldon rested his head on the wheel, taking deep breaths. Peter cradled Sara in his arms. After a second Weldon leaned back, picked up the radio mike, and thumbed the switch open. "Jack," he said. "This is Hugh. You copy?"

"Loud and clear, Chief."

"We got us a problem out in Madaket." Weldon swallowed hard and gave a little twitch of his head. "I want you to set up a roadblock 'bout five miles from town. No closer. And don't let nobody through, y'understand?"

"What's happenin' out there, Chief? Alice Cuddy called in and said somethin' 'bout a freak wind, but the phone went dead and I couldn't get her back."

"Yeah, we had us some wind." Weldon exchanged a glance with Peter. "But the main problem's a chemical spill. It's under control for now, but you keep everybody away. Madaket's in quarantine."

"You need some help?"

"I need you to do what I told you! Get on the horn and call everyone livin' 'tween the roadblock and Madaket. Tell 'em to head for Nantucket as quick as they can. Put the word on the radio, too."

"What 'bout folks comin' from Madaket? Do I let 'em through?"

"Won't be nobody comin' that way," said Weldon.

Silence. "Chief, you okay?"

"Hell, yes!" Weldon switched off.

"Why didn't you tell them?" asked Peter.

"Don't want 'em thinkin' I'm crazy and comin' out to check on me," said Weldon. "Ain't no point in them dyin', too." He shifted into reverse. "I'm gonna tell everyone to get in their cellars and wait this damn thing out. Maybe we can figure out somethin' to do. But first I'll take you home and let Sara get some rest."

"I'm all right," she said, lifting her head from Peter's chest.

"You'll feel better after a rest," he said, forcing her head back down: it was an act of tenderness, but also he did not want her to catch sight of the field. Dappled with cloud shadow; glowing palely; some quality of light different from that which shone upon the squad car; it seemed at a strange distance from the road, a view into an alternate universe where things were familiar yet not quite the same. The grasses were rippling more furiously than ever, and every so often a column of yellow stalks would whirl high into the air and scatter, as if an enormous child were running through the field, ripping up handfuls of them to celebrate his exuberance.

.   .   .

"I'm not sleepy," Sara complained; she still hadn't regained her color, and one of her eyelids had developed a tic.

Peter sat beside her on the bed. "There's nothing you can do, so why not rest?"

"What are you going to do?"

"I thought I'd have another go at the combs."

The idea distressed her. He started to explain why he had to, but instead bent and kissed her on the forehead. "I love you," he said. The words slipped out so easily that he was amazed. It had been a very long time since he had spoken them to anyone other than a memory.

"You don't have to tell me that just because things look bad," she said, frowning.

"Maybe that's why I'm telling you now," he said. "But I don't believe it's a lie."

She gave a dispirited laugh. "You don't sound very confident."

He thought it over. "I was in love with someone once," he said, "and that relationship colored my view of love. I guess I believed that it always had to happen the same way. A nuclear strike. But I'm beginning to understand it can be different, that you can build toward the sound and the fury."

"It's nice to hear," she said, and then, after a pause, "but you're still in love with her, aren't you?"

"I still think about her, but. . . ." He shook his head. "I'm trying to put it behind me, and maybe I'm succeeding. I had a dream about her this morning."

She arched an eyebrow. "Oh?"

"It wasn't a sweet dream," he said. "She was telling me how she'd cemented over her feelings for me. 'All that's left,' she said, 'is this little hard place on my breast.' And she told me that sometimes it moved around, twitched, and she showed me. I could see the damn thing jumping underneath her blouse, and when I touched it—she wanted me to—it was unbelievably hard. Like a pebble lodged beneath her skin. A heart stone. That was all that was left of us. Just this piece of hardness. It pissed me off so much that I threw her on the floor. Then I woke up." He scratched his beard, embarrassed by confession. "It was the first time I've ever had a violent thought about her."

Sara stared at him, expressionless.

"I don't know if it's meaningful," he said lamely. "But it seemed so."

She remained silent. Her stare made him feel guilty for having had the dream, sorry that he had mentioned it.

"I don't dream about her very much," he said.

"It's not important," she said.

"Well." He stood. "Try and get some sleep, okay?"

She reached for his hand. "Peter?"

"Yeah?"

"I love you. But you knew that, right?"

It hurt him to see how hesitantly she said it, because he knew that he was to blame for her hesitancy. He bent down and kissed her again. "Sleep," he said. "We'll talk about it later."

He closed the door behind him gently. Mills was sitting at the table, gazing out at 'Sconset Sally, who was pacing the yard, her lips moving, waving her arms, as if arguing with an invisible playmate. "That ol' gal sure's gone down these last years," said Mills. "Used to be sharp as a tack, but she's actin' pretty crazy now."

"Can't blame her," said Peter, sitting down across from Mills. "I'm feeling pretty crazy myself."

"So." Mills tamped tobacco into the bowl of his pipe. "You got a line on what this thing is?"

"Maybe it's the Devil." Peter leaned against the wall. "I don't really know, but I'm starting to think that Gabriela Pascual was right about it being an animal."

Mills chomped on the stem of his pipe and fished in his pocket for a lighter. "How's that?"

"Like I said, I don't really know for sure, but I've been getting more and more sensitized to it ever since I found the combs. At least it seems that way. As if the connection between us were growing stronger." Peter spotted a book of matches tucked under his sugar bowl and slid them across to Mills. "I'm beginning to have some insights into it. When we were out on the road just now, I felt that it was exhibiting an animal trait. Staking out territory. Protecting it from invaders. Look who it's attacked. Ambulances, bicyclists. People who were entering its territory. It attacked us when we visited the aggregate."

"But it didn't kill us," said Mills.

The logical response to Mills's statement surfaced from Peter's thoughts, but he didn't want to admit to it and shunted it aside. "Maybe I'm wrong," he said.

"Well, if it is an animal, then it can take a hook. All we got to do is find its mouth." Mills grunted laughter, lit his pipe, and puffed bluish smoke. "After you been out on the water a coupla weeks, you can feel when something strange is hard by . . . even if you can't see it. I ain't no psychic, but seems to me I brushed past this thing once or twice."

Peter glanced up at him. Though Mills was a typical barroom creature, an old salt with a supply of exotic tales, every now and then Peter could sense about him the sort of specific gravity that accrues to those who have spent time in the solitudes. "You don't seem afraid," he said.

"Oh, don't I?" Mills chuckled. "I'm afraid. I'm just too old to be runnin' 'round in circles 'bout it."

The door flew open, and Sally came in. "Hot in here," she said; she went to the stove and laid a finger against it. "Hmph! Must be all this shit I'm wearin'." She plumped herself down beside Mills, squirmed into a comfortable position, and squinted at Peter. "Goddamn wind won't have me," she said. "It wants you."

Peter was startled. "What do you mean?"

Sally pursed her lips as if she had tasted something sour. "It would take me if you wasn't here, but you're too strong. I can't figure a way 'round that."

"Leave the boy alone," said Mills.

"Can't." Sally glowered at him. "He's got to do it."

"You know what she's talkin' 'bout?" asked Mills.

"Hell, yes! He knows! And if he don't, all he's got to do is go talk to it. You understand me, boy. It wants *you*."

An icy fluid squirted down Peter's spine. "Like Gabriela," he said. "Is that what you mean?"

"Go on," said Sally. "Talk to it." She pointed a bony finger at the door. "Just take a stand out there, and it'll come to you."

Behind the cottage, walled off by the spread of two Japanese pines and a toolshed, was a field that the previous tenant had used for a garden. Peter had let it go to seed, and the entire plot was choked with weeds and litter: gas cans, rusty nails, a plastic toy truck, the decaying hide of a softball, cardboard scraps, this and more resting upon a matte of desiccated vines. It reminded him of the aggregate, and thus seemed an appropriate place to stand and commune with the wind . . . if such a communion weren't the product of 'Sconset Sally's imagination. Which Peter hoped it was. The afternoon was waning, and it had grown colder. Silver blares of wintery sunlight edged the blackish-gray clouds scudding overhead, and the wind was a steady pour off the sea. He could detect no presence in it, and he was beginning to feel foolish, thinking about going back inside, when a bitter-smelling breeze rippled across his face. He stiffened. Again he felt it: it was acting independent of the offshore wind, touching delicate fingers to his lips, his eyes, fondling him the way a blind man would in trying to know your shape in his brain. It feathered his hair and pried under the pocket flaps of his army jacket like a pet mouse searching for cheese; it frittered with his shoelaces and stroked him between the legs, shriveling his groin and sending a chill washing through his body.

He did not quite understand how the wind spoke to him, yet he had an image of the process as being similar to how a cat will rub against your hand and transmit a static charge. The charge was actual, a mild stinging and popping. Somehow it was translated into knowledge, doubtless by means of his gift. The knowledge was personified, and he was aware that his conceptions were human renderings of inhuman impulses; but at the same time he was certain that they were basically accurate. Most of all it was lonely. It was the only one of its kind, or, if there were others, it had never encountered them. Peter felt no sympathy for its loneliness, because it felt no sympathy for him. It wanted him not as a friend or companion but as a witness to its power. It would enjoy preening for him, showing

off, rubbing against his sensitivity to it and deriving some un-
fathomable pleasure. It was very powerful. Though its touch
was light, its vitality was undeniable, and it was even stronger
over water. The land weakened it, and it was eager to return to
the sea with Peter in tow. Gliding together through the wild
canyons of the waves, into a chaos of booming darkness and
salt spray, traveling the most profound of all deserts—the sky
above the sea—and testing its strength against the lesser
powers of the storms, seizing flying fish and juggling them like
silver blades, gathering nests of floating treasures and playing
for weeks with the bodies of the drowned. Always at play. Or
perhaps "play" was not the right word. Always employed in
expressing the capricious violence that was its essential quality. Gabriela Pascual might not have been exact in calling it an
animal, but what else could you call it? It was of nature, not of
some netherworld. It was ego without thought, power without
morality, and it looked upon Peter as a man might look upon a
clever toy: something to be cherished for a while, then ne-
glected, then forgotten.

Then lost.

Sara waked at twilight from a dream of suffocation. She sat
bolt upright, covered with sweat, her chest heaving. After a
moment she calmed herself and swung her legs onto the floor
and sat staring into space. In the half-light the dark grain of
the boards looked like a pattern of animal faces emerging from
the wall; out the window she could see shivering bushes and
banks of running clouds. Still feeling sluggish, she went into
the front room, intending to wash her face; but the bathroom
door was locked and 'Sconset Sally cawed at her from inside.
Mills was snoozing on the sofa bunk, and Hugh Weldon was
sitting at the table, sipping a cup of coffee; a cigarette smol-
dered in the saucer, and that struck her as funny: she had
known Hugh all her life and had never seen him smoke.

"Where's Peter?" she asked.

"Out back," he said moodily. "Buncha damn foolishness, if
you ask me."

"What is?"

He gave a snort of laughter. "Sally says he's talkin' to the goddamn wind."

Sara felt as if her heart had constricted. "What do you mean?"

"Beats the hell outta me," said Weldon. "Just more of Sally's nonsense." But when their eyes met she could sense his hopelessness and fear.

She broke for the door. Weldon grabbed at her arm, but she shook free and headed for the Japanese pines back of the cottage. She brushed aside the branches and stopped short, suddenly afraid. The bending and swaying of the weeds revealed a slow circular passage of wind, as if the belly of a great beast were dragging across them, and at the center of the field stood Peter. His eyes were closed, his mouth open, and strands of hair were floating above his head like the hair of a drowned man. The sight stabbed into her, and forgetting her fear, she ran toward him, calling his name. She had covered half the distance between them when a blast of wind smashed her to the ground.

Stunned and disoriented, she tried to get to her feet, but the wind smacked her flat again, pressing her into the damp earth. As had happened out on the aggregate, garbage was rising from the weeds. Scraps of plastic, rusty nails, a yellowed newspaper, rags, and directly overhead, a large chunk of kindling. She was still dazed, yet she saw with peculiar clarity how the bottom of the chunk was splintered and flecked with whitish mold. It was quivering, as if the hand that held it were barely able to restrain its fury. And then, as she realized it was about to plunge down, to jab out her eyes and pulp her skull, Peter dived on top of her. His weight knocked the breath out of her, but she heard the piece of kindling *thunk* against the back of his head; she sucked in air and pushed at him, rolling him away, and came to her knees. He was dead-pale.

"Is he all right?"

It was Mills, lumbering across the field. Behind him, Weldon had hold of 'Sconset Sally, who was struggling to escape. Mills had come perhaps a third of the way when the garbage, which had fallen back into the weeds, once more was

lifted into the air, swirling, jiggling, and—as the wind produced one of its powerful gusts—hurtling toward him. For a
second he was surrounded by a storm of cardboard and plastic; then this fell away, and he took a staggering step forward.
A number of dark dots speckled his face. Sara thought at first
they were clots of dirt. Then blood seeped out around them.
They were rusty nailheads. Piercing his brow, his cheeks, pinning his upper lip to his gum. He gave no cry. His eyes bulged,
his knees buckled, he did an ungainly pirouette and pitched
into the weeds.

Sara watched dully as the wind fluttered about Hugh
Weldon and Sally, belling their clothes; it passed beyond them,
lashing the pine boughs and vanishing. She spotted the hump
of Mills's belly through the weeds. A tear seemed to be carving
a cold groove in her cheek. She hiccuped, and thought what a
pathetic reaction to death that was. Another hiccup, and another. She couldn't stop. Each successive spasm made her
weaker, more unsteady, as if she were spitting up tiny fragments of her soul.

VII

As darkness fell, the wind poured through the streets of the
village, playing its tricks with the living, the inanimate, and
the dead. It was indiscriminate, the ultimate free spirit doing
its thing, and yet one might have ascribed a touch of frustration to its actions. Over Warren's Landing it crumpled a sea
gull into a bloody rag, and near the mouth of Hither Creek it
scattered field mice into the air. It sent a spare tire rolling down
the middle of Tennessee Avenue and skied shingles from the
roof of the AHAB-ITAT. For a while it flowed about aimlessly;
then, increasing to tornado-force, it uprooted a Japanese pine,
just yanked it from the ground, dangling huge black root
balls, and chucked it like a spear through the side of a house
across the street. It repeated the process with two oaks and a
hawthorn. Finally it began to blast holes in the walls of the
houses and snatch the wriggling creatures inside. It blew off
old Julia Stackpole's cellar door and sailed it down into the

shelves full of preserves behind which she was hiding; it gathered the broken glass into a hurricane of knives that slashed her arms, her face, and—most pertinently—her throat. It found even older George Coffin (who wasn't about to hide, because in his opinion Hugh Weldon was a damned fool) standing in his kitchen, having just stepped back in after lighting his barbecue; it swept up the coals and hurled them at him with uncanny accuracy. Over the space of a half hour it killed twenty-one people and flung their bodies onto their lawns, leaving them to bleed pale in the accumulating dusk. Its fury apparently abated, it dissipated to a breeze and—zipping through shrubs and pine boughs—it fled back to the cottage, where something it now wanted was waiting in the yard.

VIII

'Sconset Sally sat on the woodpile, sucking at a bottle of beer that she'd taken from Peter's refrigerator. She was as mad as a wet hen because she had a plan—a good plan—and that brainless wonder Hugh Weldon wouldn't hear it, wouldn't listen to a damn word she said. Stuck on being a hero, he was.

The sky had deepened to indigo, and a big lopsided silver moon was leering at her from over the roof of the cottage. She didn't like its eye on her, and she spat toward it. The elemental caught the gob of spit and spun it around high in the air, making it glisten oysterlike. Fool thing! Half monster, half a walloping, invisible dog. It reminded her of that outsized old male of hers, Rommel. One second he'd be going for the mailman's throat, and the next he'd be on his back and waggling his paws, begging for a treat. She screwed her bottle into the grass so it wouldn't spill and picked up a stick of kindling. "Here," she said, and shied the stick. "Fetch." The elemental caught the stick and juggled it for a few seconds, then let it fall at her feet. Sally chuckled. "Me'n you might get along," she told the air. "'Cause neither one of us gives a shit!" The beer bottle lifted from the grass. She made a grab for it and missed. "Goddamn it!" she yelled. "Bring that back!" The bottle sailed to a height of about twenty feet and tipped over; the beer spilled out, collected in half a dozen large drops that—one by one—exploded into spray, showering her. Sputtering, she jumped to her feet and started to wipe her face; but the elemental knocked her back down. A trickle of fear welled up inside her. The bottle still hovered above her; after a second it plopped into the grass, and the elemental curled around her, fidgeting with her hair, her collar, slithering inside her raincoat; then, abruptly, as if something else had attracted its attention, it was gone. She saw the grass flatten as it passed over, moving toward the street. She propped herself against the woodpile and finished wiping her face; she spotted Hugh Weldon through the window, pacing, and her anger was rekindled. Thought he was so goddamn masterful, did he? He didn't know piss about the elemental, and there he was, laughing at her plan.

Well, screw him!

He'd find out soon enough that his plan wouldn't work, that hers was the reasonable one, the surefire one.

A little scary, maybe, but surefire all the same.

IX

It had come full dark by the time Peter regained consciousness. He moved his head, and the throbbing nearly caused him to black out. He lay still, getting his bearings. Moonlight spilled through the bedroom window, and Sara was leaning beside it, her blouse glowing a phosphorescent white. From the tilt of her head he judged that she was listening to something, and he soon distinguished an unusual pattern to the wind: five notes followed by a glissando, which led to a repetition of the passage. It was heavy, angry music, an ominous hook that might have been intended to signal the approach of a villain. Shortly thereafter the pattern broke into a thousand skirling notes, as if the wind were being forced through the open stops of a chorus of flutes. Then another passage, this of seven notes, more rapid but equally ominous. A chill, helpless feeling stole over Peter, like the drawing of a morgue sheet. That breathy music was being played for him. It was swelling in volume, as if—and he was certain this was the case—the elemental was heralding his awakening, was once again sure of his presence. It was impatient, and it would not wait for him much longer. Each note drilled that message home. The thought of being alone with it on the open sea terrified him. Yet he had no choice. There was no way to fight it, and it would simply keep on killing until he obeyed. If it weren't for the others he would refuse to go; he would rather die here than submit to that harrowing unnatural relationship. Or was it unnatural? It occurred to him that the history of the wind and Gabriela Pascual had a great deal in common with the histories of many human relationships. Desiring; obtaining; neglecting; forgetting. It might be that the elemental was some sort of core existence, that at the heart of every relationship lay a howling emptiness, a chaotic music.

"Sara," he said, wanting to deny it.

The moonlight seemed to wrap around her as she turned. She came to sit beside him. "How are you feeling?"

"Woozy." He gestured toward the window. "How long's that been going on?"

"It just started," she said. "It's punched holes in a lot of houses. Hugh and Sally were out a while ago. More people are dead." She brushed a lock of hair from his forehead. "But . . ."

"But what?"

"We have a plan."

The wind was playing eerie triplets, an agitated whistling that set Peter's teeth on edge. "It better be a doozy," he said.

"Actually, it's Hugh's plan," she said. "He noticed something out in the field. The instant you touched me, the wind withdrew from us. If it hadn't, if it had hurled that piece of wood at you instead of letting it drop, you would have died. And it didn't want that . . . at least that's what Sally says."

"She's right. Did she tell you what it does want?"

"Yes." She looked away, and her eyes caught the moonlight; they were teary. "Anyway, we think it was confused, that when we're close together it can't tell us apart. And since it doesn't want to hurt you or Sally, Hugh and I are safe as long as we maintain proximity. If Mills had just stayed where he was. . . ."

"Mills?"

She told him.

After a moment, still seeing Mills's nail-studded face in his mind's eye, he asked, "What's the plan?"

"I'm going to ride in the jeep with Sally, and you're going with Hugh. We'll drive toward Nantucket, and when we reach the dump . . . you know that dirt road there that leads off into the moors?"

"The one that leads to Altar Rock? Yeah."

"At that point you'll jump into the jeep with us, and we'll head for Altar Rock. Hugh will keep going toward Nantucket. Since it seems to be trying to isolate this end of the island, he figures it'll come after him and we might be able to get beyond its range, and with both of us heading in different directions, we might be able to confuse it enough so that it won't react quickly, and he'll be able to escape, too." She said all this in a rush that reminded Peter of the way a teenager would try to convince her parents to let her stay out late, blurting out the good reasons before they had time to raise any objections.

"You might be right about it not being able to tell us apart when we're close to each other," he said. "God knows how it senses things, and that seems plausible. But the rest is stupid. We don't know whether its territoriality is limited to this end of the island. And what if it does lose track of me and Sally? What's it going to do then? Just blow away? Somehow I doubt it. It might head for Nantucket and do what it's done here."

"Sally says she has a backup plan."

"Christ, Sara!" Gingerly, he eased up into a sitting position. "Sally's nuts. She doesn't have a clue."

"Well, what choice do we have?" Her voice broke. "You can't go with it."

"You think I want to? Jesus!"

The bedroom door opened, and Weldon appeared silhouetted in a blur of orange light that hurt Peter's eyes. "Ready to travel?" said Weldon. 'Sconset Sally was at his rear, muttering, humming, producing a human static.

Peter swung his legs off the bed. "This is nuts, Weldon." He stood and steadied himself on Sara's shoulder. "You're just going to get killed." He gestured toward the window and the constant music of the wind. "Do you think you can outrun that in a squad car?"

"Mebbe this plan ain't worth a shit. . . ." Weldon began.

"You got that right!" said Peter. "If you want to confuse the elemental, why not split me and Sally up? One goes with you, the other with Sara. That way at least there's some logic to this."

"Way I figure it," said Weldon, hitching up his pants, "it ain't your job to be riskin' yourself. It's mine. If Sally, say, goes with me, you're right, that'd confuse it. But so might this. Seems to me it's as eager to keep us normal people in line as it is to run off with freaks like you 'n Sally."

"What . . ."

"Shut up!" Weldon eased a step closer. "Now if my way don't work, you try it yours. And if *that* don't do it, then you can go for a cruise with the damn thing. But we don't have no guarantees it's gonna let anybody live, no matter what you do."

"No, but . . ."

"No buts about it! This is my bailiwick, and we're gonna do what I say. If it don't work, well, then you can do what you have to. But 'til that happens. . . ."

"'Til that happens you're going to keep on making an ass of yourself," said Peter. "Right? Man, all day you've been looking for a way to assert your fucking authority! You don't have any authority in this situation. Don't you understand?"

Weldon went jaw to jaw with him. "Okay," he said. "You go on out there, Mr. Ramey. Go ahead. Just march on out there. You can use Mills's boat, or if you want something bigger, how 'bout Sally's." He snapped a glance back at Sally. "That okay with you, Sally?" She continued muttering, humming, and nodded her head. "See!" Weldon turned to Peter. "She don't mind. So you go ahead. You draw that son of a bitch away from us if you can." He hitched up his pants and exhaled; his breath smelled like a coffee cup full of cigarette butts. "But if it was me, I'd be 'bout ready to try anything else."

Peter's legs felt rooted to the floor. He realized that he had been using anger to muffle fear, and he did not know if he could muster up the courage to take a walk out into the wind, to sail away into the terror and nothingness that Gabriela Pascual had faced.

Sara slipped her hand through his arm. "Please, Peter," she said. "It can't hurt to try."

Weldon backed off a step. "Nobody's blamin' you for bein' scared, Mr. Ramey," he said. "I'm scared myself. But this is the only way I can figure to do my job."

"You're going to die." Peter had trouble swallowing. "I can't let you do that."

"You ain't got nothin' to say 'bout it," said Weldon. "'Cause you got no more authority than me. 'Less you can tell that thing to leave us be. Can you?"

Sara's fingers tightened on Peter's arm, but relaxed when he said, "No."

"Then we'll do 'er my way." Weldon rubbed his hands together in what seemed to Peter hearty anticipation. "Got your keys, Sally?"

"Yeah," she said, exasperated; she moved close to Peter and put a bird-claw hand on his wrist. "Don't worry, Peter. This don't work, I got somethin' up my sleeve. We'll pull a fast one on that devil." She cackled and gave a little whistle, like a parrot chortling over a piece of fruit.

As they drove slowly along the streets of Madaket, the wind sang through the ruined houses, playing passages that sounded mournful and questioning, as if it were puzzled by the movements of the jeep and the squad car. The light of a three-quarter moon illuminated the destruction: gaping holes in the walls, denuded bushes, toppled trees. One of the houses had been given a surprised look, an O of a mouth where the door had been, flanked by two shattered windows. Litter covered the lawns. Flapping paperbacks, clothing, furniture, food, toys. And bodies. In the silvery light their flesh was as pale as Swiss cheese, the wounds dark. They didn't seem real; they might have been a part of a gruesome environment created by an avant-garde sculptor. A carving knife skittered along the blacktop, and for a moment Peter thought it would jump into the air and hurtle toward him. He glanced over at Weldon to see how he was taking it all. Wooden Indian profile, eyes on the road. Peter envied him his pose of duty; he wished he had such a role to play, something that would brace him up, because every shift in the wind made him feel frail and rattled.

They turned onto the Nantucket road, and Weldon straightened in his seat. He checked the rearview mirror, keeping an eye on Sally and Sara, and held the speed at twenty-five. "Okay," he said as they neared the dump and the road to Altar Rock. "I ain't gonna come to a full stop, so when I give the word you move it."

"All right," said Peter; he took hold of the door handle and let out a calming breath. "Good luck."

"Yeah." Weldon sucked at his teeth. "Same to you."

The speed indicator dropped to fifteen, to ten, to five, and the moonlit landscape inched past.

"Go!" shouted Weldon.

Peter went. He heard the squad car squeal off as he sprinted toward the jeep; Sara helped haul him into the back, and then they were veering onto the dirt road. Peter grabbed the frame of Sara's seat, bouncing up and down. The thickets that covered the moors grew close to the road, and branches whipped the sides of the jeep. Sally was hunched over the wheel, driving like a maniac; she sent them skipping over potholes, swerving around tight corners, grinding up the little hills. There was no time to think, only to hold on and be afraid, to await the inevitable appearance of the elemental. Fear was a metallic taste in Peter's mouth; it was in the white gleam of Sara's eyes as she glanced back at him and the smears of moonlight that coursed along the hood; it was in every breath he took, every trembling shadow he saw. But by the time they reached Altar Rock, after fifteen minutes or so, he had begun to hope, to half-believe, that Weldon's plan had worked.

The rock was almost dead-center of the island, its highest point. It was a barren hill atop which stood a stone where the Indians had once conducted human sacrifices—a bit of history that did no good whatsoever for Peter's nerves. From the crest you could see for miles over the moors, and the rumpled pattern of depressions and small hills had the look of a sea that had been magically transformed to leaves during a moment of fury. The thickets—bayberry and such—were dusted to a silvery-green by the moonlight, and the wind blew steadily, giving no evidence of unnatural forces.

Sara and Peter climbed from the jeep, followed after a second by Sally. Peter's legs were shaky and he leaned against the hood; Sara leaned back beside him, her hip touching his. He caught the scent of her hair. Sally peered toward Madaket. She was still muttering, and Peter made out some of the words.

"Stupid . . . never would listen to me . . . never would . . . son of a bitch . . . keep it to my goddamn self. . . ."

Sara nudged him. "What do you think?"

"All we can do is wait," he said.

"We're going to be all right," she said firmly; she rubbed the heel of her right hand against the knuckles of her left. It seemed the kind of childish gesture intended to insure good luck, and it inspired him to tenderness. He pulled her into an embrace. Standing there, gazing past her head over the moors, he had an image of them as being the standard lovers on the cover of a paperback, clinging together on a lonely hill, with all probability spread out around them. A corny way of looking at things, yet he felt the truth of it, the dizzying immersion that a paperback lover was supposed to feel. It was not as clear a feeling as he had once had, but perhaps clarity was no longer possible for him. Perhaps all his past clarity had simply been an instance of faulty perception, a flash of immaturity, an adolescent misunderstanding of what was possible. But whether or not that was the case, self-analysis would not solve his confusion. That sort of thinking blinded you to the world, made you disinclined to take risks. It was similar to what happened to academics, how they became so committed to their theories that they began to reject facts to the contrary, to grow conservative in their judgments and deny the inexplicable, the magical. If there was magic in the world—and he knew there was—you could only approach it by abandoning the constraints of logic and lessons learned. For more than a year he had forgotten this and had constructed defenses against magic; now in a single night they had been blasted away, and at a terrible cost he had been made capable of risking himself again, of hoping.

Then he noticed something that wasted hope.

Another voice had been added to the natural flow of wind from the ocean, and in every direction, as far as the eye could see, the moon-silvered thickets were rippling, betraying the presence of far more wind than was evident atop the hill. He pushed Sara away. She followed his gaze and put a hand to her mouth. The immensity of the elemental stunned Peter. They might have been standing on a crag in the midst of a troubled sea, one that receded into an interstellar dark. For the first time, despite his fear, he had an apprehension of the elemental's beauty, of the precision and intricacy of its power. One moment it could be a tendril of breeze, capable of delicate manipulations, and the next it could become an entity the size of a city. Leaves and branches—like flecks of black space—were streaming up from the thickets, forming into columns. Six of them, at regular intervals about Altar Rock, maybe a hundred yards away. The sound of the wind evolved into a roar as they thickened and grew higher. And they grew swiftly. Within seconds the tops of the columns were lost in darkness. They did not have the squat, conical shapes of tornadoes, nor did they twist and jab down their tails; they merely swayed, slender and graceful and menacing. In the moonlight their whirling was almost undetectable and they looked to be made of shining ebony, like six enormous savages poised to attack. They began moving toward the hill. Splintered bushes exploded upward from their bases, and the roaring swelled into a dissonant chord: the sound of a hundred harmonicas being blown at once. Only much, much louder.

The sight of 'Sconset Sally scuttling for the jeep waked Peter from his daze; he pushed Sara into the rear seat and climbed in beside Sally. Though the engine was running, it was drowned out by the wind. Sally drove even less cautiously than before; the island was criss-crossed by narrow dirt roads, and it seemed to Peter that they almost crashed on every one of them. Skidding sideways through a flurry of bushes, flying over the crests of hills, diving down steep slopes. The thickets grew too

high in most places for him to see much, but the fury of the
wind was all around them, and once, as they passed a place
where the bushes had been burned off, he caught a glimpse of
an ebony column about fifty yards away. It was traveling
alongside them, he realized. Harrowing them, running them
to and fro. Peter lost track of where they were, and he could
not believe that Sally had any better idea. She was trying to do
the impossible, to drive out the wind, which was everywhere,
and her lips were drawn back in a grimace of fear. Suddenly—
they had just turned east—she slammed on the brakes. Sara
flew halfway into the front seat, and if Peter had not been
braced he might have gone through the windshield. Farther
along the road one of the columns had taken a stand, blocking
their path. It looked like God, he thought. An ebony tower
reaching from the earth to the sky, spraying clouds of dust and
plant litter from its bottom. And it was moving toward them.
Slowly. A few feet per second. But definitely on the move. The
jeep was shaking, and the roar seemed to be coming from the
ground beneath them, from the air, from Peter's body, as if the
atoms of things were all grinding together. Frozen-faced, Sally
wrangled with the gearshift. Sara screamed, and Peter, too,
screamed as the windshield was sucked out of its frame and
whirled off. He braced himself against the dash, but his arms
were weak and with a rush of shame he felt his bladder go. The
column was less than a hundred feet away, a great spinning
pillar of darkness. He could see how the material inside it
aligned itself into tightly packed rings like the segments of a
worm. The air was syrupy, hard to breathe. And then, miracu-
lously, they were swerving away from it, away from the roaring, backing along the road. They turned a corner, and Sally
got the jeep going forward; she sent them grinding up a largish
hill . . . and braked. And let her head drop onto the steering
wheel in an attitude of despair. They were once again at Altar
Rock.

And Hugh Weldon was waiting for them.

He was sitting with his head propped against the boulder
that gave the place its name. His eyes were filled with shadows.
His mouth was open, and his chest rose and fell. Labored

breathing, as if he had just run a long way. There was no sign of the squad car. Peter tried to call to him, but his tongue was stuck to his palate and all that came out was a strangled grunt. He tried again.

"Weldon!"

Sara started to sob, and Sally gasped. Peter didn't know what had frightened them and didn't care; for him the process of thought had been thinned down to following one track at a time. He climbed from the jeep and went over to the chief. "Weldon," he said again.

Weldon sighed.

"What happened?" Peter knelt beside him and put a hand on his shoulder; he heard a hiss and felt a tremor pass through the body.

Weldon's right eye began to bulge. Peter lost his balance and sat back hard. Then the eye popped out and dropped into the dust. With a high-pitched whistling, wind and blood sprayed from the empty socket. Peter fell backward, scrabbling at the dirt in an effort to put distance between himself and Weldon. The corpse toppled onto its side, its head vibrating as the wind continued to pour out, boiling up dust beneath the socket. There was a dark smear marking the spot on the boulder where the head had rested.

Until his heart rate slowed, Peter lay staring at the moon, as bright and distant as a wish. He heard the roaring of the wind from all sides and realized that it was growing louder, but he didn't want to admit to it. Finally, though, he got to his feet and gazed out across the moors.

It was as if he were standing at the center of an unimaginably large temple, one forested with dozens upon dozens of shiny black pillars rising from a dark green floor. The nearest of them were about a hundred yards away, and those were unmoving; but as Peter watched, others farther off began to slew back and forth, gliding in and out of the stationary ones, like dancing cobras. There was a fever in the air, a pulse of heat and energy, and this as much as the alienness of the sight was what transfixed him and held him immobile. He found that he had gone beyond fear. You could no more hide from the ele-

mental than you could from God. It would lead him on to the
sea to die, and its power was so compelling that he almost
acknowledged its right to do this. He climbed into the jeep.
Sara looked beaten. Sally touched his leg with a palsied hand.

"You can use my boat," she said.

On the way back to Madaket, Sara sat with her hands clasped
in her lap, outwardly calm but inwardly turbulent. Thoughts
fired across her brain so quickly that they left only partial impressions, and those were seared away by lightning strokes of
terror. She wanted to say something to Peter, but words seemed
inadequate to all she was feeling. At one point she decided to
go with him, but the decision sparked a sudden resentment.
He didn't love her! Why should she sacrifice herself for him?
Then, realizing that he was sacrificing himself for her, that he
did love her or that at least this was an act of love, she decided
that if she went it would make his act meaningless. That decision caused her to question whether or not she was using his
sacrifice to obscure her true reason for staying behind: her
fear. And what about the quality of her feelings for him? Were
they so uncertain that fear could undermine them? In a blaze
of irrationality she saw that he was pressuring her to go with
him, to prove her love, something she had never asked him to
do. What right did he have? With half her mind she understood the unreasonableness of these thoughts, yet she couldn't
stop thinking them. She felt all her emotions winnowing, leaving her hollow . . . like Hugh Weldon, with only the wind
inside him, propping him up, giving him the semblance of life.
The grotesqueness of the image caused her to shrink further
inside herself, and she just sat there, growing dim and empty,
saying nothing.

"Buck up," said Sally out of the blue, and patted Peter's leg.
"We got one thing left to try." And then, with what seemed to
Sara an irrational good cheer, she added: "But if that don't
work, the boat's got fishin' tackle and a coupla cases of cherry
brandy on board. I was too damn drunk to unload 'em yesterday. Cherry brandy be better'n water for where you're headed."

Peter gave no reply.

As they entered the village, the elemental chased beside them, whirling up debris, scattering leaves, tossing things high into the air. Playing, thought Sara. It was playing. Frisking along like a happy pup, like a petulant child who'd gotten his way and now was all smiles. She was overwhelmed with hatred for it, and she dug her nails into the seat cushion, wishing she had a way to hurt it. Then, as they passed Julia Stackpole's house, the corpse of Julia Stackpole sat up. Its bloody head hung down, its frail arms flapping. The entire body appeared to be vibrating, and with a horrid disjointed motion, amid a swirling of papers and trash, it went rolling over and over and came to rest against a broken chair. Sara shrank back into a corner of the seat, her breath ragged and shallow. A thin cloud swept free of the moon, and the light measurably brightened, making the gray of the houses seem gauzy and immaterial; the holes in their sides looked real enough—black, cavernous—as if the walls and doors and windows had only been a facade concealing emptiness.

Sally parked next to a boathouse a couple of hundred yards north of Smith Point: a rickety wooden structure the size of a garage. Beyond it a stretch of calm black water was figured by a blaze of moonlight. "You gonna have to row out to the boat," Sally told Peter. "Oars are in here." She unlocked the door and flicked on a light. The inside of the place was as dilapidated as Sally herself. Raw boards; spiderwebs spanning between paint cans and busted lobster traps; a jumble of two-by-fours. Sally went stumping around, mumbling and kicking things, searching for the oars; her footsteps set the light bulb dangling from the roof to swaying, and the light slopped back and forth over the walls like dirty yellow water. Sara's legs were leaden. It was hard to move, and she thought maybe this was because there weren't any moves left. Peter took a few steps toward the center of the boathouse and stopped, looking lost. His hands twitched at his sides. She had the idea that his expression mirrored her own: slack, spiritless, with bruised crescents under his eyes. She moved, then. The dam that had been holding back her emotions burst, and her arms were around him, and she was telling him that she couldn't let him go alone, telling him half-sentences, phrases that didn't connect. "Sara," he said, "Jesus." He held her very tightly. The next second, though, she heard a dull *thonk* and he sagged against her, almost knocking her down, and slumped to the floor. Brandishing a two-by-four, Sally bent to him and struck again.

"What are you doing?" Sara screamed it and began to wrestle with Sally. Their arms locked, they waltzed around and around for a matter of seconds, the light bulb jiggling madly. Sally sputtered and fumed; spittle glistened on her lips. Finally, with a snarl, she shoved Sara away. Sara staggered back, tripped over Peter, and fell sprawling beside him.

"Listen!" Sally cocked her head and pointed to the roof with the two-by-four. "Goddamn it! It's workin'!"

Sara came warily to her feet. "What are you talking about?"

Sally picked up her fisherman's hat, which had fallen off during the struggle, and squashed it down onto her head. "The wind, goddamn it! I told that stupid son of a bitch Hugh Weldon, but oh, no! He never listened to nobody."

The wind was rising and fading in volume, doing so with such a regular rhythm that Sara had the impression of a creature made of wind running frantically back and forth. Something splintered in the distance.

"I don't understand," said Sara.

"Unconscious is like dead to it," said Sally; she gestured at Peter with the board. "I knew it was so, 'cause after it did for Mills it came for me. It touched me up all over, and I could tell it'd have me, then. But that stupid bastard wouldn't listen. Had to do things his goddamn way!"

"It would have you?" Sara glanced down at Peter, who was unstirring, bleeding from the scalp. "You mean instead of Peter?"

"'Course that's what I mean." Sally frowned. "Don't make no sense him goin'. Young man with all his future ahead. Now me . . ." She yanked at the lapel of her raincoat as if intending to throw herself away. "What I got to lose? A coupla years of bein' alone. I ain't eager for it, y'understand. But it don't make sense any other way. Tried to tell Hugh that, but he was stuck on bein' a goddamn hero."

Her bird-bright eyes glittered in the webbed flesh, and Sara had a perception of her that she had not had since childhood: the zany old spirit, half-mad but with one eye fixed on some corner of creation that nobody else could see. She remembered all the stories. Sally trying to signal the moon with a hurricane lamp; Sally rowing through a nor'easter to pluck six sailors off Whale Shoals; Sally passing out dead-drunk at the ceremony the Coast Guard had given in her honor; Sally loosing her dogs on the then-junior senator from Massachusetts when he had come to present her a medal. Crazy Sally. She suddenly seemed valuable to Sara.

"You can't. . . ." she began, but broke off and stared at Peter.

"Can't not," said Sally, and clucked her tongue. "You see somebody looks after my dogs."

Sara nodded.

"And you better check on Peter," said Sally. "See if I hit him too hard."

Sara started to comply but was struck by a thought. "Won't it know better this time? Peter was knocked out before. Won't it have learned?"

"I suppose it can learn," said Sally. "But it's real stupid, and I don't think it's figured this out." She gestured at Peter. "Go ahead. See if he's all right."

The hairs on Sara's neck prickled as she knelt beside Peter, and she was later to reflect that in the back of her mind she had known what was about to happen. But even so she was startled by the blow.

X

It wasn't until late the next afternoon that the doctors allowed Peter to have visitors other than the police. He was still suffering from dizziness and blurred vision, and mentally speaking, he alternated between periods of relief and depression. Seeing in his mind's eye the mutilated bodies, the whirling black pillars. Tensing as the wind prowled along the hospital walls. In general he felt walled off from emotion, but when Sara came into the room those walls crumbled. He drew her down beside him and buried his face in her hair. They lay for a long time without speaking, and it was Sara who finally broke the silence.

"Do they believe you?" she asked. "I don't think they believe me."

"They don't have much choice," he said. "I just think they don't want to believe it."

After a moment she said, "Are you going away?"

He pulled back from her. She had never looked more beautiful. Her eyes were wide, her mouth drawn thin, and the strain of all that had happened to them seemed to have carved an unnecessary ounce of fullness from her face. "That depends on whether or not you'll go with me," he said. "I don't want to stay. Whenever the wind changes pitch, every nerve in my body signals an air raid. But I won't leave you. I want to marry you."

Her reaction was not what he had expected. She closed her eyes and kissed him on the forehead—a motherly, understanding kiss; then she settled back on the pillow, gazing calmly at him.

"That was a proposal," he said. "Didn't you catch it?"

"Marriage?" She seemed perplexed by the idea.

"Why not? We're qualified." He grinned. "We both have concussions."

"I don't know," she said. "I love you, Peter, but. . . ."

"But you don't trust me?"

"Maybe that's part of it," she said, annoyed. "I don't know."

"Look." He smoothed down her hair. "Do you know what really happened in the boathouse last night?"

"I'm not sure what you mean."

"I'll tell you. What happened was that an old woman gave her life so you and I could have a chance at something." She started to speak, but he cut her off. "That's the bones of it. I admit the reality's a bit more murky. God knows why Sally did what she did. Maybe saving lives was a reflex of her madness, maybe she was tired of living. Maybe it just seemed a good idea at the time. And as for us, we haven't exactly been Romeo and Juliet. I've been confused, and I've confused you. And aside from whatever problems we might have as a couple, we have a lot to forget. Until you came in I was feeling shell-shocked, and that's a feeling that's probably going to last for a while. But like I said, the heart of the matter is that Sally died to give us a chance. No matter what her motives, what our circumstance, that's what happened. And we'd be fools to let that chance slip away." He traced the line of her cheekbone with a finger. "I love you. I've loved you for a long time and tried to deny it, to hold on to a dead issue. But that's all over."

"We can't make this sort of decision now," she murmured.

"Why not?"

"You said it yourself. You're shell-shocked. So am I. And I don't know how I feel about . . . everything."

"Everything? You mean me?"

She made a noncommittal noise, closed her eyes, and after a moment she said, "I need time to think."

In Peter's experience when women said they needed time to think, nothing good ever came of it. "Jesus!" he said angrily. "Is this how it has to be between people? One approaches, the other avoids, and then they switch roles. Like insects whose mating instincts have been screwed up by pollution." He registered what he had said and had a flash-feeling of horror. "Come on, Sara! We're past that kind of dance, aren't we? It doesn't have to be marriage, but let's commit to something. Maybe we'll make a mess of it, maybe we'll end up boring each other. But let's try. It might not be any effort at all." He put his arms around her, brought her tight against him, and was immersed in a cocoon of heat and weakness. He loved her, he realized, with an intensity that he had not believed he could recapture. His mouth had been smarter than his brain for once—either that or he had talked himself into it. The reasons didn't matter.

"For Christ's sake, Sara!" he said. "Marry me. Live with me. Do something with me!"

She was silent; her left hand moved gently over his hair. Light, distracted touches. Tucking a curl behind his ear, toying with his beard, smoothing his mustache. As if she were making him presentable. He remembered how that other long-ago woman had become increasingly silent and distracted and gentle in the days before she had dumped him.

"Damn it!" he said with a growing sense of helplessness. "Answer me!"

XI

On the second night out 'Sconset Sally caught sight of a winking red light off her port bow. Some ship's riding light. It brought a tear to her eye, making her think of home. But she wiped the tear away with the back of her hand and had another slug of cherry brandy. The cramped wheelhouse of the lobster boat was cozy and relatively warm; beyond, the moonlit plain of the sea was rising in light swells. Even if you didn't have nowhere good to go, she thought, wheels and keels and wings gave a boost to your spirit. She laughed. Especially if you had a supply of cherry brandy. She had another slug. A breeze curled around her arm and tugged at the neck of the bottle. "Goddamn it!" she squawked. "Get away!" She batted at the air as if she could shoo away the elemental, and hugged the bottle to her breast. Wind uncoiled a length of rope on the deck behind her, and then she could hear it moaning about the hull. She staggered to the wheelhouse door. "Whoo-oo-ooh!" she sang, mocking it. "Don't be making your godawful noises at me, you sorry bastard! Go kill another goddamn fish if you want somethin' to do. Just leave me alone to my drinkin'."

Waves surged up on the port side. Big ones, like black teeth. Sally almost dropped the bottle in her surprise. Then she saw they weren't really waves but shapes of water made by the elemental. "You're losin' your touch, asshole!" she shouted. "I seen better'n that in the movies!" She slumped down beside the door, clutching the bottle. The word *movies* conjured flashes of old films she'd seen, and she started singing songs from them. She did "Singin' in the Rain" and "Blue Moon" and "Love Me Tender." She knocked back swallows of brandy in between the verses, and when she felt primed enough she launched into her favorite. "The sound that you hear," she bawled, "is the sound of Sally! A joy to be heard for a thousand years." She belched. "The hills are alive with the sound of Sally. . . ." She couldn't recall the next line, and that ended the concert.

The wind built to a howl around her, and her thoughts sank into a place where there were only dim urges and nerves fizzling and blood whining in her ears. Gradually she surfaced from it and found that her mood had become one of regret. Not about anything specific. Just general regrets. General Regrets. She pictured him as an old fogey with a white walrus mustache and a Gilbert-and-Sullivan uniform. Epaulets the size of skateboards. She couldn't get the picture out of her head, and she wondered if it stood for something important. If it did, she couldn't make it come clear. Like that line of her favorite song, it had leaked out through one of her cracks. Life had leaked out the same way, and all she could remember of it was a muddle of lonely nights and sick dogs and scallop shells and half-drowned sailors. Nothing important sticking up from the muddle. No monument to accomplishment or romance. Hah! She'd never met the man who could do what men said they could. The most reasonable men she'd known were those shipwrecked sailors, and their eyes big and dark as if they'd seen into some terrible bottomland that had sheared away their pride and stupidity. Her mind began to whirl, trying to get a fix on life, to pin it down like a dead butterfly and know its patterns, and soon she realized that she was literally whirling. Slowly, but getting faster and faster. She hauled herself up and clung to the wheelhouse door and peered over the side. The lobster boat was spinning around and around on the lip of a bowl of black water several hundred yards across. A whirlpool. Moonlight struck a glaze down its slopes but didn't reach the bottom. Its roaring, heart-stopping power scared her, made her giddy and faint. But after a moment she banished fear. So this was death. It just opened up and swallowed you whole. All right. That was fine by her. She slumped against the wheelhouse and drank deeply of the cherry brandy, listening to the wind and the singing of her blood as she went down not giving a damn. It sure beat puking up life a gob at a time in some hospital room. She kept slurping away at the brandy, guzzling it, wanting to be as looped as possible when the time came. But the time didn't come, and before too long she noticed that the boat had stopped spinning. The wind had quieted and the sea was calm.

A breeze coiled about her neck, slithered down her breast, and began curling around her legs, flipping the hem of her dress. "You bastard," she said soddenly, too drunk to move. The elemental swirled around her knees, belling the dress, and touched her between the legs. It tickled, and she swatted at it ineffectually, as if it were one of the dogs snooting at her. But a second later it prodded her there again, a little harder than before, rubbing back and forth, and she felt a quiver of arousal. It startled her so that she went rolling across the deck, somehow keeping her bottle upright. That quiver stuck with her, though, and for an instant a red craving dominated the broken mosaic of her thoughts. Cackling and scratching herself, she staggered to her feet and leaned on the rail. The elemental was about fifty yards off the port bow, shaping itself a waterspout, a moonstruck column of blackness, from the placid surface of the sea.

"Hey!" she shouted, wobbling along the rail. "You come on back here! *I'll* teach you a new trick!"

The waterspout grew higher, a glistening black serpent that *whooshed* and sucked the boat toward it; but it didn't bother Sally. A devilish joy was in her, and her mind crackled with lightnings of pure craziness. She thought she had figured out something. Maybe nobody had ever taken a real interest in the elemental, and maybe that was why it eventually lost interest in them. Wellsir! She had an interest in it. Damn thing couldn't be any more stupid than some of her Dobermans. Snooted like one, for sure. She'd teach it to roll over and beg and who knows what else. Fetch me that fish, she'd tell it. Blow me over to Hyannis and smash the liquor-store window and bring me six bottles of brandy. She'd show it who was boss. And could be one day she'd sail into the harbor at Nantucket with the thing on a leash. 'Sconset Sally and her pet storm, Scourge of the Seven Seas.

The boat was beginning to tip and slew sideways in the pull

of the waterspout, but Sally scarcely noticed. "Hey!" she shouted again, and chuckled. "Maybe we can work things out! Maybe we're meant for each other!" She tripped over a warp in the planking, and the arm holding the bottle flailed above her head. Moonlight seemed to stream down into the bottle, igniting the brandy so that it glowed like a magic elixir, a dark red ruby flashing from her hand. Her maniacal laugh went sky-high.

"You come on back here!" she screeched at the elemental, exulting in the wild frequencies of her life, at the thought of herself in league with this idiot god, and unmindful of her true circumstance, of the thundering around her and the tiny boat slipping toward the foaming base of the waterspout. "Come back here, damn it! We're two of a kind! We're birds of a feather! I'll sing you to sleep each night! You'll serve me my supper! I'll be your old cracked bride, and we'll have a hell of a honeymoon while it lasts!"

Black Coral

~~~~~~~~~~~~~~~~~~~~~~~~~~~~~~~~ The bearded young man who
~~~~~~~~~~~~~~~~~~~~~~~~~~~~~~~~ didn't give a damn about
anyone (or so he'd just shouted—whereupon the bartender
had grabbed his scaling knife and said, "Dat bein' de way of it,
you can do your drinkin' elsewhere!") came staggering out of
the bar and shielded his eyes against the afternoon glare. Violet afterimages flared and fizzled under his lids. He eased
down the rickety stair, holding on to the rail, and stepped into
the street, still blinking. And then, as he adjusted to the brightness, a ragged man with freckled cocoa-colored skin and a
prophet's beard swung into view, blocking out the sun.

"Hot enough de sun duppy be writhin' in de street, ain't it,
Mr. Prince?"

Prince choked. Christ! That damned St. Cecilia rum was
eating holes in his stomach! He reeled. The rum backed up
into his throat and the sun blinded him again, but he squinted
and made out old Spurgeon James, grinning, rotten teeth angled like untended tombstones, holding an empty Coke bottle
whose mouth was crusted with flies.

"Gotta go," said Prince, lurching off.

"You got work for me, Mr. Prince?"

Prince kept walking.

Old Spurgeon would lean on his shovel all day, reminisce
about "de back time," and offer advice ("Dat might go easier
with de barrow, now") while Prince sweated like a donkey and

lifted concrete blocks. Work! Still, for entertainment's sake alone he'd be worth more than most of the black trash on the island. And the ladinos! ("De dommed Sponnish!") They'd work until they had enough to get drunk, play sick, then vanish with your best tools. Prince spotted a rooster pecking at a mango rind by the roadside, elected him representative of the island's work force, and kicked; but the rooster flapped up, squabbling, lit on an overturned dinghy, and gave an assertive cluck.

"Wait dere a moment, Mr. Prince!"

Prince quickened his pace. If Spurgeon latched on, he'd never let loose. And today, January 18, marked the tenth anniversary of his departure from Vietnam. He didn't want any company.

The yellow dirt road rippled in a heat haze that made the houses—rows of weathered shanties set on pilings against the storm tides—appear to be dancing on thin rubbery legs. Their tin roofs were buckled, pitched at every angle, showing patches of rust like scabs. That one—teetering on splayed pilings over a dirt front yard, the shutter hung by a single hinge, gray flour-sack curtain belling inward—it always reminded him of a cranky old hen on her roost trying grimly to hatch a nonexistent egg. He'd seen a photograph of it taken seventy years before, and it had looked equally dejected and bedraggled then. Well, almost. There *had* been a sapodilla tree overspreading the roof.

"Givin' out a warnin', Mr Prince! Best you listen!"

Spurgeon, rags tattering in the breeze, stumbled toward him and nearly fell. He waved his arms to regain his balance, like a drunken ant, toppled sideways, and fetched up against a palm trunk, hugging it for support. Prince, in dizzy sympathy with the sight, tottered backward and caught himself on some shanty steps, for a second going eye to eye with Spurgeon. The old man's mouth worked, and a strand of spittle eeled out onto his beard.

Prince pushed off from the steps. Stupidity! That was why nothing changed for the better on Guanoja Menor (derived from the Spanish *guano* and *hoja,* a fair translation being

Lesser Leaf-shaped Piece of Bird Shit), why unemployable drunks hounded you in the street, why the rum poisoned you, why the shanties crashed from their perches in the least of storms. Unwavering stupidity! The islanders built outhouses on piers over the shallows where they bathed and fished the banks with no thought for conservation, then wondered why they stank and went hungry. They cut off their fingers to win bets that they wouldn't; they smoked black coral and inhaled gasoline fumes for escape; they fought with conch shells, wrapping their hands around the inner volute of the shell so it fit like a spiky boxing glove. And when the nearly as stupid ladinos had come from the Honduran mainland, they'd been able to steal and swindle half the land on the island.

Prince had learned from their example.

"Mr. Prince!"

Spurgeon again, weaving after him, his palm outstretched. Angrily, Prince dug out a coin and threw it at his feet.

"Dass so nice, dass so kind of you!" Spurgeon spat on the coin. But he stooped for it and, in stooping, lost his balance and fell, smashing his Coke bottle on a stone. There went fifty centavos. There went two glasses of rum. The old man rolled in the street, too drunk to stand, smearing himself with yellow dirt. "Even de sick dog gots teeth," he croaked. "Just you re-member dat, Mr. Prince!"

Prince couldn't keep from laughing.

Meachem's Landing, the town ("a quaint seaport, steeped in pirate legend," prattled the guidebook), lay along the curve of a bay inset between two scrub-thatched hills and served as the island capital. At midpoint of the bay stood the government office, a low white stucco building with sliding glass doors like a cheap motel. Three prosperous-looking Spanish men were sitting on oil drums in its shade, talking to a soldier wearing blue fatigues. As Prince passed, an offshore breeze kicked up and blew scents of rotted coconut, papaya, and creosote in from the customs dock, a concrete strip stretching one hundred yards or so into the glittering cobalt reach of the water.

There was a vacancy about the scene, a lethargy uniformly

affecting its every element. Cocals twitched the ends of their
fronds, leaning in over the tin roofs; a pariah dog sniffed at a
dried lobster claw in the dust; ghost crabs scuttered under the
shanties. It seemed to Prince that the tide of event had withdrawn, leaving the bottom dwellers exposed, creating a lull
before some culminative action. And he remembered how it
had been the same on bright afternoons in Saigon when pass-
ersby stopped and listened to the whine of an incoming rocket,
how the plastic flags on the Hondas parked in front of the bars
snapped in the wind, how a prostitute's monkey had screamed
in its cage on hearing the distant *crump* and everyone had
laughed with relief. He felt less irritable, remembering, more
at rights with the commemorative nature of the day.

Beyond the government office, past the tiny public square
and its dusty-leaved acacia, propped against the cement wall
of the general store, clinging to it like a gaudy barnacle, was a
shanty whose walls and trim had been painted crimson and
bright blue and pink and quarantine yellow. Itchy-sounding
reggae leaked from the closed shutter. Ghetto Liquors. He
tramped heavily on the stair, letting them know within that the
drunkest mother on the island, Neal His Bloody Majesty
Prince, was about to integrate their little rainbow paradise,
and pushed into the hot, dark room.

"Service!" he said, kicking the counter.

"What you want?"

Rudy Welcomes stirred behind the bar. A slash of light from
a split seam in the roof jiggled on his shaved skull.

"Saint Cecilia!" Prince leaned on the bar, reconnoitering.
Two men sat at a rear table, their hair in spiky dreadlocks,
wraiths materializing from the dark. The darkness was picked
out by the purplish glow of black lights illuminating four Jimi
Hendrix posters. Though of island stock, Rudy was
American-born and, like Prince, a child of the sixties and a
veteran. He said that the lights and posters put him in mind of
a brothel on Tu Do Street, where he had won the money with
which to establish Ghetto Liquors; and Prince, recalling similar brothels, found that the lights provided an excellent frame
of reference for the thoughtful, reminiscent stages of his

drunk. The eerie purple radiance escaping the slender black cannisters seemed the crystallized expression of war, and he fancied the color emblematic of evil energies and sluggish tropical demons.

"So this your big day for drinkin'." Rudy slid a pint bottle along the bar and resettled on his stool. "Don't you be startin' that war-buddy crap with me, now. I ain't in the mood."

"Shucks, Rudy!" Prince adopted a Southern accent. "You know I ain't war buddies with no nigger."

Rudy stiffened but let it pass; he gave a disaffected grunt. "Don't know why not, man. You could pass *yourself*. Way your hair's gotten all crispy and your skin's gone dark. See here?"

He laid his hand on Prince's to compare the color, but Prince knocked it aside and stared, challenging.

"Damn! Seem like Clint Eastwood done wandered into town!" Rudy shook his head in disgust and moved off along the bar to change the record. The two men at the rear drifted across the room and whispered with him, casting sly looks at Prince.

Prince basked in the tension. It further fleshed out his frame of reference. Confident that he'd established dominance, he took a table beside the shutter, relaxed, and sipped his rum. Through a gap in the boards he saw a girl stringing up colored lights on the shanty opposite the bar. His private holiday had this year coincided with Independence Day, always celebrated upon the third Friday in January. Stalls would sprout in the public square, offering strips of roast turtle and games of chance. Contending music would blare from the bars—reggae and salsa. Prince enjoyed watching street dancers lose their way in the mishmash of rhythms. It emphasized the fact that neither the Spanish nor the islanders could cope with the other's presence and further emphasized that they were celebrating two different events—on the day that Queen Victoria had granted the islands their freedom, the Honduran military had sailed in and established governance.

More stupidity.

The rum was sitting easier on his stomach. Prince mellowed

and went with the purple lights, seeing twisted black branches in them, seeing the twilit jungle in Lang Biang, and he heard the hiss of the walkie-talkie and Leon's stagy whisper, "Hey, Prince! I got a funny shadow in that bombax tree. . . ." He had turned his scope on the tree, following the course of the serpentine limbs through the grainy empurpling air. And then the stutter of automatic fire, and he could hear Leon's screams in the air *and* carrying over the radio. . . .

"Got somethin' for help you celebrate, Mr. Prince."

A thin hawk-faced man wearing frayed shorts dropped into the chair next to him, his dreadlocks wriggling. George Ebanks.

Prince gripped the rum bottle, angry, ready to strike, but George thrust out a bristling something—a branch of black coral.

"Dis de upful stuff, Mr. Prince," he said. "Rife with de island's secret." He pulled out a knife and whittled at the branch. Curly black shavings fell onto the table. "You just scrapes de color off and dass what you smokes."

The branch intrigued Prince; it was dead black, unshining, hard to tell where each stalk ended and the room's darkness began. He'd heard the stories. Old Spurgeon said it drove you crazy. And even older John Anderson McCrae had said, "De coral so black dat when you smokes it de color will rush into your eyes and allow you vision of de spirit world. And will allow dem sight of you."

"What's it do?" he asked, tempted.

"It make you more a part of things. Dass all, Mr. Prince. Don't fret. We goin' to smoke it with you."

Rudy and the third man—wiry, short Jubert Cox—sidled up behind George's shoulder, and Rudy winked at Prince. George loaded the knife blade with black shavings and tamped them into a hash pipe, then lit it, drawing hard until the hollows of his cheeks reflected the violet-red coal. He handed the pipe across, a wisp of smoke curling from his tight-lipped smile, and watched Prince toke it down.

The smoke tasted vile. It had a mustiness he associated with the thousands of dead polyps (was it thousands per lungful or merely hundreds?) he'd just inhaled, but it was so cool that he did not concern himself with taste and noticed only the coolness.

Cold black stone lined his throat.

The coolness spread to his arms and legs, weighting them down, and he imagined it questing with black tendrils through veins and arteries, finding out secret passages unknown even to his blood. Drifty stuff . . . and dizzying. He wasn't sure if he was sweating or not, but he *was* a little nauseous. And he didn't seem to be inhaling anymore. Not really. The smoke seemed to be issuing of its own volition from the pipestem, a silken rope, a cold strangler's cord tying a labyrinthine knot throughout his body . . .

"Take but a trifle, don't it, Mr. Prince?" Jubert giggled.

Rudy lifted the pipe from his numbed fingers.

. . . and involving the fissures of his brain in an intricate design, binding his thoughts into a coralline structure. The bright gaps in the shutter planking dwindled, receded, until they were golden straws adrift in the blackness, then golden pinpricks, then gone. And though he was initially fascinated by this production of the drug, as it progressed Prince became worried that he was going blind.

"Wuh . . ." His tongue wouldn't work. His flesh was choked with black dust, distant from him, and the coolness had deepened to a penetrating chill. And as a faint radiance suffused the dark, he imagined that the process of the drug had been reversed, that now he was flowing up the pipestem into the heart of the violet-red coal.

"Oh, dis de upful stuff all right, Mr. Prince," said George, from afar. "Dat what grows down to de root of de island."

Rippling kelp beds faded in from the blackness, illuminated by a violet glow, and Prince saw that he was passing above them toward a dim wall (the reef?) at whose base thousands upon thousands of witchy fires burned, flickering, ranging in color from indigo to violet-white, all clinging (he saw, drawing near) to the stalks and branches of black coral—a bristling jungle of coral, stalks twenty and thirty feet high, and more. The fires were smaller than candle flames and did not seem as much presences as they did peepholes into a cold furnace behind the reef. Maybe they were some sort of copepod, bioluminescent and half-alive. He descended among the stalks, moving along the channels between them. Barracuda, sleek triggerfish . . . There! A grouper—four hundred pounds if it was an ounce—angelfish and rays . . . bones showed in negative through their luminous flesh. Schools of smaller fish darted as one, stopped, darted again, into and out of the black branches. The place had a strange kinetic geometry, as if it were the innards of an organic machine whose creatures performed its functions by maneuvering in precise patterns through its interstices, and in which the violet fires served as the insane, empowering thoughts within an inky skull. Beautiful! Thomas De Quincey Land. A jeweled shade, an occulted paradise. Then, rising into the murk above him, an *immense* stalk—a shadowy, sinister Christmas tree poxed with flickering decorations. Sharks circled its upper reaches, cast in silhouette by the glow. Several of the fires detached from a branch and drifted toward him, eddying like slow moths.

"Dey just markin' you, Mr. Prince. Don't be troubled."

Where was George's voice coming from? It sounded right inside his ear. Oh, well . . . He wasn't troubled. The fires were weird, lovely. One drifted to within a foot of his eyes, hovering there, its violet-tipped edges shifting, not with the randomness of flame but with a flowing, patterned movement, a complex pulse; its center was an iridescent white. Must not be copepods.

It drifted closer.

Very lovely. A wash of violet spread from its edges in and was absorbed by the whiteness.

It brushed against his left eye.

Prince's vision went haywire, spinning. He had a glimpse of the sentinel sharks, a blurred impression of the latticework of shadow on the reef wall, then darkness. The cold touch, brief as it had been, a split second, had burned him, chilled him, as if a hypodermic had ever so slightly pricked the humor and flooded him with an icy serum, leaving him shuddering.

"Dey bound him!" George?

"Be watchful down dere, Mr. Prince." Jubert.

The shutter banged open, and bright, sweet, warming sunlight poured in. He realized he had fallen. His legs were entangled in an unyielding something that must be the chair.

"You just had a little fit, man. Happens sometimes the first time. You gonna be fine."

They pulled him up and helped him out onto the landing and down the stair. He tripped and fell the last three steps, weak and drunk, still shivering, fuddled by the sunlight.

Rudy pressed the rum bottle into his hands. "Keep in the sun for a while, man. Get your strength back."

"Oh, Mr. Prince!" A skinny black arm waved from the window of the gaudy box on stilts, and he heard smothered giggles. "You got work for me, Mr. Prince?"

Severe physical punishment was called for! Nobody was going to get away with bad-tripping him!

Prince drank, warmed himself, and plotted his revenge on the steps of the dilapidated Hotel Captain Henry. (The hotel was named for Henry Meachem, the pirate whose crews had interbred with Carib and Jamaican women, thereby populating the island, and whose treasure was the focal point of many tall tales.) A scrawny, just-delivered bitch growled at him from the doorway. Between growls she worried her inflamed teats, a nasty sucking that turned Prince's saliva thick and ropy. He gave old Mike, the hotel flunky, twenty-five centavos to chase her off, but afterward old Mike wanted more.

"I be a bitch, mon! I strip de shadow from your back!" He danced around Prince, flicking puny left jabs. Filthy, wearing colorless rags and a grease-stained baseball cap, flecks of egg yolk clotting his iron-gray whiskers.

Prince flipped him another coin and watched as he ran off to bury it. The stories said that Mike had been a miser, had gone mad when he'd discovered all his money eaten by mice and insects. But Roblie Meachem, owner of the hotel, said, "He just come home to us one mornin'. Didn't have no recollection of his name, so we call him Mike after my cousin in Miami." Still, the stories persisted. It was the island way. ("Say de thing long enough and it be so.") And perhaps the stories had done some good for old Mike, effecting a primitive psychotherapy and giving him a legend to inhabit. Mike returned from his hiding place and sat beside the steps, drawing circles in the dust with his finger and rubbing them out, mumbling, as if he couldn't get them right.

Prince flung his empty bottle over a shanty roof, caring not where it fell. The clarity of his thoughts annoyed him; the coral had sobered him somewhat, and he needed to regain his lost momentum. If Rita Steedly wasn't home, well, he'd be within a half mile of his own bar, the Sea Breeze; but if she was. . . . Her husband, an ecologist working for the government, would be off island until evening, and Prince felt certain that a go-round with Rita would reorient him and reinstitute the mean drunken process which the coral had interrupted.

Vultures perched on the pilings of Rita Steedly's dock, making them look like carved ebony posts. Not an uncommon sight on the island, but one Prince considered appropriate as to the owner's nature, more so when the largest of them flapped up and landed with a crunch in a palm top overlooking the sun deck where she lay. The house was blue stucco on concrete pilings standing in a palm grove. Between the trunks, the enclosed waters of the reef glittered in bands and swirls of aquamarine, lavender, and green according to the varying depth and bottom. Sea grape grew close by the house, and the point of land beyond it gave out into mangrove radicle.

As he topped the stairs, Rita propped herself on her elbows, pushed back her sunglasses, and weakly murmured, "Neal," as if summoning her lover to a deathbed embrace. Then she collapsed again upon the blanket, the exhausted motion of a pale dead frond. Her body glistened with oils and sweat, and her bikini top was unhooked and had slipped partway off.

Prince mixed a rum and papaya juice from the serving cart by the stair. "Just smoked some black coral with the boys down at Ghetto Liquors." He looked back at her over his shoulder and grinned. "De spirits tol' me dat I must purify myself wit de body of a woman fore de moon is high."

"I *thought* your eyes were very yellow today. You should know better." She sat up; the bikini top dropped down onto her arms. She lifted a coil of hair which had stuck to her breast, patting it into place behind her ear. "There ain't anything on this island that's healthy anymore. Even the fruit's poisoned! Did I tell you about the fruit?"

She had. Her little girl's voice grated on Prince, but he found her earnestness amusing, attractive for its perversity. Her obsession with health seemed no less a product of trauma than did his own violent disposition.

"It was just purple lights and mild discomfort," he said, sitting beside her. "But a headache and a drowsy sensation would be a good buzz to those black hicks. They tried to mess with my mind, but. . . ." He leaned over and kissed her. "I made good my escape and came straightaway."

"Jerry said he saw purple lights, too." A grackle holding a cigarette butt in its beak hopped up on the railing, and Rita shooed it off.

"*He* smoked it?"

"He smokes it all the time. He wanted me to try it, but I'm not poisoning myself any more than I have to with this . . . this garbage heap." She checked his eyes. "They're getting as bad as everyone else's. Still, they aren't as bad as the people's in Arkansas. They were so yellow they almost glowed in the dark. Like phosphorescent urine!" She shuddered dramatically, sighed, and stared glumly up into the palms. "God! I hate this place!"

Prince dragged her down to face him. "You're a twitch," he said.

"I'm not!" she said angrily, but fingered loose the buttons of his shirt as she talked. "Everything's polluted down here. Dying. And it's worse in the States. You can see the wasting in people's faces if you know how to look for it. I've tried to talk Jerry into leaving, but he says he's committed. Maybe I'll leave him. Maybe I'll go to Peru. I've heard good things about Peru."

"You'll see the wasting in *their* faces," said Prince.

Her arms slid around his back, and her eyes opened and closed, opened and closed, the eyes of a doll whose head you manipulated. Barely seeing him, seeing something else in his place, some bad sign or ugly rumor.

As his own eyes closed, as he stopped thinking, he gazed out past her head to the glowing, many-colored sea and saw in the pale sky along the horizon a flash of the way it had been after a burn-off: the full-bore immensity and silence of the light; the clear, innocent air over paddies and palms blackened like matchsticks; and how they'd moved through the dead land, crunching the scorched, brittle stalks underfoot, unafraid, because every snake within miles was now just a shadow in the cinders.

Drunk, blind, old John Anderson McCrae was telling stories at the Sea Breeze, and Prince wandered out onto the beach for some peace and quiet. The wind brought fragments of the creaky voice. ". . . dat cross were studded with emeralds . . . and sapphires . . ." The story about Meachem's gold cross (supposedly buried off the west end of the island) was John's masterpiece, told only at great expense to the listener. He told how Meachem's ghost appeared each time his treasure was threatened, huge, a constellation made of the island stars. ". . . and de round end of his peg leg were de moon shine down . . ." Of course, Meachem had had two sound legs, but the knowledge didn't trouble John. "A mon's ghost may suffer injury every bit as de mon," he'd say; and then, to any further challenge, "Well, de truth may be lackin' in it, but it capture de spirit of de truth." And he'd laugh, spray his rummy breath in the tourists' faces, and repeat his commonplace pun. And they would pay him more because they thought he was cute, colorful, and beneath them.

White cumulus swelled from the horizon, and the stars blazed overhead so bright and jittery they seemed to have a pulse in common with the rattle of the Sea Breeze's generator. The reef crashed and hissed. Prince screwed his glass into the sand and settled back against a palm trunk, angled so he could see the deck of the bar. Benches and tables were built around coconut palms that grew up through the deck; orange lights in the form of plastic palms were mounted on the trunks. Not an unpleasant place to sit and watch the sea.

But the interior of the Sea Breeze bordered on the monstrous: lamps made of transparent-skinned blowfish with bulbs in their stomachs; treasure maps and T-shirts for sale; a giant jukebox glowing red and purple like the crown jewels in a protective cage of two-by-fours; garish pirate murals on the walls; and skull-and-crossbones pennants hanging from the thatched roof. The bar had been built and painted to simulate a treasure chest with its lid ajar. Three Carib skulls sat on shelves over the bottles, with red bulbs in their jaws that winked on and off for birthdays and other celebrations. It was his temple to the stupidity of Guanoja Menor; and, being his first acquisition, memorialized a commitment he had made to the grotesque heart of acquisition itself.

A burst of laughter, shouts of "Watch out!" and "Good luck!" and old John appeared at the railing, groping his way along until he found the stair and stumbled down onto the beach. He weaved back and forth, poking the air with his cane, and sprawled in the sand at Prince's feet. A withered brown dummy stuffed into rags and flung overboard. He sat up, cocking his head. "Who's dere?" The lights from the Sea Breeze reflected off his cataracts; they looked like raw silver nuggets embedded in his skull.

"Me, John."

"Is dat you, Mr. Prince? Well, God bless you!" John patted the sand, feeling for his cane, then clutched it and pointed out to sea. "Look, Mr. Prince. Dere where de *Miss Faye* go turtlin' off to de Chinchorro Bank."

Prince saw the riding lights moving toward the horizon, the indigo light rocking on the masthead, then wondered how in the hell. . . . The indigo light swooped at him, darting across miles of wind and water in an instant, into his eyes. His vision went purple, normalized, purpled again, as if the thing were a police flasher going around and around in his head.

And it was cold.

Searing, immobilizing cold.

"Ain't dis a fine night, Mr. Prince? No matter how blind a mon gets, he can recognize a fine night!"

With a tremendous effort Prince clawed at the sand, but old John continued talking.

"Dey say de island take hold of a mon. Now dat hold be gentle 'cause de island bear no ill against dem dat dwell upon it in de lawful way. But dose dat lords it over de island, comes a night dere rule is done."

Prince wanted badly to scream because that might release the cold trapped inside him; but he could not even strain. The cold possessed him. He yearned after John's words, not listening but stretching out toward them with his wish. They issued from the soft tropic air like the ends of warm brown ropes dangling just beyond his frozen grasp.

"Dis island poor! And de people fools! But I know you hear de sayin' dat even de sick dog gots teeth. Well, dis island gots teeth dat grows down to de center of things. De Carib say dat dere's a spirit from before de back time locked into de island's root, and de Baptist say dat de island be a fountainhead of de Holy Spirit. But no matter what de truth, de people have each been granted a portion of dat spirit. And dat spirit legion now!"

The light behind Prince's eyes whirled so fast he could no longer distinguish periods of normal vision, and everything he saw had a purplish cast. He heard his entire agony as a tiny, scratchy sound deep in his throat. He toppled on his side and saw out over the bumpy sand, out to a point of land where wild palms, in silhouette against a vivid purple sky, shook their fronds like plumed African dancers, writhing up, ecstatic.

"Dat spirit have drove off de English! And one day it will drive de Sponnish home! It slow, but it certain. And dat is why we celebrate dis night. . . . 'Cause on dis very night all dose not of de spirit and de law must come to judgment."

John's shoes scraped on the sand.

"Well, I'll be along now, Mr. Prince. God bless you."

Even when his head had cleared and the cold dissipated, Prince couldn't work it out. If Jerry Steedly smoked this stuff all the time, then *he* must be having an abnormal reaction. A flashback. The thing to do would be to overpower the drug with depressants. But how could old John have seen the turtling boat? Maybe it never happened? Maybe the coral simply twitched reality a bit, and everything since Ghetto Liquors had been a real-life fantasy of amazing exactitude. He finished his drink, had another, steadied himself, and then hailed the jitney when it passed on its way to town, on *his* way to see Rudy and Jubert and George.

Vengeance would be the best antidote of all for this black sediment within him.

Independence Day.

The shanties dripped with colored lights, and the dirt road glowed orange, crisscrossed by dancers and drunks who collided and fell. Skinny black casualties lay underneath the shanties, striped by light shining down through the floorboards. Young women danced in the bar windows; older, fatter women, their hair in turbans, glowering, stood beside tubs of lobster salad and tables laden with coconut bread and pastries. The night was raucous, blaring, hooting, shouting. All the dogs were in hiding.

Prince stuffed himself on the rich food, drank, and then went from bar to bar asking questions of men who pawed his shirt, rolled their eyes, and passed out for an answer. He could find no trace of Rudy or George, but he tracked Jubert down in a shanty bar whose sole designation as a bar was a cardboard sign, tacked on a palm tree beside it, which read FRENLY CLUB NO RIOT. Prince lured him outside with the promise of marijuana, and Jubert, stupidly drunk, followed to a clearing behind the bar where dirt trails crossed, a patch of ground bounded by two other shanties and banana trees. Prince smiled a smile of good fellowship, kicked him in the groin and the stomach, and broke Jubert's jaw with the heel of his hand.

"Short cut draw blood," said Prince. "Ain't dat right. You don't trick with de mighty."

He nudged Jubert's jaw with his toe.

Jubert groaned; blood welled from his mouth, puddling black in the moonlight.

"Come back at me and I'll kill you," said Prince.

He sat cross-legged beside Jubert. Moonlight saturated the clearing, and the tattered banana leaves seemed made of gray-green silk. Their trunks showed bone white. A plastic curtain in a shanty window glowed with mystic roses, lit by the oil lamp inside. Jukebox reggae chip-chipped at the soft night, distant laughter. . . .

He let the clearing come together around him. The moon brightened as though a film had washed from its face; the light tingled his shoulders. Everything—shanties, palms, banana trees, and bushes—sharpened, loomed, grew more encircling. He felt a measure of hilarity on seeing himself as he'd been in the jungle of Lang Biang, freakishly alert. It conjured up cli-chéd movie images. Prince, the veteran maddened by memory and distanced by trauma, compelled to relive his nightmares and hunt down these measly offenders in the derelict town. The violent American legend. The war-torn Prince of the cin-ema. He chuckled. His life, he knew, was devoid of such the-matic material.

He was free of compulsion.

Thousands of tiny shake-hands lizards were slithering under the banana trees, running over the sandy soil on their hind legs. He could see the disturbance in the weeds. A hibiscus blossom nodded from behind a shanty, an exotic lure dangling out of the darkness, and the shadows beneath the palms were deep and restless . . . not like the shadows in Lang Biang, still and green, high in the vaulted trees. Spirits had lived in those trees, so the stories said, demon-things with iron beaks who'd chew your soul into rags. Once he had shot one. It had been (they told him) only a large fruit bat, deranged, probably by some chemical poison, driven to fly at him in broad daylight. But *he* had seen a demon with an iron beak sail from a green shadow and fired. Nearly every round must have hit, because all they'd found had been scraps of bloody, leathery wing. Afterward they called him Deadeye and described how he'd bounced the bat along through the air with bursts of unbeliev-able accuracy.

He wasn't afraid of spirits.

"How you doin', Jube?" Prince asked.

Jubert was staring at him, wide-eyed.

Clouds swept across the moon, and the clearing went dark, then brightened.

"Dere's big vultures up dere, Jubert, flyin' cross de moon and screamin' your name."

Prince was a little afraid of the drug, but less afraid of the islanders—nowhere near as afraid as Jubert was of him right now. Prince had been much more afraid, had cried and soiled himself; but he'd always emptied his gun into the shadows and stayed stoned and alert for eleven months. Fear, he'd learned, had its own continuum of right actions. He could handle it.

Jubert made a gurgling noise.

"Got a question, Jube?" Prince leaned over, solicitous.

A sudden gust of wind sent a dead frond crashing down, and the sound scared Jubert. He tried to lift his head and passed out from the pain.

Somebody shouted, "Listen to dat boy sing! Oh, he slick, mon!" and turned up the jukebox. The tinny music broke Prince's mood. Everything looked scattered. The moonlight showed the grime and slovenliness of the place, the sprinkles of chicken droppings and the empty crab shells. He'd lost most of his enthusiasm for hunting down Rudy and George, and he decided to head for Maud Price's place, the Golden Dream. Sooner or later everyone stopped in at the Dream. It was the island's gambling center, and because it was an anomaly among the shanties, with their two stucco rooms lit by naked light bulbs, drinking there conferred a certain prestige.

He thought about telling them in the bar about Jubert, but decided no and left him for someone else to rob.

Rudy and George hadn't been in, said Maud, smacking down a bottle on the counter. Bar flies buzzed up from the spills and orbited her like haywire electrons. Then she went back to chopping fish heads, scaling and filleting them. Monstrously fat and jet black, bloody smears on her white dress. The record player at her elbow ground out warped Freddy Fender tunes.

Prince spotted Jerry Steedly (who didn't seem glad to see Prince) sitting at a table along the wall, joined him, and told him about the black coral.

"Everybody sees the same things," said Steedly, uninterested. "The reef, the fires . . ."

"What about flashbacks? Is that typical?"

"It happens. I wouldn't worry about it." Steedly checked his watch. He was in his forties, fifteen years older than Rita, a gangly Arkansas hick whose brush-cut red hair was going gray.

"I'm not worried," said Prince. "It was fine except for the fires or whatever they were. I thought they were copepods at first, but I guess they were just part of the trip."

"The islanders think they're spirits." Steedly glanced toward the door, nervous, then looked at Prince, dead serious, as if he were considering a deep question. He kicked back in his chair and leaned against the wall, decided, half smiling. "Know what I think they are? Aliens."

Prince made a show of staring goggle-eyed, gave a dumb laugh, and drank.

"No kiddin', Neal. Parasites. Actually, copepods might not be so far off. They're not intelligent. They're reef dwellers from the next continuum over. The coral opens the perceptual gates or lets them see the gates that are already there, and . . . Wham! They latch right on. They induce a low-grade telepathy in human hosts. Among other things."

Steedly scraped back his chair and pointed at the adjoining room where people thronged, waving cards and money, shouting, losers threatening winners. "I gotta go lose some money, Neal. You take it easy."

"Are you trying to mess me around?" Prince asked with mild incredulity.

"Nope. It's just a theory of mine. They exhibit colonial behavior like a lot of small crustaceans. But they *may* be spirits. Maybe spirits aren't anything more than vague animal things slopping over from another world and setting their hooks in your soul, infecting you, dwelling in you. Who knows? I wouldn't worry about it, though."

He walked away.

"Say hi to Rita for me," Prince called.

Steedly turned, struggling with himself, but he smiled.

"Hey, Neal," he said. "It's not over."

. . .

Prince nursed his rum, cocked an eye toward the door whenever anyone entered (the place was rapidly filling), and watched Maud gutting fish. A light-bulb sun dangled inches over her head, and he imagined her with a necklace of skeletons, reaching down into a bucketful of little silver-scaled men. The thunk of her knife punctuated the babble around him. He drowsed. Idly, he began listening to the conversation of three men at the next table, resting his head against the wall. If he nodded out, Maud would wake him.

"De mon ain't got good sense, always spittin' and fumin'!"

"He harsh, mon! Dere's no denyin'."

"Harsh? De mon worse den dat. Now de way Arlie tell it . . ."

Arlie? He wondered if they meant Arlie Brooks, who tended bar at the Sea Breeze.

". . . dat Mary Ebanks bled to death. . . ."

"Dey say dat de stain where she bled still shine at night on de floor of de Sea Breeze!"

Maybe it was Arlie.

"Dat be fool duppy talk, mon!"

"Well, never mind dat! *He* never shot her. Dat was Eusebio Conejo from over at Sandy Bar. But de mon might have saved her with his knowledge of wounds if he had not run off at de gunshot!"

"Ain't he de one dat stole dat gold cross from old Byrum Waters?"

"Correct! Told him dat de gold have gone bad and dass why it so black. And Byrum, not mindful of de ways of gold, didn't know dat was only tarnish!"

"Dat was de treasure lost by old Meachem? Am I right?"

"Correct! De Carib watched him bury it, and when he gone dey move it to de hills. And den when Byrum found it he told his American friend. Hah! And dat friend become a wealthy mon and old Byrum go to de ground wrapped in a blanket!"

That was *his* cross! That was *him* they were talking about! Outraged, Prince came up out of his stupor and opened his eyes.

Then he sat very still.

The music, the shouts from the back room, the conversations had died, been sheared away without the least whisper or cough remaining, and the room had gone black . . . except the ceiling. And it brimmed, seethed with purple fire: swirls of indigo and royal purple and violet-white, a pattern similar to the enclosed waters of the reef, as if it, too, signaled varying depths and bottoms; incandescent-looking, though, a rectangle of violent, shifting light, like a corpse's first glimpse of sky when his coffin is opened up in hell . . . and cold.

Prince ducked, expecting they would swoop at him, pin him against the freezing darkness. But they did not. One by one the fires separated from the blazing ceiling and flowed down over the walls, settling on the creases and edges of things, outlining them in points of flickering radiance. Their procession seemed almost ordered, stately, and Prince thought of a congregation filing into their allotted pews preparatory to some great function. They illuminated the rumples in ragged shirts (and the ragged ends, as well) and the wrinkles in faces. They traced the shapes of glasses, bottles, tables, spiderwebs, the electric fan, light bulbs and their cords. They glowed nebular in the liquor, they became the smoldering ends of cigarettes, they mapped the spills on the counter and turned them into miniature phosphorescent seas. And when they had all taken their places, their design complete, Prince sat dumbstruck in the midst of an incredibly detailed constellation, one composed of ghostly purple stars against an ebony sky—the constellation of a tropic barroom, of Maud Price's Golden Dream.

He laughed, a venturing laugh; it sounded forced even to his own ears. There was no door, he noticed, no window outlined in purple fire. He touched the wall behind him for reassurance and jerked his hand away: it was freezing. Nothing moved other than the flickering, no sound. The blackness held him fast to his chair as though it were a swamp sucking him under.

"I hurt bad, mon! It hurt inside my head!" A bleary and distressed voice. Jubert's voice!

"Mon, I hurt you bad myself and you slip me de black coral!"

"Dass de truth!"

"De mon had de right to take action!"

Other voices tumbled forth in argument, most of them drunken, sodden, and seeming to issue from starry brooms and chairs and glassware. Many of them took his side in the matter of Jubert's beating—*that,* he realized, was the topic under discussion. And he was winning! But still other voices blurted out, accusing him.

"He took dat fat Yankee tourist down to print old Mrs. Ebanks with her camera, and Mrs. Ebanks shamed by it!"

"No, mon! I not dat shamed! Let not dat be against him!"

"He pay me for de three barracuda and take de five!"

"He knock me down when I tell him how he favor dat cousin of mine dat live in Ceiba!"

"He beat me. . . ."

"He cheat me. . . ."

"He curse me. . . ."

The voices argued points of accuracy, mitigating circumstances, and accused each other of exaggeration. Their logic was faulty and stupidly conceived. It had the feel of malicious, drunken gossip, as if a group of islanders were loitering on some dusty street and disputing the truth of a tall tale. But in this case it was *his* tale they disputed; for though Prince did not recognize all the voices, he did recognize his crimes, his prideful excesses, his slurs and petty slights. Had it not been so cold, he might have been amused, because the general consensus appeared to be that he was no worse or better than any of his accusers and therefore merited no outrageous judgment.

But then a wheezy voice, the expression of a dulled, ancient sensibility, said, "I found dat gold cross in a cave up on Hermit's Ridge. . . ."

Prince panicked, sprang for the door, forgetting there was none, scrabbled at the stony surface, fell, and crawled along, probing for an exit. Byrum's voice harrowed him.

"And I come to him and say, 'Mr. Prince, I got dis terrible pain in de chest. Can't you give me money? I know dat your money come from meltin' down de gold cross.' And he say, 'Byrum, I don't give jack-shit about your chest!' And den he show me de door!"

Prince collapsed in a corner, eyes fixed on the starry record player from which the old man's voice came. No one argued against Byrum. When he had finished there was a silence.

"The bastard's been sleeping with my wife," said a twangy American voice.

"Jerry!" Prince yelled. "Where are you?"

A constellate bottle of rum was the source of the voice. "Right here, you son . . ."

"Dere's to be no talkin' with de mon before judgment!"

"Dass right! De spirits make dat clear!"

"These damn things aren't spirits. . . ."

"If dey ain't, den why Byrum Waters in de Dream tonight?"

"De mon can't hear de voices of de spirits 'cause he not *of* de island hisself!"

"Byrum's not here! I've told you people so many times I'm sick of it! These things induce telepathy in humans. That means you can hear each others' minds, that your thoughts resonate and amplify each others', maybe even tap into some kind of collective unconscious. That's how. . . ."

"I believe somebody done pelt a rock at de mon's head! He crazy!"

The matter of the purple fires was tabled, and the voices discussed Prince's affair with Rita Steedly ("Dere's no proof de mon been messin' with your wife!"), reaching a majority opinion of guilty on what seemed to Prince shaky evidence indeed. The chill in the room had begun to affect him, and though he noticed that unfamiliar voices had joined the dialogue— British voices whose speech was laden with archaisms, guttural Carib voices—he did not wonder at them. He was far more concerned by the trembling of his muscles and the slow, flabby rhythm of his heart; he hugged his knees and buried his head in them for warmth. And so he hardly registered the verdict announced in Byrum Waters's cracked whisper ("De island never cast you out, Mr. Prince") nor did he even hear the resultant argument ("Dat all you goin' to tell him?" "De mon have a right to hear his fate!") except as a stupid hypnotic round that dazed him further and increased the chill, then turned into ghostly laughter. And he did not notice for quite a while that

the chill had lessened, that the light filtering through his lids
was yellow, and that the laughter was not voiced by spectral
fires but by ragged drunks packed closely around him, sweating, howling, and slopping their drinks on his feet. Their gap-
toothed mouths opened wider and wider in his dimming sight,
as if he were falling into the jaws of ancient animals who had
waited in their jungle centuries for such as he. Fat moths
danced around them in the air.

Prince pushed feebly at the floor, trying to stand. They
laughed louder, and he felt his own lips twitch in a smile, an
involuntary reaction to all the good humor in the room.

"Oh, damn!" Maud slammed the flat of her hand down on
the counter, starting up the bar flies and hiccuping Freddy
Fender's wail. Her smile was fierce and malefic. "How you like
dat, Mr. Prince? You one of us now!"

He must've passed out. They must've dumped him in the street
like a sack of manure! His head swam as he pulled himself up
by the window ledge; his hip pocket clinked on the stucco
wall . . . rum bottle. He fumbled it out, swallowed, gagged,
but felt it strengthen him. The town was dead, lightless, and
winded. He reeled against the doorway of the Dream and saw
the moldering shanties swing down beneath running banks of
moonlit cloud. Peaked and eerie, witches' hats, the sharp jut of
folded black wings. He couldn't think.

Dizzy, he staggered between the shanties and fell on all fours
in the shallows, then soaked his head in the wavelets lapping
the shingle. There were slippery things under his hands. No
telling what . . . hog guts, kelp. He sat on a piling and let the
wind shiver him and straighten him out. Home. Better than
fighting off the rabid dog at the Hotel Captain Henry, better
than passing out again right here. Two and a half miles across
island, no more than an hour even in his condition. But watch
out for the purple fires! He laughed. The silence gulped it up.
If this were just the drug doing tricks . . . God! You could make
a fortune selling it in the States.

"You scrapes off de color and dass what you smokes," he
sang, calypso style. "De black coral takes, boom-boom, just
one toke."

He giggled. But what the hell *were* those purple fires?

Duppies? Aliens? How 'bout the purple souls of the niggers? The niggers' stinging purple souls!

He took another drink. "Better ration it, pilgrim," he said to the dark road in his best John Wayne. "Or you'll never reach the fort alive!"

And like John Wayne, he'd be back, he'd chew out the bullet with his teeth and brand himself clean with a red-hot knife and blow holes in the bad guys.

Oh, yeah!

But suppose they were spirits? Aliens? Not hallucinations? So what!

"I one of dem, now!" he shouted.

He breezed the first two miles. The road wound through the brush-covered hills at an easy grade. Stars shone in the west, but the moon had gone behind the clouds and the darkness was as thick as mud. He wished he'd brought his flashlight. . . . That had been the first thing that had attracted him to the island: how the people carried flashlights to show their paths in the hills, along the beaches, in the towns after the generators had been shut down. And when an ignorant, flashlightless stranger came by, they'd shine a path from your feet to theirs and ask, "How de night?"

"Beautiful," he'd replied; or, "Fine, just fine." And it *had* been. He'd loved everything about the island—the stories, the musical cadences of island speech, the sea-grape trees with their funny round leathery leaves, and the glowing, many-colored sea. He'd seen that the island operated along an ingenious and flexible principle, one capable of accommodating any contrary and eventually absorbing it through a process of calm acceptance. He'd envied the islanders their peaceful, unhurried lives. But that had been before Vietnam. During the war something inside him had gone irreversibly stone-cold sober, screwed up his natural high, and when he returned their idyllic lives had seemed despicable, listless, a bacterial culture shifting on its slide.

Every now and then he saw the peak of a thatched roof in silhouette against the stars, strands of barbed wire hemming in a few acres of scrub and bananas. He stayed dead center in the road, away from the deepest shadow, sang old Stones and Dylan, and fueled himself with hits of rum. It had been a good decision to head back, because a norther was definitely brewing. The wind rushed cold in his face, spitting rain. Storms blew up quickly at this time of year, but he could make it home and secure his house before the worst of the rains.

Something crashed in the brush. Prince jumped away from the sound, looking wildly about for the danger. The tufted hillock on his right suddenly sprouted horns against the starlight and charged at him, bellowing, passing so raw and close that he could hear the breath articulated in the huge red throat. Christ! It had sounded more like a demon's bellow than a cow's, which it was. Prince lost his balance and sprawled in the dirt, shaking. The damned thing lowed again, crunching off through a thicket. He started to get up. But the rum, the adrenaline, all the poisons of his day-long exertions roiled around in him, and his stomach emptied, spewing out liquor and lobster salad and coconut bread. Afterward he felt better—weaker, yet not on the verge of as great a weakness as before. He tore off his fouled shirt and slung it into a bush.

The bush was a blaze of purple fires.

They hung on twig ends and leaf tips and marked the twisting course of branches, outlining them as they had done at Maud's. But at the center of this tracery the fires clustered together in a globe—a wicked violet-white sun extruding spidery filaments and generating forked, leafy electricities.

Prince backed away. The fires flickered in the bush, unmoving. Maybe the drug had finished its run, maybe now that he'd burned most of it out the fires could no longer affect him as they had previously. But then a cold, cold prickle shifted along his spine and he knew—oh, God!—he knew for a certainty there were fires on his back, playing hide-and-seek where he could never find them. He beat at his shoulderblades, like a man putting out flames, and the cold stuck to his fingertips. He held them up before his eyes. They flickered, pulsing from indigo to violet-white. He shook them so hard that his joints cracked, but the fires spread over his hands, encasing his forearms in a lurid glare.

In blind panic Prince staggered off the road, fell, scrambled up, and ran, holding his glowing arms stiff out in front of him. He tumbled down an embankment and came to his feet, running. He saw that the fires had spread above his elbows and felt the chill margin inching upward. His arms lit the brush around him, as if they were the wavering beams of tinted flashlights. Vines whipped out of the dark, the lengths of a black serpent coiled everywhere, lashed into a frenzy by the purple light. Dead fronds clawed his face with sharp papery fingers. He was so afraid, so empty of everything but fear, that when a palm trunk loomed ahead he ran straight into it, embracing it with his shining arms.

There were hard fragments in his mouth, blood, more blood flowing into his eyes. He spat and probed his mouth, wincing as he touched the torn gums. Three teeth missing, maybe four. He hugged the palm trunk and hauled himself up. This was the grove near his house! He could see the lights of St. Mark's Key between the trunks, white seas driving in over the reef. Leaning on the palms as he went, he made his way to the water's edge. The wind-driven rain slashed at his split forehead. Christ! It was swollen big as an onion! The wet sand sucked off one of his tennis shoes, but he left it.

He washed his mouth and forehead in the stinging saltwater, then slogged toward the house, fumbling for his key. Damn! It had been in his shirt. But it was all right. He'd built the house Hawaiian style, with wooden slats on every side to admit the breeze; it would be easy to break in. He could barely see the roof peak against the toiling darkness of the palms and the hills behind, and he banged his shins on the porch. Distant lightning flashed, and he found the stair and spotted the conch shell lying on the top step. He wrapped his hand inside it, punched a head-sized hole in the door slats, and leaned on the door, exhausted by the effort. He was just about to reach in for the latch when the darkness within—visible against the lesser darkness of night as a coil of dead, unshining emptiness—squeezed from the hole like black toothpaste and tried to encircle him.

Prince tottered backward off the porch and landed on his side; he dragged himself away a few feet, stopped, and looked up at the house. The blackness was growing out into the night, encysting him in a thicket of coral branches so dense that he could see between them only glints of the lightning bolts striking down beyond the reef. "Please," he said, lifting his hand in supplication. And something broke in him, some grimly held thing whose residue was tears. The wind's howl and the booming reef came as a single ominous vowel, roaring, rising in pitch.

The house seemed to inhale the blackness, to suck it slithering back inside, and for a moment Prince thought it was over. But then violet beams lanced from the open slats, as if the fuming heart of a reactor had been uncovered within. The beach bloomed in livid daylight—a no-man's-land littered with dead fish, half-buried conchs, rusted cans, and driftwood logs like the broken, corroded limbs of iron statues. Inky palms thrashed and shivered. Rotting coconuts cast shadows on the sand. And then the light swarmed up from the house, scattering into a myriad fiery splinters and settling on palm tops, on the prows of dinghies, on the reef, on tin roofs set among the palms, and on sea grape and cashew trees, where they burned. The ghosts of candles illuminating a sacred shore, haunting the dark interior of a church whose anthem was wind, whose litany was thunder, and upon whose walls feathered shadows leapt and lightnings crawled.

Prince got to his knees, watching, waiting, not really afraid any longer, but gone into fear. Like a sparrow in a serpent's gaze, he saw everything of his devourer, knew with great clarity that these *were* the island people, all of them who had ever lived, and that they *were* possessed of some otherworldly vitality—though whether spirit or alien or both, he could not determine—and that they had taken their accustomed places, their ritual stands. Byrum Waters hovering in the cashew tree he had planted as a boy; John Anderson McCrae flitting above the reef where he and his father had swung lanterns to lure ships in onto the rocks; Maud Price ghosting over the grave of her infant child hidden in the weeds behind a shanty. But then he doubted his knowledge and wondered if they were not telling him this, advising him of the island's consensus, for he heard the mutter of a vast conversation becoming distinct, outvoicing the wind.

He stood, searching for an avenue of escape, not in the least hopeful of finding one, but choosing to exercise a final option. Everywhere he turned the world pitched and tossed as if troubled by his sight, and only the flickering purple fires held constant. "Oh, my God!" he screamed, almost singing it in an ecstasy of fear, realizing that the precise moment for which they'd gathered had arrived.

As one, from every corner of the shore, they darted into his eyes.

Before the cold overcame him, Prince heard island voices in his head. They ranted ("Lessee how you rank with de spirit, now! Boog man!"). They instructed ("Best you not struggle against de spirit. Be more merciful dat way."). They insulted, rambled, and construed illogics. For a few seconds he tried to follow the thread of their discourse, thinking if he could understand and comply, then they might stop. But when he could not understand he clawed his face in frustration. The voices rose to a chorus, to a mob howling separately for his attention, then swelled into a roar greater than the wind's but equally single-minded and bent on his annihilation. He dropped onto his hands and knees, sensing the beginning of a terrifying dissolution, as if he were being poured out into a shimmering violet-red bowl. And he saw the film of fire coating his chest and arms, saw his own horrid glare reflected on the broken seashells and mucky sand, shifting from violet-red into violet-white and brightening, growing whiter and whiter until it became a white darkness in which he lost all track of being.

The bearded old man wandered into Meachem's Landing early Sunday morning after the storm. He stopped for a while beside the stone bench in the public square where the sentry, a man even older than himself, was leaning on his deer rifle, asleep. When the voices bubbled up in his thoughts—he pictured his thoughts as a soup with bubbles boiling up and popping, and the voices coming from the pops—and yammered at him ("No, no! Dat ain't de mon!" "Keep walkin', old fool!"). It was a chorus, a clamor that caused his head to throb; he continued on. The street was littered with palm husks and fronds and broken bottles buried in the mud that showed only their glittering edges. The voices warned him these were sharp and would cut him ("Make it hurtful like dem gashes on your face"), and he stepped around them. He wanted to do what they told him because . . . it just seemed the way of things.

The glint of a rain-filled pothole caught his eye, and he knelt by it, looking at his reflection. Bits of seaweed clung to his crispy gray hair, and he picked them out, laying them carefully in the mud. The pattern in which they lay seemed familiar. He drew a rectangle around them with his finger and it seemed even more familiar, but the voices told him to forget about it and keep going. One voice advised him to wash his cuts in the pothole. The water smelled bad, however, and other voices warned him away. They grew in number and volume, driving him along the street until he followed their instructions and sat down on the steps of a shanty painted all the colors of the rainbow. Footsteps sounded inside the shanty, and a black bald-headed man wearing shorts came out and stretched himself on the landing.

"Damn!" he said. "Just look what come home to us this mornin'. Hey, Lizabeth!"

A pretty woman joined him, yawning, and stopped mid-yawn when she saw the old man.

"Oh, Lord! Dat poor creature!"

She went back inside and reappeared shortly carrying a towel and a basin, squatted beside him, and began dabbing at his wounds. It seemed such a kind, a human thing to be so treated, and the old man kissed her soapy fingers.

"De mon a caution!" Lizabeth gave him a playful smack. "I know dass why he in such a state. See de way de skin's all tore on his forehead dere? Must be he been fightin' with de conchs over some other mon's woman."

"Could be," said the bald man. "How 'bout that? You a fool for the ladies?"

The old man nodded. He heard a chorus of affirming voices. ("Oh, dass it!" "De mon cootin' and cootin' until he half-crazy, den he coot with de *wrong* woman!" "Must have been grazed with de conch and left for dead.")

"Lord, yes!" said Lizabeth. "Dis mon goin' to trouble all de ladies, goin' to be kissin' after dem and huggin' dem. . . ."

"Can't you talk?" asked the bald man.

He thought he could, but there were so many voices, so many words to choose from . . . maybe later. No.

"Well, I guess we'd better get you a name. How 'bout Bill? I got a good friend up in Boston's named Bill."

That suited the old man fine. He liked being associated with the bald man's good friend.

"Tell you what, Bill." The bald man reached inside the door and handed him a broom. "You sweep off the steps and pick up what you see needs pickin', and we'll pass you out some beans and bread after a while. How's that sound?"

It sounded *good,* and Bill began sweeping at once, taking meticulous care with each step. The voices died to a murmurous purr in his thoughts. He beat the broom against the pilings, and dust fell onto it from the floorboards; he beat it until no more would fall. He was happy to be among people again because. . . . ("Don't be thinkin' 'bout the back time, mon! Dat all gone." "You just get on with your clean dere, Bill. Everything goin' to work out in de end." "Dass it, mon! You goin' to clean dis whole town before you through!" "Don't vex with de mon! He doin' his work!") And he was! He picked up everything within fifty feet of the shanty and chased off a ghost crab, smoothing over the delicate slashes its legs made in the sand.

By the time Bill had cleaned for a half hour he felt so at home, so content and enwrapped in his place and purpose, that when the old woman next door came out to toss her slops into the street, he scampered up her stairs, threw his arms around her, and kissed her full on the mouth. Then he stood grinning, at attention with his broom.

Startled at first, the woman put her hands on her hips and looked him up and down, shaking her head in dismay.

"My God," she said sorrowfully. "Dis de best we can do for dis poor mon? Dis de best thing de island can make of itself?"

Bill didn't understand. The voices chattered, irritated; they didn't seem angry at him, though, and he kept on smiling. Once again the woman shook her head and sighed, but after a few seconds Bill's smile encouraged her to smile in return.

"I guess if dis de worst of it," she said, "den better must come." She patted Bill on the shoulder and turned to the door. "Everybody!" she called. "Quickly now! Come see dis lovin' soul dat de storm have let fall on Rudy Welcomes's door!"

The End of
Life as We Know It

What Lisa hated most about Mexico was the flies, and Richard said Yeah, the flies were bad, but it was the lousy attitude of the people that did him in, you know, the way the waiters ignored you and the taxi drivers sneered, the sour expressions of desk clerks—as if they were doing you a big favor by letting you stay in their fleabag hotels. All that. Lisa replied that she couldn't blame the people, because they were probably irritated by the flies; this set Richard to laughing, and though Lisa had not meant it to be funny, after a moment she joined in. They needed laughter. They had come to Mexico to Save Their Marriage, and things were not going well . . . except in bed, where things had always gone well. Lisa had never been less than ardent with Richard, even during her affair.

They were an attractive couple in their thirties, the sort to whom a healthy sex life seems an essential of style, a trendy accessory to pleasure like a Jacuzzi or a French food processor. She was a tall, fey-looking brunette with fair skin, an aerobically nurtured slimness, and a face that managed to express both sensuality and intelligence ("hooker eyes and Vassar bones," Richard had told her); he was lean from handball and weights, with an executive touch of gray in his black hair and the bland, firm-jawed handsomeness of a youthful anchorman. Once they had held to the illusion that they kept fit and beautiful for one another, but all their illusions had been tarnished and they no longer understood their reasons for maintaining them.

For a while they made a game of hating Mexico, pretending it was a new bond between them, striving to outdo each other in pointing out instances of filth and native insensitivity; finally they realized that what they hated most about the country was their own perceptions of it, and they headed south to Guatemala where—they had been informed—the atmosphere was conducive to romance. They were leery about the reports of guerrilla activity, but their informant had assured them that the dangers were overstated. He was a seasoned traveler, an elderly Englishman who had spent his last twelve winters in Central America; Richard thought he was colorful, a Graham Greene character, whereas Lisa described him in her journal as "a deracinated old fag."

"You mustn't miss Lake Atitlán," he'd told them. "It's absolutely breathtaking. Revolution there is an aesthetic impossibility."

Before boarding the plane Richard bought the latest *Miami Herald,* and he entertained himself during the flight by bemoaning the decline of Western civilization. It was his conviction that the United States was becoming part of the Third World and that their grandchildren would inhabit a mildly poisoned earth and endure lives of back-breaking drudgery under an increasingly Orwellian government. Though this conviction was hardly startling, it being evident from the newspaper that such a world was close upon them, Lisa accorded his viewpoint the status of wisdom; in fact, she had relegated wisdom in general to be his preserve, staking claim herself to the traditional feminine precincts of soulfulness and caring. Sometimes back in Connecticut, while teaching her art class at the Y or manning the telephones for PBS or Greenpeace or whatever cause had enlisted her soulfulness, looking around at the other women, all—like her—expensively kept and hopeless and with an eye cocked for the least glimmer of excitement, then she would see how marriage had decreased her wattage; and yet, though she had fallen in love with another man, she had clung to the marriage for almost a year thereafter, unable to escape the fear that this was the best she could hope for, that no matter what steps she took to change her situation, her life would always be ruled by a canon of mediocrity. That she had recently stopped clinging did not signal a slackening of fear, only that her fingers were slipping, her energy no longer sufficient to maintain a good grip.

As the plane came down into Guatemala City, passing over rumpled green hills dotted with shacks whose colors looked deceptively bright and cheerful from a height, Richard began talking about his various investments, saying he was glad he'd bought this and that, because things were getting worse every day. "The shitstorm's a-comin', babe," he said, patting her knee. "But we're gonna be awright." It annoyed Lisa no end that whenever he was feeling particularly accomplished his language became countrified, and she only shrugged in response.

After clearing customs they rented a car and drove to Panajachel, a village on the shores of Lake Atitlán. There was a fancy hotel on the shore, but in the spirit of "roughing it" Richard insisted they stay at a cheaper place on the edge of town—an old green stucco building with red trim and an arched entranceway and a courtyard choked with ferns; it catered to what he called "the bleeding-ear set," a reference to the loud rock 'n' roll that blasted from the windows. The other guests were mostly college-age vacationers, a mixture of French and Scandinavians and Americans, and as soon as they had unpacked, Lisa changed into jeans and a work shirt so she would fit in among them. They ate dinner in the hotel dining room, which was cramped and furnished with red wooden tables and chairs and had the menu painted on the wall in English and Spanish. Richard appeared to be enjoying himself; he was relaxed, and his speech was peppered with slang that he hadn't used in almost a decade. Lisa liked listening to the glib chatter around them, talk of dope and how the people treat you in Huehuetenango and watch out if you're goin' to Bogotá, man, 'cause they got packs of street kids will pick you clean. . . ." These conversations reminded her of the world in which she had traveled at Vassar before Richard had snatched her up during her junior year. He had been just back from Vietnam, a medic, full of anguish at the horrors he had seen, yet strong for having seen them; he had seemed to her a source of strength, a shining knight, a rescuer. After the wedding, though, she had not been able to recall why she had wanted to be rescued; she thought now that she had derived some cheap thrill from his aura of recent violence and had applied it to herself out of a romantic need to feel imperiled.

They lingered over dinner, watching the younger guests drift off into the evening and being watched themselves—at least in Lisa's case—by a fortyish Guatemalan man with a pencil-line mustache, a dark suit, and patent-leather hair. He stared at her as he chewed, ducking his eyes each time he speared a fresh bite, then resuming his stare. Ordinarily Lisa would have been irritated, but she found the man's conspicuous anonymity appealing and she adopted a flirtatious air, laughing too loudly and fluttering her hands, in hopes that she was frustrating him.

"His name's Raoul," said Richard. "He's a white slaver in the employ of the Generalísimo, and he's been commissioned to bring in a new *gringa* for the harem."

"He's somebody's uncle," said Lisa. "Here to settle a family dispute. He's married to a dumpy Indian woman, has seven kids, and he's wearing his only suit to impress the Americans."

"God, you're a romantic!" Richard sipped his coffee, made a face, and set it down.

Lisa bit back a sarcastic reply. "I think he's very romantic. Let's say he's staring at me because he wants me. If that's true, right now he's probably thinking how to do you in, or maybe wondering if he could trade you his truck, his means of livelihood, for a night with me. That's real romance. Passionate stupidity and bloody consequences."

"I guess," said Richard, unhappy with the definition; he took another sip of coffee and changed the subject.

At sunset they walked down to the lake. The village was charming enough—the streets cobbled, the houses whitewashed and roofed with tile; but the rows of tourist shops and the American voices acted to dispel the charm. The lake, however, was beautiful. Ringed by three volcanoes, bordered by palms, Indians poling canoes toward scatters of light on the far shore. The water was lacquered with vivid crimson and yellow reflection, and silhouetted against an equally vivid sky, the palms and volcanic cones gave the place the look of a prehistoric landscape. As they stood at the end of a wooden pier, Richard drew her into a kiss and she felt again the explosive dizziness of their first kisses; yet she knew it was a sham, a false magic born of geography and their own contrivance. They could keep traveling, keep filling their days with exotic sights, lacquering their lives with reflection, but when they stopped they would discover that they had merely been preserving the forms of the marriage. There was no remedy for their dissolution.

Roosters crowing waked her to gray dawn light. She remembered a dream about a faceless lover, and she stretched and rolled onto her side. Richard was sitting at the window, wearing jeans and a T-shirt; he glanced at her, then turned his gaze to the window, to the sight of a pale green volcano wreathed in mist. "It's not working," he said, and when she failed to respond, still half-asleep, he buried his face in his hands, muffling his voice. "I can't make it without you, babe."

She had dreaded this moment, but there was no reason to put it off. "That's the problem," she said. "You used to be able to." She plumped the pillows and leaned back against them.

He looked up, baffled. "What do you mean?"

"Why should *I* have to explain it? You know it as well as I do. We weaken each other, we exhaust each other, we depress each other." She lowered her eyes, not wanting to see his face. "Maybe it's not even us. Sometimes I think marriage is this big pasty spell of cakes and veils that shrivels everything it touches."

"Lisa, you know there isn't anything I wouldn't. . . ."

"What? What'll you do?" Angrily, she wadded the sheet. "I don't understand how we've managed to hurt each other so much. If I did, I'd try to fix it. But there's nothing left to do. Not together, anyway."

He let out a long sigh—the sigh of a man who has just finished defusing a bomb and can allow himself to breathe again.
"It's him, right? You still want to be with him."

It angered her that he would never say the name, as if the
name were what counted. "No," she said stiffly. "It's not *him*."

"But you still love him."

"That's not the point! I still love you, but love. . . ." She drew
up her legs and rested her forehead on her knees. "Christ,
Richard. I don't know what more to tell you. I've said it all a
hundred times."

"Maybe," he said softly, "maybe this discussion is prema-
ture."

"Oh, Richard!"

"No, really. Let's go on with the trip."

"Where, next? The Mountains of the Moon? Brazil? It
won't change anything."

"You can't be sure of that!" He came toward the bed, his face
knitted into lines of despair. "We'll just stay a few more days.
We'll visit the villages on the other side of the lake, where they
do the weaving."

"Why, Richard? God, I don't even understand why you still
want me. . . ."

"Please, Lisa. Please. After eleven years you can try for a few
more days."

"All right," she said, weary of hurting him. "A few days."

"And you'll try?"

I've always tried, she wanted to say; but then, wondering if
it were true, as true as it should be, she merely said, "Yes."

The motor launch that ran back and forth across the lake between Panajachel and San Augustín had seating room for fifteen, and nine of those places were occupied by Germans,
apparently members of a family—kids, two sets of parents,
and a pair of portly red-cheeked grandparents. They reeked of
crudity and good health, and made Lisa feel refined by com-
parison. The young men snapped their wives' bra straps—
grandpa almost choked with laughter each time this
happened; the kids whined; the women were heavy and hairy-
legged. They spent the entire trip taking pictures of one an-

other. They must have understood English, because when Richard cracked a joke about them, they frowned and whispered and became standoffish. Lisa and Richard moved to the stern, a superficial union imposed, and watched the shore glide past. Though it was still early, the sun reflected a dynamited white glare on the water; in the daylight the volcanoes looked depressingly real, their slopes covered by patchy grass and scrub and stunted palms.

San Augustín was situated at the base of the largest volcano, and was probably like what Panajachel had been before tourism. Weeds grew between the cobblestones, the whitewash was flaked away in places, and grimy, naked toddlers sat in the doorways, chewing sugarcane and drooling. Inside the houses it was the fourteenth century. Packed dirt floors, iron cauldrons suspended over fires, chickens pecking and pigs asleep. Gnomish old Indian women worked at handlooms, turning out strange tapestries—as for example a design of black cranelike birds against a backdrop of purple sky and green trees, the image repeated over and over—and bolts of dress material, fabric that on first impression seemed to be of a hundred colors, all in perfect harmony. Lisa wanted to be sad for the women, to sympathize with their poverty and particular female plight, and to some extent she managed it; but the women were uncomplaining and appeared reasonably content and their weaving was better work than she had ever done, even when she had been serious about art. She bought several yards of the material, tried to strike up a conversation with one of the women, who spoke neither English nor Spanish, and then they returned to the dock, to the village's only bar-restaurant—a place right out of a spaghetti western, with a hitching rail in front and skinned sapling trunks propping up the porch roof and a handful of young long-haired American men standing along the bar, having an early-morning beer. "Holy marijuana!" said Richard, winking. "Hippies! I wondered where they'd gone." They took a table by the rear window so they could see the slopes of the volcano. The scarred varnish of the table was dazzled by sunlight; flies buzzed against the heated panes.

"So what do you think?" Richard squinted against the glare.

"I thought we were going to give it a few days," she said testily.

"Jesus, Lisa! I meant what do you think about the weaving." He adopted a pained expression.

"I'm sorry." She touched his hand, and he shook his head ruefully. "It's beautiful . . . I mean the weaving's beautiful. Oh God, Richard. I don't intend to be so awkward."

"Forget it." He stared out the window, deadpan, as if he were giving serious consideration to climbing the volcano, sizing up the problems involved. "What did you think of it?"

"It was beautiful," she said flatly. The buzzing of the flies intensified, and she had the notion that they were telling her to try harder. "I know it's corny to say, but watching her work. . . . What was her name?"

"Expectación."

"Oh, right. Well, watching her I got the feeling I was watching something magical, something that went on and on. . . ." She trailed off, feeling foolish at having to legitimize with conversation what had been a momentary whimsy; but she could think of nothing else to say. "Something that went on forever," she continued. "With different hands, of course, but always that something the same. And the weavers, while they had their own lives and problems, that was less important than what they were doing. You know, like the generations of weavers were weaving something through time as well as space. A long, woven magic." She laughed, embarrassed.

"It's not corny. I know what you're talking about." He pushed back his chair and grinned. "How about I get us a couple of beers?"

"Okay," she said brightly, and smiled until his back was turned. He thought he had her now. That was his plan—to get her a little drunk, not drunk enough for a midday hangover, just enough to get her happy and energized, and then that afternoon they'd go for a ride to the next village, the next exotic attraction, and more drinks and dinner and a new hotel. He'd keep her whirling, an endless date, an infinitely prolonged seduction. She pictured the two of them as a pair of silhouetted dancers tangoing across the borders of map-colored countries. Whirling and whirling, and the thing was, the very sad thing was, that sooner or later, if he kept her whirling, she would lose her own momentum and be sucked into the spin, into that loving-the-spin-I'm-in-old-black-magic routine. Then final rinse. Final spin. Then the machine would stop and she'd be plastered to the side of the marriage like a wet blouse, needing a hand to lift her out. She should do what had to be done right now. Right this moment. Cause a scene, hit him. Whatever it took. Because if she didn't. . . . He *thunked* down a bottle of beer in front of her, and her smile twitched by reflex into place.

"Thanks," she said.

"Por nada." He delivered a gallant bow and sat down. "Listen . . ."

There was a clatter from outside, and through the door she saw a skinny bearded man tying a donkey to the hitching rail. He strode on in, dusting off his jeans cowboy-style, and ordered a beer. Richard turned to look and chuckled. The man was worth a chuckle. He might have been the Spirit of the Sixties, the Wild Hippie King. His hair was a ratty brown thatch hanging to his shoulders, and braided into it were long gray feathers that dangled still lower; his jeans were festooned with painted symbols, and there were streaks of what appeared to be green dye in his thicket of a beard. He noticed them staring, waved, and came toward them.

"Mind if I join you folks?" Before they could answer, he dropped into a chair. "I'm Dowdy. Believe it or not, that's a name, not a self-description." He smiled, and his blue eyes crinkled up. His features were sharp, thin to the point of being wizened. It was hard to tell his age because of the beard, but Lisa figured him for around thirty-five. Her first reaction had been to ask him to leave; the instant he had started talking, though, she had sensed a cheerful kind of sanity about him that intrigued her. "I live up yonder," he went on, gesturing at the volcano. "Been there goin' on four years."

"Inside the volcano?" Lisa meant it for a joke.

"Yep! Got me a little shack back in under the lip. Hot in the summer, freezin' in the winter, and none of the comforts of home. I got to bust my tail on Secretariat there"—he waved at the donkey—"just to haul water and supplies." In waving he must have caught a whiff of his underarm—he gave it an ostentatious sniff. "*And* to get me a bath. Hope I ain't too ripe for you folks." He chugged down a third of his beer. "So! How you like Guatemala?"

"Fine," said Richard. "Why do you live in a volcano?"

"Kinda peculiar, ain't it," said Dowdy by way of response; he turned to Lisa. "And how you like it here?"

"We haven't seen much," she said. "Just the lake."

"Oh, yeah? Well, it ain't so bad 'round here. They keep it nice for the tourists. But the rest of the country . . . whooeee! Violent?" Dowdy made a show of awed disbelief. "You got your death squads, your guerrillas, your secret police, not to mention your basic crazed killers. Hell, they even got a political party called the Party of Organized Violence. Bad dudes. They like to twist people's arms off. It ain't that they're evil, though. It's just the land's so full of blood and brimstone and Mayan weirdness, it fumes up and freaks 'em out. That's how come we got volcanoes. Safety valves to blow off the excess poison. But things are on the improve."

"Really?" said Richard, amused.

"Yes, indeed!" Dowdy tipped back in his chair, propping the beer bottle on his stomach; he had a little potbelly like that of a cartoon elf. "The whole world's changing. I s'pose y'all have noticed the way things are goin' to hell back in the States?"

Lisa could tell that the question had mined Richard's core of political pessimism, and he started to frame an answer, but Dowdy talked through him.

"That's part of the change," he said. "All them scientists say they figured out reasons for the violence and pollution and economic failure, but what them things really are is just the sound of consensus reality scrapin' contrary to the flow of the change. They ain't nothin' but symptoms of the real change, of everything comin' to an end."

Richard made silent speech with his eyes, indicating that it was time to leave.

"Now, now," said Dowdy, who had caught the signal.

"Don't get me wrong. I ain't talkin' Apocalypse, here. And I for sure ain't no Bible basher like them Mormons you see walkin' 'round the villages. Huh! Them suckers is so scared of life they travel in pairs so's they can keep each other from bein' corrupted. 'Watch it there, Billy! You're steppin' in some sin!'" Dowdy rolled his eyes to the ceiling in a parody of prayer. "'Sweet Jesus, gimme the strength to scrape this sin off my shoe!' Then off they go, purified, a couple of All-American haircuts with souls stuffed fulla white-bread gospel and crosses 'round their necks to keep off the vampire women. Shit!" He leaned forward, resting his elbows on the table. "But I digress. I got me a religion, all right. Not Jesus, though. I'll tell you 'bout it if you want, but I ain't gonna force it down your throat."

"Well," Richard began, but Lisa interrupted.

"We've got an hour until the boat," she said. "Does your religion have anything to do with your living in the volcano?"

"Sure does." Dowdy pulled a hand-rolled cigar from his shirt pocket, lit it, and blew out a plume of smoke that boiled into a bluish cloud against the windowpanes. "I used to smoke, drink"—he flourished his beer—"and I was a bear for the ladies. Praise God, religion ain't changed that none!" He laughed, and Lisa smiled at him. Whatever it was that had put Dowdy in such good spirits seemed to be contagious. "Actually," he said, "I wasn't a hell-raiser at all. I was a painfully shy little fella, come from backwoods Tennessee. Like my daddy'd say, town so small you could spit between the city-limits signs. Anyway, I was shy but I was smart, and with that combination it was a natural for me to end up in computers. Gave me someone I could feel comfortable talkin' to. After college I took a job designin' software out in Silicon Valley, and seven years later there I was. . . . Livin' in an apartment tract with no real friends, no pictures on the walls, and a buncha terminals. A real computer nerd. Wellsir! Somehow I got it in mind to take a vacation. I'd never had one. Guess I figured I'd just end up somewhere weird, sittin' in a room and thinkin' 'bout computers, so what was the point? But I was determined to do it this time, and I came to Panajachel. First few days I did what you folks probably been doin'. Wanderin', not meetin' anyone, buyin' a few geegaws. Then I caught the launch across the lake and ran into ol' Murciélago." He clucked his tongue against his teeth. "Man, I didn't know what to make of him at first. He was the oldest human bein' I'd ever seen. Looked centuries old. All hunched up, white-haired, as wrinkled as a walnut shell. He couldn't speak no English, just Cakchiquel, but he had this mestizo fella with him who did his interpretin', and it was through him I learned that Murciélago was a *brujo.*"

"A wizard," said Lisa, who had read Castaneda, to Richard, who hadn't.

"Yep," said Dowdy. "'Course I didn't believe it. Thought it was some kinda hustle. But he interested me, and I kept hangin' 'round just to see what he was up to. Well, one night he says to me—through the mestizo fella—'I like you,' he says. 'Ain't nothin' wrong with you that a little magic wouldn't cure. I'd be glad to make you a gift if you got no objections.' I said to myself, 'Oh-oh, here it comes.' But I reckoned it couldn't do me no harm to let him play his hand, and I told him to go ahead. So he does some singin' and rubs powder on my mouth and mutters and touches me, and that was it. 'You gonna be fine now,' he tells me. I felt sorta strange, but no finer than I had. Still, there wasn't any hustle, and that same night I realized that his magic was doin' its stuff. Confused the hell out of me, and the only thing I could think to do was to hike on up to the volcano, where he lived, and ask him about it. Murciélago was waitin' for me. The mestizo had gone, but he'd left a note explainin' the situation. Seems he'd learned all he could from Murciélago and had taken up his own post, and it was time the ol' man had a new apprentice. He told me how to cook for him, wished me luck, and said he'd be seein' me around." Dowdy twirled his cigar and watched smoke rings float up. "Been there ever since and ain't regretted it a day."

Richard was incredulous. "You gave up a job in Silicon Valley to become a sorcerer's apprentice?"

"That's right." Dowdy pulled at one of the feathers in his hair. "But I didn't give up nothin' real, Richard."

"How do you know my name?"

"People grow into their names, and if you know how to look for it, it's written everywhere on 'em. 'Bout half of magic is bein' able to see clear."

Richard snorted. "You read our names off the passenger manifest for the launch."

"I don't blame you for thinkin' that," said Dowdy. "It's hard to accept the existence of magic. But that ain't how it happened." He drained the dregs of his beer. "You were easy to read, but Lisa here was sorta hard 'cause she never liked her name. Ain't that so?"

Lisa nodded, surprised.

"Yeah, see when a person don't like their name it muddies up the writin', so to speak, and you gotta scour away a lotta half-formed names to see down to the actual one." Dowdy heaved a sigh and stood. "Time I'm takin' care of business, but tell you what! I'll bring ol' Murciélago down to the bar around seven o'clock, and you can check him out. You can catch the nine o'clock boat back. I know he'd like to meet you."

"*How* do you know?" asked Richard.

"It ain't my place to explain. Look here, Rich. I ain't gonna twist your arm, but if you go back to Panajachel you're just gonna wander 'round and maybe buy some garbage. If you stay, well, whether or not you believe Murciélago's a *brujo*, you'll be doin' somethin' out of the ordinary. Could be he'll give you a gift."

"What gift did he give you?" asked Lisa.

"The gift of gab," said Dowdy. "Surprised you ain't deduced that for yourself, Lisa, 'cause I can tell you're a perceptive soul. 'Course that was just part of the gift. The gift wrappin', as it were. It's like Murciélago says, a real gift ain't known by its name." He winked at her. "But it took pretty damn good, didn't it?"

As soon as Dowdy had gone, Richard asked Lisa if she wanted a last look at the weaving before heading back, but she told him she would like to meet Murciélago. He argued briefly, then acquiesced. She knew what he was thinking. He had no interest in the *brujo*, but he would humor her; it would be an

Experience, a Shared Memory, another increment of momentum added to the spin of their marriage. To pass the time she bought a notebook from a tiny store, whose entire inventory would have fit in her suitcases, and sat outside the bar sketching the volcanoes, the people, the houses. Richard *oohed* and *ahhed* over the sketches, but in her judgment they were lifeless—accurate, yet dull and uninspired. She kept at it, though; it beat her other options.

Toward four o'clock dark thunderheads muscled up from behind the volcano, drops of cold rain spattered down, and they retreated into the bar. Lisa did not intend to get drunk, but she found herself drinking to Richard's rhythm. He would nurse each beer for a while, shearing away the label with his thumbnail; once the label had been removed he would empty the bottle in a few swallows and bring them a couple more. After four bottles she was tipsy, and after six walking to the bathroom became an adventure in vertigo. Once she stumbled against the only other customer, a long-haired guy left over from the morning crowd, and caused him to spill his drink. "My pleasure," he said when she apologized, leering, running his hands along her hips as he pushed her gently away. She wanted to pose a vicious comeback, but was too fuddled. The bathroom served to make her drunker. It was a chamber of horrors, a hole in the middle of the floor with a ridged footprint on either side, scraps of brown paper strewn about, dark stains everywhere, reeking. There was a narrow window that—if she stood on tiptoe—offered a view of two volcanoes and the lake. The water mirrored the grayish-black of the sky. She stared through the smeared glass, watching waves pile in toward shore, and soon she realized that she was staring at the scene with something like longing, as if the storm held a promise of resolution. By the time she returned to the bar, the bartender had lit three kerosene lamps; they added a shabby glory to the place, casting rich gleams along the countertop and gemmy orange reflections in the windowpanes. Richard had brought her a fresh beer.

"They might not come, what with the rain," he said.

"Maybe not." She downed a swallow of beer, beginning to like its sour taste.

"Probably for the best," he said. "I've been thinking, and I'm sure he was setting us up for a robbery."

"You're paranoid. If he were going to rob us, he'd pick a spot where there weren't any soldiers."

"Well, he's got something in mind . . . though I have to admit that was a clever story he told. All that stuff about his own doubts tended to sandbag any notion that he was hustling us."

"I don't believe he was hustling us. Maybe he's deluded, but he's not a criminal."

"How the hell could you tell that?" He picked at a stubborn fleck of beer label. "Feminine intuition? God, he was only here a few minutes."

"You know," she said angrily, "I deserve that. I've been buying that whole feminine intuition chump ever since we were married. I've let you play the intelligent one, while I"—she affected a Southern accent and a breathy voice—"I just get these little flashes. I swear I don't know where they come from, but they turn out right so often I must be psychic or somethin'. Jesus!"

"Lisa, please."

He looked utterly defeated, but she was drunk and sick of all the futile effort and she couldn't stop. "Any idiot could've seen that Dowdy was just a nice, weird little guy. Not a threat! But you had to turn him into a threat so you could feel you were protecting me from dangers I was too naïve to see. What's that do for you? Does it wipe out the fact that I've been unfaithful, that I've walked all over your self-respect? Does it restore your masculine pride?"

His face worked, and she hoped he would hit her, punctuate the murkiness of their lives with a single instance of shock and clarity. But she knew he wouldn't. He relied on his sadness to defeat her. "You must hate me," he said.

She bowed her head, her anger emptying into the hollow created by his dead voice. "I don't hate you. I'm just tired."

"Let's go home. Let's get it over with."

She glanced up, startled. His lips were thinned, a muscle clenching in his jaw.

"We can catch a flight tomorrow. If not tomorrow, the next day. I won't try to hold you anymore."

She was amazed by the panic she felt; she couldn't tell if it resulted from surprise, the kind you feel when you haven't shut the car door properly and suddenly there you are, hanging out the side, unprepared for the sight of the pavement flowing past; or if it was that she had never really wanted freedom, that all her protest had been a means of killing boredom. Maybe, she thought, this was a new tactic on his part, and then she realized that everything between them had become tactical. They played each other without conscious effort, and their games bordered on the absurd. To her further amazement she heard herself say in a tremulous voice, "Is that what *you* want?"

"Hell, no!" He smacked his palm against the table, rattling the bottles. "I want you! I want children, eternal love . . . all those dumb bullshit things we wanted in the beginning! But you don't want them anymore, do you?"

She saw how willingly she had given him an opening in which to assert his masculinity, his moral position, combining them into a terrific left hook to the heart. *Oh Jesus, they were pathetic!* Tears started from her eyes, and she had a dizzying sense of location, as if she were looking up from a well-bottom through the strata of her various conditions. Drunk, in a filthy bar, in Guatemala, shadowed by volcanoes, under a stormy sky, and—spanning it all, binding it all together—the strange webs of their relationship.

"Do you?" He frowned at her, demanding that she finish the game, speak her line, admit to the one verity that prevented them from ever truly finishing—her uncertainty.

"I don't know," she answered; she tried to say it in a neutral tone, but it came out hopeless.

The storm's darkness passed, and true darkness slipped in under cover of the final clouds. Stars pricked out above the rim of the volcano. The food in the bar was greasy—fried fish, beans, and a salad that she was afraid to eat (stains on the lettuce)—but eating steadied her, and she managed to start a conversation about their recent meals. Remember the weird Chinese place in Mérida, hot sauce in the Lobster Cantonese? Or what had passed for crepes at their hotel in Zihuatanejo? Things like that. The bartender hauled out a portable record player and put on an album of romantic ballads sung by a man with a sexy voice and a gaspy female chorus; the needle kept skipping, and finally, with an apologetic smile and a shrug, the bartender switched it off. It came to be seven-thirty, and they talked about Dowdy not showing, about catching the eight o'clock boat. Then there he was. Standing in the door next to a tiny, shrunken old man, who was leaning on a cane. He was deeply wrinkled, skin the color of weathered mahogany, wearing grungy white trousers and a gray blanket draped around his shoulders. All his vitality seemed to have collected in an astounding shock of thick white hair that—to Lisa's drunken eyes—looked like a white flame licking up from his skull.

It took the old man almost a minute to hobble the length of the room, and a considerable time thereafter to lower himself, wheezing and shaking, into a chair. Dowdy hauled up another chair beside him; he had washed the dye from his beard, and his hair was clean, free of feathers. His manner, too, had changed. He was no longer breezy, but subdued and serious, and even his grammar had improved.

"Now listen," he said. "I don't know what Murciélago will say to you, but he's a man who speaks his mind and sometimes he tells people things they don't like to hear. Just remember he bears you no ill will and don't be upset. All right?"

Lisa gave the old man a reassuring smile, not wanting him to think that they were going to laugh; but upon meeting his eyes all thought of reassuring him vanished. They were ordinary eyes. Dark; wet-looking under the lamplight. And yet they were compelling—like an animal's eyes, they radiated strangeness and pulled you in. They made the rest of his ruined face seem irrelevant. He muttered to Dowdy.

"He wants to know if you have any questions," said Dowdy.

Richard was apparently as fascinated by the old man as was Lisa; she had expected him to be glib and sardonic, but instead he cleared his throat and said gravely, "I'd like to hear about how the world's changing."

Dowdy repeated the question in Cakchiquel, and Murciélago began to speak, staring at Richard, his voice a gravelly whisper. At last he made a slashing gesture, signaling that he was finished, and Dowdy turned to them. "It's like this," he said. "The world is not one but many. Thousands upon thousands of worlds. Even those who do not have the power of clear sight can perceive this if they consider the myriad realities of the world they do see. It's easiest to imagine the thousands of worlds as different-colored lights all focused on a single point, having varying degrees of effectiveness as to how much part they play in determinin' the character of that point. What's happenin' now is that the strongest light—the one most responsible for determinin' this character—is startin' to fade and another is startin' to shine bright and dominate. When it has gained dominance, the old age will end and the new begin."

Richard smirked, and Lisa realized that he had been putting the old man on. "If that's the case," he said snottily, "then. . . ."

Murciélago broke in with a burst of harsh, angry syllables.

"He doesn't care if you believe him," said Dowdy. "Only that you understand his words. Do you?"

"Yes." Richard mulled it over. "Ask him what the character of the new age will be."

Again, the process of interpretation.

"It'll be the first age of magic," said Dowdy. "You see, all the old tales of wizards and great beasts and warriors and undyin' kings, they aren't fantasy or even fragments of a distant past. They're visions, the first unclear glimpses seen long ago of a future that's now dawnin'. This place, Lake Atitlán, is one of those where the dawn has come early, where the light of the new age shines the strongest and its forms are visible to those who can see." The old man spoke again, and Dowdy arched an eyebrow. "Hmm! He says that because he's tellin' you this, and for reasons not yet clear to him, you will be more a part of the new age than the old."

Richard gave Lisa a nudge under the table, but she chose to ignore it. "Why hasn't someone noticed this change?" he asked.

Dowdy translated and in a moment had a response. "Murciélago says he has noticed it, and asks if you have not noticed it yourself. For instance, have you not noticed the increased interest in magic and other occult matters in your own land? And surely you must have noticed the breakdown in systems, economies, governments. This is due to the fact that the light that empowered them is fadin', not to any other cause. The change comes slowly. The dawn will take centuries to brighten into day, and then the sorrows of this age will be gone from the memories of all but those few who have the ability to draw upon the dawnin' power and live long in their mortal bodies. Most will die and be reborn. The change comes subtly, as does twilight change to dusk, an almost imperceptible merging of light into dark. It will be noticed and it will be recorded. Then, just as the last age, it will be forgotten."

"I don't mean to be impertinent," said Richard, giving Lisa another nudge, "but Murciélago looks pretty frail. He can't have much of a role to play in all this."

The old man rapped the floor with his cane for emphasis as he answered, and Dowdy's tone was peeved. "Murciélago is involved in great struggles against enemies whose nature he's only beginnin' to discern. He has no time to waste with fools. But because you're not a total fool, because you need instruction, he will answer. Day by day his power grows, and at night the volcano is barely able to contain his force. Soon he will shed this frailty and flow between the forms of his spirit. He will answer no more of your questions." Dowdy looked at Lisa. "Do you have a question?"

Murciélago's stare burned into her, and she felt disoriented, as insubstantial as one of the gleams slipping across his eyes. "I don't know," she said. "Yes. What does he think about us?"

"This is a good question," said Dowdy after consulting with Murciélago, "because it concerns self-knowledge, and all important answers relate to the self. I will not tell you what you are. You know that, and you have shame in the knowledge. What you will be is manifest, and soon you will know that. Therefore I will answer the question you have not asked, the one that most troubles you. You and the man will part and come together, part and come together. Many times. For

though you are lovers, you are not true companions and you
both must follow your own ways. I will help you in this. I will
free the hooks that tear at you and give you back your natures.
And when this is done, you and the man may share each other,
may part and come together without sadness or weakness."

Murciélago fumbled for something under his blanket, and
Dowdy glanced back and forth between Richard and Lisa.
"He wants to make you a gift," he said.

"What kind of gift?" asked Richard.

"A gift is not known by its name," Dowdy reminded him.
"But it won't be a mystery for long."

The old man muttered again and stretched out a trembling
hand to Richard; in his palm were four black seeds.

"You must swallow them one at a time," said Dowdy. "And
as you do, he will channel his power through them."

Richard's face tightened with suspicion. "It's some sort of
drug, right? Take four, and I won't care what happens."

Dowdy reverted to his ungrammatical self. "Life is a drug,
man. You think me and the ol' boy are gonna get you high and
boost your traveler's checks. Shit! You ain't thinkin' clear."

"Maybe that's exactly what you're going to do," said Richard stonily. "And I'm not falling for it."

Lisa slipped her hand into his. "They're not going to hurt
us. Why don't you try it?"

"You believe this old fraud, don't you?" He disengaged his
hand, looking betrayed. "You believe what he said about us?"

"I'd like to believe it," she said. "It would be better than what
we have, wouldn't it?"

The lamplight flickered, and a shadow veered across his
face. Then the light steadied, and so it seemed did he. It was as
if the orange glow were burning away eleven years of wrong-
thinking, and the old unparanoid sure-of-himself Richard was
shining through. Christ, she wanted to say, you're really in
there!

"Aw, hell! He who steals my purse steals only forty cents on
the dollar, right?" He plucked the seeds from Murciélago's
hand, picked one up, and held it to his mouth. "Anytime."

Before letting Richard swallow the seeds, Murciélago sang

for a while. The song made Lisa think of a comic fight in a movie, the guy carrying on a conversation in between ducking and throwing punches, packing his words into short, rushed phrases. Murciélago built it to a fierce rhythm, signaled Richard, and grunted each time a seed went down, putting—Lisa thought—some magical English on it.

"God!" said Richard afterward, eyes wide with mock awe. "I had no idea! The colors, the infinite harmony! If only . . ." He broke it off and blinked, as if suddenly waking to an unaccustomed thought.

Murciélago smiled and gave out with a growly humming noise that Lisa assumed was a sign of satisfaction. "Where are mine?" she asked.

"It's different for you," said Dowdy. "He has to anoint you, touch you."

At this juncture Richard would normally have cracked a joke about dirty old men, but he was gazing out the window at shadowy figures on the street. She asked if he were okay, and he patted her hand. "Yeah, don't worry. I'm just thinking."

Murciélago had pulled out a bottle of iodine-colored liquid and was dipping his fingers into it, wetting the tips. He began to sing again—a softer, less hurried song with the rhythm of fading echoes—and Dowdy had Lisa lean forward so the old man wouldn't have to strain to reach her. The song seemed to be all around her, turning her thoughts slow and drifty. Callused brown fingers trembled in front of her face; the calluses were split, and the splits crusted with grime. She shut her eyes. The fingers left wet, cool tracks on her skin, and she could feel the shape he was tracing. A mask. Widening her eyes, giving her a smile, drawing curlicues on her cheeks and forehead. She had the idea that he was tracing the conformation of her real face, doing what the lamplight had done for Richard. Then his fingers brushed her eyelids. There was a stinging sensation, and dazzles exploded behind her eyes.

"Keep 'em shut," advised Dowdy. "It'll pass."

When at last she opened them, Dowdy was helping Murciélago to his feet. The old man nodded but did not smile at her as he had with Richard; from the thinned set of his mouth she took it that he was either measuring her or judging his work.

"That's all, folks!" said Dowdy, grinning. "See? No dirty tricks, nothin' up his sleeve. Just good ol' newfangled stick-to-your-soul magic." He waved his arms high like an evangelist. "Can you feel it, brothers and sisters? Feel it wormin' its way through your bones?"

Richard mumbled affirmatively. He seemed lost in himself, studying the pattern of rips his thumb had scraped on the label of the beer bottle, and Lisa was beginning to feel a bit lost herself. "Do we pay him anything?" she asked Dowdy; her voice sounded small and metallic, like a recorded message.

"There'll come a day when the answer's Yes," said Dowdy. "But not now." The old man hobbled toward the door, Dowdy guiding him by the arm.

"Goodbye," called Lisa, alarmed by their abrupt exit.

"Yeah," said Dowdy over his shoulder, paying more attention to assisting Murciélago. "See ya."

They were mostly silent while waiting for the launch, limiting their conversation to asking how the other was doing and receiving distracted answers; and later, aboard the launch, the black water shining under the stars and the motor racketing, their silence deepened. They sat with their hips pressed together, and Lisa felt close to Richard; yet she also felt that the closeness wasn't important; or if it was, it was of memorial importance, a tribute to past closeness, because things were changing between them. That, too, she could feel. Old postures were being redefined, webs were tearing loose, shadowy corners of their souls were coming to light. She knew this was happening to Richard as well as to herself, and she wondered how she knew, whether it was her gift to know these things. But the first real inkling she had of her gift was when she noticed that the stars were shining different colors—red, yellow, blue, and white—and there were pale gassy shapes passing across them. Clouds, she realized. Very high clouds that she would not ordinarily have seen. The sight frightened her, but a calm presence inside her would not admit to fright; and this presence, she further realized, had been there all along. Just like the true colors of the stars. It was her fearful self that was relatively new, an obscuring factor, and it—like the clouds—was passing. She considered telling Richard, but decided that he would be busy deciphering his gift. She concentrated on her own, and as they walked from the pier to the hotel, she saw halos around leaves, gleams coursing along electrical wires, and opaque films shifting over people's faces.

They went straight up to their room and lay without talking in the dark. But the room wasn't dark for Lisa. Pointillistic fires bloomed and faded in midair, seams of molten light spread along the cracks in the wall, and once a vague human shape—she identified it as a ghostly man wearing robes—crossed from the door to the window and vanished. Every piece of furniture began to glow golden around the edges, brighter and brighter, until it seemed they each had a more ornate shape superimposed. There came to be so much light that it disconcerted her, and though she was unafraid, she wished she could have a moment's normalcy just to get her bearings. And her wish was granted. In a wink the room had reverted to dim bulky shadows and a rectangle of streetlight slanting onto the floor from the window. She sat bolt upright, astonished that it could be controlled with such ease. Richard pulled her back down beside him and asked, "What is it?" She told him some of what she had seen, and he said, "It sounds like hallucinations."

"No, that's not how it feels," she said. "How about you?"

"I'm not hallucinating, anyway. I feel restless, penned in, and I keep thinking that I'm going somewhere. I mean, I have this sense of motion, of speed, and I can almost tell where I am and who's with me. I'm full of energy; it's like I'm sixteen again or something." He paused. "And I'm having these thoughts that ought to scare me but don't."

"What, for instance?"

"For instance"—he laughed—"and this really is the most important 'for instance,' I'll be thinking about us and I'll understand that what the old guy said about us parting is true, and I don't want to accept it. But I can't help accepting it. I know it's true, for the best. All that. And then I'll have that feeling of motion again. It's like I'm sensing the shape of an event or. . . ." He shook his head, befuddled. "Maybe they did drug us, Lisa. We sound like a couple of acidheads out of the sixties."

"I don't think so," she said; and then, after a silence, she asked, "Do you want to make love?"

He trailed his fingers along the curve of her stomach. "No offense, but I'm not sure I could concentrate on it just now."

"All right. But . . ."

He rolled onto his side and pressed against her, his breath warm on her cheeks. "You think we might not have another chance?"

Embarrassed, she turned her face into his chest. "I'm just horny, is all."

"God, Lisa. You pick the weirdest times to get aroused."

"You've picked some pretty weird times yourself."

"I've always been absolutely correct in my behavior toward you, madam," he said in an English accent.

"Really? What about the time in Jim and Karen's bathroom?"

"I was drunk."

"Well? I'm nervous now. You know how that affects me."

"A common glandular condition, Fräulein." German accent this time. "Correctable by simple surgery." He laughed and dropped the accent. "I wonder what Karen and Jim would be doing in our shoes."

For a while they told stories about what their various friends might do, and afterward they lay quietly, arms around each other. Richard's heart jolted against Lisa's breast, and she thought back to the first time they had been together this way. How protected she had felt, yet how fragile the strength of his heartbeat had made him seem. She'd had the idea that she could reach into his chest and touch his heart. And she could have. You had that much power over your lover; his heart was in your care, and at moments like this it was easy to believe that you would always be caring. But the moments failed you. They were peaks, and from them you slid into a mire where caring dissolved into mistrust and selfishness, where you saw that your feeling of being protected was illusory, and the moments were few and far between. Marriage sought to institutionalize those moments, by law, to butter them over a ridiculous number of years; but all it did was lessen their intensity and open you up to a new potential for failure. Everyone talked about "good marriages," ones that evolved into hallowed friendships, an emeritus passion of the spirit. Maybe they did exist. Maybe there were—as Murciélago had implied—true companions. But most of the old marrieds Lisa had known were simply exhausted, weary of struggling, and had reached an accommodation with their mates based upon mutual despair. If Murciélago was right, if the world was changing, possibly the condition of marriage would change. Lisa doubted it, though. Hearts would have to be changed as well, and not even magic could affect their basic nature. Like with seashells, you could put your ear to one and hear the sad truth of an ocean breaking on a deserted shore. They were always empty, always unfulfilled. *Deeds fill them,* said an almost-voice inside her head, and she almost knew whose voice it had been; she pushed the knowledge aside, wanting to hold on to the moment.

Somebody shrieked in the courtyard. Not unusual. Groups of people frequently hung around the courtyard at night, smoking dope and exchanging bits of travel lore; the previous night two French girls and an American boy had been fighting with water pistols, and the girls had shrieked whenever they were hit. But this time the shriek was followed by shouts in Spanish and, in broken English, a scream of pure terror, then silence. Richard sprang to his feet and cracked the door. Lisa moved up behind him. Another shout in Spanish—she recognized the word *doctor*. Richard put a finger to his lips and slipped out into the hall. Together they edged along the wall and peeked down into the courtyard. About a dozen guests were standing against the rear wall, some with their hands in the air; facing them, carrying automatic rifles, were three young men and a girl. Teenagers. Wearing jeans and polo shirts. A fourth man lay on the ground, his hands and head swathed in bandages. The guests were very pale—at this dis-

tance their eyes looked like raisins in uncooked dough—and a
couple of the women were sobbing. One of the gunmen was
wounded, a patch of blood staining his side; he was having to
lean on the girl's shoulder, and his rifle barrel was wavering
back and forth. With all the ferns sprouting around them, the
pots of flowers hanging from the green stucco wall, the scene
had an air of mythic significance—a chance meeting between
good and evil in the Garden of Eden.

"Sssst!" A hiss behind Lisa's shoulder. It was the Guatemalan man who had watched her during dinner the night before;
he had a machine pistol in one hand, and in the other he was
flapping a leather card case. ID. He beckoned, and they moved
after him down the hall. *"Policía!"* he whispered, displaying
the ID; in the photograph he was younger, his mustache so
black it appeared to have been painted on for a joke. His nervous eyes and baggy suit and five o'clock shadow reminded
Lisa of 1940s movie heavies, the evil flunky out to kill George
Sanders or Humphrey Bogart; but the way his breath whined
through his nostrils, the oily smell of the gun, his radiation of
callous stupidity, all that reduced her romantic impression.
"Malos!" he said, pointing to the courtyard. *"Comunistas!
Guerrillas!"* He patted the gun barrel.

"Okay," said Richard, holding up both hands to show his
neutrality, his noninvolvement. But as the man crept toward
the courtyard, toward the balcony railing, Richard locked his
hands together and brought them down on the back of the
man's neck, then fell atop him, kneeing and pummeling him.
Lisa was frozen by the attack, half-disbelieving that Richard
was capable of such decisive action. He scrambled to his feet,
breathing hard, and tossed the machine pistol down into the
courtyard. *"Amigos!"* he shouted, and turned to Lisa, his
mouth still open from the shout.

Their eyes met, and that stare was a divorce, an acknowl-
edgment that something was happening to separate them,
happening right now, and though they weren't exactly sure
what, they were willing to accept the fact and allow it to happen. "I couldn't let him shoot," said Richard. "I didn't have a
choice." He sounded amazed, as if he hadn't known until this
moment why he had acted.

Lisa wanted to console him, to tell him he'd done the right thing, but her emotions were locked away, under restraint, and she sensed a gulf between them that nothing could bridge—all their intimate connections were withdrawing, receding. Hooks, Murciélago had called them.

One of the guerrillas, the girl, was sneaking up the stairs, gun at the ready. She was pretty but on the chubby side, with shiny wings of black hair falling over her shoulders. She motioned for them to move back and nudged the unconscious man with her toe. He moaned, his hand twitched. "You?" she said, pointing at Richard and then to the man.

"He was going to shoot," said Richard hollowly.

From the girl's blank expression Lisa could tell that she hadn't understood. She rummaged in the man's jacket, pulled out the ID case, and shouted in rapid-fire Spanish. "Vámonos!" she said to them, indicating that they should precede her down the stairs. As Lisa started down, there was a short burst of automatic fire from the hall; startled, she turned to see the girl lifting the barrel of her rifle from the man's head, a stippling of red droplets on the green stucco. The girl frowned and trained the rifle on her, and Lisa hurried after Richard, horrified. But before her emotional reaction could mature into fear, her vision began to erode.

Glowing white flickers were edging every figure in the room, with the exception of the bandaged man, and as they grew clearer, she realized that they were phantom human shapes; they were like the afterimages of movement you see on Benzedrine, yet sharper and slower to fade, and the movements were different from those of their originals—an arm flailing, a half-formed figure falling or running off. Each time one vanished another would take its place. She tried to banish them, to will them away, but was unsuccessful, and she found that watching them distracted her from thinking about the body upstairs.

The tallest of the guerrillas—a gangly kid with a skull face and huge dark eyes and a skimpy mustache—entered into conversation with the girl, and Richard dropped to his knees beside the bandaged man. Blood had seeped through the layers of wrapping, producing a grotesque striping around the man's head. The gangly kid scowled and prodded Richard with his rifle.

"I'm a medic," Richard told him. "*Como un doctor.*" Gingerly he peeled back some layers of bandage and looked away, his face twisted in disgust. "Jesus Christ!"

"The soldiers torture him." The kid spat into the ferns. "They think he is *guerrillero* because he's my cousin."

"And is he?" Richard was probing for a pulse under the bandaged man's jaw.

"No." The kid leaned over Richard's shoulder. "He studies at San Carlos University. But because we have killed the soldiers, now he will have to fight." Richard sighed, and the kid faltered. "It is good you are here. We think a friend is here, a doctor. But he's gone." He made a gesture toward the street. "*Pasado.*"

Richard stood and cleaned his fingers on his jeans. "He's dead."

One of the women who had been sobbing let out a wail, and the kid snapped his rifle into firing position and shouted, "*Cáyete, gringa!*" His face was stony, the vein in his temple throbbed. A balding, bearded man wearing an embroidered native shirt embraced the woman, muting her sobs, and glared fiercely at the kid; one of his afterimages raised a fist. The rest of the imprisoned guests were terrified, their Adam's apples working, eyes darting about; and the girl was arguing with the kid, pushing his rifle down. He kept shaking her off. Lisa felt detached from the tension, out of phase with existence, as if she were gazing down from a higher plane.

With what seemed foolhardy bravado, the bearded guy called out to Richard. "Hey, you! The American! You with these people or somethin'?"

Richard had squatted beside the wounded guerrilla—a boy barely old enough to shave—and was probing his side. "Or something," he said without glancing up. The boy winced and gritted his teeth and leaned on his friend, a boy not much older.

"You gonna let 'em kill us?" said the bearded guy. "That's what's happenin', y'know. The girl's sayin' to let us go, but the dude's tellin' her he wants to make a statement." Panic seeped into his voice. "Y'understand that, man? The dude's lookin' to waste us so he can make a statement."

"Take it easy," Richard got to his feet. "The bullet needs to come out," he said to the gangly kid. "I . . ."

The kid swiped at Richard's head with the rifle barrel, and Richard staggered back, clutching his brow; when he straightened up, Lisa saw blood welling from his hairline. "Your friend's going to die," he said stubbornly. "The bullet needs to come out." The kid jammed the muzzle of the rifle into Richard's throat, forcing him to tip back his head.

With a tremendous effort of will Lisa shook off the fog that had enveloped her. The afterimages vanished. "He's trying to help you," she said, going toward the kid. "Don't you understand?" The girl pushed her back and aimed her rifle at Lisa's stomach. Looking into her eyes, Lisa had an intimation of the depth of her seriousness, the ferocity of her commitment. "He's trying to help," Lisa repeated. The girl studied her, and after a moment she called over her shoulder to the kid. Some of the hostility drained from the kid's face and was replaced by suspicion.

"Why?" the kid asked Richard. "Why you help us?"

Richard seemed confused, and then he started to laugh; he wiped his forehead with the back of his hand, smearing the blood and sweat, and laughed some more. The kid was puzzled at first, but a few seconds later he smiled and nodded as if he and Richard were sharing a secret male joke. "Okay," he said. "Okay. You help him. But here is danger. We go now."

"Yeah," said Richard, absorbing this. "Yeah, okay." He stepped over to Lisa and drew her into a smothering hug. She gripped his shoulders hard, and she thought her emotions were going to break free; but when he stepped back, appearing stunned, she sensed again that distance between them. . . . He put his arm around the wounded boy and helped him through the entrance; the others were already peering out the door. Lisa followed. The rows of tourist shops and restaurants looked unreal—a deserted stage set—and the colors seemed streaky and too bright. Parked under a streetlight near the entrance, gleaming toylike in the yellow glare, was a Suzuki mini-truck, the kind with a canvas-draped frame over the rear. Beyond it the road wound away into darkened hills. The girl vaulted the tailgate and hauled the wounded boy after her; the other two climbed into the cab and fired the engine. Only Richard was left standing on the cobblestones.

"Dése prisa!" The girl banged on the tailgate.

As Richard hesitated, there was a volley of shots. The noise sent Lisa scuttling away from the entrance toward the lake. Three policemen were behind a parked car on the opposite side of the street. More shots. The girl returned the fire, blowing out the windshield of the car, and they ducked out of sight. Another shot. Sparks and stone chips were kicked up near Richard's feet. Still he hesitated.

"Richard!" Lisa had intended the shout as a caution, but the name floated out of her, not desperate-sounding at all—it had the ring of an assurance. He dove for the tailgate. The girl helped him scramble inside, and the truck sped off over the first rise. The policemen ran after it, firing; then, like Keystone Cops, they put on the brakes and ran in the opposite direction.

Lisa had a flash feeling of anguish that almost instantly began to subside, as if it had been the freakish firing of a nerve. Dazedly, she moved farther away from the hotel entrance. A jeep stuffed with policemen came swerving past, but she hardly noticed. The world was dissolving in golden light, every source of light intensifying and crumbling the outlines of things. Streetlights burned like novas, sunbursts shone from windows, and even the cracks in the sidewalk glowed; misty shapes were fading into view, overlaying the familiar with tall peak-roofed houses and carved wagons and people dressed in robes. All rippling, illusory. It was as if a fantastic illustration were coming to life, and she was the only real-life character left in the story, a contemporary Alice with designer jeans and turquoise earrings, who had been set to wander through a golden fairy tale. She was entranced, and yet at the same time she resented the fact that the display was cheating her of the right to sadness. She needed to sort herself out, and she continued toward the lake, toward the pier where she and Richard had kissed. By the time she reached it, the lake itself had been transformed into a scintillating body of light, and out on the water the ghost of a sleek sailboat, its canvas belling, glided past for an instant and was gone.

She sat at the end of the pier, dangling her feet over the edge. The cool roughness of the planks was a comfort, a proof against the strangeness of the world . . . or was it *worlds*? The forms of the new age. Was that what she saw? Weary of seeing it, she willed the light away and before she could register whether or not she had been successful, she shut her eyes and tried to think about Richard. And, as if thought were a vehicle for sight, she saw him. A ragged-edged patch of vision appeared against the darkness of her closed eyes, like a hole punched through black boards. He was sitting on the oil-smeared floor of the truck, cradling the wounded boy's head in his lap; the girl was bending over the boy, mopping his forehead, holding on to Richard's shoulder so the bouncing of the truck wouldn't throw her off-balance. Lisa felt a pang of jealousy, but she kept watching for a very long time. She didn't wonder how she saw them. It all meant something, and she knew that meaning would come clear.

When she opened her eyes, she found it had grown pitch-dark. She couldn't see her hand in front of her face, and she panicked, thinking she had gone blind; but accompanying the panic was a gradual brightening, and she realized that she must have willed away all light. Soon the world had returned to normal. Almost. Though the slopes of the volcanoes were unlighted—shadows bulking against the stars—above each of their cones blazed a nimbus of ruby glow, flickering with an inconstant rhythm. The glow above Murciélago's volcano was the brightest—at least it was for a few seconds. Then it faded, and in its place a fan of rippling white radiance sprayed from the cone, penetrating high into the dark. It was such an eerie sight, she panicked. Christ, what was she doing just sitting here and watching pretty lights? And what was she going to do? Insecurity and isolation combined into an electricity that jolted her to her feet. Maybe there was an antidote for this, maybe the thing to do would be to go see Murciélago. . . . And she remembered Dowdy's story. How he'd been afraid and had gone to Murciélago, only to find that the old apprentice had taken up his own post, leaving a vacancy. She looked back at the other two volcanoes, still pulsing with their ruby glow. Dowdy and the mestizo? It had to be. The white light was Murciélago's vacancy sign. The longer she stared at it, the more certain knowledge became.

Stunned by the prospect of setting out on such an eccentric course, by the realization that everything she knew was dissolving in light or fleeing into darkness, she walked away from the pier, following the shoreline. She wanted to hold on to Richard, to sadness—her old familiar and their common woe—but with each step her mood brightened, and she couldn't even feel guilty about not being sad. Four or five hours would take her to the far side of the lake. A long walk, alone, in the dark, hallucinations lurking behind every bush. She could handle it, though. It would give her time to work at controlling her vision, to understand some of what she saw, and when she had climbed the volcano she'd find a rickety cabin back in under the lip, a place as quirky as Dowdy himself. She saw it the same way she had seen Richard and the girl. Tilting walls; ferns growing from the roof; a door made from the side of a packing crate, with the legend THIS END UP upside down. Tacked to the door was a piece of paper, probably Dowdy's note explaining the care and feeding of wizards. And inside, the thousandfold forms of his spirit compacted into a gnarled shape, a nugget of power (she experienced an upwelling of sadness, and then she felt that power surging through her, nourishing her own strength, making her aware of the thousands of bodies of light she was, all focused upon this moment in her flesh), there Murciélago would be waiting to teach her power's usage and her purpose in the world.

Oh God, Richard, goodbye.

A Traveler's Tale

All this happened several years ago on the island of Guanoja Menor, most of it to a young American named Ray Milliken. I doubt you will have heard of him, not unless you have been blessed with an exceptional memory and chanced to read the sketchy article about his colony printed by one of the national tabloids; but in these parts his name remains something to conjure with.

"Who were dat Yankee," a drunkard will say (the average Guanojan conversation incorporates at least one), "de one who lease de Buryin' Ground and say he goin' to bring down de space duppies?"

"Dat were Ray Milliken," will be the reply, and this invariably will initiate a round of stories revolving about the theme of Yankee foolishness, as if Ray's experiences were the central expression of such a history—which they well may be.

Most Americans one meets abroad seem to fall into types. I ascribe this to the fact that when we encounter a fellow countryman, we tend to exaggerate ourselves, to adopt categorizable modes of behavior, to advertise our classifiable eccentricities and political views, anything that may later prove a bone of contention, all so we may be more readily recognizable to the other. This tendency, I believe, bears upon our reputation for being people to whom time is a precious commodity; we do not want to waste a moment of our vacations or, as in the case of expatriates like myself, our retirements, by pursuing relationships based on a mistaken affinity. My type is of a grand tradition. Fifty-eight years old, with a paunch and a salt-and-pepper beard; retired from a government accounting job to this island off the coast of Honduras; once-divorced; now sharing my days with a daughter of the island, a twenty-year-old black girl named Elizabeth, whose cooking is indifferent but whose amatory performance never lacks enthusiasm. When I tally up these truths, I feel that my life has been triangulated by the works of Maugham, Green, and Conrad. The Ex-Civil Servant Gone To Seed In A Squalid Tropic. And I look forward to evolving into a further type, a gray eminence, the sort of degenerate emeritus figure called upon to settle disputes over some trifling point of island lore.

"Better now you ask ol' Franklin Winship 'bout dat," they'll say. "De mon been here since de big storm in 'seventy-eight."

Ray's type, however, was of a more contemporary variety; he was one of those child-men who are to be found wandering the sunstruck ends of the earth, always seeming to be headed toward some rumored paradise, a beach said to be unspoiled, where they hope to achieve . . . something, the realization of a half-formed ambition whose criteria of peace and purity are so high as to guarantee failure. Travelers, they call themselves, and in truth, travel is their only area of expertise. They know the cheapest restaurant in Belize City, how to sleep for free on Buttermilk Key, the best sandalmaker in Panajachel; they have languished in Mexican jails, contracted dysentery while hiking through the wilds of Olancho, and been run out of various towns for drug abuse or lack of funds. But despite their knowledge and experience, they are curiously empty young men, methodical and unexcitable, possessing personalities that have been carefully edited to give the least effrontery to the widest spectrum of the populace. As they enter their thirties—and this was Ray's age when I met him—they will often settle for long periods in a favorite spot, and societies of even younger travelers will accrete around them. During these periods a sub-type may emerge—crypto-Charles Mansons who use their self-assurance to wield influence over the currencies of sex and drugs. But Ray was not of this mold. It seemed to me that his wanderings had robbed him of guile, of all predilection for power-tripping, and had left him a worldly innocent. He was of medium stature, tanned, with ragged sun-streaked hair and brown eyes set in a handsome but unremarkable face; he had the look of a castaway frat boy. Faint, fine lines radiated from the corners of his eyes, like scratches in sandstone. He usually dressed in shorts and a flour-sack shirt, one of several he owned that were decorated with a line drawing of a polar bear above the name of the mill and the words HARINA BLANCA.

"That's me," he would say, pointing to the words and smiling. "White bread."

I first saw him in the town square of Meachem's Landing, sitting on a stone bench beneath the square's single tree—a blighted acacia—and tying trick knots for the amusement of a clutch of spidery black children. He grinned at me as I passed, and, surprised, being used to the hostile stares with which many young Americans generally favor their elders, I grinned back and stopped to watch. I had just arrived on the island and was snarled in red tape over the leasing of land, aggravated by dealing with a lawyer who insisted on practicing his broken English when explaining things, driven to distraction by the incompetent drunks who were building my house, transforming my neat blueprints into the reality of a Cubist nightmare. I welcomed Ray's companionship as a respite. Over a span of four months we met two or three times a week for drinks at the Salón de Carmín—a ramshackle bar collapsing on its pilings above the polluted shallows of the harbor. To avoid the noise and frequent brawls, we would sit out back on the walkway from which the proprietress tossed her slops.

We did not dig into each other's souls, Ray and I; we told stories. Mine described the vicissitudes of Washington life, while his were exotic accounts of chicleros and cursed Mayan jade; how he had sailed to Guayaquil on a rock star's yacht or paddled alone up the Río de la Pasión to the unexcavated ruin of Yaxchilán; a meeting with guerrillas in Salvador. Quite simply, he was the finest storyteller I have ever known. A real spellbinder. Each of his stories had obviously been worked and reworked until the emotional valence of their events had been woven into clear, colorful prose; yet they maintained a casual edge, and when listening to him it was easy to believe that they had sprung full-blown from his imagination. They were, he told me, his stock-in-trade. Whenever times were lean, he would find a rich American and manage to weasel a few dollars by sharing his past.

Knowing he considered me rich, I glanced at him suspiciously; but he laughed and reminded me that he had bought the last two rounds.

Though he was always the protagonist of his stories, I realized that some of them must have been secondhand, otherwise he would have been a much older, much unhealthier man; but despite this I came to understand that secondhand or not, they *were* his, that they had become part of his substance in the way a poster glued to a wall eventually merges with the surface beneath through a process of the weather. In between the stories I learned that he had grown up in Sacramento and had briefly attended Cal Tech, majoring in astronomy; but thereafter the thread of his life story unraveled into a welter of anecdote. From various sources I heard that he had rented a shanty near Punta Palmetto, sharing it with a Danish girl named Rigmor and several others, and that the police had been nosing around in response to reports of nudity and drugs; yet I never impinged on this area of his life. We were drinking companions, nothing more, and only once did I catch a glimpse of the soul buried beneath his placid exterior.

We were sitting as usual with our feet propped on the walkway railing, taking shelter in the night from the discordant reggae band inside and gazing out at the heat lightning that flashed orange above the Honduran coast. Moths batted at the necklace of light bulbs strung over the door, and the black water was lacquered with reflection. On either side, rows of yellow-lit windows marked the shanties that followed the sweep of the harbor. We had been discussing women—in particular a local woman whose husband appeared to be more concerned with holding on to her than curbing her infidelities.

"Being cuckolded seems the official penalty for marriage

down here," I said. "It's as if they're paying the man back for being fool enough to marry them."

"Women are funny," said Ray; he laughed, realizing the inadequacy of the cliché. "They're into sacrifice," he said. "They'll break your heart and mean well by it." He made a gesture of frustration, unable to express what he intended, and stared gloomily down at his hands.

I had never before seen such an intense expression on his face; it was clear that he was not talking about women in the abstract. "Having trouble with Rigmor?" I asked.

"Rigmor?" He looked confused, then laughed again. "No, that's just fun and games." He went back to staring at his hands.

I was curious; I had a feeling that I had glimpsed beneath his surface, that the puzzle he presented—a bright young man wasting himself in endless wandering—might have a simple solution. I phrased my next words carefully, hoping to draw him out.

"I suppose most men have a woman in their past," I said, "one who failed to recognize the mutuality of a relationship."

Ray glanced at me sharply, but made no comment.

"Sometimes," I continued, "we use those women as justifications for our success or failure, and I guess they do deserve partial credit or blame. After all, they do sink their claws in us . . . but we let them."

He opened his mouth, and I believe he was about to tell me a story, the one story of real moment in his life; but just then old Spurgeon James, drunk, clad in tattered shirt and shorts, the tangle of his once-white beard stained a motley color by nicotine and rum, staggered out of the bar and began to urinate into the shallows. "Oh, mon!" he said. "Dis night wild!" He reeled against the wall, half-turning, the arc of his urine glistening in the yellow light and splashing near Ray's feet. When he had finished, he tried to extort money from us by relating the story that had gained him notoriety the week before—he claimed to have seen flying saucers hanging over Flowers's Bay. Anxious to hear Ray's story, I thrust a *lempira* note at Spurgeon to get rid of him; but by the time he had gone back in,

Ray had lost the impulse to talk about his past and was off instead on the subject of Spurgeon's UFOs.

"You don't believe him, do you?" I said. "Once Spurgeon gets a load on, he's liable to see the Pope driving a dune buggy."

"No," said Ray. "But I wish I could believe him. Back at Cal Tech I'd planned on joining one of the projects that were searching for extraterrestrial life."

"Well then," I said, fumbling out my wallet, "you'd probably be interested to know that there's been a more reliable sighting on the island. That is, if you consider a pirate reliable. Henry Meachem saw a UFO back in the 1700s—1793, I think." I pulled out a folded square of paper and handed it to Ray. "It's an excerpt from the old boy's journal. I had the clerk at the Historical Society run me off a Xerox. My youngest girl reads science fiction and I thought she might get a laugh out of it."

Ray unfolded the paper and read the excerpt, which I reproduce below.

May 7th, 1793. I had just gone below to my Cabin after negotiating the Reef, when I heard divers Cries of astonishment and panic echoing down the Companion-way. I return'd to the Fore-Deck and there found most of the Crew gather'd along the Port-Rail, many of them pointing to the Heavens. Almost directly overhead and at an unguessable Distance, I espi'd an Object of supernal red brilliance, round, no larger than a Ha'penny. The brightness of the Object was most curious, and perhaps brightness is not the proper Term to describe its Effect. While it was, indeed, bright, it was not sufficiently so to cause me to shield my Eyes; and yet whenever I attempt'd to direct my Gaze upon it, I experienc'd a sensation of Vertigo and so was forc'd to view it obliquely. I call'd for my Glass, but before it could be bro't there was a Windy Noise—yet not a whit more Wind—and the Object began to expand, all the while maintaining its circular Forme. Initially, I thought it to be falling towards us, as did the Crew, and several Men flung themselves into the Sea to escape immolation. However, I soon realis'd that it was merely growing larger, as tho' a

Hole were being burned thro' the Sky to reveal the flame-
lash'd Sky of Hell behind. Suddenly a Beam of Light, so
distinct as to appear a reddish-gold Wire strung between
Sky and Sea, lanc'd down from the Thing and struck the
Waters inside the Reef. There was no Splash, but a great
hissing and venting of Steam, and after this had subsided,
the Windy Noise also began to subside, and the fiery Circle
above dwindled to a point and vanish'd. I consider'd put-
ting forth a Long-Boat to discover what had fall'n, but I
was loathe to waste the Southerly Wind. I mark'd the posi-
tion of the Fall—a scant 3 miles from our Camp at Sandy
Bay—and upon our Return there will be ample Opportu-
nity to explore the Phenomenon. . . .

As I recall, Ray was impressed by the excerpt, saying that he
had never read of a sighting quite like this one. Our conversation meandered over the topics of space colonies, quasars, and
UFO nuts—whom he deprecated as having given extraterrestrial research a bad name—and though I tried to resurrect the
topic of women, I never succeeded.

At the time I was frantically busy with supervising the building of my house, maneuvering along the path of bribery and
collusion that would lead to my obtaining final residence papers, and I took for granted these meetings at the Salón de
Carmín. If I had been asked my opinion of Ray in those days, I
would have said that he was a pleasant-enough sort but rather
shallow. I never considered him my friend; in fact, I looked on
our relationship as being free from the responsibilities of
friendship, as a safe harbor from the storms of social
convention—new friends, new neighbors, new woman—that
were blowing around me. And so, when he finally left the island after four months of such conversations, I was surprised
to find that I missed him.

Islands are places of mystery. Washed by the greater mysteries
of wind and sea, swept over by tides of human event, they ac-
cumulate eerie magnetisms that attract the lawless, the eccentric, and—it is said—the supernatural; they shelter oddments

of civilization that evolve into involute societies, and their histories are less likely to reflect orderly patterns of culture than mosaics of bizarre circumstance. Guanoja's embodiment of the mystery had fascinated me from the beginning. It had originally been home to Caribe Indians, who had moved on when Henry Meachem's crews and their slaves established their colonies—their black descendants still spoke an English dotted with eighteenth- and nineteenth-century colloquialisms. Rum-running, gun-smuggling, and revolution had all had their moment in the island's tradition; but the largest part of this tradition involved the spirit world. Duppies (a word used to cover a variety of unusual manifestations, but generally referring to ghosts, both human and animal); the mystical rumors associated with the smoking of black coral; and then there was the idea that some of the spirits dwelling there were not the shades of dead men and women, but ancient and magical creatures, demigods left over from the days of the Caribe. John Anderson McCrae, the patriarch of the island's storytellers, once put it to me this way:

"Dis island may look like a chewed-up bone some dog have dropped in a puddle, and de soil may be no good for plantains, no good for corn. But when it come to de breedin' of spirits, dere ain't no soil better."

It was, as John Anderson McCrae pointed out, no tropic paradise. Though the barrier reef was lovely and nourished a half-dozen diving resorts, the interior consisted of low scrub-thatched hills and much of the coast was given over to mangrove. A dirt road ran partway around the island, connecting the shantytowns of Meachem's Landing, Spanish Harbor, and West End, and a second road crossed from Meachem's Landing to Sandy Bay on the northern coast—a curving stretch of beach that at one moment seemed beautiful, and the next abysmally ugly. That was the charm of the island, that you could be walking along a filthy beach, slapping at flies, stepping carefully to avoid dead fish and pig droppings; and then, as if a different filter had slid across the sun, you suddenly noticed the hummingbirds flitting in the sea grape, the hammocks of coco palms, the reef water glowing in bands of jade and turquoise and aquamarine. Sprinkled among the palms at Sandy Bay were a few dozen shanties set on pilings, their tin roofs scabbed by rust; jetties with gap-boarded outhouses at their seaward ends extended out over the shallows, looking like charcoal sketches by Picasso. It had no special point of attraction, but because Elizabeth's family lived nearby, I had built my house—three rooms of concrete block and a wooden porch—about a hundred yards from the terminus of the cross-island road.

A half-mile down the beach stood The Chicken Shack, and its presence had been a further inducement to build in Sandy Bay. Not that the food or decor was in the least appealing; the sole item on the menu was fried chicken, mostly bone and gristle, and the shanty was hardly larger than a chicken coop itself, containing three picnic tables and a kitchen. Mounted opposite each other on the walls was a pair of plates upon which a transient artist had painted crude likenesses of the proprietor, John James, and his wife; and these two black faces, their smiles so poorly rendered as to appear ferocious, always seemed to me to be locked in a magical duel, one whose stray energies caused the food to be overdone. If your taste was for a good meal, you would have done better elsewhere; but if you had an appetite for gossip, The Chicken Shack was unsurpassed in this regard; and it was there one night, after a hiatus of almost two years, that I next had word of Ray Milliken.

I had been out of circulation for a couple of weeks, repairing damage done to my house by the last norther, and since Elizabeth was grouchy with her monthlies, I decided to waste a few hours watching Hatfield Brooks tell fortunes at the Shack. He did so each Wednesday without fail. On arriving, I found him sitting at the table nearest the door—a thin young man who affected natty dreads but none of the hostility usually attendant to the hairstyle. Compared to most of the islanders, he was a saintly sort. Hardworking; charitable; a nondrinker; faithful to his wife. In front of him was what looked to be a bowling ball of marbled red plastic, but was actually a Zodiac Ball—a child's toy containing a second ball inside, and be-

tween the inner and outer shells, a film of water. There was a
small window at the top, and if you shook the ball, either the
word *Yes* or *No* would appear in the window, answering your
question. Sitting beside Hatfield, scrunched into the corner,
was his cousin Jimmy Mullins, a diminutive wiry man of
thirty-five. He had fierce black eyes that glittered under the
harsh light; the skin around them was puckered as if they had
been surgically removed and later reembedded. He was shirtless, his genitals partly exposed by a hole in his shorts. John
James, portly and white-haired, waved to me from behind the
counter, and Hatfield asked, "How de night goin', Mr. Winship?"

"So-so," I replied, and ordered a bottle of Superior from
John. "Not much business," I remarked to Hatfield, pressing
the cold bottle against my forehead.

"Oh, dere's a trickle now and den," he said.

All this time Mullins had said not a word. He was apparently angry at something, glowering at Hatfield, shifting un-
comfortably on the bench, the tip of his tongue darting in and
out.

"Been hunting lately?" I asked him, taking a seat at the table
by the counter.

I could tell he did not want to answer, to shift his focus from
whatever had upset him; but he was a wheedler, a borrower,
and he did not want to offend a potential source of small
loans. In any case, hunting was his passion. He did his hunting
by night, hypnotizing the island deer with beams from his
flashlight; nonetheless he considered himself a great sports-
man, and not even his bad mood could prevent him from
boasting.

"Shot me a nice little buck Friday mornin'," he mumbled;
and then, becoming animated, he said, "De minute I see he
eye, podner, I know he got to crumble."

There was a clatter on the stairs, and a teenage girl wearing
a man's undershirt and a print skirt pushed in through the
door. Junie Elkins. She had been causing the gossip mills to
run overtime due to a romance she was having with a boy from
Spanish Harbor, something of which her parents disapproved.

She exchanged greetings, handed a coin to Hatfield, and sat across from him. Then she looked back at me, embarrassed. I pretended to be reading the label of my beer bottle.

"What you after knowin', darlin'?" asked Hatfield.

Junie leaned over the table and whispered. Hatfield nodded, made a series of mystic passes, shook the ball, and Junie peered intently at the window in its top.

"Dere," said Hatfield. "Everything goin' to work out in de end."

Other Americans have used Hatfield's method of fortune-telling to exemplify the islanders' gullibility and ignorance, and even Hatfield would admit to an element of hoax. He did not think he had power over the ball; he had worked off-island on the steamship lines and had gained a measure of sophistication. Still he credited the ball with having some magical potential. "De thing made to tell fortunes even if it just a toy," he said to me once. He did not deny that it gave wrong answers, but suggested these might be blamed on changing conditions and imperfect manufacture. The way he explained it was so sweetly reasonable that I almost believed him; and I did believe that if the ball was going to work anywhere, it would be on this island, a place where the rudimentary underpinnings of culture there were still in evidence, where simpler laws obtained.

After Junie had gone, Mullins's hostility again dominated the room and we sat in silence. John set about cleaning the kitchen, and the clatter of dishes accentuated the tension. Suddenly Mullins brought his fist down on the table.

"Damn it, mon!" he said to Hatfield. "Gimme my money!"

"Ain't your money," said Hatfield gently.

"De mon has got to pay *me* for *my* land!"

"Ain't your land."

"I got testimony dat it's mine!" Again Mullins pounded the table.

John moved up to the counter. "Dere's goin' to be no riot in dis place tonight," he said sternly.

Land disputes—as this appeared to be—were common on the island and often led to duels with conch shells or machetes.

The pirates had not troubled with legal documents, and after taking over the island, the Hondurans had managed to swindle the best of the land from the blacks; though the old families had retained much of the acreage in the vicinity of Sandy Bay. But, since most of the blacks were at least marginally related, matters of ownership proved cloudy.

"What's the problem?" I asked.

Hatfield shrugged, and Mullins refused to answer; anger seemed visible above his head like heat ripples rising from a tin roof.

"Some damn fool have leased de Buryin' Ground," said John. "Now dese two feudin'."

"Who'd want that pesthole?"

"A true damn fool, dat's who," said John. "Ray Milliken."

I was startled to hear Ray's name—I had not expected to hear it again—and also by the fact that he or anyone would spend good money on the Burying Ground. It was a large acreage three miles west of Sandy Bar near Punta Palmetto, mostly mangrove swamp, and notable for its population of snakes and insects.

"It ain't de Garden of Eden, dat's true," said Hatfield. "I been over de other day watchin' dem clear stumps, and every time de blade dig down it churn up three or four snakes. *Coralitos,* yellowjaws."

"Snakes don't bother dis negro," said Mullins pompously.

His referral to himself as "dis negro" was a sure sign that he was drunk, and I realized now that he had scrunched into the corner to preserve his balance. His gestures were sluggish, and his eyes were bloodshot and rolling.

"Dat's right," he went on. "Everybody know dat if de yellowjaw bite, den you just bites de pizen back in he neck."

John made a noise of disgust.

"What's Milliken want the place for?" I asked.

"He goin' to start up a town," said Hatfield. "Least dat's what he hopin'. De lawyer say we best hold up de paperwork 'til we find out what de government think 'bout de idea."

"De fools dat goin' to live in de town already on de island," said John. "Dey stayin' over in Meachem's Landin'. Must be forty or fifty of dem. Dey go 'round smilin' all de time, sayin',

'Ain't dis nice,' and 'Ain't dat pretty.' Dey of a cult or some-thin'."

"All I know," said Hatfield, "is dat de mon come to me and say, 'Hatfield, I got three thousand *lemps,* fifteen hundred dol-lars gold, if you give me ninety-nine years on de Buryin' Ground.' And I say, 'What for you want dat piece of perdition? My cousin Arlie he lease you a nice section of beachfront.' And den he tell me 'bout how de Caribe live dere 'cause dat's where dey get together with de space duppies. . . .'"

"Aliens," said John disparagingly.

"Correct! Aliens." Hatfield stroked the Zodiac Ball. "He say de aliens talk to de Caribe 'cause de Caribe's lives is upful and just naturally 'tracts de aliens. I tell him, 'Mon, de Caribe fierce! Dey warriors!' And he say, 'Maybe so, but dey must have been doin' somethin' right or de aliens won't be comin' 'round.' And den he tell me dat dey plan to live like de Caribe and bring de aliens back to Guanoja."

"Gimme a Superior, John," said Mullins bossily.

"You got de money?" asked John, his arms folded, knowing the answer.

"No, I ain't got de money!" shouted Mullins. "Dis boog clot got my money!" He threw himself at Hatfield and tried to wrestle him to the floor; but Hatfield, being younger, stronger, and sober, caught his wrists and shoved him back into the cor-ner. Mullins's head struck the wall with a *thwack,* and he grabbed the injured area with both hands.

"Look," I said. "Even if the government permits the town, which isn't likely, do you really believe a town can survive on the Burying Ground? Hell, they'll be straggling back to Meachem's Landing before the end of the first night."

"Dat's de gospel," said John, who had come out from back of the counter to prevent further riot.

"Has any money changed hands?" I asked.

"He give me two hundred *lemps* as security," said Hatfield. "But I 'spect he want dat back if de government disallow de town."

"Well," I said, "if there's no town, there's no argument. Why not ask the ball if there's going to be a town on the Burying Ground?"

"Sound reasonable to me," said John; he gave the ball no credence, but was willing to suspend disbelief in order to make peace.

"Lemme do it!" Mullins snatched the ball up, staring cross-eyed into the red plastic. "Is dere goin' to be a town on de Buryin' Ground?" he asked solemnly; then he turned it over twice and set it down. I stood and leaned forward to see the little window.

No, it read.

"Let's have beers all around," I said to John. "And a soda for Hatfield. We'll toast the solution of a problem."

But the problem was not solved—it was only in the first stages of inception—and though the Zodiac Ball's answer eventually proved accurate, we had not asked it the right question.

This was in October, a time for every sort of inclement weather, and it rained steadily over the next few days. Fog banks moved in, transforming the sea into a mystic gray dimension, muffling the crash of waves on the reef so they sounded like bones being crunched in an enormous mouth. Not good weather for visiting the Burying Ground. But finally a sunny day dawned, and I set out to find Ray Milliken. I must admit I had been hurt by his lack of interest in renewing our acquaintance, but I had too many questions to let this stop me from hunting him up. Something about a colony built to attract aliens struck me as sinister rather than foolhardy—this being how it struck most people. I could not conceive of a person like Ray falling prey to such a crackpot notion; nor could I support the idea, one broached by Elizabeth, that he was involved in a swindle. She had heard that he had sold memberships in the colony and raised upwards of a hundred thousand dollars. The report was correct, but I doubt that Ray's original motives have much importance.

There was no road inland, only a snake-infested track, and so I borrowed a neighbor's dory and rowed along inside the reef. The tide was low, and iron-black coral heads lifted from the sea like the crenellated parapets of a drowned castle; beyond, the water was banded with sun-spattered streaks of slate and lavender. I could not help being nervous. People steered clear of the Burying Ground—it was rumored to harbor duppies . . . but then so was every other part of the island, and I suspect the actual reason for its desertion was that it had no worth to anyone, except perhaps to a herpetologist. The name of the place had come down from the Caribe; this was a puzzling fact, since all their grave sites were located high in the hills. Pottery and tools had been found in the area, but no solid evidence of burials. Two graves did exist, those belonging to Ezekiel Brooks, the son of William, a mate on Henry Meachem's privateer, and to Ezekiel's son Carl. They had lived most of their lives on the land as hermits, and it was their solitary endurance that had ratified the Brooks family's claim to ownership.

On arriving, I tied the dory to a mangrove root and immediately became lost in a stand of scrub palmetto. I had sweated off my repellent, and mosquitoes swarmed over me; I stepped cautiously, probing the weeds with my machete to stir up any lurking snakes. After a short walk I came to a clearing about fifty yards square; it had been scraped down to the raw dirt. On the far side stood a bulldozer, and next to it was a thatched shelter beneath which a group of men were sitting. The primary colors and simple shapes—yellow bulldozer, red dirt, dark green walls of brush—made the clearing look like a test for motor skills that might be given to a gigantic child. As I crossed to the shelter, one of the men jumped up and walked toward me. It was Ray. He was shirtless, wearing boots and faded jeans, and a rosy sheen of new sunburn overlaid his tan.

"Frank," he said, pumping my hand.

I was taken aback by the religious affirmation in his voice—it was as if my name were something he had long treasured.

"I was planning to drop around in a few days," he said. "After we got set up. How are you?"

"Old and tormented," I said, slapping at a mosquito.

"Here." He gestured at the shelter. "Let's get into the shade."

"How are *you*?" I asked as we walked.

"Great, Frank," he replied. "Really great." His smile seemed the product of an absolute knowledge that things, indeed, were really great.

He introduced me to the others; I cannot recall their names, a typical sampling of Jims and Daves and Toms. They all had Ray's Krishna-conscious smile, his ultrasincerity, and they delighted in sharing with me their lunch of banana fritters and coconut. "Isn't this food beautiful?" said one. There was so much beatitude around me that I, grumpy from the heat and mosquitoes, felt like a heathen among them. Ray kept staring at me, smiling, and this was the main cause of my discomfort. I had the impression that something was shining too brightly behind his eyes, a kind of manic brilliance flaring in him the way an old light bulb flares just before it goes dark for good. He began to tell me of the improvements they were planning— wells, electronic mosquito traps, generators, schools with computers, a medical clinic for the islanders, on and on. His friends chimed in with additions to the list, and I had the feeling that I was listening to a well-rehearsed litany.

"I thought you were going to live off the land like the Caribe," I said.

"Oh, no," said Ray. "There are some things they did that we're going to do, but we'll do them better."

"Suppose the government denies your permits?"

I was targeted by a congregation of imperturbable smiles. "They came through two days ago," said Ray. "We're going to call the colony Port Ezekiel."

After lunch, Ray led me through the brush to a smaller clearing where half-a-dozen shelters were erected; hammocks were strung beneath each one. His had a fringe of snakeskins tacked to the roofpoles, at least thirty of them; they were crusted with flies, shifting horribly in the breeze. They were mostly yellowjaws—the local name for the fer-de-lance—and he said they killed ten or twelve a day. He sat cross-legged on the ground and invited me to take the hammock.

"Want to hear what I've been up to?" he asked.

"I've heard some of it."

"I bet you have." He laughed. "They think we're looney." He

started as the bulldozer roared to life in the clearing behind us. "Do you remember showing me old Meachem's journal?"

"Yes."

"In a way you're responsible for all this." He waved at the dirt and the shelters. "That was my first real clue." He clasped his hands between his legs. "When I left here, I went back to the States. To school. I guess I was tired of traveling, or maybe I realized what a waste of space I'd been. I took up astronomy again. I wasn't very interested in it, but I wasn't more interested in anything else. Then one day I was going over a star chart, and I noticed something amazing. You see, while I was here I'd gotten into the Caribe culture. I used to wander around the Burying Ground looking for pottery. Found some pretty good pieces. And I'd hike up into the hills and make maps of the villages, where they'd stationed their lookouts and set their signal fires. I still had those maps, and what I'd noticed was that the pattern of the Caribe signal fires corresponded exactly to the constellation Cassiopeia. It was incredible! The size of the fires even corresponded to the magnitudes of the specific stars. I dropped out of school and headed back to the island." He gave me an apologetic look. "I tried to see you, but you were on the mainland."

"That must have been when Elizabeth's old boyfriend was giving us some trouble," I said. "We had to lie low for a while."

"I guess so." Ray reached for a pack that was propped against the wall and extracted a sheaf of 8″ by 11″ photographs; they appeared to consist chiefly of smudges and crooked lines. "I began digging through the old sites, especially here—this is the only place I found pottery with these particular designs. . . ."

From this point on I had difficulty keeping a straight face. Have you ever had a friend tell you something unbelievable, something they believed in so strongly that for you to discredit it would cause them pain? Perhaps it was a story about a transcendent drug experience or their conversion to Christianity. And did they stare at you earnestly as they spoke, watching your reactions? I mumbled affirmatively and nodded and avoided Ray's eyes. Compared to Ray's thesis, Erich von

Däniken's ravings were a model of academic discipline. From the coincidental pattern of the signal fires, the incident of Meachem's UFO and some drunken tales he had solicited, from these smudges and lines that—if you exerted your imagination—bore a vague resemblance to bipeds wearing fishbowls on their heads, Ray had concocted an intricate scenario of alien visitation. It was essentially the same story as von Däniken's—the ancient star-seeding race. But where Ray's account differed was in his insistence that the aliens had had a special relationship with the Caribe, that the Caribe could call them down by lighting their fires. The landing Meachem had witnessed had been one of the last, because with the arrival of the English the Caribe had gradually retreated from the island, and the aliens no longer had a reason for visiting. Ray meant to lure them back by means of a laser display that would cast a brighter image of Cassiopeia than the Caribe could have managed; and when the aliens returned, he would entreat them to save our foundering civilization.

He had sold the idea of the colony by organizing a society to study the possibility of extraterrestrial life; he had presented slides and lectured on the Guanojan Outer Space Connection. I did not doubt his ability to make such a presentation, but I was amazed that educated people had swallowed it. He told me that his group included a doctor, an engineer, and sundry Ph.D.s, and that they all had some college background. And yet perhaps it was not so amazing. Even today there must be in America, as there were when I left it, a great many aimless and exhausted people like Ray and his friends, people damaged by some powerful trouble in their past and searching for an acceptable madness.

When Ray had finished, he looked at me soberly and said, "You think we're nuts, don't you?"

"No," I said; but I did not meet his eyes.

"We're not," he said.

"It's not important." I tried to pass it off as a joke. "Not down here, anyway."

"It's not just the evidence that convinced me," he said. "I knew it the first time I came to the Burying Ground. I could feel it."

"Do you remember what else we talked about the night I showed you Meachem's journal?" I am not sure why I wanted to challenge him; perhaps it was simply curiosity, a desire to know how fragile his calm mask really was.

"No," he said, and smiled. "We talked about a lot of things."

"We were talking about women, and then Spurgeon James interrupted us. But I think you were on the verge of telling me about a woman who had hurt you. Badly. Is all that behind you now?"

His smile dissolved, and the expression that flared briefly in its place was terrible to see—grieving, and baffled by the grief. This time it was *his* eyes that drifted away from mine. "You're wrong about me, Frank," he said. "Port Ezekiel is going to be something very special."

Shortly thereafter I made my excuses, and he walked me down to the dory. I invited him to visit me and have a meal, but I knew he would not come. I had threatened his beliefs, the beliefs he thought would shore him up, save him, and there was now a tangible barrier between us.

"Come back anytime," he called as I rowed away.

He stood watching me, not moving at all, an insignificant figure being merged by distance into the dark green gnarl of the mangrove; even when I could barely see him, he continued to stand there, as ritually attendant as his mythical Caribe hosts might have been while watching the departure of their alien guests.

Over five weeks passed before I again gave much thought to Ray and Port Ezekiel. (Port Ezekiel! That name as much as anything had persuaded me of Ray's insanity, smacking as it did of Biblical smugness, a common shelter for the deluded.) This was a studied lack of concern on my part. I felt he was lost and wanted no involvement with his tragedy. And besides, though the colony remained newsworthy, other events came to supersede it. The shrimp fleet struck against its parent American company, and riots broke out in the streets of Spanish Harbor. The old talk of independence was revived in the bars—idle talk, but it stirred the coals of anti-Americanism. Normally smiling faces frowned at me, the prices went up when I shopped in town, and once a child yelled at me, "Get off de island!" Small things, but they shook me. And since the establishment of Port Ezekiel had been prelude to these events, I could not help feeling that Ray was somehow to blame for this peculiarly American darkness now shadowing my home.

Despite my attempt to ignore Ray's presence, I did have news of him. I heard that he had paid Hatfield in full and that Jimmy Mullins was on the warpath. Three thousand *lempira* must have seemed a king's ransom to him; he lived in a tiny shanty with his wife Hettie and two underfed children, and he had not worked for over a year. I also heard that the shipments of modern conveniences intended for Port Ezekiel had been waylaid by customs—someone overlooked in the chain of bribery, no doubt—and that the colonists had moved into the Burying Ground and were living in brushwood shacks. And then, over a span of a couple of weeks, I learned that they were deserting the colony. Groups of them turned up daily in Meachem's Landing, complaining that Ray had misled them. Two came to our door one evening, a young man and woman, both delirious, sick with dysentery and covered with infected mosquito bites. They were too wasted to tell us much, but after we had bedded them down I asked the woman what was happening at the colony.

"It was awful," she said, twisting her hand in the blanket and shivering. "Bugs and snakes . . . and . . ." Her eyes squeezed shut. "He just sits there with the snakes."

"You mean Ray?"

"I don't know," she said, her voice cracking into hysteria. "I don't know."

Then, one night as Elizabeth and I were sitting on the porch, I saw a flashlight beam weaving toward us along the beach. By the way the light wavered, swooping up to illuminate the palm crowns, down to shine upon a stoved-in dory, I could tell the bearer was very drunk. Elizabeth leaned forward, peering into the dark. "Oh, Lord," she said, holding her bathrobe closed. "It dat damn Jimmy Mullins." She rose and went into the house, pausing at the door to add, "If he after foolin' with me, you tell him I'm goin' to speak with my uncle 'bout him."

Mullins stopped at the margin of the porch light to urinate, then he staggered up onto the steps; he dropped his flashlight, and it rolled over beside my machete, which was propped by the door. He was wearing his town clothes—a white rayon shirt with the silk-screened photo of a soccer star on the back, and brown slacks spattered with urine. Threads of saliva hung from his chin.

"Mr. Frank, sir," he said with great effort. His eyes rolled up, and for a moment I thought he was going to pass out; but he pulled himself together, shook his head to clear the fog, and said, "De mon have got to pay me."

I wanted no part of his feud with Hatfield. "Why don't I give you a ride home?" I said. "Hettie'll be worried."

Blearily, he focused on me, clinging to a support post. "Dat boog Yankee clot have cheated me," he said. "You talk to him, Mr. Frank. You tell him he got to pay."

"Ray Milliken? He doesn't owe you anything."

"Somebody owe me!" Mullins flailed his arm at the night. "And I ain't got de force to war with Hatfield." He adopted a clownish expression of sadness. "I born in de summer and never get no bigger den what you seein' now."

So, sucked along by the feeble tide of anti-Americanism, Mullins had given up on Hatfield and shifted his aim to a more vulnerable target. I told him that Ray was crazy and would likely not respond to either threats or logic; but Mullins insisted that Ray should have checked Hatfield's claim before paying him. Finally I agreed to speak to Ray on his behalf and—somewhat mollified—he grew silent. He clung to the post, pouting; I settled back in my chair. It was a beautiful night, the phosphorescent manes of the breakers tossing high above the reef, and I wished he would leave us alone to the view.

"Damn boog Yankee!" He reeled away from the post and careened against the doorframe; his hand fell upon my machete. Before I could react, he picked it up and slashed at the air. "I cut dat bastard down to de deck!" he shouted, glaring at me.

The moment seemed endless, as if the flow of time had snagged on the point of the machete. Drunk, he might do anything. I felt weak and helpless, my stomach knotted by a chill. The blade looked to have the same drunken glitter as his eyes. God knows what might have happened, but at that moment Elizabeth—her robe belling open, eyes gleaming crazily—sneaked up behind him and smacked him on the neck with an ax handle. Her first blow sent him tottering forward, the machete still raised in a parody of attack; and the second drove him off the porch to sprawl facedown in the sand.

Later, after John James and Hettie had dragged Mullins home, as Elizabeth and I lay in bed, I confessed that I had been too afraid to move during the confrontation. "Don't vex yourself, Frank," she said. "Dere's enough trouble on de island dat sooner or later you be takin' care of some of mine." And after we had made love, she curled against me, tucked under my arm, and told me of a dream that had frightened her the previous night. I knew what she was doing—nothing about her was mysterious—and yet, as with every woman I have known, I could not escape the feeling that a stranger lay beside me, someone whose soul had been molded by a stronger gravity and under a hotter star.

I spent the next morning patching things up with Mullins, making him a gift of vegetable seeds and listening to his complaints, and I did not leave for the Burying Ground until midafternoon. It had rained earlier, and gray clouds were still passing overhead, hazy fans of sunlight breaking through now and again. The chop of the water pulled against me, and it was getting on toward sunset by the time I arrived—out on the horizon the sea and sky were blending in lines of blackish squalls. I hurried through the brush, intending to convey my warning as quickly as possible and be home before the winds; but when I reached the first clearing, I stopped short.

The thatch and poles of the brushwood huts were strewn over the dirt, torn apart, mixed in with charred tin cans, food wrappers, the craters of old cooking fires, broken tools, mildewed paperbacks, and dozens of conch shells, each with their whorled tops sliced off—that must have been a staple of their diet. I called Ray's name, and the only answer was an intensification in the buzzing of the flies. It was like the aftermath of a measly war, stinking and silent. I picked my way across the litter to the second clearing and again was brought up short. An identical mess carpeted the dirt and Ray's shelter remained intact, the fringe of rotting snakeskins still hanging from the roofpoles—but that was not what had drawn my attention.

A trench had been dug in front of the shelter and covered with a sheet of wire mesh; large rocks held the wire in place. Within the trench were forty or fifty snakes. *Coralitos,* yellow-jaws, Tom Goffs, cottonmouths. Their slithering, their noses scraping against the wire as they tried to escape, created a sibilance that tuned my nerves a notch higher. As I stepped over the trench and into the shelter, several of them struck at me; patches of the mesh glistened with their venom. Ray's hammock was balled up in a corner, and the ground over which it had swung had been excavated; the hole was nearly full of murky water—groundwater by the briny smell. I poked a stick into it and encountered something hard at a depth of about three feet. A boulder, probably. Aside from Ray's pack, the only other sign of habitation was a circular area of dirt that had been patted smooth; dozens of bits of oyster shell were scattered across it, all worked into geometric shapes—stars, hexagons, squares, and so forth. A primitive gameboard. I did not know what exactly to make of these things, but I knew they were the trappings of madness. There was an air of savagery about them, of a mind as tattered as its surroundings, shriveled to the simplest of considerations; and I did not believe that the man who lived here would understand any warning I might convey. Suddenly afraid, I turned to leave and was given such a shock that I nearly fell back into the water-filled pit.

Ray was standing an arm's length away, watching me. His hair was ragged, shoulder-length, and bound by a cottonmouth-skin band; his shorts were holed and filth-encrusted. The dirt smeared on his cheeks and forehead made his eyes appear round and staring. Mosquito bites speckled his chest—though not as many as had afflicted the colonists I had treated. In his right hand he carried a long stick with a twine noose at one end, and in his left hand was a burlap sack whose bottom humped and writhed.

"Ray," I said, sidling away from him.

I expected a croak or a scream of rage for an answer, but when he spoke it was in his usual voice. "I'm glad you're here," he said. He dropped the sack—it was tied at the top—beside the trench and leaned his stick against the wall of the shelter.

Still afraid, but encouraged by the normalcy of his actions, I said, "What's going on here?"

He gave me an appraising stare. "You better see her for yourself, Frank. You wouldn't believe me if I told you." He sat cross-legged beside the patch of smoothed dirt and began picking up the shell-bits. The way he picked them up fascinated me—so rapidly, pinching them up between thumb and forefinger, and funneling them back into his palm with the other three fingers, displaying an expert facility. And, I noticed, he was only picking up the hexagons.

"Sit down," he said. "We've got an hour or so to kill."

I squatted on the opposite side of the gameboard. "You can't stay here, Ray."

He finished with the hexagons, set them aside, and started on the squares. "Why not?"

I told him about Mullins, but as I had presumed he was unconcerned. All his money, he said, was tied up in investment funds; he would find a way to deal with Mullins. He was calm in the face of my arguments, and though this calm seemed to reflect a more deep-seated confidence than had been evident on my first visit, I did not trust it. To my mind the barrier between us had hardened, become as tricky to navigate as the reef around the island. I gave up arguing and sat quietly, watching him play with the shells. Night was falling, banks of dark clouds were rushing overhead, and gusts of wind shredded the thatch. Heavy seas would soon be washing over the reef, and it would be beyond my strength to row against them. But I did not want to abandon him. Under the dreary storm-light, the wreckage of Port Ezekiel looked leached of color and vitality, and I had an image of the two of us being survivors of a great disaster, stalemated in debate over the worth of restarting civilization.

"It's almost time," he said, breaking the silence. He gazed out to the swaying tops of the bushes that bounded the clearing. "This is so wild, Frank. Sometimes I can't believe it myself."

The soft astonishment in his voice brought the pathos of his situation home to me. "Jesus, Ray," I said. "Come back with me. There's nothing here."

"Tell me that when you've seen her." He stood and walked over to the water-filled pit. "You were right, Frank. I was crazy, and maybe I still am. But I was right, too. Just not in the way I expected."

"Right about what?"

He smiled. "Cassiopeia." He hunkered down by the pit. "I've got to get in the water. There has to be physical contact or else the exchange can't occur. I'll be unconscious for a while, but don't worry about it. All right?"

Without waiting for my approval, he lowered himself into the water. He seemed to be groping for something, and he shifted about until he had found a suitable position. His shoulders just cleared the surface. Then he bowed his head so that I could no longer see his face.

My thoughts were in turmoil. His references to "her," his self-baptism, and now the sight of his disembodied head and tendrils of hair floating on the water, all this had rekindled my fear. I decided that the best thing I could do for him, for both of us, would be to knock him out, to haul him back to Sandy Bay for treatment. But as I looked around for a club, I noticed something that rooted me in my tracks. The snakes had grown frantic in their efforts to escape; they were massed at the far side of the trench, pushing at the mesh with such desperation that the rocks holding it down were wobbling. And then, an instant later, I began to sense another presence in the clearing.

How did I sense this? It was similar to the feeling you have when you are alone for the first time with a woman to whom you are attracted, how it seems you could close your eyes and stopper your ears and still be aware of her every shift in position, registering these changes as thrills running along your nerves and muscles. And I knew beyond a shadow of a doubt that this presence was female. I whirled around, certain that someone was behind me. Nothing. I turned back to Ray. Tremors were passing through his shoulders, and his breath came in hoarse shudders as if he had been removed from his natural element and were having trouble with the air. Scenes from old horror movies flashed through my brain. The stranger lured to an open grave by an odd noise; the ghoul rising from the swamp, black water dripping from his talons; the maniac with the split-personality, smiling, hiding a bloody knife under his coat. And then I saw, or imagined I saw, movement on the surface of the water; it was bulging—not bubbling, but the entire surface bulging upward as if some force below were building to an explosion. Terrified, I took a backward step, and as my foot nudged the wire screen over the trench, as the snakes struck madly at the mesh, terrified themselves, I broke and ran.

I went crashing through the brush, certain that Ray was after me, possessed by some demon dredged up from his psyche . . . or by worse. I did not stop to untie the dory, but grabbed the machete from beneath the seat, hacked the rope in two, and pulled hard out into the water. Waves slopped over the bow, the dory bucked and plunged, and the noise from the reef was deafening. But even had a hurricane been raging, I would not have put back into the Burying Ground. I strained at the oars, gulping down breaths that were half salt spray, and I did not feel secure until I had passed beyond Punta Palmetto and was hidden from the view of whatever was now wandering that malarial shore.

After a night's sleep, after dosing my fears with the comforts of home, all my rational structures were re-erected. I was ashamed at having run, at having left Ray to endure his solitary hell, and I assigned everything I had seen and felt to a case of nerves or—and I did not think this impossible—to poltergeistlike powers brought on by his madness. Something had to be done for him. As soon as I had finished breakfast, I drove over to Meachem's Landing and asked the militia for their help. I explained the situation to one Sergeant Colmenares, who thanked me for my good citizenship but said he could do nothing unless the poor man had committed a crime. If I had been clearheaded, I would have invented a crime, anything to return Ray to civilization; instead, I railed at the sergeant, stumped out of the office, and drove back to Sandy Bay.

Elizabeth had asked me to buy some cooking oil, and so I stopped off at Sarah's Store, a green-painted shanty the size of a horse stall not far from The Chicken Shack. Inside, there was room for three people to stand at the counter, and behind it Sarah was enthroned on her stool. An old woman, almost ninety, with a frizzy crown of white hair and coal-black skin that took on bluish highlights under the sun. It was impossible to do business with her and not hear the latest gossip, and during our conversation she mentioned that Ray had stopped in the night before.

"He after havin' a strife wit dat Jimmy Mullins," she said. "Now Jimmy he have followed dis tourist fella down from de Sea Breeze where dey been drinkin', and he settin' up to beg de mon fah somet'ing. You know how he gets wit his lies." She did her Jimmy Mullins imitation, puffing out her chest and frowning. "'I been in Vietnam,' he say, and show de mon dat scar from when he shot himself in de leg. 'I bleed fah Oncle Sam, and now Oncle Sam goin' to take care of dis negro.' Den in walk Ray Milliken. He did not look left or right but jus' stare at de cans of fruit juice and ax how much dey was. Talkin' wit dat duppy voice. Lord! De duppy force crawlin' all over him. Now dis tourist fella have gone 'cause de sight of Ray wit his wild look and his scrapes have made de fella leery. But Jimmy jus' stand dere, watchful. And when Ray pay fah de juice, Jimmy say, 'Gimme dat money.' Ray make no reply. He drink de juice down and den he amble out de door. Jimmy follow him and he screamin'. 'You scorn me like dat!' he say. 'You scorn me like dat!' It take no wisdom to know dere's blood in de air, so I set a Superior on de counter and call out, 'Jimmy, you come here 'fore yo' beer lose de chill.' And dat lure him back."

I asked Sarah what she meant by "duppy voice," but she would only say, "Dat's what it were—de duppy voice." I paid for my oil, and as I went out the door, she called, "God bless

America!" She always said it as a farewell to her American customers; most thought she was putting them on, but knowing
Sarah's compassion for waifs and strays, her conviction that
material wealth was the greatest curse one could have, I believe
it was heartfelt.

Sarah's story had convinced me of the need for action, and that
afternoon I returned to the Burying Ground. I did not confront
Ray; I stationed myself behind some bushes twenty feet to the
right of the shelter. I planned to do as I should have done
before—hit him and drag him back to Sandy Bay. I had with
me Elizabeth's ax handle and an ample supply of bug repellent.

Ray was not at the clearing when I arrived, and he did not
put in an appearance until after five o'clock. This time he was
carrying a guitar, probably gleaned from the debris. He sat
beside the trench and began chording, singing in a sour, puny
voice that sent a chill through me despite the heat; it seemed he
was giving tongue to the stink of the rotting snakeskins, ampli-
fying the whine of the insects. The sun reflected an orange fire
on the panels of the guitar.

"Cas-si-o-pee-ee-ya," he sang, country-western style, "I'll be
yours tonight." He laughed—cracked, high-pitched laughter—
and rocked back and forth on his haunches. "Cas-si-o-pee-ee-
ya, why don't you treat me right."

Either he was bored or else that was the whole song. He set
down the guitar and for the next hour he hardly moved,
scratching, looking up to the sun as if checking its decline.
Sunset faded, and the evening star climbed above Alps of purple cumulus. Finally, stretching and shaking out the kinks, he
stood and walked to the pit and lowered himself into the water.
It was at this point that I had intended to hit him, but my
curiosity got the best of me and I decided to observe him instead; I told myself that I would be better able to debunk his
fantasies if I had some personal experience of them. I would
hit him after he had fallen asleep.

It was over an hour before he emerged from the water, and
when he did I was very glad to be hidden. Icy stars outlined the

massed clouds, and the moon had risen three-quarters full, transforming the clearing into a landscape of black and silvery-gray. Everything had a shadow, even the tattered fronds lying on the ground. There was just enough wind to make the shadows tremble, and the only noise apart from the wind was the pattering of lizards across the desiccated leaves. From my vantage I could not see if the water was bulging upward, but soon the snakes began their hissing, their pushing at the mesh, and I felt again that female presence.

Then Ray leaped from the pit.

It was the most fluid entrance I have ever seen—like a dancer mounting onto stage from a sunken level. He came straight up in a shower of silver droplets and landed with his legs straddling the pit, snapping his head from side to side. He stepped out of the shelter, pacing back and forth along the trench, and as the light struck him full, I stopped thinking of him as *he*.

Even now, at a remove from the events, I have difficulty thinking of Ray as a man; the impression of femininity was so powerful that it obliterated all my previous impressions of him. Though not in the least dainty or swishy, every one of his movements had a casual female sensuality, and his walk was potently feminine in the way of a lioness. His face was leaner, sleeker of line. Aside from these changes was the force of that presence pouring over me. I had the feeling that I was involved in a scene out of prehistory—the hominid warrior with his club spying on an unknown female, scenting her, knowing her sex along the circuits of his nerves. When he . . . when she had done pacing, she squatted beside the trench, removed one of the rocks, and lifted the edge of the screen. With incredible speed, she reached in and snatched out a wriggling yellowjaw. I heard a sickening mushy crack as she crushed its head between her thumb and forefinger. She skinned it with her teeth, worrying a rip, tearing loose long peels until the blood-rilled meat gleamed in the moonlight. All this in a matter of seconds. Watching her eat, I found I was gripping the ax handle so tightly that my hand ached. She tossed the remains of the snake into the bushes, then she stood—again, that marvelous fluidity—and turned toward the spot where I was hiding.

"Frank," she said; she barely pronounced the *a* and trilled the *r*, so that the word came out as "Frrenn-kuh."

It was like hearing one's name spoken by an idol. The ax handle slipped from my hand. I stood, weak-kneed. If her speed afoot was equal to her speed of hand, I had no chance of escape.

"I won't kill you," she said, her accent slurring the words into the rhythm of a musical phrase. She went back under the shelter and sat beside the patch of smoothed dirt.

The phrasing of her assurance did nothing to ease my fears, yet I came forward. I told myself that this was Ray, that he had created this demoness from his sick needs and imaginings; but I could not believe it. With each step I became more immersed in her, as if her soul were too large for the body and I was passing through its outer fringes. She motioned me to sit, and as I did, her strangeness lapped over me like heat from an open fire.

My throat was constricted, but I managed to say, "Cassiopeia?"

Her lips thinned and drew back from her teeth in a feral smile. "That's what Ray calls me. He can't pronounce my name. My home . . ." She glanced at the sky. "The clouds obscure it."

I gawped at her; I had so many questions, I could not frame even one. Finally I said, "Meachem's UFO. Was that your ship?"

"The ship was destroyed far from here. What Meachem saw was a ghost, or rather the opening and closing of a road traveled by one." She gestured at the pit. "It lies there, beneath the water."

I remembered the hard something I had poked with a stick; it had not felt in the least ectoplasmic, and I pointed this out.

"'Ghost' is a translation of the word for it in my language," she said. "You touched the energy fields of a . . . a machine. It was equipped with a homing capacity, but its fields were disrupted by the accident that befell my ship. It can no longer open the roads between the worlds."

"Roads?" I said.

"I don't understand the roads, and if I could explain them it would translate as metaphysics. The islanders would probably accept the explanation, but I doubt you would." She traced a line in the dirt with her forefinger. "To enter the superluminal universe the body must die and be reanimated at journey's end. The other components of the life travel with the machine. All I know of the roads is that though journeys often last for years, they appear to be direct. When Meachem saw flame in the sky, it was because I came from flame, from the destruction of my ship."

"The machine . . ." I began.

"It's an engineered life form," she said. "You see, any life consists of a system of energy fields unified in the flesh. The machine is a partial simulation of that system, a kind of phantom life that's designed to sustain the most crucial of those fields—what you'd call the *anima,* the soul—until the body can be reanimated . . . or, if the body has been destroyed, until an artificial host has been supplied. Of course there was no such host here. So the machine attracted those whose souls were impaired, those with whom a temporary exchange could be made. Without embodiment I would have gone mad." She scooped up a handful of shell-bits. "I suppose I've gone mad in spite of it. I've rubbed souls with too many madmen."

She tossed out the shell-bits. A haphazard toss, I thought; but then I noticed that they had fallen into neat rows.

"The differences between us are too great for the exchange to be other than temporary," she went on. "If I didn't reenter the machine each morning, both I and my host—and the machine—would die."

Despite the evidence of my senses, this talk of souls and energy fields—reminding me of the occult claptrap of the sixties—had renewed my doubts. "People have been digging up the Burying Ground for years," I said. "Why hasn't someone found this machine?"

"It's a very clever machine," she said, smiling again. "It hides from those who aren't meant to find it."

"Why would it choose only impaired hosts?"

"To choose an unimpaired one would run contrary to the machine's morality. And to mine."

"How does it attract them?"

"My understanding of the machine is limited, but I assume there's a process of conditioning involved. Each time I wake in a new host, it's always the same. A clearing, a shelter, the snakes."

I started to ask another question, but she waved me off.

"You act as though I must prove something," she said. "I have no wish to prove anything. Even if I did, I'm not sure I could. Most of my memories were stripped from me at the death of my body, and those that remain are those that have stained the soul. In a sense I'm as much Ray as I am myself. Each night I inherit his memories, his abilities. It's like living in a closet filled with someone else's belongings."

I continued to ask questions, with part of my mind playing the psychiatrist, eliciting answers in order to catalog Ray's insanity; yet my doubts were fading. She could not recall the purpose of her journey or even of her life, but she said that her original body had been similar to the human form—her people, too, had a myth of an ancient star-seeding race—though it had been larger, stronger, with superior organs of perception. Her world was a place of thick jungles, and her remote ancestors had been nocturnal predators. An old Caribe man had been her first host on the island; he had wandered onto the Burying Ground six months after her arrival, maddened by pain from a cancer that riddled his stomach. His wife had been convinced that a goddess had possessed him, and she had brought the tribal elders to bear witness.

"They were afraid of me," she said. "And I was equally afraid of them. Little devil-men with ruddy skins and necklaces of jaguar teeth. They built fires around me, hemming me in, and they'd dance and screech and thrust their spears at me through the flames. It was nightmarish. I knew they might lose control of their fear at any second and try to kill me. I might have defended myself, but life was sacred to me then. They were whole, vital beings. To harm them would have been to mock what remained of me."

She had cultivated them, and they had responded by providing her with new hosts, by arranging their fires to depict the constellation Cassiopeia, hoping to call down other gods to keep her company. It had been a fruitless hope, and there were other signals that would have been more recognizable to her people, but she had been touched by their concern and had not told them.

I will not pretend that I recall exactly everything she said, yet I believe what follows captures the gist of her tale. At first I was disconcerted by its fluency and humanity; but I soon realized that not only had she had two centuries in which to practice her humanity, not only was she taking advantage of Ray's gift for storytelling, but also that she had told much of it before.

For twenty-two years [she said] I inhabited Caribe bodies, most of them terribly damaged. Cripples, people with degenerative diseases, and once a young girl with a huge dent in her skull, an injury gotten during a raid. Though my energies increased the efficiency of their muscles, I endured all their agonies. But as the Caribe retreated from the island in face of the English, even this tortured existence was denied to me. I spent four years within the machine, despairing of ever leaving it again. Then, in 1819, Ezekiel Brooks stumbled onto the Burying Ground. He was a retarded boy of seventeen and had become lost in the mangrove. When his father, William, came in search of him, he found me instead. He remembered the fiery object that had fallen from the sky and was delighted to have solved a puzzle that had baffled his captain for so many years. Thereafter he visited every week and dragged old Henry Meachem along.

Meachem was in his seventies then, fat, with a doughy, wrinkled face and long gray hair done up into ringlets; he affected foppish clothes and a lordly manner. He had the gout and had to be carried through the mangrove by his slaves. They brought with them a teakwood chair, its grips carved into lions' heads, and there he'd sit, wheezing, bellowing at the slaves to keep busy with their fly whisks, plying me with questions. He did not believe my story, and on his second visit, a night much like this one, moonstruck and lightly winded, he was accompanied by a Spanish woman, a scrawny old hag enveloped in a black shawl and skirt, who he told me was a witch.

"Sit you down with Tía Claudia," he said, prodding her forward with his cane, "and she'll have the truth of you. She'll unravel your thoughts like a ball of twine."

The old woman sat cross-legged beside the pit, pulled a lump of clouded crystal from her skirt, and set it on the ground before her. Beneath the shawl her shadowed wrinkles had the look of a pattern in tree bark, and despite her apparent frailty I could feel her presence as a chill pressure on my skin. Uneasy, I sat down on the opposite side of the pit. Her eyelids drooped, her breath grew shallow and irregular, and the force of her life flooded me, intensifying in the exercise of her power. The fracture planes inside the crystal appeared to be gleaming with more than refracted moonlight, and as I stared at them, a drowsy sensation stole over me . . . but then I was distracted by a faint rushing noise from the pit.

Hatchings of fine lines were etching the surface of the water, sending up sprays of mist. The patterns they formed resembled the fracture planes of the crystal. I glanced up at Tía Claudia. She was trembling, a horror-stricken expression on her face, and the rushing noise was issuing from her parted lips as though she had been invaded by a ghostly wind. The ligature of her neck was cabled, her hands were clawed. I looked back to the pit. Beneath the surface, shrinking and expanding in a faltering rhythm, was a point of crimson light. Tía Claudia's power, I realized, was somehow akin to that of the machine. She was healing it, restoring its homing capacity, and it was opening a road! Hope blazed in me. I eased into the pit, and the fields gripped me, stronger than ever. But as the old woman let out a shriek and slumped to the ground, they weakened; the point of light shrank to nothing, gone glimmering like my hope. It had only been a momentary restoration, a product of her mind joined to the machine's.

Two of Meachem's slaves helped Tía Claudia to her feet, but she shook them off and backed out of the shelter, her eyes fixed on the pit. She leaned against Meachem's chair for support.

"Well?" he said.

"Kill him!" she said. "He's too dangerous, too powerful."

"Him?" Meachem laughed.

Tía Claudia said that I was who I claimed to be and argued that I was a threat to him. I understood that she was really concerned with my threat to her influence over Meachem, but I was so distressed by the lapsing of the machine's power that I didn't care what they did to me. Bathed in the silvery light, stars shining around their heads, they seemed emblematic of something—perhaps of all humanity—this ludicrous old pirate in his ruffled shirt, and, shaking her knobbly finger at him, the manipulative witch who wanted to be his master.

After that night, Meachem took me under his wing. I learned that he was an exile, outlawed by the English and obsessed with the idea of returning home, and I think he was happy to have met someone even more displaced than he. Occasionally he'd invite me to his house, a gabled building of pitch-coated boards that clung to a strip of iron shore east of Sandy Bay. He'd sit me down in his study and read to me for hours from his journals; he thought that—being a member of an advanced civilization—I'd have the wit to appreciate his intellect. The study was a room that reflected his obsession with England, its walls covered with Union Jacks, a riot of scarlet and blue. Sometimes, watching the flies crusting the lip of his pewter mug, his sagging face looming above them, the colors on the wall appearing to drip in the unsteady glare of the oil lamp . . . sometimes it seemed a more nightmarish environment than the Caribe's circle of fires. He'd pore over the pages, now and again saying, "Ah, here's one you'll like," and would quote the passage.

"'Wars,'" he read to me once, "'are the solstices of the human spirit, ushering in winter to a young man's thought and rekindling the spring of an old man's anger.'"

Every page was filled with aphorisms like that—high-sounding, yet empty of meaning except as regarded his own nature. He was the cruelest man I've ever known. A wife-beater, a tyrant to his slaves and children. Some nights he would have himself borne down to the beach, order torches lit,

and watch as those who had offended him were flogged—
often to the death—with stalks of withe. After witnessing one
of the floggings, I considered killing him, even though such an
act would have been in violation of everything I believed.

Then one night he brought another woman to the Burying
Ground, a young mulatto girl named Nora Mullins.

"She be weak-minded like Ezekiel," said Meachem. "She'll
make you a perfect wife."

She would have run, but his slaves herded her forward. Her
eyes darted left and right, her hands fidgeted with the folds of
her skirt.

"I don't need a wife," I said.

"Don't you now? Here's a chance to create your own lin-
eage, to escape that infernal contraption of yours. Nora'll bear
you a child, and if blood holds true, it'll be as witless as its
parents. After Ezekiel's gone, you can take up residence in
your heir." His laugh disintegrated into a hacking cough.

The idea had logic behind it, but the thought of being intimate with a member of another species, especially one whose
sex might be said to approximate my own, repelled me. Further, I didn't trust his motives. "Why are you doing this?" I
asked.

"I'm dyin'." The old monster worked up a tear over the prospect. "Nora's my legacy to you. I've always thought it a vast
irony that a high-flyin' soul such as yourself should have been
brought so low. It'll please me to think of you marooned
among generations of idiots while I'm wingin' off to my reward."

"This island is your reward," I said. "Even the soul dies."

"You know that for a fact?" He was worried.

"No," I said, relenting. "No one knows that."

"Well, then I'll come back to haunt you."

But he never did.

I had intended to send Nora away after he left, but Ezekiel—
though too timid to approach her sexually—found her attractive, and I didn't want to deprive him of her companionship.
In addition, I began to realize how lonely I had been myself.
The idea of keeping her with me and fathering a child seemed

more and more appealing, and a week later, using Ezekiel's memories to rouse lust, I set out to become a family man.

What a strange union that was! The moon sailing overhead, chased by ragged blue clouds; the wind and insects and frogs combining into a primitive music. Nora was terrified. She whimpered and rolled her eyes and halfheartedly tried to fight me off. I don't believe she was clear as to what was happening, but eventually her instincts took control. It would be hard to imagine two more inept virgins. I had a logical understanding of the act, at least one superior to Nora's; but this was counterbalanced by her sluggish coordination and my revulsion. Somehow we managed. I think it was mainly due to the fact that she sensed I was like her, female in a way that transcended anatomy, and this helped us to employ tenderness with one another. Over the succeeding nights an honest affection developed between us; though her speech was limited to strangled cries, we learned to communicate after a fashion, and our lovemaking grew more expert, more genuine.

Fourteen years we were together. She bore me three children, two stillborn, but the third a slow-witted boy whom we named Carl—it was a name that Nora could almost pronounce. By day she and Ezekiel were brother and sister, and by night she and I were husband and wife. Carl needed things the land couldn't provide, milk, vegetables, and these were given us by William Brooks; but when he died several years after Carl's birth, taking with him the secret of my identity, Nora began going into Sandy Bay to beg—or so I thought until I was visited by her brother Robert. I knew something must be wrong. We were the shame of the family; they had never acknowledged us in any way.

"Nora she dead," he told me. "Murdered."

He explained that two of her customers had been fighting over her, and that when she had tried to leave, one—a man named Halsey Brooks—had slit her throat. I didn't understand. Customers? Nothing Mullins said made sense.

"Don't you know she been whorin'?" he said. "Mon, you a worse fool dan I think. She been whorin' dese six, seven years."

"Carl," I said. "Where is he?"

"My woman takin' charge of him," he said. "I come for to bring you to dis Brooks. If you ain't mon enough, den I handle it myself. Family's family, no matter how crooked de tie."

What I felt then was purely human—loss, rage, guilt over the fact that Nora had been driven to such straits. "Show him to me," I said.

Hearing the murderousness in my voice, Robert Mullins smiled.

Halsey Brooks was drinking in a shanty bar, a single room lit by oil lamps whose glass tops were so sooty that the light penetrated them as baleful orange gleams. The rickety tables looked like black spiders standing at attention. Brooks was sitting against the rear wall, a big slack-bellied man with skin the color of sunbaked mud, wearing a shirt and trousers of sailcloth. Mullins stationed himself out of sight at the door, his machete at the ready in case I failed, and I went inside.

Catching sight of me, Brooks grinned and drew a knife from his boot. "Dat little squirt of yours be missin' you down in hell," he said, and threw the knife.

I twisted aside, and the knife struck the wall. Brooks's eyes widened. He got to his feet, wary; the other customers headed for the door, knocking over chairs in their haste.

"You a quick little nigger," said Brooks, advancing on me. "But quick won't help you now."

He would have been no match for me; but confronted by the actual task of shedding blood, I found that I couldn't go through with it. I was nauseated by the thought that I had even considered it. I backed away, tripped over a chair, and went sprawling in the corner.

"Dat de best you got to offer?" said Brooks, chuckling.

As he reached for me, Mullins slipped up behind and slashed him across the neck and back. Brooks screamed—an incredibly girlish sound for a man so large—and sank to his knees beside me, trying to pinch together the lips of his wounds. He held a hand to his face, seemingly amazed by the redness. Then he pitched forward on top of me. The reek of his blood and sweat, just the feel of him in my hands as I started to push him away, all that drove me into a fury. One of his eyes was an inch from mine, half-closed and clouding over.

He was dying, but I wanted to dig the last flicker of life out of him. I tore at his cheek with my teeth. The eye snapped open, I heard the beginning of his scream, and I remember nothing more until I threw him aside. His face was flayed to the muscle-strings, his nose was pulped, and there were brimming dark-red craters where his eyes had been.

"My God!" said Mullins, staring at the ruin of Brooks's head; he turned to me. "Go home! De thing more dan settled."

All my rage had drained and been replaced by self-loathing. Home! I *was* home. The island had eroded my spirit, transformed me into one of its violent creatures.

"Don't come 'round no more," said Mullins, wiping his blade on Brooks's trousers; he gave me a final look of disgust. "Get back to de damn Buryin' Ground where you belong."

Cassiopeia sprang to her feet and stepped out into the clearing. Her expression was grim, and I was worried that she might have worked herself into a rage by rehashing the killing. But she only walked a few paces away. Silvered by the moonlight, she looked unnaturally slim, and it seemed more than ever that I was seeing an approximation of her original form. The snakes had grown dead-still in the trench.

"You didn't really kill him," I said.

"I would have," she said. "But never again." She kicked at a pile of conch shells and sent them clattering down.

"What happened then?"

She did not answer for a moment, gazing out toward the sound of the reef. "I was sickened by the changes I'd undergone," she said. "I became a hermit, and after Ezekiel died I continued my hermitage in Carl's body. That poor soul!" She walked a little farther away. "I taught him to hide whenever men visited the Burying Ground. He lived like a wild animal, grubbing for roots, fishing with his bare hands. At the time it seemed the kindest thing I could do. I wanted to cleanse him of the taint of humanity. Of course that proved impossible . . . for both of us."

"You know," I said, "with all the technological advances these days, you might be able to contact. . . ."

"Don't you think I've considered my prospects!" she said angrily; and then, in a quieter tone, "I used to hope that human science would permit me to return home someday, but I'm not sure I want to anymore. I've been perverted by this culture. I'd be as repulsive to my people as Ezekiel was to Robert Mullins, and I doubt that I'd be comfortable among them myself."

I should have understood the finality of her loneliness—she had been detailing it in her story. But I understood now. She was a mixture of human and alien, spiritually a half-breed, gone native over a span of two centuries. She had no people, no place except this patch of sand and mangrove, no tradition except the clearing and the snakes and a game made of broken shells. "I'm sorry," I said.

"It's not your fault, Frank," she said, and smiled. "It's your American heritage that makes you tend to enshrine the obvious."

"Ray and I aren't a fair sample," I said defensively.

"I've known other Americans," she said. "They've all had that tendency. Everyone down here thought they were fools when they first came. They seemed totally unaware of the way things worked, and no one understood that their tremendous energy and capacity for deceit would compensate. But they were worse than either the pirates or the Spanish."

Without another word, she turned and walked toward the brush.

"Wait!" I said. I was eager to hear about her experiences with Americans.

"You can come back tomorrow, Frank," she said. "Though maybe you shouldn't."

"Why not?" Then, thinking that she might have some personal reason for distrusting Americans, I said, "I won't hurt you. I don't believe I'm physically capable of it."

"What a misleading way to measure security," she said. "In terms of hurt. You avoid using the word 'kill,' and yet you kill so readily. It's as though you're all pretending it's a secret."

She slipped into the brush, moving soundlessly, somehow avoiding the dry branches, the papery fronds.

I drove all over the island the next day, trying to find a tape recorder, eventually borrowing one from a tourist in Meachem's Landing. Half-baked delusions of grandeur had been roused in me. I would be the Schliemann of extraterrestrial research, uncovering the ruin of an alien beneath the waste of a human being. There would be best-sellers, talk shows, exclamations of academic awe. Of course there was no real proof. A psychiatrist would point out how conveniently pat the story was—the machine that hid itself, the loss of memory, the alien woman conjured up by a man whose disorder stemmed from a disappointment in love. He would say it was the masterwork of a gifted tale-spinner, complete with special effects. Yet I thought that whoever heard it would hear—as I had—the commonplace perfection of truth underlying its exotic detail.

I had forgotten my original purpose for visiting the Burying Ground, but that afternoon Jimmy Mullins turned up at my door, eager to learn if I had news for him. He was only moderately drunk and had his wife Hettie in tow—a slender, mahogany-skinned woman wearing a dirty blue dress. She was careworn, but still prettier than Mullins deserved. I was busy and put him off, telling him that I was exploring something with Ray that could lead to money. And, I realized, I was. Knowing his character, I had assumed Mullins was attempting to swindle Hatfield; but Nora Mullins's common-law marriage to Ezekiel Brooks gave credence to his claim. I should have explained it to him. As it was, he knew I was just getting rid of him, and Hettie had to pull him down from the porch to cut short his arguments. My news must have given him some heart, though, because a few minutes later Hatfield knocked at the door.

"What you tellin' Jimmy?" he asked. "He braggin' dat you got proof de Buryin' Ground his."

I denied the charge and told him what I had learned, but not how I had learned it.

"I never mean to cheat Jimmy," he said, scratching his head. "I just want to make sure he not cheatin' me. If he got a case . . . well, miserable as he is, he blood."

After he left, I had problems. I found I needed new batteries for the recorder and had to drive into Meachem's Landing; and when I returned home I had an argument with Elizabeth that lasted well past sunset. As a result, I did not start out for the

Burying Ground until almost ten o'clock, and while I was
stowing my pack in the dory, I saw Cassiopeia walking toward
me along the beach.

It was a clear night, the shadows of the palms sharp on the
sand, and each time she passed through a shadow, it seemed I
was seeing Ray; but then, as she emerged into the light, I
would undergo a peculiar dislocation and realize that it was
not Ray at all.

"I was on my way out to you," I said. "You didn't have to
come into town."

"I gave up being a hermit long ago, Frank," she said. "I like
coming here. Sometimes it jogs my memory to be around so
many others, though there's nothing really familiar about
them."

"What do you remember?"

"Not much. Flashes of scenery, conversations. But once I
did remember something concrete. I think it had to do with my
work, my profession. I'll show you."

She squatted, smoothed a patch of sand, and began tracing
a design. As with all her actions, this one was quick and complicated; she used three fingers of each hand, moving them in
contrary directions, adding a squiggle here, a straight line
there, until the design looked like a cross between a mandala
and a printed circuit. Watching it evolve, I was overcome by a
feeling of peace, not the drowsiness of hypnotism, but a powerful, enlivening sensation that alerted me to the peacefulness
around me. The soughing of the palms, the lapping of the water, the stillness of the reef—it was low tide. This feeling was as
potent as the effect of a strong drug, and yet it had none of the
fuzziness that I associate with drugs. By the time she had finished, I was so wrapped in contentment that all my curiosity
had abated—I was not even curious about the design—and I
put aside for the moment the idea of recording her. We strolled
eastward along the beach without talking, past Sarah's Store
and The Chicken Shack, taking in the sights. The tin roofs of
the shanties gleamed under the moonlight, and, their imperfections hidden by the darkness, the shanties themselves
looked quaint and cozy. Shadows were dancing behind the

curtains, soft reggae drifted on the breeze. Peace. When I finally broke the silence, it was not out of curiosity but in the spirit of that peace, of friendship.

"What about Ray?" I asked. "He was in pretty rough shape when I visited him the other afternoon."

"He's better off than he would be elsewhere," she said. "Calmer, steadier."

"But he can't be happy."

"Maybe not," she said. "But in a way I'm what he was always seeking, even before he began to deteriorate. He actually thinks of me in romantic terms." She laughed—a trilling note. "I'm very happy with him myself. I've never had a host with so few defects."

We were drawing near the New Byzantine Church of the Archangel, a small white-frame building set back from the shore. This being Friday, it had been turned into a movie theater. The light above the door illuminated a gaudy poster that had been inserted into the glass case normally displaying the subject of the sermon; the poster showed two bloodstained Chinese men fighting with curved knives. Several teenagers were silhouetted by the light, practicing martial-art kicks beside the steps—like stick figures come to life—and a group of men was watching them, passing a bottle. One of the men detached himself from the group and headed toward us. Jimmy Mullins.

"Mr. Milliken!" he shouted. "Dis de owner of de Buryin' Ground wantin' to speak with you!"

Cassiopeia spun on her heel and went wading out into the water. Infuriated, Mullins ran after her, and—myself infuriated at the interruption, this breach of peace—I stuck out a foot and tripped him. I threw myself on top of him, trying for a pin, but he was stronger than I had supposed. He wrenched an arm loose, stunned me with a blow to the head, and wriggled free. I clamped my arms around his leg, and he dragged me along, yelling at Cassiopeia.

"Pay me my money, bastard!"

"*I'll* pay you!" I said out of desperation.

It might have been a magic spell that I had pronounced. He

quit dragging me; I clung to his leg with one hand, and with the other I wiped a crust of mucky sand from my mouth.

"You goin' to pay me three thousand *lemps*?" he said in a tone of disbelief.

It occurred to me that he had not expected the entire amount, that he had only been hoping for a nuisance payment. But I was committed. Fifteen hundred dollars was no trifle to me, but I might be able to recoup it from Ray, and if not, well, I could make it up by foregoing my Christmas trip to the States. I pulled out my wallet and handed Mullins all the bills, about fifty or sixty *lempira*.

"That's all I've got now," I said, "but I'll get the rest in the morning. Just leave Milliken alone."

Mullins stared at the money in his hand, his little snappish eyes blinking rapidly, speechless. I stared out to sea, searching for a sign of Cassiopeia, but found none. Not at first. Then I spotted her, a slim, pale figure standing atop a coral head about fifteen yards from shore. Without taking a running start, she leaped—at that distance she looked like a white splinter being blown through the night—and landed upon another coral head some twenty, twenty-five feet away. Before I could absorb the improbability of the leap, she dived and vanished into the water beyond the reef.

"I be at your house nine o'clock sharp," said Mullins joyfully. "And we go to de bank together. You not goin' to be havin' no more strife with dis negro!"

But Mullins did not show up the next morning, not at nine o'clock or ten or eleven. I asked around and heard that he had been drinking in Spanish Harbor; he had probably forgotten the appointment and passed out beneath some shanty. I drove to the bank, withdrew the money, and returned home. Still no Mullins. I wandered the beach, hoping to find him, and around three o'clock I ran into Hettie at Sarah's Store.

"Jimmy he never home of a Saturday," she told me ruefully.

I considered giving her the money, but I suspected that she would not tell Mullins, would use it for the children, and though this would be an admirable use, I doubted that it would please Mullins. Twilight fell, and my patience was exhausted. I left a message for Mullins with Elizabeth, stashed the money in a trunk, and headed for the Burying Ground.

After mooring the dory, I switched on the recorder and secreted it in my pack. My investigative zeal of the previous day had been reborn, and not even the desolation of Port Ezekiel could dim my spirits. I had solved the ultimate problem of the retiree; I had come up with a project that was not only time-consuming but perhaps had some importance. And now that Mullins had been taken care of, nothing would interfere.

Cassiopeia was sitting beneath the shelter when I reached the clearing, a silvery star of moonlight shifting across her face from a ragged hole in the thatch. She pointed to my pack and asked, "What's that?"

"The pack?" I said innocently.

"Inside it."

I knew she meant the recorder. I showed it to her and said, "I want to document your story."

She snatched it from me and slung it into the bushes.

"You're a stupid man, Frank," she said. "What do you suppose would happen if you played a recording of me for someone? They'd say it was an interesting form of insanity, and if they could profit, or if they were driven by misguided compassion, they'd send me away for treatment. And that would be that."

For a long while afterward she would not talk to me. Clouds were passing across the moon, gradually thinning, so that each time the light brightened it was brighter than the time before, as if the clearing were being dipped repeatedly into a stream and washed free of a grimy film. Cassiopeia sat brooding over her gameboard. Having grown somewhat accustomed to her, to that strong female presence, I was beginning to be able to detect her changes in mood. And they were rapid changes, fluctuating every few seconds between hostility and sadness. I recalled her telling me that she was probably mad; I had taken the statement to be an expression of gloom, but now I wondered if any creature whose moods shifted with such rapidity could be judged sane. Nonetheless, I was about to ask her to continue her story when I heard an outboard motor, and, moments after it had been shut off, a man's voice shouting, "Mr. Milliken!"

It was Jimmy Mullins.

A woman's voice shrilled, unintelligible, and there was a crash as if someone had fallen; a second later Mullins pushed into the clearing. Hettie was clinging to his arm, restraining him; but on seeing us, he cuffed her to the ground and staggered forward. His town clothes were matted with filth and damp. Two other men crowded up behind Hettie. They were both younger than Mullins, slouching, dressed in rags and sporting natty dreads. One held a rum bottle, and the second, the taller, carried a machete.

"You owe me three thousand *lemps!*" said Mullins to Cassiopeia; his head lolled back, and silver dots of moonlight flared in his eyes.

"Sick of dis Yankee domination," said the taller men; he giggled. "Ain't dat right, Jimmy?"

"Jimmy," I said. "We had a bargain."

Mullins said nothing, his face a mask of sodden fury; he teetered on the edge of the trench, unaware of the snakes.

"Tired of dis exploitation," said the man, and his friend, who had been taking a pull from the bottle, elbowed him gleefully and said, "Dat pretty slick, mon! Listen up." He snapped his fingers in a reggae tempo and sang in a sweet, tremulous voice:

> *"Sick of dis Yankee domination,*
> *Oh yea—aa-ay,*
> *Tired of dis exploitation . . ."*

The scenario was clear—these two had encountered the drunken Mullins in a bar, listened to the story of his windfall, and, thinking that he was being had, hoping to gain by it, they had egged him into this confrontation.

"Dis my land, and you ain't legal on it," said Mullins.

"What about our bargain Jimmy?" I asked. "The money's back at the house."

He was tempted, but drunkenness and politics had infected his pride. "I ain't no beggar," he said. "I wants what's mine, and *dis* mon's money mine." He bent down and picked up one of the conch shells that were lying about; he curled his fingers around the inner curve of the shell—it fit over his hand like the spiked glove of a gladiator. He took a vicious swipe in our direction, and it *whooshed* through the air.

Cassiopeia let out a hissing breath.

It was very tense in the clearing. The two men were watching Mullins with new respect, new alertness, no longer joking. Even in the hands of a fool, conch shells were serious business; they had a ritual potency. Cassiopeia was deadpan, measuring Mullins. Her anger washed over me—I gauged it to be less anger than a cold disapproval, the caliber of emotion one experiences in reaction to a nasty child. But I was ready to intervene if her mood should escalate. Mullins was a coward at heart, and I thought that he would go to the brink but no further. I edged forward, halfway between them. My mouth was dry.

"I goin' to bash you simple, and you not pay me," said Mullins, crossing over the trench.

"Listen, Jimmy . . ." I said, raising the voice of reason.

Cassiopeia lunged for him. I threw my arms around her, and Mullins, panicked, seeing her disadvantage, swung the shell. She heaved me aside with a shrug and tried to slip the punch. But I had hampered her just enough. The shell glanced off her shoulder. She gave a cawing guttural screech that scraped a nail down the slate of my spine, and clutched at the wound.

"See dere," said Mullins to his friends, triumphant. "Dis negro take care of he own." He went reeling back over the trench, nearly tripping, and in righting himself, he caught sight of the snakes. It would have been impossible not to see them—they were thrusting frenziedly at the wire. Mullins's jaw fell, and he backed away. One of the rocks was dislodged from the screen. The snakes began to slither out, writing rippling black figures on the dirt and vanishing into the litter, rustling the dead fronds.

"Oh, Jimmy!" Hettie held out a hand to him. "Have a care!

Cassiopeia gave another of those chilling screeches and low-ered into a crouch. Her torso swaying, her hands hooked. The flesh of her left shoulder was torn, and blood webbed her arm, dripping from her fingertips, giving them the look of claws. She stepped across the trench after Mullins. Without warning, the taller of the two men sprinted toward her, his machete raised. Cassiopeia caught his wrist and flipped him one-handed into the trench as easily as she might have tossed away an empty bottle.

There were still snakes in the trench.

They struck at his arms, his legs, and he thrashed about wildly, crying out; but one must have hit a vein, for the cry was sheared off. His limbs beat a tattoo against the dirt, his eyes rolled up. Slivers of iris peeped beneath the lids. A tiny *coralito* hung like a tassel from his cheek, and a yellowjaw was coiling around his throat; its flat head poked from the spikes of his hair. I heard a squawk, a sharp crack, and looked to the center of the clearing. The second man was crumpled at Cassiopeia's feet, his neck broken. Dark blood poured from his mouth, puddling under his jaw.

"Mr. Milliken," said Mullins, backing, his bravado gone. "I goin' to make things right. Hettie she fix dat little scrape. . . ."

He stumbled, and as he flung out an arm for balance, Cas-siopeia leaped toward him, going impossibly high. It was a gorgeous movement, as smooth as the arc of a diver but more complex. She maintained a crouch in midair, and passing close to Mullins, she plucked the conch shell from his waving hand, fitted it to her own, and spun round to face him—all before she had landed.

Hettie began to scream. Short, piercing shrieks, as if she were being stabbed over and over.

Mullins ran for the brush, but Cassiopeia darted ahead of him and blocked his path. She was smiling. Again Mullins ran, and again she cut him off, keeping low, flowing across the ground. Again and again she let him run, offering him hope and dashing it, harrying him this way and that. The wind had increased, and clouds were racing overhead, strobing the moonlight; the clearing seemed to be spinning, a carousel of glare and shadow, and Hettie's screams were keeping time with the spin. Mullins's legs grew rubbery, he weaved back and forth, his arms windmilling, and at last he collapsed in a heap of fronds. Almost instantly he scrambled to his knees, yelling and tearing loose a snake that had been hanging from his wrist.

A *coralito,* I think.

"Ah!" he said. "Ah . . . ah!"

His stare lanced into my eyes, freezing me with its hopelessness; a slant of light grazed his forehead, shining his sweat to silver beads.

Cassiopeia walked over and grabbed a handful of his shirtfront, hoisting him up until his feet were dangling. He kicked feebly and made a piteous bubbling noise. Then she drove the conch shell into his face. Once. Twice. Three times. Each blow splintered bone and sent a spray of blood flying. Hettie's scream became a wail. After the final blow, a spasm passed through Mullins's body—it looked too inconsequential to be death.

I was dimly aware that Hettie had stopped screaming, that the outboard motor had been started, but I was transfixed. Cassiopeia was still holding Mullins aloft, as if admiring her handiwork. His head glistened black in the moonlight, featureless and oddly misshapen. At least a minute went by before she dropped him. The thump of the body broke the spell that the scene had cast. I eased toward the brush.

"You can leave, Frank," she said. "I won't kill you."

I was giddy with fear, and I almost laughed. She did not turn but cocked an eye at me over her shoulder—a menacing posture. I was afraid that if I tried to leave she would hunt me through the brush.

"I won't kill you," she said again. She lowered her head, and I could feel her despair, her shame; it acted to lessen my fear.

"The soldiers will be coming," I said.

She was silent, motionless.

"You should make the exchange with Ray."

I was horrified by what she had done, but I wanted her to

live. Insane or not, she was too rare to lose—a voice of mystery in all this ordinary matter.

"No more." She said it in a grim whisper. "I know it's much to ask, Frank, but will you keep me company?"

"What are you going to do?"

"Nothing. Wait for the soldiers." She inspected her wound; the blood had quit flowing. "And if they don't come before dawn, I'll watch the sunrise. I've always been curious about it."

She scarcely said a word the rest of the night. We went down to the shore and sat beside a tangle of mangrove. I tried to convince her to survive, but she warded off every argument with a slashing gesture. Toward dawn, as the first gray appeared in the east, she had a convulsion, a brief flailing of the limbs that stretched her out flat. Dawn comes swiftly on the water, and by the time she had regained consciousness, pink streaks were infiltrating the gray.

"Make the exchange," I urged her. "It's not too late, is it?"

She ignored me. Her eyes were fixed on the horizon, where the rim of the solar disc was edging up; the sea reflected a rippling path of crimson and purple leading away from it, and the bottoms of the clouds were dyed these same colors.

Ten minutes later she had a more severe convulsion. This one left a froth of bloody bubbles rimming her nostrils. She groped for my hand, and as she squeezed it, I felt my bones grinding together. My emotions were grinding together as well; my situation—like Henry Meachem's—was so similar to hers. Aliens and strangers, all of us, unable to come to grips with this melancholy island.

Shortly after her third convulsion, I heard an outboard motor. A dory was cutting toward us from the reef wall; it was not a large enough craft to be the militia, and as it drew near, I recognized Hatfield Brooks by his silhouette hunched over the tiller, his natty dreads. He switched off the motor and let the dory drift until he was about fifty feet away; then he dropped the anchor and picked up a rifle that had been leaning against the front seat. He set the stock to his shoulder.

"Keep clear of dere, Mr. Winship!" he called. "I can't vouch for de steadiness of my aim."

Behind him, shafts of light were spearing up through balconies of cloud—a cathedral of a sky.

"Don't, Hatfield!" I stepped in front of Cassiopeia, waving my arms. "She's . . . he's dying! There's no need for it!"

"Keep clear!" he shouted. "De mon have killed Jimmy, and I come for him!"

"Just let him die!"

"He don't just let Jimmy die! Hettie been sayin' how dat crazy mon batter him!" He braced himself in the stern and took aim.

With a hoarse sigh, Cassiopeia climbed to her feet. I caught her wrist. Her skin was burning hot, her pulse drummed. Nerves twitched at the corners of her eyes, and one of the pupils was twice the size of the other. It was Ray's face I was seeing in that dawn light—hollow-cheeked, dirt-smeared, haggard; but even then I saw a sleeker shape beneath. She peeled my fingers off her wrist.

"Goodbye, Frank," she said; she pushed me away and ran toward Hatfield.

Ran!

The water was waist-deep all the way to the reef, yet she knifed through it as if it were nothing, ploughing a wake like the hull of a speedboat. It was a more disturbing sight than her destruction of Mullins had been. Thoroughly inhuman. Hatfield's first shot struck her in the chest and barely slowed her. She was twenty feet from the dory when the second shot hit, and that knocked her sideways, clawing at her stomach. The third drilled a jet of blood from her shoulder, driving her back; but she came forward again. One plodding step after another, shaking her head with pain. Four, five, six. Hatfield kept squeezing off the rounds, and I was screaming for him to finish her—each shot was a hammerblow that shivered loose a new scream. An arm's length from the dory, she sank to her knees and grabbed the keel, rocking it violently. Hatfield bounced side to side, unable to bring the rifle to bear. It discharged twice. Wild misses aimed at the sky, the trees.

And then, her head thrown back, arms upflung, Cassiopeia leaped out of the water.

Out of the world.

I am not sure whether she meant to kill Hatfield or if this was just a last expression of physicality—whatever her intent, she went so high that it was more a flight than a leap. Surrounded by a halo of fiery drops, twisting above the dory, her chest striped with blood, she seemed a creation of some visionary's imagination, bursting from a jeweled egg and being drawn gracefully into the heavens. But at the peak of the leap, she came all disjointed and fell, disappearing in a splash. Moments later, she floated up—face downward—and began to drift away. The sound of the reef faded in a steady, soothing hiss. The body spun slowly on the tide; the patch of water around it was stained gold and purple, as if the wounds were leaking the colors of sunrise.

Hatfield and I stared at each other across the distance. He did not lower the rifle. Strangely enough, I was not afraid. I had come to the same conclusion as Cassiopeia, the knowledge that the years could only decline from this point onward. I felt ready to die. The soft crush of waves building louder and louder on the reef, the body drifting leisurely toward shore, the black snaky-haired figure bobbing in his little boat against the enormous flag of the sunburst—it was a perfect medium for death. The whole world was steeped in it. But Hatfield laid the rifle down. He half raised his hand to me—an aborted salute or farewell—and held the pose a second or two; he must have recognized the futility of any gesture, for he ducked his head then and fired up the motor, leaving me to take charge of the dead.

The authorities were unable to contact Ray's family. It may be that he had none; he had never spoken of them. The local cemetery refused his remains—too many Brookses and Mullinses under the soil; and so, as was appropriate, he was laid to rest beside Ezekiel and Carl on the Burying Ground. Hatfield fled off-island and worked his passage to Miami; though he is still considered something of a hero, the tide of anti-Americanism ebbed—it was as if Ray had been a surrogate for the mercenaries and development bankers who had raped the island over the years. Once more there were friendly greetings, smiling faces, and contented shrimp-workers. As for me, I married Elizabeth. I have no illusions about the relationship; in retrospect, it seems a self-destructive move. But I was shaken, haunted. If I had not committed my stupidity with the recorder, if I had not thrown my arms around Cassiopeia, would she have been able to control her anger? Would she merely have disarmed Mullins? I needed the bitter enchantment of a marriage to ground myself in the world again, to obscure the answers to these questions, to blur the meaning of these events.

And what was their meaning?

Was this a traveler's tale like none other, a weaving together of starships and pirates, madmen and ghosts, into the history of an alien being and a sorry plot of mangrove? Or was it simply an extraordinary instance of psychosis, a labyrinthine justification for a young man's lack of inner strength?

I have no proof that would be measurable by any scientific rule, though I can offer one that is purely Guanojan and therefore open to interpretation—what was seen might have been an actual event or the shade of such an event, or it might have been the relic of a wish powerful enough to outlast the brain that conceived it. Witness the testimony of Donald Ebanks, a fisherman, who put in at night to the Burying Ground for repairs several months after Cassiopeia's death. I heard him tell the story at The Chicken Shack, and since it was only the third retelling, since he had only downed two rums, it had not changed character much from the original.

"I tinkerin' wit de fuel line," he said, "when of a sudden dere's de sound of wind, and yet dere ain't no wind to feel. I 'ware dat dis de duppy sign, but I ain't fearful 'cause my mother she take me to Escuilpas as a child and have de Black Virgin bless me. After dat no duppy can do me harm. Still, I wary. I turn and dere dey is. Two of dem, bot' shinin' pale white wit dat duppy glow dat don't 'low you to see dere trut'ful colors. One were Ray Milliken, and de other . . . God! I fall back in de boat to see it. De face ain't not'ing but teeth and eyes, and dere's a fringe 'round de head like de fringe of de anemone—snappin' and twistin'. And tall! Dis duppy mus' be two foot taller dan Ray. Skinny-tall. Wearin' somet'ing dat fit tight to it frame neck-to-toe, and shine even brighter dan de glow 'round dere bodies. Now Ray he smile and come a step to me, but dis other cotch he arm and 'pear to be scoldin' him. It point behind dem, and dere, right where it pointin', some of de glow clear a spot, and de spot growin' wider and wider to a circle, and t'rough de circle I'm seein' creepers, trees . . . solid jungle like dey gots in Miskitia. Ray have a fretful look on he face, but he shrug and dey walks off into de circle. Not walkin' proper, you understand. Dey dwindlin', and de wind dwindlin' wit dem. See, dey not travelin' over de Buryin' Ground but 'pon duppy roads dat draws dem quick from de world, and dey jus' dwindlin' and dwindlin' 'til dey's not'ing but a speck of gleam and a whisper of wind. Den dey gone. Gone for good was de feelin' I got. But where, I cannot tell you."

Mengele

During the Vietnam War I served as an aerial scout, piloting a single-engine Cessna low above the jungles, spotting targets for the F-16s. It was not nearly so dangerous as it sounds; the VC preferred to risk the slim chance of being spotted rather than giving away their positions by shooting me down, and most of my flights were made in an atmosphere of relative peace and quiet. I had always been a loner, perhaps even a bit of a misanthrope, and after my tour was up, after returning to the States, I found these attitudes had hardened. War had either colored my perceptions or dropped the scales from my eyes, for everywhere I went I noticed a great dissolution. In the combat zones and shooting galleries, in the bombed-looking districts of urban decay, in the violent music and the cities teeming with derelicts and burned-out children, I saw reflected the energies that had created Vietnam; and it occurred to me that in our culture war and peace had virtually the same effects. The West, it seemed, was truly in decline. I was less in sympathy with those who preached social reform than with the wild-eyed street evangelists who proclaimed the last days and the triumph of evil. Yet evil struck me then as too emotional and unsophisicticated a term, redolent of swarming demons and medieval plagues, and I preferred to think of it as a spiritual malaise. No matter what label was given to the affliction, though, I wanted no part of it. I came to think of my wartime experiences, the clean minimalism of my solo flights, as an idyll, and thus I entered into the business of ferrying small planes (Phelan's Air Pherry I called it, until I smartened up).

My disposition to the business was similar to that of someone who is faced with the prospect of crossing a puddle too large to leap; he must plot a course between the shallow spots and then skip on tiptoe from point to point, landing as lightly as possible in order to avoid a contaminating splash. It was my intent to soar above decay, to touch down only in those places as yet unspoiled. Some of the planes I ferried carried cargos, which I did not rigorously inspect; others I delivered to their owners, however far away their homes. The farther away the better, to my mind. By my reckoning I have spent fifteen months in propeller-driven aircraft over water, a good portion of this over the North Atlantic; and so, when I was offered a substantial fee to pilot a twin-engine Beechcraft from Miami to Asunción, the capital of Paraguay, it hardly posed a challenge.

From the outset, though, the flight proved to be anything but unchallenging: the Beechcraft was a lemon. The right wing shimmied, the inside of the cabin rattled like an old jalopy, and the radio was constantly on the fritz, giving up the ghost once and for all as I crossed into Paraguayan airspace. I had to set down in Guayaquil for repairs to the electrical system, and then, as I was passing over the Gran Chaco—the great forest that sprawls across western Paraguay, a wilderness of rumpled, dark green hills—the engines died.

In those first seconds of pure silence before the weight of the world dragged me down and the wind began ripping past, I experienced an exhilaration, an irrational confidence that God had chosen to make an exception of me and had repealed the law of gravity, that I would float the rest of the way to Asunción. But as the nose of the plane tipped earthward and a chill fanned out from my groin, I shook off this notion and started fighting for my life. A river—the Pilcomayo—was glinting silver among the hills several miles to my left; I banked into a glide and headed toward it. Under ordinary conditions I would have had time to pick an optimal stretch of water, but the

Beechcraft was an even worse glider than airplane, and I had to settle for the nearest likely spot: a fairly straight section enclosed by steep piney slopes. As I flashed between the slopes, I caught sight of black-roofed cottages along the shore, a much larger house looming on the crest. Then I smacked down, skipping like a stone for at least a hundred yards. I felt the tail lift, and everything became a sickening whirl of dark green and glare, and the hard silver light of the river came up to shatter the windshield.

I must have regained consciousness shortly after the crash, for I recall a face peering in at me. There was something malformed about the face, some wrongness of hue and shape, but I was too dizzy to see clearly. I tried to speak, managed a croak, and just this slight effort caused me to lose consciousness again. The next thing I recall is waking in a high-ceilinged room whose size led me to believe that I was inside the large house I had noticed atop the slope. My head ached fiercely, and when I put a hand to my brow I found it to be bandaged. As soon as the aching had diminished, I sat up and looked around. The decor of the room had a rectitude that would have been appropriate to a mausoleum. The walls and floors were of gray marble inscribed by veins of deeper gray; the door—a featureless rectangle of ebony—was flanked by two black wooden chairs; the bed itself was spread with a black silk coverlet. I assumed the drapes overhanging the window to be black also, but on closer inspection I discovered that they were woven of a cloth that under various intensities of light displayed many colors of darkness. These were the only furnishings. Carefully, because I was still dizzy, I walked to the window and pulled back the drapes. Scattered among the pines below were a dozen or so black roofs—tile, they were— and a handful of people were visible on the paths between them. There was a terrible, slow awkwardness to their movements that brought to mind the malformed face I had seen earlier, and a nervous thrill ran across the muscles of my shoulders. Farther down the slope the pines grew more thickly, obscuring the wreckage of the plane, though patches of shining water showed through the boughs.

I heard a click behind me, and turning I saw an old man in

the doorway. He was leaning on a cane, wearing a loose gray shirt that buttoned high about his throat, and dark trousers—apparently of the same material as the drapes; he was so hunched that it was only with great difficulty he was able to lift his eyes from the floor (an infirmity, he told me later, that had led to his acquiring an interest in entomology). He was bald, his scalp mottled like a bird's egg, and when he spoke the creakiness of his voice could not disguise a thick German accent.

"I'm pleased to see you up and about, Mr. Phelan," he said, indicating by a gesture that I should sit on the bed.

"I take it I have you to thank for this," I said, pointing to my bandage. "I'm very grateful, Mr. . . . ?"

"You may call me Dr. Mengele." He shuffled toward me at a snail's pace. "I have of course learned your name from your papers. They will be returned to you."

The name Mengele, which had the sound of a dull bell ringing, was familiar; but I was neither Jewish nor a student of history, and it was not until after he had examined me, pronouncing me fit, that I began to put together the name and the facts of his age, his accent, and his presence in this remote Paraguayan village. Then I remembered a photograph I had seen as a child: a fleshy, smiling man with dark hair cut high above his ears was standing beside a surgical table, where lay a young woman, her torso draped by a sheet; her legs were exposed, and from the calves down all the flesh had been removed, leaving the skeleton protruding from the bloody casings of her knees. *Josef Mengele in his surgery at Auschwitz* had read the caption. That photograph had had quite an effect on me, because of its horrific detail and also because I had not understood what scientific purpose could have been served by this sort of mutilation. I stared at the old man, trying to match his face with the smiling, fleshy one, trying to feel the emanation of evil; but he was withered and shrunken to the point of anonymity, and the only impression I received from him was of an enormous vitality, a forceful physical glow such as might have accrued to a healthy young man.

"Mengele," I said. "Not . . ."

"Yes, yes!" he said impatiently. "*That* Mengele. The mad doctor of the Third Reich. The monster, the sadist."

I was repelled, and yet I did not feel outrage as I might have, had I been Jewish. I had been born in 1948, and the terrors of World War II, the concentration camps, Mengele's hideous pseudoscientific experiments, they had the reality of vampire movies for me. I was curious, intensely so, in the way a child becomes fascinated with a crawling thing he has turned up from beneath a stone: he is inclined to crush it, but more likely to watch it ooze along.

"Come with me," said Mengele, shuffling toward the door. "I can offer you dinner, but afterward I'm afraid you must leave. We have but one law here, and that is that no stranger may pass the night within our borders." I had not observed any roads leading away from the village, and when I asked if I might have use of a radio, he laughed. "We have no communication with the outside world. We are self-sufficient here. None of the villagers ever leave, and rarely do we have visitors. You will have to make your way as best you can."

"Are you saying I'll have to walk?" I asked.

"You have no choice. If you head south along the river, some twenty or twenty-five kilometers, you will reach another village and there you will find a radio."

The prospect of being thrown out into the Gran Chaco made me even less eager for his company, but if I was going on a twenty-five-kilometer hike I needed food. His pace was so slow that our walk to the dining room effectively constituted a tour of the house. He talked as we went, telling me—surprisingly enough—of his conversion to Nazism (National Socialism, he termed it) and his work at the camps. Whenever I asked a question he would pause, his expression would go blank, and after a moment he would pose a complicated answer. I had the idea that his answers were prerehearsed, that he had long ago anticipated every possible question and during those pauses he was rummaging through a file. In truth I only half listened to him, being disconcerted by the house. It seemed less a house than a bleak mental landscape, and though I was accompanied by the man whose mind it no doubt reflected, I felt imperiled, out of my element. We passed room after room of gray marble and black furnishings identical to those I have already noted, but with an occasional variant: a pedestal supporting nothing but an obsidian surface; a bookshelf containing rows of black volumes; a carpet of so lusterless and deep a black that it looked to be an opening into some negative dimension. The silence added to my sense of endangerment, and as we entered the dining room, a huge marble cell distinguished from the other rooms by a long ebony table and an iron chandelier, I forced myself to pay attention to him, hoping the sound of his voice would steady my nerves. He had been telling me, I realized, about his flight from Germany.

"It hardly felt like an escape," he said. "It had more the air of a vacation. Packing, hurried goodbyes, and as soon as I reached Italy and met my Vatican contact, it all became quite relaxing. Good dinners, fine wines, and at last a leisurely sea voyage." He seated himself at one end of the table and rang a small black bell: it had been muffled in some way and barely produced a note. "It will be several minutes before you are served, I fear," he went on. "I did not know when you would be sufficiently recovered to eat."

I took a seat at the opposite end of the table. The strangeness of the environment, meeting Mengele, and now his reminiscences, all coming on the heels of my crash . . . it had left me fuddled. I felt as if I were phasing in and out of existence; at one moment I would be alert, intent upon his words, and the next I would be wrapped in vagueness and staring at the walls. The veins of the marble appeared to be writhing, spelling out messages in an archaic script.

"This house," I said suddenly, interrupting him. "Why is it like it is? It doesn't seem a place in which a man—even one with your history—would choose to live."

Again, that momentary blankness. "I believe you may well be a kindred spirit, Mr. Phelan," he said, and smiled. "Only one other has asked that particular question, and though he did not understand my answer at first, he came to understand it as you may someday." He cleared his throat. "You see, several years after I had settled in Paraguay I underwent a crisis of conscience. Not that I had regrets concerning my actions during the war. Oh, I had nightmares now and again, but no more than such as come to every man. No, I had faith in my work, despite the fact that it had been countenanced as evil, and as it turned out, that work proved to be the foundation of consequential discoveries. But perhaps, I thought, it *was* evil. If this were the case, I freely admitted to it . . . and yet I had never seen myself as an evil man. Only a committed one. And now the focus of my commitment—National Socialism—had failed. It was inconceivable to me, though, that the principles underlying it had failed, and I came to the conclusion that the failure could probably be laid to a misapprehension of those principles. Things had happened too fast for us. We had always been in a hurry, overborne by the needs of the country; we had been too pressured to act coherently, and the movement had become less a religion than a church. Empty, pompous ritual had taken the place of contemplated action. But now I had no pressure and all the time in the world, and I set out to understand the nature of evil."

He sighed and drummed his fingers on the table. "It was a slow process. Years of study, reading philosophy and natural history and cabalistic works, anything that might have a bearing on the subject. And when finally I did understand, I was amazed that I had not done so sooner. It was obvious! Evil was not—as it had been depicted for centuries—the tool of chaos. Creation was the chaotic force. Why, you can see this truth in every mechanism of the natural world, in the clouds of pollen, the swarms of flies, the migrations of birds. There is precision in those events, but they are nonetheless chaotic. Their precision is one born of overabundance, a million pellets shot and several dozen hitting the mark. No, evil was not chaotic. It was simplicity, it was system, it was the severing stroke of a knife. And most of all, it was inevitable. The entropic resolution of good, the utter simplification of the creative. Hitler had always known this, and National Socialism had always embodied it. What were the blitzkrieg and the concentration camps if not tactical expressions of that simplicity? What is this house if not its esthetic employment?" Mengele smiled, apparently amused by something he saw written on my face. "This understanding of mine may not strike you as revelatory, yet once I did understand everything I had been doing, all my researches began to succeed whereas previously they had failed. By understanding, of course, I do not mean that I merely acknowledged the principle. I absorbed it, I dissolved in it, I let it rule me like magic. I *understood*!"

I am not sure what I might have said—I was revolted by the depth of his madness, his iniquity—but at that moment he turned to the door and said, "Ah! Your dinner." A man dressed in the same manner as Mengele was shuffling across the room, carrying a tray. I barely glanced at him, intent upon my host. The man moved behind my chair and, leaning in over my shoulder, began to lay down plates and silverware. Then I noticed his hand. The skin was ashen gray, the fingers knobbly and unnaturally long—the fingers of a demon—and the nails were figured by half-moons of dead white. Startled, I looked up at him.

He had almost finished setting my place, and I doubt I stared at him for more than a few seconds, but those seconds passed as slowly as drops of water welling from a leaky tap. His face had a horrid simplicity that echoed the decor of the house. His mouth was a lipless slit, his eyes narrow black ovals, his nose a slight swelling perforated by two neat holes; he was bald, his skull elongated, and each time he inclined his head I could see a ridge of bone bisecting the scalp like the sagittal crest of a lizard. All his movements had that awful slowness I had observed in the people of the village. I wanted to fling myself away from the table, but I maintained control and waited until he had gone before I spoke.

"My God!" I said. "What's wrong with him?"

Mengele pursed his lips in disapproval. "The deformed are ever with us, Mr. Phelan. Surely you have seen worse in your time."

"Yes, but . . ."

"Tell me of an instance." He leaned forward, eager to hear.

I was nonplused, but I told him how one night in New York City—my home—I had been walking in the East Village when a man had come toward me from the opposite corner; his collar had been turned up, his chin tucked in, so that most of his face was obscured; yet as he had passed, the flare of the streetlight had revealed a grimacing mouth set vertically just beneath his cheekbone, complete with tiny teeth. I had not been able to tell if he had in addition a normal mouth, and over the years I had grown uncertain as to whether or not it had been a hallucination. Mengele was delighted and asked me to supply more descriptive details, as if he planned to add the event to his file.

"But your servant," I asked. "What of him?"

"Merely a decoration," he said. "A creature of my design. The village and the woods abound with them. No doubt you will encounter a fair sampling on your walk along the Pilcomayo."

"Your design!" I was enraged. "You made him that way?"

"You cannot have expected my work to have an angelic character." Mengele paused, thoughtful. "You must understand that what you see here, the villagers, the house, everything, is a memorial to my work. It has the reality of one of those glass baubles that contain wintry rural scenes and when shaken produce whirling snowstorms. The same actions are repeated over and over, the same effects produced. There is nothing for you to be upset about. The people here are content to serve me in this fashion. They understand." He pointed to the plates in front of me. "Eat, Mr. Phelan. Time is pressing."

I looked down at the plates. They were black ceramic. One held a green salad, and the other slices of roast beef swimming in blood. I have always enjoyed rare beef, but in that place it seemed an obscenity. Nonetheless, I was hungry, and I ate. And while I did, while Mengele told me of his work in genetics—work that had created monstrosities such as his servant—I determined to kill him. We were natural enemies, he and I. For though I had no personal score to settle, he exulted in the dissolution that I had spent most of my postwar life in avoiding. It was time, I thought, to do more than avoid it. I decided to take the knife with which I cut my beef and slash his throat. Perhaps he would appreciate the simplicity.

"Naturally," he said, "the creation of grotesques was not the pinnacle of my achievements. That pinnacle I reached nine years ago when I discovered a means of chemically affecting the mechanisms that underlie gene regulation, specifically those that control cell breakdown and rebuilding."

Being no scientist, I was not sure what he meant. "Cell breakdown?" I said. "Are you. . . ."

"Simply stated," he said, "I learned to reverse the process of aging. It may be that I have discovered the secret of immortality, though it is not yet clear how many treatments the body will accept."

"If that's true, why haven't you treated yourself?"

"Indeed," he said with a chuckle. "Why not?"

There was no doubt in my mind that he was lying about his great triumph, and this lie—which put into an even darker perspective the malignancy of his work, showing it to be purposeless, serving no end other than to further the vileness of his ego—this lie firmed my resolve to kill him. I gripped the knife and started to push back my chair; but then a disturbing thought crossed my mind. "Why have you revealed yourself to me?" I asked. "Surely you know that I'm liable to mention this to someone."

"First, Mr. Phelan, you may never have a chance to mention it; a twenty-five-kilometer walk along the Pilcomayo is no Sunday stroll. Second, whom would you tell? The officialdom of this country are my associates."

"What about the Israelis? If they knew of this place, they'd be swarming all over you."

"The Israelis!" Mengele made a noise of disgust. "They would not find me here. Tell them if you wish. I will give you proof." He opened a drawer in the end of the table and from it removed an ink bottle and a sheet of paper; he poured a few drops of ink onto the paper, and after a moment pressed his thumb down to make a print; then he blew on the paper and slid it toward me. "Show that to the Israelis and tell them I am not afraid of their reprisals. My work will go on."

I picked up the paper. "I suppose you've altered your prints, and this will only prove to the Israelis that I'm a madman."

"These fingerprints have not been altered."

"Good." I folded the paper and stuck it into my shirt pocket. Knife in hand, I stood and walked along the table toward him. I am certain he knew my intention, yet his bemused expression did not falter; and when I reached his side he looked me in the eyes. I wanted to say something, pronounce a curse that would harrow him to hell; his calm stare, however, unnerved me. I put my left hand behind his neck to steady him and prepared to draw the blade across his jugular. But as I did, he seized my wrist in a powerful grip, holding me immobile. I clubbed him on the brow with my left hand, and his head scarcely wobbled. Terrified, I tried to wrench free and managed to stagger a few paces away, pulling him after me. He did not attack; he only laughed and maintained his grip. I battered him again and again, I clawed at his face, his neck, and in so doing I tore the buttons from his shirt. The two halves fell open, and I screamed at what I saw.

He flung me to the floor and shrugged off the torn shirt. I was transfixed. Though he was still hunched, his torso was smooth-skinned and powerfully muscled, the torso of a young man from which a withered neck had sprouted; his arms, too, bulged with muscle and evolved into gnarled, liver-spotted hands. There was no trace of surgical scarring; the skin flowed from youth to old age in the way a tributary changes color upon merging with the mainstream. "Why not?" he had answered when I asked why he did not avail himself of his treatments. Of course he had, and—in keeping with his warped sensibilities—he had transformed himself into a monster. The sight of that shrunken face perched atop a youthful body was enough to shred the last of my rationality. Ablaze with fear, I scrambled to my feet and ran from the room, bursting through the main doors and down the piney slope, with Mengele's laughter echoing behind.

Night had fallen, a three-quarter moon rode high, and as I plunged along the path toward the river, in the slants of silvery light piercing the boughs I saw the villagers standing by the doors of their cottages. Some moved after me, stretching out their arms . . . whether in supplication or aggression, I was unable to tell. I did not stop to take note of their particular deformities, but glimpsed oblate heads, strangely configured hands, great bruised-looking eyes that seemed patches of velvet woven into their skins rather than organs with humors and capillaries. Breath shrieked in my throat as I zigzagged among them, eluding their sluggish attempts to touch me. And then I was splashing through the shallows, past the wreckage of my plane, past those godforsaken slopes, panicked, falling, crawling, sending up silvery sprays of water that were like shouts, pure expressions of my fear.

Twenty-five kilometers along the Río Pilcomayo. Fifteen miles. Twelve hours. No measure could encompass the terrors of that walk. Mengele's creatures did, indeed, abound. Once, while pausing to catch my breath, I spotted an owl on a branch that overhung the water. A jet-black owl, its eyes glowing faintly orange. Once a vast bulk heaved up from midstream, just the back of the thing, an expanse of smooth dark skin: it may have been thirty feet long. Once, at a point where the Pilcomayo fell into a gorge and I was forced to go overland, something heavy pursued me through the brush, and at last, fearing it more than the rapids, I dove into the river; as the current bore me off, I saw its huge misshapen head leaning over the cliff, silhouetted against the stars. All around I heard cries that I did not believe could issue from an earthly throat. Bubbling screeches, grinding roars, eerie whistles that reminded me of the keening made by incoming artillery rounds. By the time I reached the village of which Mengele had spoken, I was incoherent and I remember little of the flight that carried me to Asunción.

The authorities questioned me about my accident. I told them my compass had malfunctioned, that I had no idea where I had crashed. I was afraid to mention Mengele. These men were his accomplices, and besides, if his creatures flourished along the Pilcomayo, could not some of them be here? What had he said? "The deformed are ever with us, Mr. Phelan." True enough, but since my experiences in his house it seemed I had become sensitized to their presence. I picked them out of crowds, I encountered them on street corners, I saw the potential for deformity in every normal face. Even after returning to New York, every subway ride, every walk, every meal out, brought me into contact with men and women who hid their faces—all having the gray city pallor—yet who could not quite disguise some grotesque disfigurement. I suffered nightmares; I imagined I was being watched. Finally, in hopes of exorcising these fears, I went to see an old Jewish man, a colleague of Simon Wiesenthal, the famous Nazi hunter.

His office in the East Seventies was a picture of clutter, with stacks of papers and folios teetering on his desk, overflowing file cabinets. He was as old a man as Mengele had appeared, his forehead tiered by wrinkles, cadaverous cheeks, weepy brown eyes. I took a seat at the desk and handed him the paper on which Mengele had made his thumbprint. "I'd like this identified," I said. "I believe it belongs to Josef Mengele."

He stared at it a moment, then hobbled over to a cabinet and began shuffling through papers. After several minutes he clicked his tongue against his teeth and came back to the desk. "Where did you get this?" he asked with a degree of urgency.

"Does it match?"

He hesitated. "Yes, it matches. Now where did you get it?"

As I told my story, he leaned back and closed his eyes and nodded thoughtfully, interrupting me to ask an occasional question. "Well," I said when I had finished. "What are you going to do?"

"I don't know. There may be nothing I can do."

"What do you mean?" I said, dumbfounded. "I can give you the exact position of the village. Hell, I can take you there myself!"

He let out a weary sigh. "This"—he tapped the paper—"this is not Mengele's thumbprint."

"He must have altered it," I said, desperate to prove my case. "He *is* there! I swear it! If you would just. . . ." And then I realized something. "You said it matched?"

The old man's face seemed to have sagged further into decay. "Six years ago a man came to the office and told me almost verbatim the story you have told. I thought he was insane and threw him out, but before he left he thrust a paper at me, one that bore a thumbprint. That print matches yours. But it does not belong to Mengele."

"Then it is proof!" I said excitedly. "Don't you see? He may have altered it, but this proves that he exists, and the existence of the village where he lives."

"Does he live there?" he asked. "I'm afraid there is another possibility."

I was not sure what he meant at first; then I remembered Mengele's description of the village. ". . . what you see here, the villagers, the house, everything, is a memorial to my work. It has the reality of one of those glass baubles that contain wintry rural scenes and when shaken produce whirling snow-storms." The key word was "everything." I had likened the way he had paused before giving answers to rummaging through a file, but it was probably more accurate to say he had been re-calling a memorized biography. It had been a stand-in I had met, a young man made old or the reverse. Mengele was many years gone from the village, gone God knows where and in God knows what disguise, doing his work. Perhaps he was once again the fleshy, smiling man whose photograph I had seen as a child.

The old man and I had little else to say to one another. He was anxious to be rid of me; I had, after all, shed a wan light on his forty years of vengeful labor. I asked if he had an address for the other man who had told him of the village; I thought he alone might be able to offer me solace. The old man gave it to me—an address in the West Twenties—and promised to initi-ate an investigation of the village; but I think we both knew that Mengele had won, that *his* principle, not ours, was in accord with the times. I felt hopeless, stunned, and on step-ping outside I became aware of Mengele's victory in an even more poignant way.

It was a gray, blustery afternoon, a few snowflakes whirling between the drab facades of the buildings; the windows were glinting blackly, reflecting opaque diagonals of the sky. Gar-bage was piled in the gutters, spilling onto the sidewalks, and wedges of grimy crusted snow clung to the bumpers of the cars. Hunched against the wind, holding their coat collars closed over their faces, pedestrians struggled past. What I could see of their expressions was either hateful or angry or worried. It was a perfect Mengelian day, all underpinnings visible, everything pared down to ordinary bone; and as I walked along, I wondered for how much of it he was directly responsible. Oh, he was somewhere turning out grotesques, working scientific charms, but I doubted his efforts were essential to that gray principle underlying the factory air, the principle he worshiped, whose high priest he was. He had been right. Good *was* eroding into evil, bright into dark, abundance into uniformity. Everywhere I went I saw that truth reflected. In the simple shapes and primary colors of the cars, in the mad eyes of the bag ladies, in the featureless sky, in the single-minded stares of businessmen. We were all suffering a reduction to simpler forms, a draining of spirit and vitality.

I walked aimlessly, but I was not surprised to find myself some time later standing before an apartment building in the West Twenties; nor was I any more surprised when shortly thereafter a particularly gray-looking man came down the steps, his face muffled by a scarf and a wool hat pulled low over his brow. He shuffled across the street toward me, unwrapping the scarf. I knew I would be horrified by his deformity, yet I was willing to accept him, to listen, to hear what comforts deformity bestowed; because, though I did not understand Mengele's principle, though I had not dissolved in it or let it rule me, I had acknowledged it and sensed its inevitability. I could almost detect its slow vibrations ringing the changes of the world with—like the syllables of Mengele's name—the sullen, unmusical timbre of a deadened bell.

The Man Who Painted the Dragon Griaule

*O*ther than the Sichi Collection, Cattanay's only
surviving works are to be found in the Municipal Gallery at Regensburg, a group of eight oils-on-canvas,
most notable among them being Woman With Or-
anges. These paintings constitute his portion of a student exhibition hung some weeks after he had left the
city of his birth and traveled south to Teocinte, there
to present his proposal to the city fathers; it is unlikely
he ever learned of the disposition of his work, and
even more unlikely that he was aware of the general
critical indifference with which it was received. Perhaps the most interesting of the group to modern
scholars, the most indicative as to Cattanay's later
preoccupations, is the Self-Portrait, painted at the age
of twenty-eight, a year before his departure.

The majority of the canvas is a richly varnished
black in which the vague shapes of floorboards are
presented, barely visible. Two irregular slashes of gold
cross the blackness, and within these we can see a section of the artist's thin features and the shoulder panel
of his shirt. The perspective given is that we are looking down at the artist, perhaps through a tear in the
roof, and that he is looking up at us, squinting into
the light, his mouth distorted by a grimace born of

intense concentration. On first viewing the painting, I was struck by the atmosphere of tension that radiated from it. It seemed I was spying upon a man imprisoned within a shadow having two golden bars, tormented by the possibilities of light beyond the walls. And though this may be the reaction of the art historian, not the less knowledgeable and therefore more trustworthy response of the gallery-goer, it also seemed that this imprisonment was self-imposed, that he could have easily escaped his confine; but that he had realized a feeling of stricture was an essential fuel to his ambition, and so had chained himself to this arduous and thoroughly unreasonable chore of perception. . . .

—FROM MERIC CATTANAY:
THE POLITICS OF CONCEPTION
BY READE HOLLAND, PH.D.

I

In 1853, in a country far to the south, in a world separated from this one by the thinnest margin of possibility, a dragon named Griaule dominated the region of the Carbonales Valley, a fertile area centering upon the town of Teocinte and renowned for its production of silver, mahogany, and indigo. There were other dragons in those days, most dwelling on the rocky islands west of Patagonia—tiny, irascible creatures, the largest of them no bigger than a swallow. But Griaule was one of the great Beasts who had ruled an age. Over the centuries he had grown to stand 750 feet high at the midback, and from the tip of his tail to his nose he was six thousand feet long. (It should be noted here that the growth of dragons was due not to caloric intake, but to the absorption of energy derived from the passage of time.) Had it not been for a miscast spell, Griaule would have died millennia before. The wizard entrusted with the task of slaying him—knowing his own life would be forfeited as a result of the magical backwash—had experienced a last-second twinge of fear, and, diminished by this ounce of courage, the spell had flown a mortal inch awry. Though the wizard's whereabouts was unknown, Griaule had remained alive. His heart had stopped, his breath stilled, but his mind continued to seethe, to send forth the gloomy vibrations that enslaved all who stayed for long within range of his influence.

This dominance of Griaule's was an elusive thing. The people of the valley attributed their dour character to years of living under his mental shadow, yet there were other regional populations who maintained a harsh face to the world and had no dragon on which to blame the condition; they also attributed their frequent raids against the neighboring states to Griaule's effect, claiming to be a peaceful folk at heart—but again, was this not human nature? Perhaps the most certifiable proof of Griaule's primacy was the fact that despite a standing offer of a fortune in silver to anyone who could kill him, no one had succeeded. Hundreds of plans had been put forward, and all had failed, either through inanition or impracticality. The archives of Teocinte were filled with schematics for enormous steam-powered swords and other such improbable devices, and the architects of these plans had every one stayed too long in the valley and become part of the disgruntled populace. And so they went on with their lives, coming and going, always returning, bound to the valley, until one spring day in 1853, Meric Cattanay arrived and proposed that the dragon be painted.

He was a lanky young man with a shock of black hair and a pinched look to his cheeks; he affected the loose trousers and shirt of a peasant, and waved his arms to make a point. His eyes grew wide when listening, as if his brain were bursting with illumination, and at times he talked incoherently about "the conceptual statement of death by art." And though the city fathers could not be sure, though they allowed for the possibility that he simply had an unfortunate manner, it seemed he was mocking them. All in all, he was not the sort they were inclined to trust. But, because he had come armed with such a wealth of diagrams and charts, they were forced to give him serious consideration.

"I don't believe Griaule will be able to perceive the menace in a process as subtle as art," Meric told them. "We'll proceed as if we were going to illustrate him, grace his side with a work of true vision, and all the while we'll be poisoning him with the paint."

The city fathers voiced their incredulity, and Meric waited impatiently until they quieted. He did not enjoy dealing with these worthies. Seated at their long table, sour-faced, a huge smudge of soot on the wall above their heads like an ugly thought they were sharing, they reminded him of the Wine Merchants Association in Regensburg, the time they had rejected his group portrait.

"Paint can be deadly stuff," he said after their muttering had died down. "Take Vert Veronese, for example. It's derived from oxide of chrome and barium. Just a whiff would make you keel over. But we have to go about it seriously, create a real piece of art. If we just slap paint on his side, he might see through us."

The first step in the process, he told them, would be to build a tower of scaffolding, complete with hoists and ladders, that would brace against the supraorbital plates above the dragon's eye; this would provide a direct route to a seven-hundred-foot-square loading platform and base station behind the eye. He estimated it would take eight-one-thousand board feet of lumber, and a crew of ninety men should be able to finish construction within five months. Ground crews accompanied by chemists and geologists would search out limestone deposits (useful in priming the scales) and sources of pigments, whether organic or minerals such as azurite and hematite. Other teams would be set to scraping the dragon's side clean of algae, peeled skin, any decayed material, and afterward would laminate the surface with resins.

"It would be easier to bleach him with quicklime," he said. "But that way we lose the discolorations and ridges generated by growth and age, and I think what we'll paint will be defined by those shapes. Anything else would look like a damn tattoo!"

There would be storage vats and mills: edge-runner mills to separate pigments from crude ores, ball mills to powder the pigments, pug mills to mix them with oil. There would be boiling vats and calciners—fifteen-foot-high furnaces used to produce caustic lime for sealant solutions.

"We'll build most of them atop the dragon's head for purposes of access," he said. "On the frontoparietal plate." He checked some figures. "By my reckoning, the plate's about 350 feet wide. Does that sound accurate?"

Most of the city fathers were stunned by the prospect, but one managed a nod, and another asked, "How long will it take for him to die?"

"Hard to say," came the answer. "Who knows how much poison he's capable of absorbing? It might just take a few years. But in the worst instance, within forty or fifty years, enough chemicals will have seeped through the scales to have weakened the skeleton and he'll fall in like an old barn."

"Forty years!" exclaimed someone. "Preposterous!"

"Or fifty." Meric smiled. "That way we'll have time to finish the painting." He turned and walked to the window and stood gazing out at the white stone houses of Teocinte. This was going to be the sticky part, but if he read them right, they would not believe in the plan if it seemed too easy. They needed to feel they were making a sacrifice, that they were nobly bound to a great labor. "If it does take forty or fifty years," he went on, "the project will drain your resources. Timber, animal life, minerals. Everything will be used up by the work. Your lives will be totally changed. But I guarantee you'll be rid of him."

The city fathers broke into an outraged babble.

"Do you really want to kill him?" cried Meric, stalking over to them and planting his fists on the table. "You've been waiting centuries for someone to come along and chop off his head or send him up in a puff of smoke. That's not going to happen! There is no easy solution. But there is a practical one, an elegant one. To use the stuff of the land he dominates to destroy him. It will *not* be easy, but you *will* be rid of him. And that's what you want, isn't it?"

They were silent, exchanging glances, and he saw that they now believed he could do what he proposed and were wondering if the cost was too high.

"I'll need five hundred ounces of silver to hire engineers and artisans," said Meric. "Think it over. I'll take a few days and go see this dragon of yours . . . inspect the scales and so forth. When I return, you can give me your answer."

The city fathers grumbled and scratched their heads, but at last they agreed to put the question before the body politic. They asked for a week in which to decide and appointed Jarcke, who was the mayoress of Hangtown, to guide Meric to Griaule.

The valley extended seventy miles from north to south, and was enclosed by jungled hills whose folded sides and spiny backs gave rise to the idea that beasts were sleeping beneath them. The valley floor was cultivated into fields of bananas and cane and melons, and where it was not cultivated, there were stands of thistle palms and berry thickets and the occasional giant fig brooding sentinel over the rest. Jarcke and Meric tethered their horses a half-hour's ride from town and began to ascend a gentle incline that rose into the notch between two hills. Sweaty and short of breath, Meric stopped a third of the way up; but Jarcke kept plodding along, unaware he was no longer following. She was by nature as blunt as her name—a stump beer keg of a woman with a brown weathered face. Though she appeared to be ten years older then Meric, she was nearly the same age. She wore a gray robe belted at the waist with a leather band that held four throwing knives, and a coil of rope was slung over her shoulder.

"How much farther?" called Meric.

She turned and frowned. "You're standin' on his tail. Rest of him's around back of the hill."

A pinprick of chill bloomed in Meric's abdomen, and he stared down at the grass, expecting it to dissolve and reveal a mass of glittering scales.

"Why don't we take the horses?" he asked.

"Horses don't like it up here." She grunted with amusement. "Neither do most people, for that matter." She trudged off.

Another twenty minutes brought them to the other side of the hill high above the valley floor. The land continued to slope upward, but more gently than before. Gnarled, stunted

oaks pushed up from thickets of chokecherry, and insects siz-
zled in the weeds. They might have been walking on a natural
shelf several hundred feet across; but ahead of them, where the
ground rose abruptly, a number of thick greenish-black
columns broke from the earth. Leathery folds hung between
them, and these were encrusted with clumps of earth and bro-
caded with mold. They had the look of a collapsed palisade
and the ghosted feel of ancient ruins.

"Them's the wings," said Jarcke. "Mostly they's covered, but
you can catch sight of 'em off the edge, and up near Hangtown
there's places where you can walk in under 'em . . . but I
wouldn't advise it."

"I'd like to take a look off the edge," said Meric, unable to
tear his eyes away from the wings; though the surfaces of the
leaves gleamed in the strong sun, the wings seemed to absorb
the light, as if their age and strangeness were proof against
reflection.

Jarcke led him to a glade in which tree ferns and oaks
crowded together and cast a green gloom, and where the earth
sloped sharply downward. She lashed her rope to an oak and
tied the other end around Meric's waist. "Give a yank when
you want to stop, and another when you want to be hauled
up," she said, and began paying out the rope, letting him walk
backward against her pull.

Ferns tickled Meric's neck as he pushed through the brush,
and the oak leaves pricked his cheeks. Suddenly he emerged
into bright sunlight. On looking down, he found his feet were
braced against a fold of the dragon's wing, and on looking up,
he saw that the wing vanished beneath a mantle of earth and
vegetation. He let Jarcke lower him a dozen feet more, yanked,
and gazed off northward along the enormous swell of
Griaule's side.

The scales were hexagonals thirty feet across and half that
distance high; their basic color was a pale greenish gold, but
some were whitish, draped with peels of dead skin, and others
were overgrown by viridian moss, and the rest were scrolled
with patterns of lichen and algae that resembled the characters
of a serpentine alphabet. Birds had nested in the cracks, and

ferns plumed from the interstices, thousands of them lifting in
the breeze. It was a great hanging garden whose scope took
Meric's breath away—like looking around the curve of a fossil
moon. The sense of all the centuries accreted in the scales
made him dizzy, and he found he could not turn his head, but
could only stare at the panorama, his soul shriveling with a
comprehension of the timelessness and bulk of this creature to
which he clung like a fly. He lost perspective on the scene—
Griaule's side was bigger than the sky, possessing its own potent gravity, and it seemed completely reasonable that he
should be able to walk out along it and suffer no fall. He
started to do so, and Jarcke, mistaking the strain on the rope
for a signal, hauled him up, dragging him across the wing,
through the dirt and ferns, and back into the glade. He lay
speechless and gasping at her feet.

"Big 'un, ain't he," she said, and grinned.

After Meric had gotten his legs under him, they set off
toward Hangtown; but they had not gone a hundred yards,
following a trail that wound through the thickets, before
Jarcke whipped out a knife and hurled it at a racoon-sized
creature that leaped out in front of them.

"Skizzer," she said, kneeling beside it and pulling the knife
from its neck. "Calls 'em that 'cause they hisses when they
runs. They eats snakes, but they'll go after children what ain't
careful."

Meric dropped down next to her. The skizzer's body was
covered with short black fur, but its head was hairless, corpse-
pale, the skin wrinkled as if it had been immersed too long in
water. Its face was squinty-eyed, flat-nosed, with a dispropor-
tionately large jaw that hinged open to expose a nasty set of
teeth.

"They's the dragon's critters," said Jarcke. "Used to live in
his bunghole." She pressed one of its paws, and claws curved
like hooks slid forth. "They'd hang around the lip and drop on
other critters what wandered in. And if nothin' wandered
in. . . ." She pried out the tongue with her knife—its surface
was studded with jagged points like the blade of a rasp. "Then
they'd lick Griaule clean for their supper."

Back in Teocinte, the dragon had seemed to Meric a simple thing, a big lizard with a tick of life left inside, the residue of a dim sensibility; but he was beginning to suspect that this tick of life was more complex than any he had encountered.

"My gram used to say," Jarcke went on, "that the old dragons could fling themselves up to the sun in a blink and travel back to their own world, and when they come back, they'd bring the skizzers and all the rest with 'em. They was immortal, she said. Only the young ones came here 'cause later on they grew too big to fly on Earth." She made a sour face. "Don't know as I believe it."

"Then you're a fool," said Meric.

Jarcke glanced up at him, her hand twitching toward her belt.

"How can you live here and *not* believe it!" he said, surprised to hear himself so fervently defending a myth. "God! This . . ." He broke off, noticing the flicker of a smile on her face.

She clucked her tongue, apparently satisfied by something. "Come on," she said. "I want to be at the eye before sunset."

The peaks of Griaule's folded wings, completely overgrown by grass and shrubs and dwarfish trees, formed two spiny hills that cast a shadow over Hangtown and the narrow lake around which it sprawled. Jarcke said the lake was a stream flowing off the hill behind the dragon, and that it drained away through the membranes of his wing and down onto his shoulder. It was beautiful beneath the wing, she told him. Ferns and waterfalls. But it was reckoned an evil place. From a distance the town looked picturesque—rustic cabins, smoking chimneys. As they approached, however, the cabins resolved into dilapidated shanties with missing boards and broken windows; suds and garbage and offal floated in the shallows of the lake. Aside from a few men idling on the stoops, who squinted at Meric and nodded glumly at Jarcke, no one was about. The grass-blades stirred in the breeze, spiders scuttled under the shanties, and there was an air of torpor and dissolution.

Jarcke seemed embarrassed by the town. She made no attempt at introductions, stopping only long enough to fetch another coil of rope from one of the shanties, and as they walked between the wings, down through the neck spines—a forest of greenish gold spikes burnished by the lowering sun—she explained how the townsfolk grubbed a livelihood from Griaule. Herbs gathered on his back were valued as medicine and charms, as were the peels of dead skin; the artifacts left by previous Hangtown generations were of some worth to various collectors.

"Then there's scale hunters," she said with disgust. "Henry Sichi from Port Chantay'll pay good money for pieces of scale, and though it's bad luck to do it, some'll have a go at chippin' off the loose 'uns." She walked a few paces in silence. "But there's others who've got better reasons for livin' here."

The frontal spike above Griaule's eyes was whorled at the base like a narwhal's horn and curved back toward the wings. Jarcke attached the ropes to eyebolts drilled into the spike, tied one about her waist, the other about Meric's; she cautioned him to wait, and rappelled off the side. In a moment she called for him to come down. Once again he grew dizzy as he descended; he glimpsed a clawed foot far below, mossy fangs jutting from an impossibly long jaw; and then he began to spin and bash against the scales. Jarcke gathered him in and helped him sit on the lip of the socket.

"Damn!" she said, stamping her foot.

A three-foot-long section of the adjoining scale shifted slowly away. Peering close, Meric saw that while in texture and hue it was indistinguishable from the scale, there was a hairline division between it and the surface. Jarcke, her face twisted in disgust, continued to harry the thing until it moved out of reach.

"Call 'em flakes," she said when he asked what it was. "Some kind of insect. Got a long tube that they pokes down between the scales and sucks the blood. See there?" She pointed off to where a flock of birds was wheeling close to Griaule's side; a chip of pale gold broke loose and went tumbling down to the valley. "Birds pry 'em off, let 'em bust open, and eats the innards." She hunkered down beside him and after a moment asked, "You really think you can do it?"

"What? You mean kill the dragon?"

She nodded.

"Certainly," he said, and then added, lying, "I've spent years devising the method."

"If all the paint's goin' to be atop his head, how're you goin' to get it to where the paintin's done?"

"That's no problem. We'll pipe it to wherever it's needed."

She nodded again. "You're a clever fellow," she said; and when Meric, pleased, made as if to thank her for the compliment, she cut in and said, "Don't mean nothin' by it. Bein' clever ain't an accomplishment. It's just somethin' you come by, like bein' tall." She turned away, ending the conversation.

Meric was weary of being awestruck, but even so he could not help marveling at the eye. By his estimate it was seventy feet long and fifty feet high, and it was shuttered by an opaque membrane that was unusually clear of algae and lichen, glistening, with vague glints of color visible behind it. As the westering sun reddened and sank between two distant hills, the membrane began to quiver and then split open down the center. With the ponderous slowness of a theater curtain opening, the halves slid apart to reveal the glowing humor. Terrified by the idea that Griaule could see him, Meric sprang to his feet, but Jarcke restrained him.

"Stay still and watch," she said.

He had no choice—the eye was mesmerizing. The pupil was slit and featureless black, but the humor . . . he had never seen such fiery blues and crimsons and golds. What had looked to be vague glints, odd refractions of the sunset, he now realized were photic reactions of some sort. Fairy rings of light developed deep within the eye, expanded into spoked shapes, flooded the humor, and faded—only to be replaced by another and another. He felt the pressure of Griaule's vision, his ancient mind, pouring through him, and as if in response to this pressure, memories bubbled up in his thoughts. Particularly sharp ones. The way a bowlful of brush water had looked after freezing over during a winter's night—a delicate, fractured flower of murky yellow. An archipelago of orange peels that his girl had left strewn across the floor of the studio. Sketching atop Jokenam Hill one sunrise, the snow-capped roofs of Regensburg below pitched at all angles like broken paving stones, and silver shafts of the sun striking down through a leaden overcast. It was as if these things were being drawn forth for his inspection. Then they were washed away by what also seemed a memory, though at the same time it was wholly unfamiliar. Essentially it was a landscape of light, and he was plunging through it, up and up. Prisms and lattices of iridescent fire bloomed around him, and everything was a roaring fall into brightness, and finally he was clear into its white furnace heart, his own heart swelling with the joy of his strength and dominion.

It was dusk before Meric realized the eye had closed. His mouth hung open, his eyes ached from straining to see, and his tongue was glued to his palate. Jarcke sat motionless, buried in shadow.

"Th . . ." He had to swallow to clear his throat of mucus. "This is the reason you live here, isn't it?"

"Part of the reason," she said. "I can see things comin' way up here. Things to watch out for, things to study on."

She stood and walked to the lip of the socket and spat off the edge; the valley stretched out gray and unreal behind her, the folds of the hills barely visible in the gathering dusk.

"I seen you comin'," she said.

A week later, after much exploration, much talk, they went down into Teocinte. The town was a shambles—shattered windows, slogans painted on the walls, glass and torn banners and spoiled food littering the streets—as if there had been both a celebration and a battle. Which there had. The city fathers met with Meric in the town hall and informed him that his plan had been approved. They presented him a chest containing five hundred ounces of silver and said that the entire resources of the community were at his disposal. They offered a wagon and a team to transport him and the chest to Regensburg and asked if any of the preliminary work could be begun during his absence.

Meric hefted one of the silver bars. In its cold gleam he saw the object of his desire—two, perhaps three years of freedom, of doing the work he wanted and not having to accept commissions. But all that had been confused. He glanced at Jarcke; she was staring out the window, leaving it to him. He set the bar back in the chest and shut the lid.

"You'll have to send someone else," he said. And then, as the city fathers looked at each other askance, he laughed and laughed at how easily he had discarded all his dreams and expectations.

> *It had been eleven years since I had been to the valley, twelve since work had begun on the painting, and I was appalled by the changes that had taken place. Many of the hills were scraped brown and treeless, and there was a general dearth of wildlife. Griaule, of course, was most changed. Scaffolding hung from his back; artisans, suspended by webworks of ropes, crawled over his side; and all the scales to be worked had either been painted or primed. The tower rising to his eye was swarmed by laborers, and at night the calciners and vats atop his head belched flame into the sky, making it seem there was a mill town in the heavens. At his feet was a brawling shantytown populated by prostitutes, workers, gamblers, ne'er-do-wells of every sort, and soldiers: the burdensome cost of the project had encouraged the city fathers of Teocinte to form a regular militia, which regularly plundered the adjoining states and had posted occupation forces to some areas. Herds of frightened animals milled in the slaughtering pens, waiting to be rendered into oils and pigments. Wagons filled with ores and vegetable products rattled in the streets. I myself had brought a cargo of madder roots from which a rose tint would be derived.*
>
> *It was not easy to arrange a meeting with Cattanay. While he did none of the actual painting, he was always busy in his office consulting with engineers and artisans, or involved in some other part of the*

logistical process. When at last I did meet with him, I found he had changed as drastically as Griaule. His hair had gone gray, deep lines scored his features, and his right shoulder had a peculiar bulge at its midpoint—the product of a fall. He was amused by the fact that I wanted to buy the painting, to collect the scales after Griaule's death, and I do not believe he took me at all seriously. But the woman Jarcke, his constant companion, informed him that I was a responsible businessman, that I had already bought the bones, the teeth, even the dirt beneath Griaule's belly (this I eventually sold as having magical properties).

"Well," said Cattanay, "I suppose someone has to own them."

He led me outside, and we stood looking at the painting.

"You'll keep them together?" he asked.

I said, "Yes."

"If you'll put that in writing," he said, "then they're yours."

Having expected to haggle long and hard over the price, I was flabbergasted; but I was even more flabbergasted by what he said next.

"Do you think it's any good?" he asked.

Cattanay did not consider the painting to be the work of his imagination; he felt he was simply illuminating the shapes that appeared on Griaule's side and was convinced that once the paint was applied, new shapes were produced beneath it, causing him to make constant changes. He saw himself as an artisan more than a creative artist. But to put his question into perspective, people were beginning to flock from all over the world and marvel at the painting. Some claimed they saw intimations of the future in its gleaming surface; others underwent transfiguring experiences; still others—artists themselves—attempted to capture something of the work on canvas, hopeful of establishing reputations merely by being competent

copyists of Cattanay's art. The painting was nonrep-
resentational in character, essentially a wash of pale
gold spread across the dragon's side; but buried be-
neath the laminated surface were a myriad tints of iri-
descent color that, as the sun passed through the
heavens and the light bloomed and faded, solidified
into innumerable forms and figures that seemed to
flow back and forth. I will not try to categorize these
forms, because there was no end to them; they were as
varied as the conditions under which they were
viewed. But I will say that on the morning I met with
Cattanay, I—who was the soul of the practical man,
without a visionary bone in my body—felt as though I
were being whirled away into the painting, up
through geometries of light, latticeworks of rainbow
color that built the way the edges of a cloud build,
past orbs, sprials, wheels of flame. . . .

—FROM THIS BUSINESS OF GRIAULE
BY HENRY SICHI

II

There had been several women in Meric's life since he arrived in the valley; most had been attracted by his growing fame and his association with the mystery of the dragon, and most had left for the same reasons, feeling daunted and unappreciated. But Lise was different in two respects. First, because she loved Meric truly and well; and second, because she was married—albeit unhappily—to a man named Pardiel, the foreman of the calciner crew. She did not love him as she did Meric, yet she respected him and felt obliged to consider carefully before ending the relationship. Meric had never known such an introspective soul. She was twelve years younger than he, tall and lovely, with sun-streaked hair and brown eyes that went dark and seemed to turn inward whenever she was pensive. She was in the habit of analyzing everything that affected her, drawing back from her emotions and inspecting them as if they were a clutch of strange insects she had discovered crawling on her skirt. Though her penchant for self-examination kept her from him, Meric viewed it as a kind of baffling virtue. He had the classic malady and could find no fault with her. For almost a year they were as happy as could be expected; they talked long hours and walked together on those occasions when Pardiel worked double shifts and was forced to bed down by his furnaces, they spent the nights making love in the cavernous spaces beneath the dragon's wing.

It was still reckoned an evil place. Something far worse than skizzers or flakes was rumored to live there, and the ravages of this creature were blamed for every disappearance, even that of the most malcontented laborer. But Meric did not give credence to the rumors. He half believed Griaule had chosen him to be his executioner and that the dragon would never let him be harmed; and besides, it was the only place where they could be assured of privacy.

A crude stair led under the wing, handholds and steps hacked from the scales—doubtless the work of scale hunters. It was a treacherous passage, six hundred feet above the valley floor; but Lise and Meric were secured by ropes, and over the months, driven by the urgency of passion, they adapted to it. Their favorite spot lay fifty feet in (Lise would go no farther; she was afraid even if he was not), near a waterfall that trickled over the leathery folds, causing them to glisten with a mineral brilliance. It was eerily beautiful, a haunted gallery. Peels of dead skin hung down from the shadows like torn veils of ectoplasm; ferns sprouted from the vanes, which were thicker than cathedral columns; swallows curved through the black air. Sometimes, lying with her hidden by a tuck of the wing, Meric would think the beating of their hearts was what really animated the place, that the instant they left, the water ceased flowing and the swallows vanished. He had an unshakable faith in the transforming power of their affections, and one morning as they dressed, preparing to return to Hangtown, he asked her to leave with him.

"To another part of the valley?" She laughed sadly. "What good would that do? Pardiel would follow us."

"No," he said. "To another country. Anywhere far from here."

"We can't," she said, kicking at the wing. "Not until Griaule dies. Have you forgotten?"

"We haven't tried."

"Others have."

"But we'd be strong enough. I know it!"

"You're a romantic," she said gloomily, and stared out over the slope of Griaule's back at the valley. Sunrise had washed the hills to crimson, and even the tips of the wings were glowing a dull red.

"Of course I'm a romantic!" He stood, angry. "What the hell's wrong with that?"

She sighed with exasperation. "You wouldn't leave your work," she said. "And if we did leave, what work would you do? Would . . ."

"Why must everything be a problem in advance!" he shouted. "I'll tattoo elephants! I'll paint murals on the chests of giants, I'll illuminate whales! Who else is better qualified?"

She smiled, and his anger evaporated.

"I didn't mean it that way," she said. "I just wondered if you could be satisfied with anything else."

She reached out her hand to be pulled up, and he drew her into an embrace. As he held her, inhaling the scent of vanilla water from her hair, he saw a diminutive figure silhouetted against the backdrop of the valley. It did not seem real—a black homunculus—and even when it began to come forward, growing larger and larger, it looked less a man than a magical keyhole opening in a crimson-set hillside. But Meric knew from the man's rolling walk and the hulking set of his shoulders that it was Pardiel; he was carrying a long-handled hook, one of those used by artisans to maneuver along the scales.

Meric tensed, and Lise looked back to see what had alarmed him. "Oh, my God!" she said, moving out of the embrace.

Pardiel stopped a dozen feet away. He said nothing. His face was in shadow, and the hook swung lazily from his hand. Lise took a step toward him, then stepped back and stood in front of Meric as if to shield him. Seeing this, Pardiel let out an inarticulate yell and charged, slashing with the hook. Meric pushed Lise aside and ducked. He caught a brimstone whiff of the calciners as Pardiel rushed past and went sprawling, tripped by some irregularity in the scale. Deathly afraid, knowing he was no match for the foreman, Meric seized Lise's hand and ran deeper under the wing. He hoped Pardiel would be too frightened to follow, leery of the creature that was rumored to live there; but he was not. He came after them at a measured pace, tapping the hook against his leg.

Higher on Griaule's back, the wing was dimpled downward by hundreds of bulges, and this created a maze of small chambers and tunnels so low that they had to crouch to pass along them. The sound of their breathing and the scrape of their feet were amplified by the enclosed spaces, and Meric could no longer hear Pardiel. He had never been this deep before. He had thought it would be pitch-dark; but the lichen and algae adhering to the wing were luminescent and patterned every surface, even the scales beneath them, with whorls of blue and green fire that shed a sickly radiance. It was as if they were giants crawling through a universe whose starry matter had not yet congealed into galaxies and nebulas. In the wan light, Lise's face—turned back to him now and again—was teary and frantic; and then, as she straightened, passing into still another chamber, she drew in breath with a shriek.

At first Meric thought Pardiel had somehow managed to get ahead of them; but on entering he saw that the cause of her fright was a man propped in a sitting position against the far wall. He looked mummified. Wisps of brittle hair poked up from his scalp, the shapes of his bones were visible through his skin, and his eyes were empty holes. Between his legs was a scatter of dust where his gentials had been. Meric pushed Lise toward the next tunnel, but she resisted and pointed at the man.

"His eyes," she said, horror-struck.

Though the eyes were mostly a negative black, Meric now realized they were shot through by opalescent flickers. He felt compelled to kneel beside the man—it was a sudden, motiveless urge that gripped him, bent him to its will, and released him a second later. As he rested his hand on the scale, he brushed a massive ring that was lying beneath the shrunken

fingers. Its stone was black, shot through by flickers identical
to those within the eyes, and incised with the letter S. He
found his gaze was deflected away from both the stone and the
eyes, as if they contained charges repellent to the senses. He
touched the man's withered arm; the flesh was rock-hard, petrified. But alive. From that brief touch he gained an impression
of the man's life, of gazing for centuries at the same patch of
unearthly fire, of a mind gone beyond mere madness into a
perverse rapture, a meditation upon some foul principle. He
snatched back his hand in revulsion.

There was a noise behind them, and Meric jumped up,
pushing Lise into the next tunnel. "Go right," he whispered.
"We'll circle back toward the stair." But Pardiel was too close
to confuse with such tactics, and their flight became a wild
chase, scrambling, falling, catching glimpses of Pardiel's
smoke-stained face, until finally—as Meric came to a large
chamber—he felt the hook bite into his thigh. He went down,
clutching at the wound, pulling the hook loose. The next moment Pardiel was atop him; Lise appeared over his shoulder,
but he knocked her away and locked his fingers in Meric's hair
and smashed his head against the scale. Lise screamed, and
white lights fired through Meric's skull. Again his head was
smashed down. And again. Dimly, he saw Lise struggling with
Pardiel, saw her shoved away, saw the hook raised high and the
foreman's mouth distorted by a grimace. Then the grimace
vanished. His jaw dropped open, and he reached behind him
as if to scratch his shoulder blade. A line of dark blood eeled
from his mouth and he collapsed, smothering Meric beneath
his chest. Meric heard voices. He tried to dislodge the body,
and the effects drained the last of his strength. He whirled
down through a blackness that seemed as negative and inex-
haustible as the petrified man's eyes.

Someone had propped his head on their lap and was bathing
his brow with a damp cloth. He assumed it was Lise, but when
he asked what had happened, it was Jarcke who answered,
saying, "Had to kill him." His head throbbed, his leg throbbed
even worse, and his eyes would not focus. The peels of dead

skin hanging overhead appeared to be writhing. He realized they were out near the edge of the wing.

"Where's Lise?"

"Don't worry," said Jarcke. "You'll see her again." She made it sound like an indictment.

"Where is she?"

"Sent her back to Hangtown. Won't do you two bein' seen hand in hand the same day Pardiel's missin'."

"She wouldn't have left. . . ." He blinked, trying to see her face; the lines around her mouth were etched deep and reminded him of the patterns of lichen on the dragon's scale. "What did you do?"

"Convinced her it was best," said Jarcke. "Don't you know she's just foolin' with you?"

"I've got to talk to her." He was full of remorse, and it was unthinkable that Lise should be bearing her grief alone; but when he struggled to rise, pain lanced through his leg.

"You wouldn't get ten feet," she said. "Soon as your head's clear, I'll help you with the stairs."

He closed his eyes, resolving to find Lise the instant he got back to Hangtown—together they would decide what to do. The scale beneath him was cool, and that coolness was transmitted to his skin, his flesh, as if he were merging with it, becoming one of its ridges.

"What was the wizard's name?" he asked after a while, recalling the petrified man, the ring and its incised letter. "The one who tried to kill Griaule. . . ."

"Don't know as I ever heard it," said Jarcke. "But I reckon it's him back there."

"You saw him?"

"I was chasin' a scale hunter once what stole some rope, and I found him instead. Pretty miserable sort, whoever he is."

Her fingers trailed over his shoulder—a gentle, treasuring touch. He did not understand what it signaled, being too concerned with Lise, with the terrifying potentials of all that had happened; but years later, after things had passed beyond remedy, he cursed himself for not having understood.

At length Jarcke helped him to his feet, and they climbed up

to Hangtown, to bitter realizations and regrets, leaving Pardiel
to the birds or the weather or worse.

It seems it is considered irreligious for a woman in
love to hesitate or examine the situation, to do anything other than blindly follow the impulse of her
emotions. I felt the brunt of such an attitude—people
judged it my fault for not having acted quickly and
decisively one way or another. Perhaps I was overcau-
tious. I do not claim to be free of blame, only innocent
of sacrilege. I believe I might have eventually left
Pardiel—there was not enough in the relationship to
sustain happiness for either of us. But I had good reason for cautious examination. My husband was not
an evil man, and there were matters of loyalty between us.

I could not face Meric after Pardiel's death, and I
moved to another part of the valley. He tried to see me
on many occasions, but I always refused. Though I
was greatly tempted, my guilt was greater. Four years
later, after Jarcke died—crushed by a runaway
wagon—one of her associates wrote and told me
Jarcke had been in love with Meric, that it had been
she who had informed Pardiel of the affair, and that
she may well have staged the murder. The letter acted
somewhat to expiate my guilt, and I weighed the possibility of seeing Meric again. But too much time had
passed, and we had both assumed other lives. I decided against it. Six years later, when Griaule's influence had weakened sufficiently to allow emigration, I
moved to Port Chantay. I did not hear from Meric for
almost twenty years after that, and then one day I received a letter, which I will reproduce in part:

". . . My old friend from Regensburg, Louis Dardano, has been living here for the past few years, engaged in writing my biography. The narrative has a
breezy feel, like a tale being told in a tavern, which—if
you recall my telling you how this all began—is quite

*appropriate. But on reading it, I am amazed my life
has had such a simple shape. One task, one passion.
God, Lise! Seventy years old, and I still dream of you.
And I still think of what happened that morning under the wing. Strange, that it has taken me all this time
to realize it was not Jarcke, not you or I who was cul-
pable, but Griaule. How obvious it seems now. I was
leaving, and he needed me to complete the expression
on his side, his dream of flying, of escape, to grant
him the death of his desire. I am certain you will think
I have leaped to this assumption, but I remind you
that it has been a leap of forty years' duration. I know
Griaule, know his monstrous subtlety. I can see it at
work in every action that has taken place in the valley
since my arrival. I was a fool not to understand that
his powers were at the heart of our sad conclusion.*

*"The army now runs everything here, as no doubt
you are aware. It is rumored they are planning a winter campaign against Regensburg. Can you believe it!
Their fathers were ignorant, but this generation is
brutally stupid. Otherwise, the work goes well and
things are as usual with me. My shoulder aches, children stare at me on the street, and it is whispered I am
mad. . . ."*

—FROM UNDER GRIAULE'S WING
BY LISE CLAVERIE

III

Acne-scarred, lean, arrogant, Major Hauk was a very young
major with a limp. When Meric had entered, the major had
been practicing his signature—it was a thing of elegant loops
and flourishes, obviously intended to have a place in posterity.
As he strode back and forth during their conversation, he
paused frequently to admire himself in the window glass, settling the hang of his red jacket or running his fingers along the
crease of his white trousers. It was the new style of uniform,

the first Meric had seen at close range, and he noted with amusement the dragons embossed on the epaulets. He wondered if Griaule was capable of such an irony, if his influence was sufficiently discreet to have planted the idea for this comic-opera apparel in the brain of some general's wife.

". . . not a question of manpower," the major was saying, "but of. . . ." He broke off, and after a moment cleared his throat.

Meric, who had been studying the blotches on the backs of his hands, glanced up; the cane that had been resting against his knee slipped and clattered to the floor.

"A question of matériel," said the major firmly. "The price of antimony, for example . . ."

"Hardly use it anymore," said Meric. "I'm almost done with the mineral reds."

A look of impatience crossed the major's face. "Very well," he said; he stooped to his desk and shuffled through some papers. "Ah! Here's a bill for a shipment of cuttlefish from which you derive. . . ." He shuffled more papers.

"Syrian brown," said Meric gruffly. "I'm done with that, too. Golds and violets are all I need anymore. A little blue and rose." He wished the man would stop badgering him; he wanted to be at the eye before sunset.

As the major continued his accounting, Meric's gaze wandered out the window. The shantytown surrounding Griaule had swelled into a city and now sprawled across the hills. Most of the buildings were permanent, wood and stone, and the cant of the roofs, the smoke from the factories around the perimeter, put him in mind of Regensburg. All the natural beauty of the land had been drained into the painting. Blackish gray rain clouds were muscling up from the east, but the afternoon sun shone clear and shed a heavy gold radiance on Griaule's side. It looked as if the sunlight were an extension of the gleaming resins, as if the thickness of the paint were becoming infinite. He let the major's voice recede to a buzz and followed the scatter and dazzle of the images; and then, with a start, he realized the major was sounding him out about stopping the work.

The idea panicked him at first. He tried to interrupt, to raise objections; but the major talked through him, and as Meric thought it over, he grew less and less opposed. The painting would never be finished, and he was tired. Perhaps it was time to have done with it, to accept a university post somewhere and enjoy life for a while.

"We've been thinking about a temporary stoppage," said Major Hauk. "Then if the winter campaign goes well. . . ." He smiled. "If we're not visited by plague and pestilence, we'll assume things are in hand. Of course we'd like your opinion."

Meric felt a surge of anger toward this smug little monster. "In my opinion, you people are idiots," he said. "You wear Griaule's image on your shoulders, weave him on your flags, and yet you don't have the least comprehension of what that means. You think it's just a useful symbol. . . ."

"Excuse me," said the major stiffly.

"The hell I will!" Meric groped for his cane and heaved up to his feet. "You see yourselves as conquerors. Shapers of destiny. But all your rapes and slaughters are Griaule's expressions. *His* will. You're every bit as much his parasites as the skizzers."

The major sat, picked up a pen, and began to write.

"It astounds me," Meric went on, "that you can live next to a miracle, a source of mystery, and treat him as if he were an oddly shaped rock."

The major kept writing.

"What are you doing?" asked Meric.

"My recommendation," said the major without looking up.

"Which is?"

"That we initiate stoppage at once."

They exchanged hostile stares, and Meric turned to leave; but as he took hold of the doorknob, the major spoke again.

"We owe you so much," he said; he wore an expression of mingled pity and respect that further irritated Meric.

"How many men have you killed, Major?" he asked, opening the door.

"I'm not sure. I was in the artillery. We were never able to be sure."

"Well, I'm sure of my tally," said Meric. "It's taken me forty years to amass it. Fifteen hundred and ninety-three men and women. Poisoned, scalded, broken by falls, savaged by animals. Murdered. Why don't we—you and I—just call it even."

Though it was a sultry afternoon, he felt cold as he walked toward the tower—an internal cold that left him light-headed and weak. He tried to think what he would do. The idea of a university post seemed less appealing away from the major's office; he would soon grow weary of worshipful students and in-depth dissections of his work by jealous academics. A man hailed him as he turned into the market. Meric waved but did not stop, and heard another man say, "*That's* Cattanay?" (That ragged old ruin?)

The colors of the market were too bright, the smells of charcoal cookery too cloying, the crowds too thick, and he made for the side streets, hobbling past one-room stucco houses and tiny stores where they sold cooking oil by the ounce and cut cigars in half if you could not afford a whole one. Garbage, tornadoes of dust and flies, drunks with bloody mouths. Somebody had tied wires around a pariah dog—a bitch with slack teats; the wires had sliced into her flesh, and she lay panting in an alley mouth, gaunt ribs flecked with pink lather, gazing into nowhere. She, thought Meric, and not Griaule, should be the symbol of their flag.

As he rode the hoist up the side of the tower, he fell into his old habit of jotting down notes for the next day. *What's that cord of wood doing on level five? Slow leak of chrome yellow from pipes on level twelve.* Only when he saw a man dismantling some scaffolding did he recall Major Hauk's recommendation and understand that the order must already have been given. The loss of his work struck home to him then, and he leaned against the railing, his chest constricted and his eyes brimming. He straightened, ashamed of himself. The sun hung in a haze of iron-colored light low above the western hills, looking red and bloated and vile as a vulture's ruff. That polluted sky was his creation as much as was the painting, and it would be good to leave it behind. Once away from the valley, from all the influences of the place, he would be able to consider the future.

A young girl was sitting on the twentieth level just beneath the eye. Years before, the ritual of viewing the eye had grown to cultish proportions; there had been group chanting and praying and discussions of the experience. But these were more practical times, and no doubt the young men and women who had congregated here were now manning administrative desks somewhere in the burgeoning empire. They were the ones about whom Dardano should write; they, and all the eccentric characters who had played roles in this slow pageant. The gypsy woman who had danced every night by the eye, hoping to charm Griaule into killing her faithless lover—she had gone away satisfied. The man who had tried to extract one of the fangs—nobody knew what had become of him. The scale hunters, the artisans. A history of Hangtown would be a volume in itself.

The walk had left Meric weak and breathless; he sat down clumsily beside the girl, who smiled. He could not remember her name, but she came often to the eye. Small and dark, with an inner reserve that reminded him of Lise. He laughed inwardly—most women reminded him of Lise in some way.

"Are you all right?" she asked, her brow wrinkled with concern.

"Oh, yes," he said; he felt a need for conversation to take his mind off things, but he could think of nothing more to say. She was so young! All freshness and gleam and nerves.

"This will be my last time," she said. "At least for a while. I'll miss it." And then, before he could ask why, she added, "I'm getting married tomorrow, and we're moving away."

He offered congratulations and asked her who was the lucky fellow.

"Just a boy." She tossed her hair, as if to dismiss the boy's importance; she gazed up at the shuttered membrane. "What's it like for you when the eye opens?" she asked.

"Like everyone else," he said. "I remember . . . memories of my life. Other lives, too." He did not tell her about Griaule's memory of flight; he had never told anyone except Lise about that.

"All those bits of souls trapped in there," she said, gesturing

at the eye. "What do they mean to him? Why does he show
them to us?"

"I imagine he has his purposes, but I can't explain them."

"Once I remembered being with you," said the girl, peeking
at him shyly through a dark curl. "We were under the wing."

He glanced at her sharply. "Tell me."

"We were . . . together," she said, blushing. "Intimate, you
know. I was very afraid of the place, of the sounds and
shadows. But I loved you so much, it didn't matter. We made
love all night, and I was surprised because I thought that kind
of passion was just in stories, something people had invented
to make up for how ordinary it really was. And in the morning
even that dreadful place had become beautiful, with the wing
tips glowing red and the waterfall echoing. . . ." She lowered
her eyes. "Ever since I had that memory, I've been a little in love
with you."

"Lise," he said, feeling helpless before her.

"Was that her name?"

He nodded and put a hand to his brow, trying to pinch back
the emotions that flooded him.

"I'm sorry." Her lips grazed his cheek, and just that slight
touch seemed to weaken him further. "I wanted to tell you how
she felt in case she hadn't told you herself. She was very troubled by something, and I wasn't sure she had."

She shifted away from him, made uncomfortable by the intensity of his reaction, and they sat without speaking. Meric
became lost in watching how the sun glazed the scales to reddish gold, how the light was channeled along the ridges in
molten streams that paled as the day wound down. He was
startled when the girl jumped to her feet and backed toward
the hoist.

"He's dead," she said wonderingly.

Meric looked at her, uncomprehending.

"See?" She pointed at the sun, which showed a crimson silver above the hill. "He's dead," she repeated, and the expression on her face flowed between fear and exultation.

The idea of Griaule's death was too large for Meric's mind
to encompass, and he turned to the eye to find a counter-

proof—no glints of color flickered beneath the membrane. He heard the hoist creak as the girl headed down, but he continued to wait. Perhaps only the dragon's vision had failed. No. It was likely not a coincidence that work had been officially terminated today. Stunned, he sat staring at the lifeless membrane until the sun sank below the hills; then he stood and went over to the hoist. Before he could throw the switch, the cables thrummed—somebody heading up. Of course. The girl would have spread the news, and all the Major Hauks and their underlings would be hurrying to test Griaule's reflexes. He did not want to be there when they arrived, to watch them pose with their trophy like successful fishermen.

It was hard work climbing up to the frontoparietal plate. The ladder swayed, the wind buffeted him, and by the time he clambered onto the plate he was giddy, his chest full of twinges. He hobbled forward and leaned against the rust-caked side of a boiling vat. Shadowy in the twilight, the great furnaces and vats towered around him, and it seemed this system of fiery devices reeking of cooked flesh and minerals was the actual machinery of Griaule's thought materialized above his skull. Energyless, abandoned. They had been replaced by more efficient equipment down below, and it had been—what was it?—almost five years since they were last used. Cobwebs veiled a pyramid of firewood; the stairs leading to the rims of the vats were crumbling. The plate itself was scarred and coated with sludge.

"Cattanay!"

Someone shouted from below, and the top of the ladder trembled. God, they were coming after him! Bubbling over with congratulations and plans for testimonial dinners, memorial plaques, specially struck medals. They wold have him draped in bunting and bronzed and covered with pigeon shit before they were done. All these years he had been among them, both their slave and their master, yet he had never felt at home. Leaning heavily on his cane, he made his way past the frontal spike—blackened by years of oily smoke—and down between the wings to Hangtown. It was a ghost town, now. Weeds overgrowing the collapsed shanties; the lake a stinking pit, drained after some children had drowned in the summer of '91. Where Jarcke's home had stood was a huge pile of animal bones, taking a pale shine from the half-light. Wind keened through the tattered shrubs.

"Meric!" "Cattanay."

The voices were closer.

Well, there was one place where they would not follow.

The leaves of the thickets were speckled with mold and brittle, flaking away as he brushed them. He hesitated at the top of the scale hunters' stair. He had no rope. Though he had done the climb unaided many times, it had been quite a few years. The gusts of wind, the shouts, the sweep of the valley and the lights scattered across it like diamonds on gray velvet— it all seemed a single inconstant medium. He heard the brush crunch behind him, more voices. To hell with it! Gritting his teeth against a twinge of pain in his shoulder, hooking his cane over his belt, he inched onto the stair and locked his fingers in the handholds. The wind whipped his clothes and threatened to pry him loose and send him pinwheeling off. Once he slipped; once he froze, unable to move backward or forward. But at last he reached the bottom and edged upslope until he found a spot flat enough to stand.

The mystery of the place suddenly bore in upon him, and he was afraid. He half turned to the stair, thinking he would go back to Hangtown and accept the hurly-burly. But a moment later he realized how foolish a thought that was. Waves of weakness poured through him, his heart hammered, and white dazzles flared in his vision. His chest felt heavy as iron. Rattled, he went a few steps forward, the cane pocking the silence. It was too dark to see more than outlines, but up ahead was the fold of wing where he and Lise had sheltered. He walked toward it, intent on revisiting it; then he remembered the girl beneath the eye and understood that he had already said that goodbye. And it *was* goodbye—that he understood vividly. He kept walking. Blackness looked to be welling from the wing joint, from the entrances to the maze of luminous tunnels where they had stumbled onto the petrified man. Had it really been the old wizard, doomed by magical justice to molder and live on and on? It made sense. At least it accorded with what happened to wizards who slew their dragons.

"Griaule?" he whispered to the darkness, and cocked his head, half-expecting an answer. The sound of his voice pointed up the immensity of the great gallery under the wing, the emptiness, and he recalled how vital a habitat it had once been. Flakes shifting over the surface, skizzers, peculiar insects fuming in the thickets, the glum populace of Hangtown, waterfalls. He had never been able to picture Griaule fully alive—that kind of vitality was beyond the powers of the imagination. Yet he wondered if by some miracle the dragon were alive now, flying up through his golden night to the sun's core. Or had that merely been a dream, a bit of tissue glittering deep in the cold tons of his brain? He laughed. Ask the stars for their first names, and you'd be more likely to receive a reply.

He decided not to walk any farther—it was really no decision. Pain was spreading through his shoulder, so intense he imagined it must be glowing inside. Carefully, carefully, he lowered himself and lay propped on an elbow, hanging on to the cane. Good, magical wood. Cut from a hawthorn atop Griaule's haunch. A man had once offered him a small fortune for it. Who would claim it now? Probably old Henry Sichi would snatch it for his museum, stick it in a glass case next to his boots. What a joke! He decided to lie flat on his stomach, resting his chin on an arm—the stony coolness beneath acted to muffle the pain. Amusing, how the range of one's decision dwindled. You decided to paint a dragon, to send hundreds of men searching for malachite and cochineal beetles, to love a woman, to heighten an undertone here and there, and finally to position your body a certain way. He seemed to have reached the end of the process. What next? He tried to regulate his breathing, to ease the pressure on his chest. Then, as something rustled out near the wing joint, he turned on his side. He thought he detected movement, a gleaming blackness flowing toward him . . . or else it was only the haphazard firing of his nerves playing tricks with his vision. More surprised than afraid, wanting to see, he peered into the darkness and felt his heart beating erratically against the dragon's scale.

It's foolish to draw simple conclusions from complex events, but I suppose there must be both moral and truth to this life, these events. I'll leave that to the gadflies. The historians, the social scientists, the expert apologists for reality. All I know is that he had a fight with his girlfriend over money and walked out. He sent her a letter saying he had gone south and would be back in a few months with more money than she could ever spend. I had no idea what he'd done. The whole thing about Griaule had just been a bunch of us sitting around the Red Bear, drinking up my pay—I'd sold an article—and somebody said, "Wouldn't it be great if Dardano didn't have to write articles, if we didn't have to paint pictures that color-coordinated with people's furniture or slave at getting the gooey smiles of little nieces and nephews just right?" All sorts of improbable moneymaking schemes were put forward. Robberies, kidnappings. Then the idea of swindling the city fathers of Teocinte came up, and the entire plan was fleshed out in minutes. Scribbled on napkins, scrawled on sketchpads. A group effort. I keep trying to remember if anyone got a glassy look in their eye, if I felt a cold tendril of Griaule's thought stirring my brains. But I can't. It was a half-hour's sensation, nothing more. A drunken whimsy, an art-school metaphor. Shortly thereafter, we ran out of money and staggered into the streets. It was snowing—big wet flakes that melted down our collars. God, we were drunk! Laughing, balancing on the icy railing of the University Bridge. Making faces at the bundled-up burghers and their fat ladies who huffed and puffed past, spouting steam and never giving us a glance, and none of us—not even the burghers—knowing that we were living our happy ending in advance. . . .

—FROM THE MAN WHO PAINTED
THE DRAGON GRIAULE
BY LOUIS DARDANO

A Spanish Lesson

That winter of '64, when I was seventeen and prone to obey the impulses of my heart as if they were illuminations produced by years of contemplative study, I dropped out of college and sailed to Europe, landing in Belfast, hitchhiking across Britain, down through France and Spain, and winding up on the Costa del Sol—to be specific, in a village near Málaga by the name of Pedregalejo—where one night I was to learn something of importance. What had attracted me to the village was not its quaintness, its vista of the placid Mediterranean and neat white stucco houses and little bandy-legged fishermen mending nets; rather, it was the fact that the houses along the shore were occupied by a group of expatriates, mostly Americans, who posed for me a bohemian ideal.

The youngest of them was seven years older than I, the eldest three times my age, and among them they had amassed a wealth of experience that caused me envy and made me want to become like them: bearded, be-earringed, and travel-wise. There was, for example, Leonard Somstaad, a Swedish poet with the poetic malady of a weak heart and a fondness for *marjoun* (hashish candy); there was Art Shapiro, a wanderer who had for ten years migrated between Pedregalejo and Istanbul; there was Don Washington, a black ex-GI and blues singer, whose Danish girlfriend—much to the delight of the locals—was given to nude sunbathing; there was Robert Braehme, a New York actor who, in the best theatrical tradition, attempted halfheartedly to kill several of the others, suffered a nervous breakdown, and had to be returned to the States under restraint.

And then there was Richard Shockley, a tanned, hook-nosed man in his late twenties, who was the celebrity of the group. A part-time smuggler (mainly of marijuana) and a writer of some accomplishment. His first novel, *The Celebrant,* had created a minor critical stir. Being a fledgling writer myself, it was he whom I most envied. In appearance and manner he suited my notion of what a writer should be. For a while he took an interest in me, teaching me smuggling tricks and lecturing on the moral imperatives of art; but shortly thereafter he became preoccupied with his own affairs and our relationship deteriorated.

In retrospect I can see that these people were unremarkable; but at the time they seemed impossibly wise, and in order to align myself with them I rented a small beach house, bought a supply of notebooks, and began to fill them with page after page of attempted poetry.

Though I had insinuated myself into the group, I was not immediately accepted. My adolescence showed plainly against the backdrop of their experience. I had no store of anecdotes, no expertise with flute or guitar, and my conversation was lacking in hip savoir faire. In their eyes I was a kid, a baby, a clever puppy who had learned how to beg, and I was often the object of ridicule. Three factors saved me from worse ridicule: my size (six foot three, one-ninety), my erratic temper, and my ability to consume enormous quantities of drugs. This last was my great trick, my means of gaining respect. I would perform feats of ingestion that would leave Don Washington, a consummate doper, shaking his head in awe. Pills, powders, herbs—I was indiscriminate, and I initiated several dangerous dependencies in hopes of achieving equal status.

Six weeks after moving to the beach, I raised myself a notch in the general esteem by acquiring a girlfriend, a fey California blonde named Anne Fisher. It amuses me to recall the event that led Anne to my bed, because it smacked of the worst of cinema verité, an existential moment opening onto a bittersweet romance. We were walking on the beach, a rainy day, sea and sky blending in a slate fog toward Africa, both of us stoned near to the point of catatonia, when we happened upon a drowned kitten. Had I been unaccompanied, I might have inspected the corpse for bugs and passed on; but as it was, being under Anne's scrutiny, I babbled some nonsense about "this inconstant image of the world," half of which I was parroting from a Eugenio Montale poem, and proceeded to give the kitten decent burial beneath a flat rock.

After completing this nasty chore, I stood and discovered Anne staring at me wetly, her maidenly nature overborne by my unexpected sensitivity. No words were needed. We were alone on the beach, with Nina Simone's bluesy whisper issuing from a window of one of the houses, gray waves slopping at our feet. As if pressed together by the vast emptiness around us, we kissed. Anne clawed my back and ground herself against me: you might have thought she had been thirsting for me all her nineteen years, but I came to understand that her desperation was born of philosophical bias and not sexual compulsion. She was deep into sadness as a motif for passion, and she liked thinking of us as two worthless strangers united by a sudden perception of life's pathetic fragility. Fits of weeping and malaise alternating with furious bouts of lovemaking were her idea of romantic counterpoint.

By the time she left me some months later, I had grown thoroughly sick of her; but she had—I believed—served her purpose in establishing me as a full-fledged expatriate.

Wrong. I soon found that I was still the kid, the baby, and I realized that I would remain so until someone of even lesser status moved to the beach, thereby nudging me closer to the mainstream. This didn't seem likely, and in truth I no longer cared; I had lost respect for the group: had I not, at seventeen, become as hiply expatriated as they, and wouldn't I, when I reached their age, be off to brighter horizons? Then, as is often the case with reality, presenting us with what we desire at the moment desire begins to flag, two suitably substandard people rented the house next to mine.

Their names were Tom and Alise, and they were twins a

couple of years older than I, uncannily alike in appearance, and hailing from—if you were to believe their story—Canada. Yet they had no knowledge of things Canadian, and their accent was definitely northern European. Not an auspicious entrée into a society as picky as Pedregalejo's. Everyone was put off by them, especially Richard Shockley, who saw them as a threat. "Those kind of people make trouble for everyone else," he said to me at once. "They're just too damn weird." (It has always astounded me that those who pride themselves on eccentricity are so quick to deride this quality in strangers.) Others as well testified to the twins' weirdness: they were secretive, hostile; they had been seen making strange passes in the air on the beach, and that led some to believe they were religious nuts; they set lanterns in their windows at night and left them burning until dawn. Their most disturbing aspect, however, was their appearance. Both were scarcely five feet tall, emaciated, pale, with black hair and squinty dark eyes and an elfin cleverness of feature that Shockley described as "prettily ugly, like Munchkins." He suggested that this look might be a product of inbreeding, and I thought he might be right: the twins had the sort of dulled presence that one associates with the retarded or the severely tranquilized. The fishermen treated them as if they were the devil's spawn, crossing themselves and spitting at the sight of them, and the expatriates were concerned that the fishermen's enmity would focus the attention of the Guardia Civil upon the beach.

The Guardia—with their comic-opera uniforms, their machine guns, their funny patent-leather hats that from a distance looked like Mickey Mouse ears—were a legitimate menace. They had a long-standing reputation for murder and corruption, and were particularly fond of harassing foreigners. Therefore I was not surprised when a committee led by Shockley asked me to keep an eye on my new neighbors, the idea being that we should close ranks against them, even to the point of reporting any illegalities. Despite knowing that refusal would consolidate my status as a young nothing, I told Shockley and his pals to screw off. I'm not able to take pride in this— had they been friendlier to me in the past, I might have gone

along with the scheme; but as it was, I was happy to reject
them. And further, in the spirit of revenge, I went next door to
warn Tom and Alise.

My knock roused a stirring inside the house, whispers, and
at last the door was cracked and an eye peeped forth. "Yes?"
said Alise.

"Uh," I said, taken aback by this suspicious response. "My
name's Lucius. From next door. I've got something to tell you
about the people around here." Silence. "They're afraid of
you," I went on. "They're nervous because they've got dope
and stuff, and they think you're going to bring the cops down
on them."

Alise glanced behind her, more whispers, and then she said,
"Why would we do that?"

"It's not that you'd do it on purpose," I said. "It's just that
you're . . . different. You're attracting a lot of attention, and
everyone's afraid that the cops will investigate you and then
decide to bust the whole beach."

"Oh." Another conference, and finally she said, "Would you
please come in?"

The door swung open, creaking like a coffin lid centuries
closed, and I crossed the threshold. Tom was behind the door,
and after shutting it, Alise ranged herself beside him. Her
chest was so flat, their features so alike, it was only the length of
her hair that allowed me to tell them apart. She gestured at a
table-and-chairs set in the far corner, and, feeling a prickle of
nervousness, I took a seat there. The room was similar to the
living room of my house: whitewashed walls, unadorned and
flaking; cheap production-line furniture (the signal difference
being that they had two beds instead of one); a gas stove in a
niche to the left of the door. Mounted just above the light
switch was a plastic crucifix; a frayed cord ran up behind the
cross to the fixture on the ceiling, giving the impression that
Christ had some role to play in the transmission of the current.
They had kept the place scrupulously neat; the one sign of
occupancy was a pile of notebooks and a sketchpad lying on
the table. The pad was open to what appeared to be a render-
ing of complex circuitry. Before I could get a better look at it,

Tom picked up the pad and tossed it onto the stove. Then they sat across from me, hands in their laps, as meek and quiet as two white mice. It was dark in the room, knife-edges of golden sunlight slanting through gaps in the shutter boards, and the twins' eyes were like dirty smudges on their pale skins.

"I don't know what more to tell you," I said. "And I don't have any idea what you should do. But I'd watch myself." They did not exchange glances or in any way visibly communicate, yet there was a peculiar tension to their silence, and I had the notion that they were again conferring: this increased my nervousness.

"We realize we're different," said Tom at length; his voice had the exact pitch and timbre of Alise's, soft and faintly blurred. "We don't want to cause harm, but there's something we have to do here. It's dangerous, but we have to do it. We can't leave until it's done."

"We think you're a good boy," chimed in Alise, rankling me with this characterization. "We wonder if you would help us?"

I was perplexed. "What can I do?"

"The problem is one of appearances," said Tom. "We can't change the way we look, but perhaps we can change the way others perceive us. If we were to become more a part of the community, we might not be so noticeable."

"They won't have anything to do with you," I told him. "They're too. . . ."

"We have an idea," Alise cut in.

"Yes," said Tom. "We thought if there was the appearance of a romantic involvement between you and Alise, people might take us more for granted. We hoped you would be agreeable to having Alise move in with you."

"Now wait!" I said, startled. "I don't mind helping you, but I. . . ."

"It would only be for appearance' sake," said Alise, deadpan. "There'd be no need for physical contact, and I would try not to be an imposition. I could clean for you and do the shopping."

Perhaps it was something in Alise's voice or a subtle shift in attitude, but for whatever reason, it was then that I sensed their desperation. They were very, very afraid . . . of what, I had no inkling. But fear was palpable, a thready pulse in the air. It was a symptom of my youth that I did not associate their fear with any potential threat to myself; I was merely made the more curious. "What sort of danger are you in?" I asked.

Once again there was that peculiar nervy silence, at the end of which Tom said, "We ask that you treat this as a confidence."

"Sure," I said casually. "Who am I gonna tell?"

The story Tom told was plausible; in fact, considering my own history—a repressive, intellectual father who considered me a major disappointment, who had characterized my dropping out as "the irresponsible actions of a glandular case"—it seemed programmed to enlist my sympathy. He said that they were not Canadian but German, and had been raised by a dictatorial stepfather after their mother's death. They had been beaten, locked in closets, and fed so poorly that their growth had been affected. Several months before, after almost twenty years of virtual confinement, they had managed to escape, and since then they had kept one step ahead of detectives hired by the stepfather. Now, penniless, they were trying to sell some antiquities that they had stolen from their home; and once they succeeded in this, they planned to travel east, perhaps to India, where they would be beyond detection. But they were afraid that they would be caught while waiting for the sale to go through; they had had too little practice with the world to be able to pass as ordinary citizens.

"Well," I said when he had finished. "If you want to move in"—I nodded at Alise—"I guess it's all right. I'll do what I can to help you. But first thing you should do is quit leaving lanterns in your window all night. That's what really weirds the fishermen out. They think you're doing some kind of magic or something." I glanced back and forth between them. "What are you doing?"

"It's just a habit," said Alise. "Our stepfather made us sleep with the lights on."

"You'd better stop it," I said firmly; I suddenly saw myself playing Anne Sullivan to their Helen Keller, paving their way to a full and happy life, and this noble self-image caused me to wax enthusiastic. "Don't worry," I told them. "Before I'm through, you people are going to pass for genu-*wine* All-American freaks. I guarantee it!"

If I had expected thanks, I would have been disappointed. Alise stood, saying that she'd be right back, she was going to pack her things, and Tom stared at me with an expression that—had I not been so pleased with myself—I might have recognized for pained distaste.

The beach at Pedregalejo inscribed a grayish white crescent for about a hundred yards along the Mediterranean, bounded on the west by a rocky point and on the east by a condominium under construction, among the first of many that were gradually to obliterate the beauty of the coast. Beyond the beachfront houses occupied by the expatriates were several dusty streets lined with similar houses, and beyond them rose a cliff of ocher rock surmounted by a number of villas, one of which had been rented by an English actor who was in the area shooting a bullfighting movie: I had been earning my living of late as an extra on the film, receiving the equivalent of five dollars a day and lunch (also an equivalent value, consisting of a greasy sandwich and soda pop).

My house was at the extreme eastern end of the beach and differed from the rest in that it had a stucco porch that extended into the water. Inside, as mentioned, it was almost identical to the twins' house; but despite this likeness, when Alise entered, clutching an airline bag to her chest, she acted as if she had walked into an alien spacecraft. At first, ignoring my invitation to sit, she stood stiffly in the corner, flinching every time I passed; then, keeping as close to the walls as a cat exploring new territory, she inspected my possessions, peeking into my backpack, touching the strings of my guitar, studying the crude watercolors with which I had covered up flaking spots in the whitewash. Finally she sat at the table, knees pressed tightly together and staring at her hands. I tried to draw her into a conversation but received mumbles in reply, and eventually, near sunset, I took a notebook and a bagful of dope, and went out onto the porch to write.

When I was even younger than I was in 1964, a boy, I'd
assumed that all seas were wild storm-tossed enormities, rife
with monsters and mysteries; and so, at first sight, the relatively tame waters of the Mediterranean had proved a disappointment. However, as time had passed, I'd come to
appreciate the Mediterranean's subtle shifts in mood. On
that particular afternoon the sea near to shore lay in a rippled
sheet stained reddish orange by the dying light; farther out,
a golden haze obscured the horizon and made the skeletal
riggings of the returning fishing boats seem like the crawling of huge insects in a cloud of pollen. It was the kind of
antique weather from which you might expect the glowing
figure of Agamemnon, say, or of some martial Roman soul
to emerge with ghostly news concerning the sack of Troy
or Masada.

I smoked several pipefuls of dope—it was Moroccan kef, a
fine grade of marijuana salted with flecks of white opium—
and was busy recording the moment in overwrought poetry
when Alise came up beside me and, again reminding me of a
white mouse, sniffed the air. "What's that?" she asked, pointing at the pipe. I explained and offered a toke. "Oh, no," she
said, but continued peering at the dope and after a second
added, "My stepfather used to give us drugs. Pills that made us
sleepy."

"This might do the same thing," I said airily, and went back
to my scribbling.

"Well," she said a short while later. "Perhaps I'll try a little."

I doubt that she had ever smoked before. She coughed and
hacked, and her eyes grew red-veined and weepy, but she denied that the kef was having any effect. Gradually, though, she
lapsed into silence and sat staring at the water; then, perhaps
five minutes after finishing her last pipe, she ran into the house
and returned with a sketchpad. "This is wonderful," she said.
"Wonderful! Usually it's so hard to see." And began sketching
with a charcoal pencil.

I giggled, taking perverse delight in having gotten her high,
and asked, "What's wonderful?" She merely shook her head,
intent on her work. I would have pursued the question, but at
that moment I noticed a group of expatriates strolling toward

us along the beach. "Here's your chance to act normal," I said, too stoned to recognize the cruelty of my words.

She glanced up. "What do you mean?"

I nodded in the direction of the proto-hippies. They appeared to be as ripped as we were: one of the women was doing a clumsy skipping dance along the tidal margin, and the others were staggering, laughing, shouting encouragement. Silhouetted against the violent colors of sunset, with their floppy hats and jerky movements, they had the look of shadow actors in a medieval mystery play. "Kiss me," I suggested to Alise. "Or act affectionate. Reports of your normalcy will be all over the beach before dark."

Alise's eyes widened, but she set down her pad. She hesitated briefly, then edged her chair closer; she leaned forward, hesitated again, waiting until the group had come within good viewing range, and pressed her lips to mine.

Though I was not in the least attracted to Alise, kissing her was a powerful sexual experience. It was a chaste kiss. Her lips trembled but did not part, and it lasted only a matter of seconds; yet for its duration, as if her mouth had been coated with some psychochemical, my senses sharpened to embrace the moment in microscopic detail. Kissing had always struck me as a blurred pleasure, a smashing together of pulpy flesh accompanied by a flurry of groping. But with Alise I could feel the exact conformation of our lips, the minuscule changes in pressure as they settled into place, the rough material of her blouse grazing my arm, the erratic measures of her breath (which was surprisingly sweet). The delicacy of the act aroused me as no other kiss had before, and when I drew back I half expected her to have been transformed into a beautiful princess. Not so. She was as ever small and pale. Prettily ugly.

Stunned, I turned toward the beach. The expatriates were gawping at us, and their astonishment reoriented me. I gave them a cheery wave, put my arm around Alise, and inclining my head to hers in a pretense of young love, I led her into the house.

That night I went to sleep while she was off visiting Tom. I tried to station myself on the extreme edge of the bed, leaving her enough room to be comfortable; but by the time she returned I had rolled onto the center of the mattress, and when she slipped in beside me, turning on her side, her thin buttocks cupped spoon-style by my groin, I came drowsily awake and realized that my erection was butting between her legs. Once again physical contact with her caused a sharpening of my senses, and due to the intimacy of the contact my desire, too, was sharpened. I could no more have stopped myself than I could have stopped breathing. Gently, as gently as though she were the truest of trueloves—and, indeed, I felt that sort of tenderness toward her—I began moving against her, thrusting more and more forcefully until I had eased partway inside. All this time she had made no sound, no comment, but now she cocked her leg back over my hip, wriggled closer, and let me penetrate her fully.

It had been a month since Anne had left, and I was undeniably horny; but not even this could explain the fervor of my performance that night. I lost track of how many times we made love. And yet we never exchanged endearments, never spoke or in any way acknowledged one another as lovers. Though Alise's breath quickened, her face remained set in that characteristic deadpan, and I wasn't sure if she was deriving pleasure from the act or simply providing a service, paying rent. It didn't matter. I was having enough fun for both of us. The last thing I recall is that she had mounted me, female superior, her skin glowing ghost-pale in the dawn light, single-scoop breasts barely jiggling; her charcoal eyes were fixed on the wall, as if she saw there an important destination toward which she was galloping me posthaste.

My romance with Alise—this, and the fact that she and Tom had taken to smoking vast amounts of kef and wandering the beach glassy-eyed, thus emulating the behavior of the other expatriates—had more or less the desired effect upon everyone . . . everyone except Richard Shockley. He accosted me on my way to work one morning and told me in no uncertain terms that if I knew what was good for me, I should break all ties with the twins. I had about three inches and thirty pounds on him, and—for reasons I will shortly explain—I was in an irascible mood; I gave him a push and asked him to keep out of my business or suffer the consequences.

"You stupid punk!" he said, but backed away.

"Punk?" I laughed—laughter has always been for me a spark to fuel rage—and followed him. "Come on, Rich. You can work up a better insult than that. A verbal guy like you. Come on! Give me a reason to get really crazy."

We were standing in one of the dusty streets back of the beach, not far from a bakery, a little shop with dozens of loaves of bread laid neatly in the window, and at that moment a member of the Guardia Civil poked his head out the door. He was munching a sweet roll, watching us with casual interest: a short, swarthy man, wearing an olive green uniform with fancy epaulets, an automatic rifle slung over his shoulder, and sporting one of those goofy patent-leather hats. Shockley blanched at the sight, wheeled around, and walked away. I was about to walk away myself, but the guardsman beckoned. With a sinking feeling in the pit of my stomach, I went over to him.

"*Cobarde*," he said, gesturing at Shockley.

My Spanish was poor, but I knew that word: *coward*. "Yeah," I said. "In *inglés, cobarde* means chickenshit."

"Cheek-sheet," he said; then, more forcefully: "Cheek-sheet!"

He asked me to teach him some more English; he wanted to know all the curse words. His name was Francisco, he had fierce bad breath, and he seemed genuinely friendly. But I knew damn well that he was most likely trying to recruit me as an informant. He talked about his family in Seville, his girlfriend, how beautiful it was in Spain. I smiled, kept repeating, "*Sí, sí*," and was very relieved when he had to go off on his rounds.

Despite Shockley's attitude, the rest of the expatriates began to accept the twins, lumping us together as weirdos of the most perverted sort, yet explicable in our weirdness. From Don Washington I learned that Tom, Alise, and I were thought to be involved in a ménage à trois, and when I attempted to deny this, he said it was no big thing. He did ask, however, what I saw in Alise; I gave some high-school reply about it all being the same in the dark, but in truth I had no answer to his question. Since Alise had moved in, my life had assumed a distinct pattern. Each morning I would hurry off to Málaga to work on the movie set; each night I would return home and enter into brainless rut with Alise. I found this confusing. Separated from Alise, I felt only mild pity for her, yet her proximity would drive me into a lustful frenzy. I lost interest in writing, in Spain, in everything except Alise's undernourished body. I slept hardly at all, my temper worsened, and I began to wonder if she were a witch and had ensorcelled me. Often I would come home to discover her and Tom sitting stoned on my porch, the floor littered with sketches of those circuitlike designs (actually they less resembled circuits than a kind of mechanistic vegetation). I asked once what they were. "A game," replied Alise, and distracted me with a caress.

Two weeks after she moved in, I shouted at the assistant director of the movie (he had been instructing me on how to throw a wineskin with the proper degree of adulation as the English actor-matador paraded in triumph around the bullring) and was fired. After being hustled off the set, I vowed to get rid of Alise, whom I blamed for all my troubles. But when I arrived home, she was nowhere to be seen. I stumped over to Tom's house and pounded on the door. It swung open, and I peeked inside. Empty. Half a dozen notebooks were scattered on the floor. Curiosity overrode my anger. I stepped in and picked up a notebook.

The front cover was decorated with a hand-drawn swastika, and while it is not uncommon to find swastikas on notebook covers—they make for entertaining doodling—the sight of this one gave me a chill. I leafed through the pages, noticing that though the entries were in English, there were occasional words and phrases in German, these having question marks beside them; then I went back and read the first entry.

The Führer had been dead three days, and still no one had ventured into the office where he had been exposed to the

*poisoned blooms, although a servant had crawled along
the ledge to the window and returned with the news that
the corpse was stiffened in its leather tunic, its cheeks bristling with a dead man's growth, and strings of desiccated
blood were hanging from its chin. But as we well remembered his habit of reviving the dead for a final bout of torture, we were afraid that he might have set an igniter in his
cells to ensure rebirth, and so we waited while the wine in
his goblet turned to vinegar and then to a murky gas that
hid him from our view. Nothing had changed. The garden
of hydrophobic roses fertilized with his blood continued to
lash and slather, and the hieroglyphs of his shadow selves
could be seen patrolling the streets. . . .*

The entry went on in like fashion for several pages, depicting a magical-seeming Third Reich, ruled by a dead or mori-
bund Hitler, policed by shadow men known collectively as The
Disciples, and populated by a terrified citizenry. All the entries
were similar in character, but in the margins were brief nota-
tions, most having to do with either Tom's or Alise's physical
state, and one passage in particular caught my eye:

*Alise's control of her endocrine system continues to out-
pace mine. Could this simply be a product of male and
female differences? It seems likely, since we have all else in
common.*

Endocrine? Didn't that have something to do with glands
and secretions? And if so, couldn't this be a clue to Alise's se-
ductive powers? I wished that old Mrs. Adkins (General Science, fifth period) had been more persevering with me. I
picked up another notebook. No swastika on the cover, but on
the foreleaf was written: "Tom and Alise, 'born' 12 March
1944." The entire notebook contained a single entry, apparently autobiographical, and after checking out the window to
see if the twins were in sight, I sat down to read it.

Five pages later I had become convinced that Tom was either
seriously crazy or that he and Alise were the subjects of an

insane Nazi experiment . . . or both. The word *clone* was not then in my vocabulary, but this was exactly what Tom claimed that he and Alise were. They, he said, along with eighteen others, had been grown from a single cell (donor unknown), part of an attempt to speed up development of a true Master Race. A successful attempt, according to him, for not only were the twenty possessed of supernormal physical and mental abilities, but they were stronger and more handsome than the run of humanity: this seemed to me wish fulfillment, pure and simple, and other elements of the story—for example, the continuation of an exotic Third Reich past 1945—seemed delusion. But upon reading further, learning that they had been sequestered in a cave for almost twenty years, being educated by scientific personnel, I realized that Tom and Alise could have been told these things and have assumed their truth. One could easily make a case for some portion of the Reich having survived the war.

I was about to put down the notebook when I noticed several loose sheets of paper stuck in the rear; I pulled them out and unfolded them. The first appeared to be a map of part of a city, with a large central square labeled "Citadel," and the rest were covered in a neat script that—after reading a paragraph or two—I deduced to be Alise's.

Tom says that since I'm the only one ever to leave the caves (before we all finally left them, that is), I should set down my experiences. He seems to think that having even a horrid past is preferable to having none, and insists that we should document it as well as we can. For myself, I would like to forget the past, but I'll write down what I remember to satisfy his compulsiveness.

When we were first experimenting with the tunnel, we knew nothing more about it than that it was a metaphysical construct of some sort. Our control of it was poor, and we had no idea how far it reached or through what medium it penetrated. Nor had we explored it to any great extent. It was terrifying. The only constant was that it was always dark, with fuzzy different-colored lights shining at what seemed tremendous distances away. Often you would feel disembodied, and sometimes your body was painfully real, subject to odd twinges and shocks. Sometimes it was hard to move—like walking through black glue, and other times it was as if the darkness were a frictionless substance that squeezed you along faster than you wanted to go. Horrible afterimages materialized and vanished on all sides—monsters, animals, things to which I couldn't put a name. We were almost as frightened of the tunnel as we were of our masters. Almost.

One night after the guards had taken some of the girls into their quarters, we opened the tunnel and three of us entered it. I was in the lead when our control slipped and the tunnel began to constrict. I started to turn back, and the next I knew I was standing under the sky, surrounded by window less buildings. Warehouses, I think. The street was deserted, and I had no idea where I was. In a panic, I ran down the street and soon I heard the sounds of traffic. I turned a corner and stopped short. A broad avenue lined with gray buildings—all decorated with carved eagles—led away from where I stood and terminated in front of an enormous building of black stone. I recognized it at once from pictures we had been shown—Hitler's Citadel.

Though I was still very afraid, perhaps even more so, I realized that I had learned two things of importance. First, that no matter through what otherworldly medium it stretched, the tunnel also negotiated a worldly distance. Second, I understood that the portrait painted of the world by our masters was more or less accurate. We had never been sure of this, despite having been visited by Disciples and other of Hitler's creatures, their purpose being to frighten us into compliance.

I only stood a few minutes in that place, yet I'll never be able to forget it. No description could convey its air of menace, its oppressiveness. The avenue was thronged with people, all—like our guards—shorter and less attractive than I and my siblings, all standing stock-still, silent, and gazing at the Citadel. A procession of electric cars was passing through their midst, blowing horns, apparently to celebrate a triumph, because no one was obstructing their path. Several Disciples were prowling the fringes of the crowd, and overhead a huge winged shape was flying. It was no aircraft; its wings beat, and it swooped and soared like a live thing. Yet it must have been forty or fifty feet long. I couldn't make out what it was; it kept close to the sun, and therefore was always partly in silhouette. (I should mention that although the sun was at meridian, the sky was a deep blue such as I have come to associate with the late-afternoon skies of this world, and the sun itself was tinged with red, its globe well defined—I think it may have been farther along the path to dwarfism than the sun of this world.) All these elements contributed to the menace of the scene, but the dominant force was the Citadel. Unlike the other buildings, no carvings adorned it. No screaming eagles, no symbols of terror and war. It was a construct of simple curves and straight lines; but that simplicity implied an animal sleekness, communicated a sense of great power under restraint, and I had the feeling that at any moment the building might come alive and devour everyone within its reach. It seemed to give its darkness to the air.

I approached a man standing nearby and asked what was going on. He looked at me askance, then checked around to see if anyone was watching us. "Haven't you heard?" he said.

"I've been away," I told him.

This, I could see, struck him as peculiar, but he accepted the fact and said, "They thought he was coming back to life, but it was a false alarm. Now they're offering sacrifices."

The procession of cars had reached the steps of the Citadel, and from them emerged a number of people with their hands bound behind their backs, and a lesser number of very large men, who began shoving them up the steps toward the main doors. Those doors swung open, and from the depths of the Citadel issued a kind of growling music overlaid with fanfares of trumpets. A reddish glow—feeble at first, then brightening to a blaze—shone from within. The light and the music set my heart racing. I backed away, and as I did, I thought I saw a face forming in the midst of that red glow. Hitler's face, I believe. But I didn't wait to validate this. I ran, ran as hard as I could back to the street behind the warehouses, and there, to my relief, I discovered that the tunnel had once again been opened.

I leaned back, trying to compare what I had read with my knowledge of the twins. Those instances of silent communication. Telepathy? Alise's endocrinal control. Their habit of turning lamps on to burn away the night—could this be some residual behavior left over from cave life? Tom had mentioned that the lights had never been completely extinguished, merely dimmed. Was this all an elaborate fantasy he had concocted to obscure their pitiful reality? I was certain this was the case with Alise's testimony; but whatever, I found that I was no longer angry at the twins, that they had been elevated in my thoughts from nuisance to mystery. Looking back, I can see that my new attitude was every bit as discriminatory as my previous one. I felt for them an adolescent avidity such as I might have exhibited toward a strange pet. They were neat, weird, with the freakish appeal of Venus's-flytraps and sea monkeys. Nobody else had one like them, and having them to myself made me feel superior. I would discover what sort of tricks they could perform, takes notes on their peculiarities, and then, eventually growing bored, I'd move along to a more consuming interest. Though I was intelligent enough to understand that this attitude was—in its indulgence and lack of concern for others—typically ugly-American, I saw no harm in adopting it. Why, they might even benefit from my attention.

At that moment I heard voices outside. I skimmed the notebook toward the others on the floor and affected nonchalance. The door opened; they entered and froze upon seeing me. "Hi," I said. "Door was open, so I waited for you here. What you been up to?"

Tom's eyes flicked to the notebooks, and Alise said, "We've been walking."

"Yeah?" I said this with great good cheer, as if pleased that they had been taking exercise. "Too bad I didn't get back earlier. I could have gone with you."

"Why *are* you back?" asked Tom, gathering the notebooks.

I didn't want to let on about the loss of my job, thinking that the subterfuge would give me a means of keeping track of them. "Some screw-up on the set," I told him. "They had to put off filming. What say we go into town?"

From that point on, no question I asked them was casual; I was always testing, probing, trying to ferret out some of their truth.

"Oh, I don't know," said Tom. "I thought I'd have a swim."

I took a mental note: why do subjects exhibit avoidance of town? For an instant I had an unpleasant vision of myself, a teenage monster gloating over his two gifted white mice, but this was overborne by my delight in the puzzle they presented. "Yeah," I said breezily. "A swim would be nice."

That night making love with Alise was a whole new experience. I wasn't merely screwing; I was exploring the unknown, penetrating mystery. Watching her pale, passionless face, I imagined the brain behind it to be a strange glowing jewel, with facets instead of convolutions. *National Enquirer* headlines flashed through my head. NAZI MUTANTS ALIVE IN SPAIN. AMERICAN TEEN UNCOVERS HITLER'S SECRET PLOT. Of course there would be no such publicity. Even if Tom's story was true—and I was far from certain that it was—I had no intention of betraying them. I wasn't that big a jerk.

For the next month I maintained the illusion that I was still employed by the film company and left home each morning at dawn; but rather than catching the bus into Málaga, I would hide between the houses, and as soon as Tom and Alise went off on one of their walks (they always walked west along the beach, vanishing behind a rocky point), I would sneak into Tom's house and continue investigating the notebooks. The more I read, the more firmly I believed the story. There was a flatness to the narrative tone that reminded me of a man I had heard speaking about the concentration camps, dully recounting atrocities, staring into space, as if the things he said were putting him into a trance. For example:

> . . . It was on July 2nd that they came for Urduja and Klaus. For the past few months they had been making us sleep together in a room lit by harsh fluorescents. There were no mattresses, no pillows, and they took our clothes so we could not use them as covering. It was like day under those trays of white light, and we lay curled around each other for warmth. They gassed us before they entered, but we had long since learned how to neutralize the gas, and so we were all awake, linked, pretending to be asleep. Three of them came into the room, and three more stood at the door with guns. At first it seemed that this would be just another instance of rape. The three men violated Urduja, one after the other. She kept up her pretense of unconsciousness, but she felt everything. We tried to comfort her, sending out our love and encouragement. But I could sense her hysteria, her pain. They were rough with her, and when they had finished, her thighs were bloody. She was very brave and gave no cry; she was determined not to give us away. Finally they picked her and Klaus up and carried them off. An hour later we felt them die. It was horrible, as if part of my mind had short-circuited, a corner of it left forever dim.
>
> We were angry and confused. Why would they kill what they had worked so hard to create? Some of us, Uwe and Peter foremost among them, wanted to give up the tunnel and revenge ourselves as best we could; but the rest of us managed to calm things down. Was it revenge we wanted, we asked, or was it freedom? If freedom was to be our choice, then the tunnel was our best hope. Would I—I wonder—have lobbied so hard for the tunnel if I had known that only Alise and I would survive it?

The story ended shortly before the escape attempt was to be made; the remainder of the notebooks contained further de-

pictions of that fantastic Third Reich—genetically created
giants who served as executioners, fountains of blood in
the squares of Berlin, dogs that spoke with human voices and
spied for the government—and also marginalia concerning the
twins' abilities, among them being the control of certain forms
of energy: these particular powers had apparently been used to
create the tunnel. All this fanciful detail unsettled me, as did
several elements of the story. Tom had stated that the usual
avenues of escape had been closed to the twenty clones, but
what was a tunnel if not a usual avenue of escape? Once he had
mentioned that the tunnel was "unstable." What did that
mean? And he seemed to imply that the escape had not yet
been effected.

By the time I had digested the notebooks, I had begun to
notice the regular pattern of the twins' walks; they would dis-
appear around the point that bounded the western end of the
beach, and then, a half hour later, they would return, looking
worn-out. Perhaps, I thought, they were doing something
there that would shed light on my confusion, and so one
morning I decided to follow them.

The point was a spine of blackish rock shaped like a lizard's
tail that extended about fifty feet out into the water. Tom and
Alise would always wade around it. I, however, scrambled up
the side and lay flat like a sniper atop it. From my vantage I
overlooked a narrow stretch of gravelly shingle, a little trough
scooped out between the point and low brown hills that rolled
away inland. Tom and Alise were sitting ten or twelve feet below, passing a kef pipe, coughing, exhaling billows of smoke.

That puzzled me. Why would they come here just to get
high? I scrunched into a more comfortable position. It was a
bright, breezy day; the sea was heaving with a light chop, but
the waves slopping onto the shingle were ripples. A few fishing
boats were herding a freighter along the horizon. I turned my
attention back to the twins. They were standing, making peculiar gestures that reminded me of T'ai Chi, though these were
more labored. Then I noticed that the air above the tidal margin had become distorted as with a heat haze . . . yet it was not
hot in the least. I stared at the patch of distorted air—it was
growing larger and larger—and I began to see odd translucent

shapes eddying within it: they were similar to the shapes that
the twins were always sketching. There was a funny pressure in
my ears; a drop of sweat slid down the hollow of my throat,
leaving a cold track.

Suddenly the twins broke off gesturing and leaned against
each other; the patch of distorted air misted away. Both were
breathing heavily, obviously exhausted. They sat down a couple of feet from the water's edge, and after a long silence Tom
said, "We should try again to be certain."

"Why don't we finish it now?" said Alise. "I'm so tired of this
place."

"It's too dangerous in the daylight." Tom shied a pebble out
over the water. "If they're waiting at the other end, we might
have to run. We'll need the darkness for cover."

"What about tonight?"

"I'd rather wait until tomorrow night. There's supposed to
be a storm front coming, and nobody will be outside."

Alise sighed.

"What's wrong?" Tom asked. "Is it Lucius?"

I listened with even more intent.

"No," she said. "I just want it to be over."

Tom nodded and gazed out to sea. The freighter appeared to
have moved a couple of inches eastward; gulls were flying under the sun, becoming invisible as they passed across its glaring face, and then swooping away like bits of winged matter
blown from its core. Tom picked up the kef pipe. "Let's try it
again," he said.

At that instant someone shouted, "Hey!" Richard Shockley
came striding down out of the hills behind the shingle. Tom
and Alise got to their feet. "I can't believe you people are so
fucking uncool," said Shockley, walking up to them; his face
was dark with anger, and the breeze was lashing his hair as if
it, too, were enraged. "What the hell are you trying to do? Get
everyone busted?"

"We're not doing anything," said Alise.

"Naw!" sneered Shockley. "You're just breaking the law in
plain view. Plain fucking view!" His fists clenched, and I
thought for a moment he was going to hit them. They were so

much smaller than he that they looked like children facing an irate parent.

"You won't have to be concerned with us much longer," said Tom. "We're leaving soon."

"Good," said Shockley. "That's real good. But lemme tell you something, man. I catch you smoking out here again, and you might be leaving quicker than you think."

"What do you mean?" asked Alise.

"Don't you worry about what I fucking mean," said Shockley. "You just watch your behavior. We had a good scene going here until you people showed up, and I'll be damned if I'm going to let you blow it." He snatched the pipe from Tom's hand and slung it out to sea. He shook his finger in Tom's face. "I swear, man! One more fuckup, and I'll be on you like white on rice!" Then he stalked off around the point.

As soon as he was out of sight, without a word exchanged between them, Tom and Alise waded into the water and began groping beneath the surface, searching for the pipe. To my amazement, because the shallows were murky and full of floating litter, they found it almost instantly.

I was angry at Shockley, both for his treatment of the twins and for his invasion of what I considered my private preserve, and I headed toward his house to tell him to lay off. When I entered I was greeted by a skinny, sandy-haired guy—Skipper by name—who was sprawled on pillows in the front room; from the refuse of candy wrappers, crumpled cigarette packs, and empty pop bottles surrounding him, I judged him to have been in this position for quite some time. He was so opiated that he spoke in mumbles and could scarcely open his eyes, but from him I learned the reason for Shockley's outburst. "You don't wanna see him now, man," said Skipper, and flicked out his tongue to retrieve a runner of drool that had leaked from the corner of his mouth. "Dude's on a rampage, y'know?"

"Yeah," I said. "I know."

"Fucker's paranoid," said Skipper. "Be paranoid myself if I was holding a key of smack."

"Heroin?"

"King H," said Skipper with immense satisfaction, as if pronouncing the name of his favorite restaurant, remembering past culinary treats. "He's gonna run it up to Copenhagen soon as—"

"Shut the hell up!" It was Shockley, standing in the front door. "Get out," he said to me.

"Be a pleasure." I strolled over to him. "The twins are leaving tomorrow night. Stay off their case."

He squared his shoulders, trying to be taller. "Or what?"

"Gee, Rich," I said. "I'd hate to see anything get in the way of your mission to Denmark."

Though in most areas of experience I was a neophyte compared to Shockley, he was just a beginner compared to me as regarded fighting. I could tell a punch was coming from the slight widening of his eyes, the tensing of his shoulders. It was a silly school-girlish punch. I stepped inside it, forced him against the wall, and jammed my forearm under his chin. "Listen, Rich," I said mildly. "Nobody wants trouble with the Guardia, right?" My hold prevented him from speaking, but he nodded. Spit bubbled between his teeth. "Then there's no problem. You leave the twins alone, and I'll forget about the dope. Okay?" Again he nodded. I let him go, and he slumped to the floor, holding his throat. "See how easy things go when you just sit down and talk about them?" I said, and grinned. He glared at me. I gave him a cheerful wink and walked off along the beach.

I see now that I credited Shockley with too much wisdom; I assumed that he was an expert smuggler and would maintain a professional calm. I underestimated his paranoia and gave no thought to his reasons for dealing with a substance as volatile as heroin: they must have involved a measure of desperation, because he was not a man prone to taking whimsical risks. But I wasn't thinking about the consequences of my actions. After what I had seen earlier beyond the point, I believed that I had figured out what Tom and Alise were up to. It seemed implausible, yet equally inescapable. And if I was right, this was my chance to witness something extraordinary. I wanted nothing to interfere.

Gray clouds blew in the next morning from the east, and a steady downpour hung a silver beaded curtain from the eaves of my porch. I spent the day pretending to write and watching Alise out of the corner of my eye. She went about her routines, washing the dishes, straightening up, sketching—the sketching was done with a bit more intensity than usual. Finally, late that afternoon, having concluded that she was not going to tell me she was leaving, I sat down beside her at the table and initiated a conversation. "You ever read science fiction?" I asked.

"No," she said, and continued sketching.

"Interesting stuff. Lots of weird ideas. Time travel, aliens . . ." I jiggled the table, causing her to look up, and fixed her with a stare. "Alternate worlds."

She tensed but said nothing.

"I've read your notebooks," I told her.

"Tom thought you might have." She closed the sketchpad.

"And I saw you trying to open the tunnel yesterday. I know that you're leaving."

She fingered the edge of the pad. I couldn't tell if she was nervous or merely thinking.

I kept after her. "What I can't figure out is *why* you're leaving. No matter who's chasing you, this world can't be as bad as the one described in the notebooks. At least we don't have anything like The Disciples."

"You've got it wrong," she said after a silence. "The Disciples are of my world."

I had more or less deduced what she was admitting to, but I hadn't really been prepared to accept that it was true, and for a moment I retrenched, believing again that she was crazy, that she had tricked me into swallowing her craziness as fact. She must have seen this in my face or read my thoughts, because she said then, "It's the truth."

"I don't understand," I said. "Why are you going back?"

"We're not; we're going to collapse the tunnel, and to do that we have to activate it. It took all of us to manage it before;

Tom and I wouldn't have been able to see the configurations clearly enough if it hadn't been for your drugs. We owe you a great deal." A worry line creased her brow. "You mustn't spy on us tonight. It could be dangerous."

"Because someone might be waiting," I said. "The Disciples?"

She nodded. "We think one followed us into the tunnel and was trapped. It apparently can't control the fields involved in the tunnel, but if it's nearby when we activate the opening. . . ." She shrugged.

"What'll you do if it is?"

"Lead it away from the beach," she said.

She seemed assured in this, and I let the topic drop. "What are they, anyway?" I asked.

"Hitler once gave a speech in which he told us they were magical reproductions of his soul. Who knows? They're horrid enough for that to be true."

"If you collapse the tunnel, then you'll be safe from pursuit. Right?"

"Yes."

"Then why leave Pedregalejo?"

"We don't fit in," she said, and let the words hang in the air a few seconds. "Look at me. Can you believe that in my world I'm considered beautiful?"

An awkward silence ensued. Then she smiled. I'd never seen her smile before. I can't say it made her beautiful—her skin looked dead-pale in the dreary light, her features asexual—but in the smile I could detect the passive confidence with which beauty encounters the world. It was the first time I had perceived her as a person and not as a hobby, a project.

"But that's not the point," she went on. "There's somewhere we want to go."

"Where?"

She reached into her airline bag, which was beside the chair, and pulled out a dog-eared copy of *The Tibetan Book of the Dead*. "To find the people who understand this."

I scoffed. "You believe that crap?"

"What would you know?" she snapped. "It's chaos inside

the tunnel. It's. . . ." She waved her hand in disgust, as if it weren't worth explaining anything to such an idiot.

"Tell me about it," I said. Her anger had eroded some of my skepticism.

"If you've read the notebooks, you've seen my best attempt at telling about it. Ordinary referents don't often apply inside the tunnel. But it appears to pass by places described in this book. You catch glimpses of lights, and you're drawn to them. You seem to have an innate understanding that the lights are the entrances to worlds, and you sense that they're fearsome. But you're afraid that if you don't stop at one of them, you'll be killed. The others let themselves be drawn. Tom and I kept going. This light, this world, felt less fearsome than the rest." She gave a doleful laugh. "Now I'm not so sure."

"In one of the notebooks," I said, "Tom wrote that the others didn't survive."

"He doesn't really know," she said. "Perhaps he wrote that to make himself feel better about having wound up here. That would be like him."

We continued talking until dark. It was the longest time I had spent in her company without making love, and yet— because of this abstinence—we were more lovers then than we had ever been before. I listened to her not with an eye toward collecting data, but with genuine interest, and though everything she told me about her world smacked of insanity, I believed her. There were, she said, rivers that sprang from enormous crystals, birds with teeth, bats as large as eagles, cave cities, wizards, winged men who inhabited the thin Andean air. It was a place of evil grandeur, and at its heart, its ruler, was the dead Hitler, his body uncorrupting, his death a matter of conjecture, his terrible rule maintained by a myriad of servants in hopes of his rebirth.

At the time Alise's world seemed wholly alien to me, as distinct from our own as Jupiter or Venus. But now I wonder if— at least in the manner of its rule—it is not much the same: are we not also governed by the dead, by the uncorrupting laws they have made, laws whose outmoded concepts enforce a logical tyranny upon a populace that no longer meets their stan-

dards of morality? And I wonder further if each alternate
world (Alise told me they were infinite in number) is but a
distillation of the one adjoining, and if somewhere at the heart
of this complex lies a compacted essence of a world, a blazing
point of pure principle that plays cosmic Hitler to its shadow
selves.

The storm that blew in just after dark was—like the Mediterranean—an age-worn elemental. Distant thunder, a few
strokes of lightning, spreading glowing cracks down the sky, a
blustery wind. Alise cautioned me again against following her
and told me she'd be back to say goodbye. I told her I'd wait,
but as soon as she and Tom had left, I set out toward the point.
I would no more have missed their performance than I would
have turned down, say, a free ticket to see the Rolling Stones. A
few drops of rain were falling, but a foggy moon was visible
through high clouds inland. Shadows were moving in the
lighted windows of the houses; shards of atonal jazz alternated
with mournful gusts of wind. Once Tom and Alise glanced
back, and I dropped down on the mucky sand, lying flat until
they had waded around the point. By the time I reached the top
of the rocks, the rain had stopped. Directly below me were two
shadows and the glowing coal of the kef pipe. I was exhila-
rated. I wished my father were there so I could say to him, "All
your crap about 'slow and steady wins the race,' all your ratio-
nalist bullshit, it doesn't mean anything in the face of this.
There's mystery in the world, and if I'd stayed in school, I'd
never have known it."

I was so caught up in thinking about my father's reactions
that I lost track of Tom and Alise. When I looked down again,
I found that they had taken a stand by the shore and were per-
forming those odd, graceful gestures. Just beyond them, its
lowest edge level with the water, was a patch of darkness
blacker than night, roughly circular, and approximately the
size of a circus ring. Lightning was still striking down out to
sea, but the moon had sailed clear of the clouds, staining silver
the surrounding hilltops, bringing them close, and in that light
I could see that the patch of darkness had depth . . . depth,
and agitated motion. Staring into it was like staring into a fire

while hallucinating, watching the flames adopt the forms of monsters; only in this case there were no flames but the vague impressions of monstrous faces melting up from the tunnel walls, showing a shinier black, then fading. I was at an angle to the tunnel, and while I could see inside it, I could also see that it had no exterior walls, that it was a hole hanging in mid-air, leading to an unearthly distance. Every muscle in my body was tensed, pressure was building in my ears, and I heard a static hiss overriding the grumble of thunder and the mash of the waves against the point.

My opinion of the twins had gone up another notch. Any-one who would enter that fuming nothingness was worthy of respect. They looked the image of courage: two pale children daring the darkness to swallow them. They kept on with their gestures until the depths of the tunnel began to pulse like a black gulping throat. The static hiss grew louder, oscillating in pitch, and the twins tipped their heads to the side, admiring their handiwork.

Then a shout in Spanish, a beam of light probing at the twins from the seaward reach of the point.

Seconds later Richard Shockley splashed through the shallows and onto shore; he was holding a flashlight, and the wind was whipping his hair. Behind him came a short dark-skinned man carrying an automatic rifle, wearing the hat and uniform of the Guardia Civil. As he drew near I recognized him to be Francisco, the guardsman who had tried to cozy up to me. He had a Band-Aid on his chin, which—despite his weapon and traditions—made him seem an innocent. The two men's atten-tion was fixed on the twins, and they didn't notice the tunnel, though they passed close to its edge. Francisco began to ha-rangue the twins in Spanish, menacing them with his gun. I crept nearer and heard the word *heroína*. Heroin. I managed to hear enough to realize what had happened. Shockley, either for the sake of vengeance or—more likely—panicked by what he considered a threat to his security, had planted heroin in Tom's house and informed on him, hoping perhaps to divert suspicion and ingratiate himself with the Guardia. Alise was denying the charges, but Francisco was shouting her down.

And then he caught sight of the tunnel. His mouth fell open, and he backed against the rocks directly beneath me. Shockley spotted it, too. He shined his flashlight into the tunnel, and the beam was sheared off where it entered the blackness, as if it had been bitten in half. For a moment they were frozen in a tableau. Only the moonlight seemed in motion, coursing along Francisco's patent-leather hat.

What got into me then was not bravery or any analogue thereof, but a sudden violent impulse such as had often landed me in trouble. I jumped feetfirst onto Francisco's back. I heard a grunt as we hit the ground, a snapping noise, and the next I knew I was scrambling off him, reaching for his gun, which had flown a couple of yards away. I had no clue of how to operate the safety or even of where it was located. But Shockley wasn't aware of that. His eyes were popped, and he sidled along the rocks toward the water, his head twitching from side to side, searching for a way out.

Hefting the cold, slick weight of the gun gave me a sense of power—a feeling tinged with hilarity—and as I came to my feet, aiming at Shockley's chest, I let out a purposefully demented laugh. "Tell me, Rich," I said. "Do you believe in God?"

He held out a hand palm-up and said, "Don't," in a choked voice.

"Remember that garbage you used to feed me about the moral force of poetry?" I said. "How you figure that jibes with setting up these two?" I waved the rifle barrel at the twins; they were staring into the tunnel, unmindful of me and Shockley.

"You don't understand," said Shockley.

"Sure I do, Rich." I essayed another deranged-teenage-killer laugh. "You're not a nice guy."

In the moonlight his face looked glossy with sweat. "Wait a minute," he said. "I'll. . . ."

Then Alise screamed, and I never did learn what Shockley had in mind. I spun around and was so shocked that I nearly dropped the gun. The tunnel was still pulsing, its depths shrinking and expanding like the gullet of a black worm, and in front of it stood a . . . my first impulse is to say "a shadow," but that description would not do justice to the Disciple. To picture it you must imagine the mold of an androgynous human body constructed from a material of such translucency that you couldn't see it under any condition of light; then you must further imagine that the mold contains a black substance (negatively black) that shares the properties of both gas and fluid, which is slipping around inside, never filling the mold completely—at one moment presenting to you a knife-edge, the next a frontal silhouette, and at other times displaying all the other possible angles of attitude, shifting among them. Watching it made me dizzy. Tom and Alise cowered from it, and when it turned full face to me, I, too, cowered. Red glowing pinpricks appeared in the places where its eyes should have been; the pinpricks swelled, developing into real eyes. The pupils were black planets eclipsing bloody suns.

I wanted to run, but those eyes held me. Insanity was like a heat in them. They radiated fury, loathing, hatred, and I wonder now if anything human, even some perverted fraction of mad Hitler's soul, could have achieved such an alien resolve. My blood felt as thick as syrup, my scrotum tightened. Then something splashed behind me, and though I couldn't look away from the eyes, I knew that Shockley had run. The Disciple moved after him. And how it moved! It was as if it were turning sideways and vanishing, repeating the process over and over, and doing this so rapidly that it seemed to be strobing, winking in and out of existence, each wink transporting it several feet farther along. Shockley never had a chance. It was too dark out near the end of the point for me to tell what really happened, but I saw two shadows merge and heard a bubbling scream.

A moment later the Disciple came whirling back toward the shore. Instinctively I clawed the trigger of Francisco's gun—the safety had not been on. Bullets stitched across the Disciple's torso, throwing up geysers of blackness that almost instantly were reabsorbed into its body, as if by force of gravity. Otherwise they had no effect. The Disciple stopped just beyond arm's reach, nailing me with its burning gaze, flickering with the rhythm of a shadow cast by a fire. Only its eyes were constant, harrowing me.

Someone shouted—I think it was Tom, but I'm not sure; I

had shrunk so far within myself that every element of the scene except the glowing red eyes had a dim value. Abruptly the Disciple moved away. Tom was standing at the mouth of the tunnel. When the Disciple had come half the distance toward him, he took a step forward and—like a man walking into a black mirror—disappeared. The Disciple sped into the tunnel after him. For a time I could see their shapes melting up and fading among the other, more monstrous shapes.

A couple of minutes after they had entered it, the tunnel collapsed. Accompanied by a keening hiss, the interior walls constricted utterly and flecks of ebony space flew up from the mouth. Night flowed in to take its place. Alise remained standing by the shore, staring at the spot where the tunnel had been. In a daze, I walked over and put an arm around her shoulder, wanting to comfort her. But she shook me off and went a few steps into the water, as if to say that she would rather drown than accept my consolation.

My thoughts were in chaos, and needing something to focus them, I knelt beside Francisco, who was still lying facedown. I rolled him onto his back, and his head turned with a horrid grating sound. Blood and sand crusted his mouth. He was dead, his neck broken. For a long while I sat there, noticing the particulars of death, absorbed by them: how the blood within him had begun to settle to one side, discoloring his cheek; how his eyes, though glazed, had maintained a bewildered look. The Band-Aid on his chin had come unstuck, revealing a shaving nick. I might have sat there forever, hypnotized by the sight; but then a bank of clouds overswept the moon, and the pitch-darkness shocked me, alerted me to the possible consequences of what I had done.

From that point on I was operating in a panic, inspired by fear to acts of survival. I dragged Francisco's body into the hills; I waded into the water and found Shockley's body floating in the shallows. Every inch of his skin was horribly charred, and as I hauled him to his resting place beside Francisco, black flakes came away on my fingers. After I had covered the bodies with brush, I led Alise—by then unresisting—back to the house, packed for us both, and hailed a taxi for the airport. There I had a moment of hysteria, realizing that she would not have a passport. But she did. A Canadian one, forged in Málaga. We boarded the midnight flight to Casablanca, and the next day—because I was still fearful of pursuit—we began hitchhiking east across the desert.

Our travels were arduous. I had only three hundred dollars, and Alise had none. Tom's story about their having valuables to sell had been more or less true, but in our haste we had left them behind. In Cairo, partly due to our lack of funds and partly to medical expenses incurred by Alise's illness (amoebic dysentery), I was forced to take a job. I worked for a perfume merchant in the Khan el-Khalili Bazaar, steering tourists to his shop, where they could buy rare essences and drugs and change money at the black market rates. In order to save enough to pay our passage east, I began to cheat my employer, servicing some of his clients myself, and when he found me out I had to flee with Alise, who had not yet shaken her illness.

I felt responsible for her, guilty about my role in the proceedings. I'd come to terms with Francisco's death. Naturally I regretted it, and sometimes I would see that dark, surprised face in my dreams. But acts of violence did not trouble my heart then as they do now. I had grown up violent in a violent culture, and I was able to rationalize the death as an accident. And, too, it had been no saint I had killed. I could not, however, rationalize my guilt concerning Alise, and this confounded me. Hadn't I tried to save her and Tom? I realized that my actions had essentially been an expression of adolescent fury, yet they had been somewhat on the twins' behalf. And no one could have stood against the Disciple. What more could I have done? Nothing, I told myself. But this answer failed to satisfy me.

In Afghanistan, Alise suffered a severe recurrence of her dysentery. This time I had sufficient funds (money earned by smuggling, thanks to Shockley's lessons) to avoid having to work, and we rented a house on the outskirts of Kabul. We lived there three months until she had regained her health. I fed her yogurt, red meat, vegetables; I bought her books and a

tape recorder and music to play on it; I brought people in
whom I thought she might be interested to visit her. I wish I
could report that we grew to be friends, but she had withdrawn into herself and thus remained a mystery to me, something curious and inexplicable. She would lie in her room—a
cubicle of whitewashed stone—with the sunlight slanting in
across her bed, paling her further, transforming her into a
piece of ivory sculpture, and would gaze out the window for
hours, seeing, I believe, not the exotic traffic on the street—
robed horsemen from the north, ox-drawn carts, and Chinese-
made trucks—but some otherworldly vista. Often I wanted to
ask her more about her world, about the tunnel and Tom and
a hundred other things. But while I could not institute a new
relationship with her, I did not care to reinstitute our previous
one. And so my questions went unasked. And so certain
threads of this narrative must be left untied, reflecting the
messiness of reality as opposed to the neatness of fiction.

Though this story is true, I do not ask that you believe it. To
my mind it is true enough, and if you have read it to the end,
then you have sufficiently extended your belief. In any case, it
is a verity that the truth becomes a lie when it is written down,
and it is the art of writing to wring as much truth as possible
from its own dishonest fabric. I have but a single truth to offer,
one that came home to me on the last day I saw Alise, one that
stands outside both the story and the act of writing it.

We had reached the object of our months-long journey, the
gates of a Tibetan nunnery on a hill beneath Dhaulagiri in Nepal, a high blue day with a chill wind blowing. It was here that
Alise planned to stay. Why? She never told me more than she
had in our conversation shortly before she and Tom set out to
collapse the tunnel. The gates—huge wooden barriers carved
with the faces of gods—swung open, and the female lamas
began to applaud, their way of frightening off demons who
might try to enter. They formed a crowd of yellow robes and
tanned, smiling faces that seemed to me another kind of barrier, a deceptively plain facade masking some rarefied contentment. Alise and I had said a perfunctory goodbye, but as she
walked inside, I thought—I hoped—that she would turn back
and give vent to emotion.

She did not. The gates swung shut, and she was gone into the only haven that might accept her as commonplace.

Gone, and I had never really known her.

I sat down outside the gates, alone for the first time in many months, with no urgent destination or commanding purpose, and took stock. High above, the snowy fang of Dhaulagiri reared against a cloudless sky; its sheer faces deepened to gentler slopes seamed with the ice-blue tongues of glaciers, and those slopes eroded into barren brown hills such as the one upon which the nunnery was situated. That was half the world. The other half, the half I faced, was steep green hills terraced into barley fields, and winding through them a river, looking as unfeatured as a shiny aluminum ribbon. Hawks were circling the middle distance, and somewhere, perhaps from the monastery that I knew to be off among the hills, a horn sounded a great bass note like a distant dragon signaling its hunger or its rage.

I sat at the center of these events and things, at the dividing line of these half-worlds that seemed to me less in opposition than equally empty, and I felt that emptiness pouring into me. I was so empty, I thought that if the wind were to strike me at the correct angle, I might chime like a bell . . . and perhaps it did, perhaps the clarity of the Himalayan weather and this sudden increment of emptiness acted to produce a tone, an illumination, for I saw myself then as Tom and Alise must have seen me. Brawling, loutish, indulgent. The two most notable facts of my life were negatives: I had killed a man, and I had encountered the unknown and let it elude me. I tried once again to think what more I could have done, and this time, rather than arriving at the usual conclusion, I started to understand what lesson I had been taught on the beach at Pedregalejo.

Some years ago a friend of mine, a writer and a teacher of writing, told me that my stories had a tendency to run on past the climax, and that I frequently ended them with a moral, a technique he considered outmoded. He was, in the main, correct. But it occurs to me that sometimes a moral—whether or not clearly stated by the prose—is what provides us with the real climax, the good weight that makes the story resonate beyond the measure of the page. So, in this instance, I will go contrary to my friend's advice and tell you what I learned, because it strikes me as being particularly applicable to the American consciousness, which is insulated from much painful reality, and further because it relates to a process of indifference that puts us all at risk.

When the tragedies of others become for us diversions, sad stories with which to enthrall our friends, interesting bits of data to toss out at cocktail parties, a means of presenting a pose of political concern, or whatever . . . when this happens we commit the gravest of sins, condemn ourselves to ignominy, and consign the world to a dangerous course. We begin to justify our casual overview of pain and suffering by portraying ourselves as do-gooders incapacitated by the inexorable forces of poverty, famine, and war. "What can I do?" we say. "I'm only one person, and these things are beyond my control. I care about the world's trouble, but there are no solutions."

Yet no matter how accurate this assessment, most of us are relying on it to be true, using it to mask our indulgence, our deep-seated lack of concern, our pathological self-involvement. In adopting this attitude we delimit the possibilities for action by letting events progress to a point at which, indeed, action becomes impossible, at which we can righteously say that nothing can be done. And so we are born, we breed, we are happy, we are sad, we deal with consequential problems of our own, we have cancer or a car crash, and in the end our actions prove insignificant. Some will tell you that to feel guilt or remorse over the vast inaction of our society is utter foolishness; life, they insist, is patently unfair, and all anyone can do is to look out for his own interest. Perhaps they are right; perhaps we are so mired in our self-conceptions that we can change nothing. Perhaps this is the way of the world. But, for the sake of my soul and because I no longer wish to hide my sins behind a guise of mortal incapacity, I tell you it is not.

About the Author

"Just keep it simple," advised Lucius Shepard when asked to provide information for this biographical sketch. Born forty years ago in Lynchburg, Virginia, Shepard "raised hell in high school and hallucinated for a year and a half at the University of North Carolina" before dropping out to travel extensively in Europe, the Middle East, Latin America, and the Carribean. During this peripatetic period of his life, the author smuggled marijuana, taught Spanish at a diplomatic school, owned a T-shirt company, worked as a janitor in a nuclear facility and bouncer at a whorehouse in Malaga, and, most recently, "beat his brains out" as a rock musician. After graduating from the Clarion Science Fiction Writers' Workshop in 1980 (where he returned as a teacher in 1988), Shepard sold his first novel, *Green Eyes,* which appeared as an Ace Special in 1984. Having won the John W. Campbell Award as best new writer in 1985, his work has since won numerous awards, including the Nebula for the short story "R & R" and the 1988 World Fantasy Award for this very collection. Shepard's second novel, the Bantam New Fiction title *Life During Wartime,* is presently a nominee for the 1988 Arthur C. Clarke Award in England. He is currently at work on his new novel, *The End of Life As We Know It.*